R E G I O N
A R O U S E D

FOCUSING ON WAYS
TO MAKE THE REGIONAL PROCESS
WORK BETTER, 1999 - 2003

June 2003

BY
FRANK W. OSGOOD, AICP
Regional Planner

RoseDog Books

PITTSBURGH, PENNSYLVANIA 15222

ISBN # 0-8059-9362-2
Printed in the United States of America

First Printing

For information or to order additional books, please write:
RoseDog Books
701 Smithfield St.
Pittsburgh, PA 15222
U.S.A.
1-800-834-1803
Or visit our web site and
on-line bookstore at www.rosedogbookstore.com

To my parents, Earle and Blanche Osgood, who inspired me to help others less fortunate and volunteer to protect our freedoms.

Also, to my supportive family: Sisters, Jean and Ruth; Brother, Don. Daughter, Anne; and son, Frank, Jr.

CONTENTS

PART FOUR
APRIL 2001 - SEPTEMBER 2001

PART FIVE
2003 FORWARD INTO FUTURE

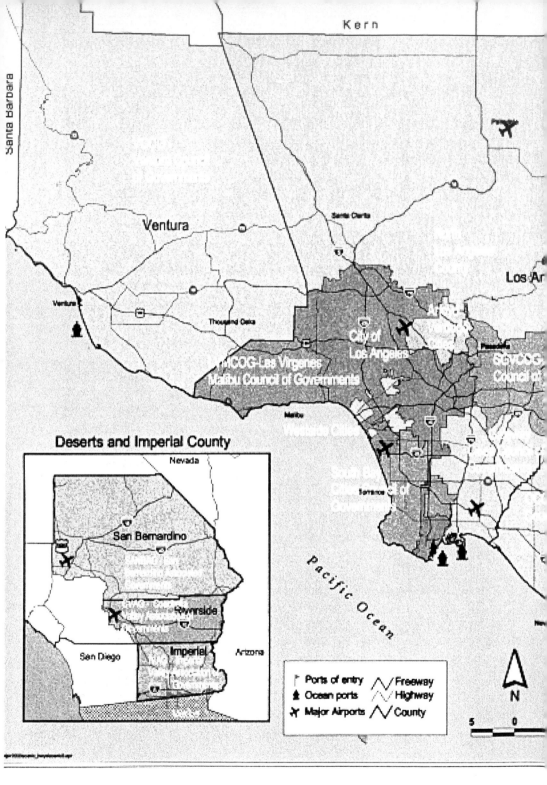

Counties and Su

Source: SCAG 2002
        Thomas Bros. Network

Figure

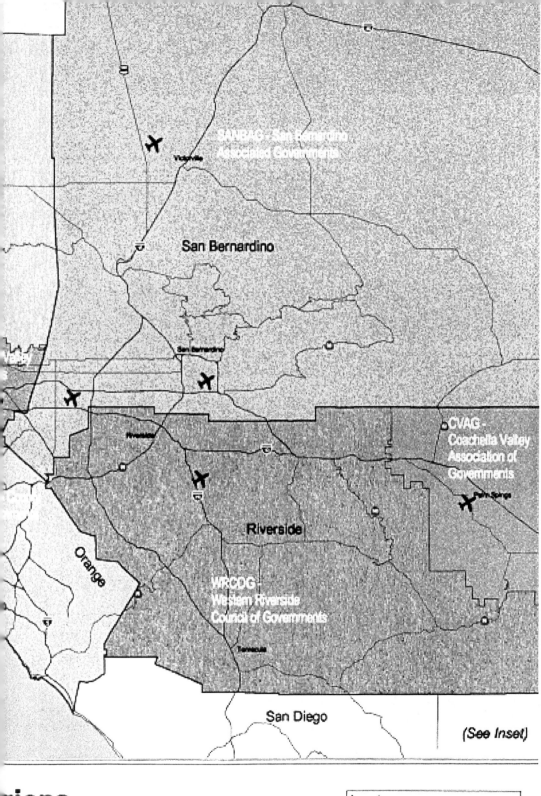

SANBAG - San Bernardino
Associated Governments

San Bernardino

San Bernardino

Victorville

CVAG -
Coachella Valley
Association of
Governments

Palm Springs

Riverside

Riverside

WRCOG -
Western Riverside
Council of Governments

Temecula

Orange

San Diego

(See Inset)

gions

2004 EIR UPDATE

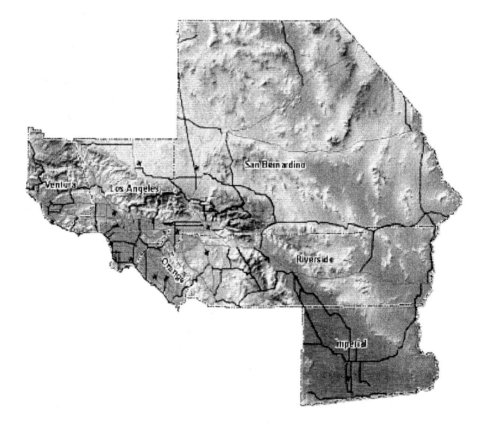

FOREWORD

"Why did you write this book about the L.A. Region and its regional planning organization, the Southern California Association of Governments (SCAG)?" I am often asked. "They have been around a long time and accomplished too little." I did it because I wanted to get Regional Citizens more involved in the L.A. Region and all across the nation. Dilemmas in ethics and morality affected by the regional process desperately needed discussion.

I could have written a scholarly book about SCAG. Instead, I wanted to give this serious subject new life by mixing a documentary analysis with a little fiction. Although frowned on by many in the writing field, I felt it was important to develop regional planning issues in ways that could entertain people with a plot that can educate them about the need to strengthen regional planning. I hope the story line I developed will catch the interest of potential Regional Citizens.

Some warned, "Don't replay the past and make a lot of Regional Council (RC) members angry unless you can give them a stronger regional vision." My intent in this docudrama is to constructively improve regional planning and development in the L.A. Region by critiquing SCAG and other agencies involved in the process. I wanted to help arouse the Region from its state of constant TURMOIL–that only works against itself–into a REGION AROUSED.

From the beginning, I realized that my book on the unnecessarily dull regional planning process would not be read by significant numbers of influential people unless it held human interest. I designed this docudrama to be a riveting story of people concerned enough about making their city–and their Region–more livable, more workable and more fulfilling. Although the storyline has fictional elements, the planning process I document covers possibly ninety percent of the action and is very real. By this focus on fact, I hope to draw future regional citizens into the real process as active participants dedicated to making the L.A. Region a better place.

As I continued this book's research with no assurance of success, many friends encouraged me. They kept my dream for a better Region alive. The issues covered, when combined with a plan, carry the hope of a better region. Their synergy will accomplish far more than if done separately–results greater than with its collective parts.

* * *

ix

Frank W. Osgood

This docudrama focuses on the planning and politics of developing SCAG's 2001 Regional Plan (RTP). It covers the major elements of the regional planning process for the six-county L.A. Region over the last two years of the three year RTP update cycle. Understanding this process took me through hundreds of hours of meetings in many committees, SCAG's Regional Council and the Regional Advisory Council (RAC). To fairly critique SCAG's involvement, I also sifted through minutes, notes and news articles on meetings, observed the political process first hand.

As I observed the regional process over time, I became increasingly intrigued. I joined the Regional Advisory Council, representing non-elected officials, that advised the Regional Council (SCAG's policy board). Eventually elected Vice Chair and then Chair of the RAC, I helped evaluate the actions taken during the last two years of the 2001 Regional Transportation Plan (RTP). As Chair, I attended several hundred SCAG meetings and was able to critique the regional process in depth.

My experience in writing motivated me to transform the voluminous meeting notes I had taken and reviews of numerous reports into a story line, leading characters, and a plot. The two key participants–House Speaker Juan Rodriguez and RC member Jim Simpson–are purely fictional characters. An investigative journalist was added to probe the effectiveness of the regional process, and help the story-telling process take place more effectively and effortlessly by introducing dialogue. Certain characters in the book parallel actual roles and persons, with their names and other characteristics changed to protect their privacy. These people were involved in a wide range of committee and subregion meetings to focus on regional needs.

My professional training and long experience in regional planning across much of the nation has been capped by intimate involvement in a wide range of public and private planning studies throughout the L.A. Region over the 1980's and early 1990's.

* * *

Appreciation is given to the novel's editor, Bruce D. McDowell, senior consultant and project director in the Management Studies Center of the National Academy of Public Administration (NAPA), Washington, D.C. An old friend and planning colleague, Bruce has been involved in the regional planning movement all his professional life, through various federal agencies. Formerly with the National Association of Regional Councils (NARC), Patricia S. Atkins is a Professor with George Washington University's Institute of Public Policy in Washington, who provided important advice and assistance on regions and subregions.

In researching the book, I gained numerous insights from Myron Orfield's *Metropolitics* book to understand regional change through the political process at the state and regional levels. William Fulton's book, *The Reluctant Metropolis,* was helpful for its fascinating background and history of the L.A. Region's political and planning process. Appreciation is also extended to my Cypress readers group, which also helped me significantly in the book's initial development. Community-based organizations and readers were also helpful in the overall writing process.

In interweaving fact with some fiction in this docudrama to create an interesting plot, I have greatly simplified planning and legal terms and used dialogue freely to express both actual and contrived situations.

The whistle-blowing element expressed through investigative journalism was tied to the *L.A. Times* because it is the Region's newspaper. Although I considered giving the paper a fictitious name, that idea was discarded as being too contrived.

Part One
October 1999-March 2000

CHAPTER 1
NEEDED REGIONAL
REFORMS

Juan Rodriguez, State House Speaker, although heckled by the opposition at a Long Beach rally, began a drive to pass his bill for a statewide regional planning initiative. Leaked information by staff to enemy intent on destroying him creates problems.

"Everything big in life involves a little terror."
Author unknown

An impatient, unruly crowd gathered at the Long Beach Auditorium on a Thursday evening in October 1999 to discuss more effective regional cooperation. Looking out at the assemblage from the podium, Juan Rodriguez, state House Speaker, frowned uneasily. The audience scattered throughout the hall looked more like a lynching mob than a group gathered to rationally discuss how the region could work better.

Over 500 people had already arrived, though the meeting wasn't scheduled to begin for another 15 minutes. His spirits rose when he saw that many civic groups were represented. Where else could he find representatives drawn from such diverse groups as the Sierra Club, unions, community-based organizations, elected officials from many cities, and prominent builders. Also represented were various business and professional groups and the media, all anxious to discuss regional matters.

He had laboriously called old political "friends" dedicated to the continued successful evolvement of the regional process, encouraging them to attend, and saw a few in the crowd. But he also spotted a large number of political "enemies." The meeting had been well publicized by the press, radio and TV.

Why did he feel uneasy? He sensed that this broad-based gathering arrayed round a number of powerful pressure groups could get out-of-hand if not handled adroitly. Priding himself on being able to size up a political gathering, he began adapting his remarks to defuse the problems that inevitably emerge when a wide mix of people from all walks of life, each with different political agendas, come together.

As he surveyed the scene, several in the crowd stood out. One woman in particular–white, about forty, with gray hair–screamed to those around her:

"Let's roil up the crowd so Rodriguez has problems being heard."

"Right," cried a red-faced young man near her who paced about irritably. "Let's yell back and forth to get their attention." He seemed possessed of a continuously running mouth.

"Friends. Rodriguez isn't here to help us–only to snow us with his propaganda," the white-haired woman yelled, moving around to get noticed. Dressed in red, with well groomed hair, her anger was easy to focus on.

"Yeah," shouted a huge balding, heavyset man, over six feet, waving his arms overhead, "Rodriguez ignores the common person. He loves developing controversial legislation to get reelected."

"Do you want to be snowed by his bull? This is your chance to beat this creep at his own game," the woman screeched, glaring disdainfully up at Juan, as she plowed through the crowd gathered near the dais.

"Let's boo him when he's introduced," the fiery, red-faced man bellowed, obviously enjoying the potential rancor being created.

The nearby crowd began to feed on their energy. The noise level picked up. People began restlessly moving around, irritated that the meeting hadn't started yet.

Juan recognized the crowd psychology inflaming the situation, and knew this group would be increasingly difficult to speak to as their tension and impatience grew. He got up to calm the situation.

"Folks! Glad to see so many here tonight," he exclaimed, nervously glancing out at the throng. "We're waiting for a few speakers who haven't arrived yet, but we'll begin in 15 minutes–on schedule. Please be pa—."

"Start now," piped up a middle-aged concerned woman sitting in the front row. "Get the show on the road." Others echoed her feelings.

"Please be patient. We'll begin at 8 P.M.." A loud chorus of boos greeted him from every corner of the hall as he sat down.

Amid the rising noise, the other participants arrived and took their seats on the dais, and held a hurried conference. Since the audience had swelled to almost one thousand and was becoming increasingly impatient and belligerent, they decided to start early.

One of Juan's aides, Fred Smith, stepped to the podium and asked for quiet. He thanked the crowd for coming and amidst the continued grumbling, announced the meeting's purpose.

"We're here tonight to discuss what needs to be done to 'jump-start' the proposed regional bill being crafted in committee. Since only limited funds are available, we want to maximize Federal, state and local funds available for regional airports, highways, transit and housing. We want to prevent growing traffic gridlock–on the ground and in the air. Juan Rodriguez, Speaker of the House, has taken time from his busy schedule to talk with you about an important subject which is–as you well know–close to his heart. Let me present . . . House Speaker Juan Rodriguez!"

Juan, who normally received enthusiastic applause when speaking, was concerned by the lukewarm response. A harbinger of things to come, he wondered? He moved into his short speech, providing more details on the various programs highlighted in the proposed bill. He explained his focus on maximizing the use of Federal funds for reducing L.A.'s well-known sprawl by guiding growth and building new highways. He then asked for questions from the floor.

They came quickly. "Why are you sponsoring a bill that'll take away local control from your constituents?" asked Hazel, a city council representative from a community in the San Fernando Valley.

"Trust me, local autonomy won't be affected. Our approach will be explained when our complete program is introduced," Juan indicated tactfully. "It will be taken care of soon."

"You support legislation that increases residential densities to extreme levels," Jacob, a member of the Sierra Club, accused. "And you claim to be an environmentalist."

"Residential densities will increase very little overall. When the details are provided, all of this will make sense, Jacob," Juan emphasized, making eye contact with the questioner.

"Again, bear with me. I know you'll be pleased with the final results."

"Some of the money being used for mass transportation could have been added desperately needed freeway extensions and interchange improvements. Don't you think that's unfair?" Lila Moore, a striking blonde from the Construction Industry Group, definitely easy on the eyes, posed it.

"Plans for freeway maintenance and interchange improvements are still scheduled to take place. Again, Lila, get in touch with us so we can provide you with all the details as they become available. As our legislation is developed, all elements of our Transportation Plan will be presented for approval by your Regional Council representatives. It's too early to spell out all the details now, since they're still being determined at the committee level," Juan explained to her.

As he fielded these and other questions throughout the evening, he sensed that some powerful pressure groups had banded together to get him. Demands continued thick and fast:

- His not backing more affordable housing for minority groups in inner city and suburbs.

- Undesirability of mixed-use development by single family and low density advocates.

- How to handle Brownfields and other deteriorating urban areas by environmentalists.

Juan wondered why these pressure groups had come tonight to attack him? What big issue had united them?

The answer came when Daisy, an elderly woman representing the Senior Citizens asked: "Why did you—our state representative—sell out to the lobbyists by authoring and sponsoring HB 150? It puts strict state controls on the development of regional guidelines, eliminating input on what could be done locally."

This stunned him. Who had distorted his intent so much, he wondered? He spent the remainder of the evening defending his fledgling bill—which wasn't even out of committee yet.

The other speakers on the dais tried to help, but quickly realized that they were likely to be smeared if they became too passionate in Juan's defense. Juan ended up fielding almost all the questions himself and asking for extra time to more fully present his position.

The media circled like vultures. They sensed a front-page story for the morning edition and angled for more sound bites for the late evening TV news. They interviewed the questioners and speakers. Each one searched for 15 minutes of fame and glory. Juan pleaded again for more time to answer questions—but to no avail. They wanted instant explanations to difficult questions where previous answers had been slanted, distorted or taken out of context.

The meeting disintegrated into a media frenzy rather than the intended coming together of reasonable minds. The discussion of how to prevent the Southern California Region from continuing its downward spiral toward transportation gridlock had been buried beneath hostility and shouting matches. Juan became heartsick, astounded that people despised his position enough to attempt to destroy him. He knew this had to be true because many of the evening's questions covered materials which were being put together in issue papers coming only from his office. Someone close to him or working for him in Sacramento was involved.

As Juan gathered his materials to go home to his family in north Long Beach, Bea Johnson, a Los Angeles Times journalist and sometimes TV reporter, caught his eye and asked for an interview. In an effort to salvage something from the evening, he agreed to meet with her in an adjoining room away from all the clamor. He respected Bea, an investigative journalist who often wrote on regional affairs. She would give him a chance to put a good spin on the event, he hoped.

"How can I help you Speaker?" Bea asked. "You've done a lot in Sacramento to champion the regional cause. I know you can't go into much detail but I'm willing to cover your position in greater depth when you're ready to respond to the accusations made tonight."

"Thanks, Bea, it would help if you mentioned this meeting briefly in your column and indicate we spoke one on one. Let the readers know I'll respond soon with more details on our legislative program. You've been doing a great job covering regional affairs."

"Speaker...hang in there. You'll get your day in court. Call me when you're ready." Bea wanted to focus more on regional affairs, knowing the importance of championing Los Angeles as one of the world's leading metropolitan regions. She realized her opportunity to make it happen through her ongoing investigative activities. Wanting to begin a series on regional matters, this could be the door opener. Investigative journalism was definitely her strength and she felt that Juan could help her begin the process with his creative programs.

* * *

Jim Robinson, veteran of many Regional Council and Southern California Association of Governments (SCAG) battles, left his law office after a busy day. He was kicking himself for not having the foresight to attend the Long Beach speech which his old friend, Juan Rodriguez, had given tonight. Although they had drifted apart since college at USC, he still respected Juan for the drive and vision which had allowed him to reach his current lofty perch as Speaker in the California State House. Their friendship had been limited by their entirely different agendas but his respect for Juan remained strong. When Jim heard that Juan had had a tough meeting in Long Beach without his involvement, Jim felt bad. Admittedly, he might be considered to be jealous of Juan's rapid rise in politics while he was chasing a football around in the National Football Association. But he was beginning to make waves through his efforts at SCAG, and he would be reckoned with in the future.

It would be a busy day tomorrow, as the Regional Council (RC) would be meeting, so Jim began preparing for it, as well as the policy meeting with the Transportation group beforehand. As chair of the influential Long Range Transportation Finance Task Force, he had to cover the latest task force proposals to finance the 2001 Regional Transportation Plan, which would be up for adoption. His ambition to be nominated for Regional Council chair was another step toward catching up with Juan. Maybe the Long Beach extravaganza would slow Juan down some. Time would tell. Until then, he would keep his eyes open.

* * *

As Juan wearily wended his way home through the late evening traffic, he felt the stress of another long, challenging day. He looked forward to seeing his wife, Marie, and their three children, Roslyn, Jose and Juan, Jr. He always worried that he wasn't home enough and his family suffered. He wished he could change, but he couldn't.

From the 710 Freeway, he exited onto the Pacific Coast Highway eastward, turned north on Bellflower Blvd, near the Cal State-Long Beach campus and passed through the adjacent attractive residential neighbor-hood where he and his family had lived for 20 years. His home was straight ahead. He had been away several weeks. Where did the time go?

Entering the driveway, he parked his blue BMW in the attached garage, got out, and looked with pride at his sprawling California-style single level home. Quite a change from the ghetto house where he was raised in East L.A. When he walked in the door, the Rodriguez brood mobbed him.

"Dad, we've been waiting for you," yelled Roslyn, his 10 year old daughter. She put her arms around him and hugged. What a dynamo, he thought fondly, just like her mother, willowy, with long brown hair and dark brown eyes.

Marie came swiftly to him, her face aglow, as they gathered in the fam-ily room. Her "man" was finally home. He swept her into his arms, grate-ful for her understanding ways.

"A bad day, Juan? Let me warm dinner for you," she said, bustling around.

Buzz pulled at his shirt. "Dad, Jose and I want to show you something. We made it just for you." Juan, Jr., 12, was somewhat subdued tonight. Normally he was more out-going, displaying feelings characteristic of his nickname, Buzz, exuding energy.

Last but not least, Jose, 8, was also upset, exclaiming: "What took so long, Dad? We thought that you would be here a long time ago. Buzz and I have been waiting for hours to show you our project."

6

Marie came to his aid. "Boys, boys, don't you know your father is tired and hungry! Give him a chance to relax. The project can wait a few minutes. Go play." Turning to Juan, she stated, "They've been so impatient lately about your being away so much. How about a drink, dear?"

Declining, Juan followed Marie into the kitchen, putting his arm around her. "The meeting didn't go well," he stated resignedly. But just telling her about the event and feeling her understanding response helped. Marie understood and always seemed to say the right thing and get him laughing again. He knew everything would be okay.

He went to see what was happening in his children's lives. He knew he must somehow spend more time with them.

* * *

Juan returned to the State Capital Monday after his disaster in Long Beach, determined to put the trip behind him. He couldn't shake his concern about what was behind the previous night's embarrassing setup and who was behind it. Was it his bill? His pent up emotions pushed him to get the bill out of committee as quickly as possible to prevent any other road blocks from developing. As Juan entered the historic caucus room, he marveled at the ornateness of the statutory and wall trimmings. He also noted that his dedicated committee members were already there, patiently waiting to begin the day's meeting. Joe Vargas and Otto Wong, his trusted associates, were also there, coffee cups in hand.

"Thanks for breaking away from your busy schedules. I wanted to bring you up-to-date on the Long Beach meeting," he said.

"Were there problems? How can we help?" asked Pedro, a committee member from San Fernando Valley.

"We'll cover approaches later. We've got to get this bill out of committee soon. There seem to be some legislative leaks, as well as strong opposition."

"Juan, we're ready to move, " replied Erwin, another member of the committee from San Francisco. "Just give the order."

"Good. Its doubly important to get this bill drafted and ready for final committee review ASAP. It proposes a program to achieve a greater sense of community and stability in achieving better education, more security and less traffic congestion for the voters. It's been tried with some success in Minnesota. Myron Orfield, as a member of the Minnesota House of Representatives, worked hard during the '90's to build a broad, powerful political coalition of central and older suburban communities to reform regional governance, housing, land use and transportation policies. I want to get him to participate in a workshop here to ensure it fits the uniqueness of California's major metropolitan areas." He paced back and forth, impatient to get the whole process going. "Only through a strong, inclusive regional response will regional polarization be countered."

Pedro broke in, "Yes, our region's problems are worsening and the opposition's growing. We need to get your bill passed now. Otherwise, we'll never solve our urban problems."

"Right. To stabilize the central cities and older suburbs," Juan went on, "we know we need six separate and independent reforms on a metropolitan scale covering housing, finance, urban reinvestment, better land planning, welfare reform and growth controls. They're interrelated and they reinforce each other legally, morally and politically. We'll also need a reform changing the voting process."

"Can we accomplish all these reforms quickly?" Erwin questioned, with a frown etching his forehead. "Maybe we should gradually test the waters with only a few reforms."

"No! We've got to take a chance. Give the legislature the whole program," Juan said, pounding the table for emphasis. "If it fails the first time, at least we'll educate them. Then we can make necessary changes and reintroduce the bill in 2001. Some bills take time before they're accepted."

"Since this is a major bill and needs a shift in thinking about how to solve urban problems," Hank, another committee member, agreed, "this will take time and a lot of education."

"We'll be in good shape when the first reform is achieved," Jasper, another advocate, enthused, "Companion bills on land use controls and growth management are in various stages of development. In addition, welfare reform meeting Federal requirements is well along."

"Also, bond issues for substantial public works, highway transportation and transit have been introduced within committees," broke in Roger. "What you're proposing in these other reforms should jell things so that everything needed will be available in a regional program to achieve quality urban development."

"I'm glad you brought this up since we need all the help we can get in the days ahead. Do you all think that you can get some strong backing from those working on these other measures?"

"You bet. I'll make a few calls," responded Erwin. "Pedro, let's get on this today."

"No problem. I've already made some calls. Let's move on them together."

Juan went on, "The proliferation of cities in the Los Angeles Megalopolis–currently there are 185 municipalities with land use powers–regulating the land use practices of one market leads to such over-reg-ulation. It results in barriers in the new suburbs to the affordable housing or mixed-use developments the market needs in the job-rich communities. Can you imagine Newport Beach or Laguna Hills accepting these devel-opments? But they need to be involved to make it work."

Juan paused for emphasis.

"What I'm trying to do," he slowed to space out each word, "is create a *less regulated setting*."

With this, he asked for and got volunteers for assignments in key small-er committees to continue the necessary grunt work on the various seg-ments of the bill.

"That's all for today. We've got a lot to do. We'll meet again at one tomorrow afternoon. Thanks for your support."

Juan pulled Joe and Otto aside before they left the Caucus Room. "You may have heard about how the audience was prepared for what I was going to say at Long Beach. We need to find out who my enemies are, why they're aligned against me, and what can be done to prevent any further damage to our proposed bill."

They agreed on an approach to achieve good damage control within the office.

With that they disbanded, agreeing to meet again at nine the next morn-ing.

*   *   *

Juan arrived at the state capitol at six the next morning and caught up on paper work, with instructions left through notes and tapes on handling many of the phone calls, faxes and e-mails which came to his attention every day. He also sent out faxes, e-mails and drafts of letters needing responses. Without a well-managed program to handle these communica-tions, his time in state government would end quickly. He couldn't say enough about his great staff. They were intensely loyal, did a terrific job of shielding and advising him so he could continue to do the work he had been elected to do.

Before his nine o'clock meeting, Juan decided to clear his head by tak-ing a stroll in one of the parks surrounding the capitol. He loved nature and found a few minutes in the fresh air helped him keep perspective in Sacramento's power-hungry atmosphere. The beautiful shrubbery, tree cover and flowers rested his eyes. For a moment, he drank in the scene, complete with the chattering squirrels and cawing birds, as the human problems and greed of politics dissipated. Thinking back on his life also helped him keep his balance on those things most important to him.

Lost in thoughts about how much the environment had been a happy part of his youth, he came back to the present when a pigeon landed cooing at his feet. Reinvigorated, he rose and strode back to his office prepared for the upcoming meeting.

* * *

Joe and Otto, tired and concerned, waited in his office. From the bags under their eyes, he knew they'd had little sleep.

"We thought it would be easy to trace what's been happening," Joe began wryly, shaking his head at the thought. "But it wasn't. We asked some key staff members if any outsider had been asking questions about our legislative program. No luck."

"Yeah, we kept asking around. We'd almost given up when Jody, a legislative assistant, gave us some gossip that she'd heard," Otto related. "She was only too happy to help," he chuckled. When she said, 'You must be talking about Amy Fuller,' I was taken aback. I hadn't mentioned names."

Otto continued. "She said 'I know it's Amy because she's such a gossip, always bad mouthing people. She's been dating Jake Posse, a CIG lobbyist. She loves to talk about things going on in the office to visitors. A real chatterbox who's easy to draw out. I'm sure she's been giving him information which might have seemed of little value. He probably started complimenting her and leading her on. It just flowed. Now she's really infatuated with him and things probably got out of hand. You know how pillow talk goes.'"

"I checked back with Jody," Otto said, "and she said that Rose confirmed Amy was sleeping with Jake and may have blabbed some information to him."

Otto had egged her on. "What types of information? " He was careful to not push her too much.

"Amy said that she had given him some memos and reports that Jake said Mr. Rodriguez had agreed to provide him. Also, data on some bills scheduled to be passed in committee. She had such a crush on him, she didn't think about why he needed these or when Jake had asked for them."

Otto thanked her, realizing all this information probably gave Jake a snapshot of almost everything of importance going on with Juan over the past six months.

Juan was devastated. "Just when I thought that I could trust all of my staff. Amy has to go–now! " he growled.

"Maybe. But I've been thinking maybe we could learn more by keeping her awhile," Otto suggested quickly. "What do you think?"

"I see where you're going, Otto," Juan countered quickly. "I agree. We could feed her false formation which could lead CIG in wrong directions. We might also be able to determine who to target other than Jake Posse. Let's keep her on and see what we might be able to do on this. I'm incensed CIG would try to do something like this. Guess I'm on their endangered species list of people to destroy." He went on, "This could prove to be very interesting."

"That's only the tip of the iceberg," Joe said. " I uncovered evidence linking a number of lobbyists with legislators against your efforts in the past. Based on the flimsy material and comments I gathered from my contacts overnight, there have been a number of meetings among those which attacked you in Long Beach."

Juan scowled–but knew he had been too naive about the vicious steps that some would take to protect their self-interests. Obviously, there were other staff leaks in addition to that woman. A definite concentrated effort to find out what was happening in Juan's office would likely hit more pay dirt. Although he would get more information on CIG's activities in the days ahead, this was enough to make Juan think about getting out of politics. Who could he trust? Were greed and lust the only issues which he needed to worry about? How could he accomplish his mission in the face of this determined opposition which would do anything to achieve their objectives? He now realized even more how desperate others could get to keep their good life and, in the process, prevent needed changes to occur. As a result, the gap between the rich and poor continued to widen. Was there no honor?

Realizing more and more the uphill battle Juan was waging, Joe and Otto agreed to keep him advised over the next few days as more information came in. They couldn't develop any strategy until they knew more about what to expect. Then they could counterattack effectively.

Juan went on, " Also, more detail about how, why, when and future directions planned have to be uncovered. The only thing to do now is to feed Amy and any other person we have doubts about, false information. Additional safeguards have to be developed. This means better controls on paperwork and dissemination–fax, e-mail, phone and internet."

Juan tried to push all this out of his mind as he left the meeting. He might get depressed if he continued to dwell on it. These things had happened– maybe for good reason. The depth of his faith was being tested now. He must not only pray about it but also remain optimistic. God had a way of continually testing you. Otherwise, you couldn't remain strong.

Returning to his office, he thought more about what to do. His office, littered as it was, offered him a haven for getting a lot of work done.

However, he made sure of his accessibility to his staff, with his door always open. It took a lot of effort but was worth it as they were able to keep him apprised of all the little things happening which maximized his effectiveness.

He must move ahead. He knew his enemies were threatened by his proposed legislation and would take measures to stop him. But people depended on him. His leadership skills would be tested. No matter what some people said about him or did to him, he must not give up. He must give his enemies the other cheek, whether they laughed at him, ridiculed him, or spread lies. He must put it behind him!

The one thing he had to do as soon as possible was get in touch with those political and personal friends who might be able to help. He mulled over those who could help the most. Certainly, the first to contact would be Jim Robinson, an old buddy from college days. They went back a long way, through football and even double-dating with their eventual wives. They had lost touch when Jim had gone into professional football. But he was back. The only difficulty was whether he would be a good backer; he had never been even in SC days. He was too used to the adulation from football stardom to be a team player. He didn't see him at the Long Beach meeting. Oh well, time would tell if they could find common ground in politics.

Also, Gavin O'Neil, with the Gateway Cities Partnership and Mike Nelson, Executive Director of the Gateway Cities COG. Juan had met Gavin in Ireland during a vacation and had been impressed with him, encouraging him to migrate to Southern California. Realizing Mike was a natural to get involved in regional affairs, he had interested him in getting Gateway Cities going from the Lakewood area. where he had been City Manager.

Who else? Possibly Carla Hawks, a member of the Gateway Cities COG, and, of course, Marcine Simpson, who was with an Alameda Corridor job training organization. Carla was another of his regional converts who became interested through the Brownfields toxic soils program which he had championed. Toxic soil problems wracked the Gateway Cities Subregion.

Anyone else? There were several others but he needed people he could trust who were with regional organizations in his district. Oh, yeah. Henry Ferrotte, an economic development consultant who was currently Vice Chair of the Regional Advisory Council, an important regional citizen organization serving the SCAG region. He and Henry had tested each other under difficult circumstances early in their development as regional planning enthusiasts.

He thought they all would work well together, and they needed to be involved as a team. Some already knew each other–a big plus. He would have his secretary develop a schedule to fit them in either here in Sacramento or, if need be, in Los Angeles/Long Beach.

He smiled in anticipation. It would be great to get together again. They should be able to help each other. He thought back to how they'd worked well together in the past. He felt he could trust each of them. That was so important. Operating as a team, each providing their expertise, contacts and political instincts. They came from a variety of backgrounds, their careers shaped by their experiences in government and life.

He knew the next two years would be extremely important in developing strong regions in Southern California. Much needed to be done, but it would be difficult. His recent experience in Long Beach, and now within his own offices in Sacramento, had shown that. Mis-guided special interests were threatening to destroy the future of our cities and metropolitan regions. He and his compadres must be prepared to do whatever was necessary to protect their way of life.

CHAPTER 2
RISE OF A SUBREGION

*More than 100 toxic sites exist in the built-out, lower
income Gateway Cities Subregion which needs
industrial land to attract firms focusing on machinery
and other skilled jobs. These jobs are needed for
retrained, unemployed workers with which Gateway
Cities Partnership, development arm of subregion, is
concerned. Brownfields must be saved for industry,
not other uses like education and retail.*

"I brought you into a fertile land to eat its fruit
and rich produce. But you came and defiled my land
and made my inheritance detestable."
Jeremiah, 2:7; Old Testament, Bible

"Any vision of our subregion's future must consider our present problems and condition. We can't change it without significant efforts to renew our built-out areas," said Mike Nelson, addressing the Gateway Cities Executive Committee at its monthly meeting. "We're falling behind in renewing our deteriorating areas and will have difficulty catching up. Don't forget our toxic waste problems, obsolete land uses and dilapidated, overcrowded housing."

Carla Hawks, frowning with concern, asked: "How can we revitalize areas without treating the toxic soils that permeate our key sites?"

"We can't. Our future depends on eliminating toxic soils on key sites through a strong management plan," replied Mike. "The biggest needs are industry, followed by affordable housing. We must act now if the subregion is to have a strong future."

"What should we do then?" Carla asked, drumming her fingers nervously, thinking about her city and its pressing economic decline worsened by Brownfields.

"We need to visit a Brownfields area to see what we can learn. The South Gate site currently in the news as suitable for two new schools. How about there?" Mike asked, straightening his glasses as he looked around at the committee.

"Let's go next Tuesday. I can get several key members to attend if you and Gavin can handle the tour."

"Fine. Let's meet at the site at nine Tuesday morning," Mike replied.

* * *

The Brownfields site, covering over 100 acres at Firestone and Atlantic in the inner-city portion of Southeast Los Angeles County, was bisected by the decaying 710 Long Beach Freeway and flood-prone, concrete encased Los Angeles River. Nine people–including Bea's cameraman–arrived in the early morning for the tour. Stretching out before them was a tired clump of land filled with faded, dilapidated, old factory buildings. They rose pathetically amid a clutter and hodgepodge of streets, railroad tracks and overhead transmission lines, assaulting each other in a chaotic scene.

Gavin gave them a tour by car and on foot this early morning in November 1999. There were foundries, product recyclers, cement-making outfits, oil-barrel storage areas, truck-holding areas, warehousing and other heavy industry spewing their distinctive noises and odors into the cramped area. They were haphazardly connected by rail spurs, street stubs and irregular on-street parking.

"What's that putrid smell? It's overpowering," groaned Carla.

"Delightful, isn't it?" said Gavin, the official tour leader. "That nauseating mix," he explained, "is produced by oil, foundry metals and rubber."

"Yuck!" Mike Nelson wrinkled his nose as he walked around the site near their cars. "Without all the smog, the San Gabriel Mountains framing the sky would be majestic and beautiful. As it is, they just look faded."

"Right," said Gavin. "Remember though, those are visual and smell reactions. This area is in even poorer condition than it looks. The leached soil and horrible mix of toxic wastes were caused by oil spills, foundry wastes and other materials deposited over many years when there were no protections.

"I can barely hear you," yelled Marcine, cupping her ear to hear comments.

"Those loud, deafening sounds are coming from the roar of diesel trucks and constant high-pitched freeway traffic," Mike yelled back, raising his voice and cupping his hands to form a megaphone. "Can you imagine living adjacent to this area?"

"No, but it's still in better shape then dozens of other sites that litter the Gateway Cities," Gavin said. "All of them need expensive and time-consuming cleanup if the area is to be revitalized."

"How crappy can you get?" Bea asked, thinking about her job reporting all this. "Look at those buildings with rusting corrugated siding painted in garish colors, interspersed with rusted fence. And all sorts of ugly transmission lines circulating aimlessly overhead. Think how this will look on TV."

"Yeah. There are even some apartment units and an abandoned elementary school crammed in among these industrial uses," stated Gavin.

"The more I look at the area, the worse it gets," said Bea, squinting her eyes. "Why?"

"Because the many types of pollution you see violate your senses," replied Gavin. "High noise levels, irritating odors, rough, narrow streets, poor drainage, weird tree cover. Also, poor or non-existent street lighting, rampant graffiti, and the rusted fencing everywhere–all combine in a massive assault on our senses. The only oasis I see is a plant nursery wedged–somehow–into one small corner of the site."

"Even the haphazard street system's not safe and its flow is impeded by its poor condition," Mike stated. "Plus the decaying freeway interchanges siphon the value from abutting retail uses."

"The worst of it is that you can't see the leached soil and polluted ground water problems here," continued Gavin. "We'll have to remove several feet of soil and make many other costly adjustments to take care of these problems."

"What about the structures? Must all structures be removed, even those in good condition?" asked Marcine.

"Yes, since all top soil must be stripped. It will take several years of treatment before the area can be returned to full, efficient use." Gavin scowled at the thought.

"Scary–the time and cost factors alone," Marcine frowned. "Then you must consider the jobs needed to fill the space and provide needed income. Can we speed up the job retraining process?"

"We'll have to. Land for machine tool firms is needed, as well as retraining for the underemployed workforce. A critical time period for Gateway Cities," emphasized Gavin. "All the Brownfields require similar action–or even more, depending on the degree of toxic waste penetration discovered."

Such an eye-opening experience for all–including Bea, the media/TV rep. She busily scrawled notes as she supervised the video taping.

"We never dreamed such a mess would result from decades of carelessness and neglect," Mike said. "Now we can see the uphill task to save our inner cities. And this is just the beginning! Gateway and other older subregions face many other problems as well."

"Wasn't the school district planning to put two schools on this site without treating the soils?" said Carla. "It's unbelievable they could foist

16

that on our kids. They may have problems finding sites, but that's no way to rationalize the problem. Thanks, Gavin and Mike, for the tour. Very enlightening–and alarming. It will help our approach to Brownfields."

* * *

"Such a challenge to get this subregion back to its former vitality. How can I help make things happen? Hope Mike has some insights that will help," Carla mused to herself. She worried about keeping harmony between 26 abutting cities, a difficult task with conflict and bad feelings never ceasing.

As she sat at her desk waiting for the COG's Executive Director, Mike Nelson, to arrive, she thought about the region's evolution. In the past, such issues as zoning, street widenings, changes in land use and other administrative matters had been handled separately by each city. Any city border problems could cause bad feelings between the adjoining cities, making it difficult for them to cooperate. Now she must work one-on-one with the cities to develop a cooperative spirit among them. She enjoyed doing it since she had a happy, bubbly spirit and "thrived on people," as she called it.

Mike Nelson, the middle-aged former City Manager of Lakewood, arrived. He was one of the prime movers behind the formation of the Subregion and Carla needed his help to get a better grasp on where they should go.

"Sorry I'm late, Carla. Too many back-to-back meetings," he said wearily as he shook hands and sat down. "I like your office," he said, looking around "The family photos and mementos give it a comfortable feeling."

"I spend a lot of time here, so I wanted it to feel like home," Carla replied. "I hope you're ready to go to work?"

"You bet. I brought some materials on the Subregion," Mike replied. "You know it's been a struggle to get the cities to work together. Of course, nothing's changed. It's funny," he joked, "Many visiting state and Federal officials leave shaking their heads. They've never seen such a dysfunctional group of cities, and wish us luck on getting things done."

"Yes," she laughed at the thought. "I know the challenge we face. I've been through this in my city's relations with surrounding cities. Could you give me some background on how all this came about, Mike?"

"It didn't happen overnight. Around 30 years ago, the mayors of several Southeast L.A. County (SELAC) cities began informal meetings to socialize and discuss topics of mutual interest. Then another group called the SELAC Study Committee began getting together before the Mayors meeting to consider future options. Funding would come through Southern California Association of Governments (SCAG) which was a very ineffectual 'top-down' regional agency at the time."

"There's a long history of informal efforts to communicate–not cooperate. But, it was a much different time. They were all newly formed suburbs then," remarked Carla, shaking her head. "Remember when we used to get together for a beer after a hard week, Mike. Of course," she chuckled, "we were just kids learning the ropes back then."

"Ah. Those were the days." Mike said, smiling at the memories. "Anyway, this was followed by a group of city managers establishing the Southeast L.A. County Management Group, formed to carry on a similar monthly dialogue. Over the years, various combinations of planning directors and other city officials also worked together on specific joint planning projects, such as air quality, water quality and transportation plans."

"It wasn't very effective though, was it?" Carla said. "When did things start getting serious?"

"Well, it began quite innocently in early 1992 when Lakewood felt that it wasn't getting enough help from SCAG in finding state and Federal money for its street improvements. L.A. City had the inside track on most of the money coming through. A Lakewood planner started checking around and discovered that where subregions had been formed, their strength from the numbers of cities working together tended to counter L.A.'s power plays. So, Lakewood officials contacted staff in surrounding cities and found considerable interest in forming a group to explore the development of a subregion for the Southeast L.A. County area."

"Yes, I know," Carla broke in. "My city was a part of that group."

"Right. So initially, officials of several cities met to explore some options. At first, there were problems in setting any direction because the various cities interests differed so much. What is now the Gateway Cities is composed of clusters of cities. For example, 15 cities north of the 91 Freeway and along the 710 Freeway share inner-city, urban core types of problems. Long Beach, Signal Hill and Lakewood to the south had other interests, due to their size, cultural diversity, and their relationship to the Port of Long Beach as well as the ocean-front. To complicate things, the seven cities in the eastern cluster share the suburban lifestyle. So you can understand the difficulty in getting cities to work together around a common theme."

"You covered it well, Mike. All the cities face the problems daily. When you include racial, income and housing problems, it gets even more complicated. What happened next?"

"Well, this group of cities found even greater social and economic problems emerging regionally. Genuine distress reigned over the limited resources the local governments had to cope with these problems. The relentless pace of growth, fueled by waves of in-migrants, and their impacts on the already stressed physical and social infrastructure grid-locked the system. This breakdown threatened the stability of many SELAC communities. Impacts of overcrowding on water and sewer systems, streets, housing and education were at a 'breaking point'. Overcrowding was a cultural issue, not just one of insufficient numbers of affordable, larger units. The change in ethnic composition created similar problems. As you can see, the whole area was in deep trouble."

"Wow. I didn't know it was that bad." Carla's concern increased rapidly. "How did they finally create Gateway Cities?"

"To simplify, different committees representing city managers, planning directors and elected officials began meeting almost monthly in 1993 and early 1994. They thrashed out some issues of streets and highways, air quality, water quality, and growth. In March 1994, Lakewood, representing 14 cities mostly in the northern portion of the current Gateway Cities, entered into an agreement with the Metropolitan Transportation Agency (MTA), and planned to develop and implement a Transportation Management Program for the Southeast Area. They studied this and other programs such as air quality. A Joint Powers Agreement was negotiated to create the mechanism which is now the Gateway Cities COG. Originally, it was called the Southeast L.A. County Subregion. The number of cities belonging fluctuated considerably. Cities struggled with the regional concept which, to some," he dead-panned, "seemed like a form of Communism."

"Well, your summary certainly helps me understand what I'm faced with. I still remember the all-day conference we had at the Cerritos Performing Arts Center in April 1994. Do you remember plowing through all those consultant studies and finally realizing that 'Eureka, we really do have a blood and guts subregion here?' It felt so rewarding."

"Heady days, Carla. I didn't realize at the time how much effort it would take to get us from there to here. Remember the SELAC Study Committee which preceded the COG? You, Hetty, Doug, Raul Perez and Harry Galvin were the core group. I recall some of the city managers approaching me in late 1994 about being Executive Director. Don Drake chaired the Study Committee and then the COG. It took about a year to enlist all the cities and to put together Southeast L.A. County Subregion. The resolution was adopted in mid-1997, and we had our first annual meeting in November 1997 when we became known as Gateway Cities.

"Great memories, Mike. Do you think I should visit all these cities now?" Carla asked.

"You bet! You have a talent for being able to convince people what you believe in–and what they should believe in."

"Thanks. Then, here's what I'll do," said Carla, as she chattered away, excited by the opportunity. "Brownfields and their toxic soils are a major issue which almost all the cities face. I'll talk about what good Brownfields and environmental justice programs can mean to them. Also, the importance of good regional planning if their citizens are to achieve a good life. I'll get my assistant, Jan, to set up a meeting with the City Manager of Downey that should get the ball rolling. Downey seems to think regional more than any of the other surrounding cities."

"Sounds great, Carla. You have my support. Let Lenny, my assistant, know what you need. She'll provide all the maps and data." Mike felt ecstatic about this breakthrough.

* * *

Carla kept moving, meeting with Jack Rowe, the Downey City Manager and some of his department heads the next day.

"Jack, you know how important considering regional matters is when you plot the future of your city. Can we depend on your total support in Brownfields involvement?

"You bet. We can get $200,000 per site in planning money from EDA."

"We also need you to get other less knowledgeable cities involved too. You know the Gateway Cities Partnership is deeply involved in Brownfields and needs the support of all cities."

"Carla, we'll help all we can. We took major hits in the 80's with job losses in aerospace. I'll encourage all my friends in nearby cities to get involved."

"That's great. We have a lot of problems in housing, poverty, education and retraining, but some cities seem to feel if they ignore them, they'll go away. Even when they understand, they don't encourage discussion. But these problems aren't going away. Overcrowding, congestion, lack of municipal resources, and poverty have to be faced. Any ideas on how to get these cities to develop programs to turn things around?"

"We've got to list our problems and consider how we might cooperate on a subregion basis to solve them. Then move ahead through various federal and state grant programs to achieve breakthroughs. How about an all-day workshop?"

"A great idea. Thanks for your input, Jack," said Carla.

Region Aroused

* * *

Carla approached other cities about the workshop and got enthusiastic support. The six small, poor Hub Cities (including Cudahy and Huntington Park), usually hard nuts to crack, but wanting desperately to be an important part of things, came on board. Historically, they'd worked together because of their similar circumstances. Long Beach and Cerritos, more advanced in approaching urban matters, as usual were "gung ho." Even Norwalk and Whittier, conservative bastions, realized the importance of the proposal, and joined in.

Pleased with the results, Carla began to spend more time away from work. Consumed by politics, she had become a workaholic. A widow, she bottled up her grief from the loss of her husband to cancer two years ago by immersing herself in her politics. But now, she wanted variety and planned to pursue a more balanced life. She knew that her life hadn't been easy, but it'd been interesting.

Carla remembered growing up in the 50's and 60's as a black in Compton in a far different environment than Gateway Cities now provided. So much had taken place in the past 50 years with decline of the inner city. She remembered hearing about the importance of Firestone and other area industries to the World War II effort. Even after the war, the area continued to prosper, known worldwide for its automotive machine tools.

Her family had suffered, especially in the 80's and 90's, as computer industries evolved and the Berlin Wall came down, putting many skilled people out-of-work. Gateway City communities were hit hard and the neighborhoods declined. Her father and many friends and relatives lost their jobs at Firestone when it closed. Her husband, Jed, ultimately lost his job and she scurried around to develop a career of her own to help out. Her political career grew from the jobs she got with several Gateway cities. All this made a big impression on her. She realized only too well how important jobs, housing, and decent incomes are to helping urban areas cope. She wanted to help get the Gateway Cities back to its former glory. She knew that only hard work and good planning would make it happen, and that prepared her for yet another work day.

Carla had thoughts on the changing family and what needed to be done in the area of education. Also, problems with too much TV, computer games and the internet chat rooms. These issues must be faced head on, she knew, and she resolved to help lead the way.

* * *

Mike moved ahead, encouraged by his meeting with Carla. She'd accomplished a lot of what he wanted done, but knew must come from the

Gateway Cities leadership. Now, if he could get SCAG to correct its poor management, he would feel more comfortable. This was a high priority because he'd had problems with SCAG in getting invoices paid on time and other matters.

In November 1999, an article on SCAG by Bea Johnson, L.A. Times' investigative reporter, created a crisis. The headlines charged, "Broad Lack of Oversight Found for Governing Agency." At the next SCAG meeting, Mike asked Bea about the breakdowns in the agency:

"Bea, you wrote the article about SCAG's bungling. What gives?"

"Oh, you saw my article detailing widespread financial, accounting and contracting problems at SCAG," she replied. "Well, they're getting sloppy and needed to be called on it."

"Yeah, I know. The Times editorial several days later also said that the agency 'has failed to become a strong voice for regional leadership,'" Mike quipped.

"They were awarding contracts without competitive bidding, in some cases going to relatives, friends or associates of board members or former members."

"You've heard the joke?" Mike kidded. "SCAG stands for 'Spousal Contract Award Group.'"

"It's not far from the truth," Bea laughingly answered. "Have you seen the numbers on responses to proposals lately?"

"No, although I know it's not good."

"Three responses out of over 100 requests sent out. And those three were insiders who seemed always to get contracts."

"It's a waste of time to spend time and money to submit. It really hurts the smaller firms who don't have deep pockets," Mike grunted.

"The RC should really get tough with them," Bea remarked heatedly. "They need to get rid of a few high priced deadbeats and get some strong management. This has got to be SCAG's worst crisis so far. And they've had a few."

Just then Jim Robinson, chair of SCAG's influential Transportation Finance Task Force, came up, overhearing some of the conversation.

"You can rest assured that something will get done on this," he exploded. "I'm outraged that SCAG should screw up so bad and let our dirty linen be aired in the paper. I'm going to make sure we get rid of some of the old timers who are not only out of touch with planning but think the world owes them. They've got lazy after 15 years on the job. The recent audit should result in some 'righting of the ship' but the entrenched leadership is still there. They won't be pressured to accomplish reforms unless we put the screws to them. I promise we will."

* * *

Gavin angrily tugged at the red tie his wife had insisted was the ultimate sign of power. "Why is this happening now just when everything was going great?" he said to himself. He paced the room, face flushed and scowling. Despite his evident despair, the tailored charcoal suit and blue shirt framing his trim athletic build, showed a man in his prime. His gray hair and ruddy complexion accentuated his good looks.

"I'm the President and CEO of the Gateway Cities Partnership. I've faced worse situations than this before and won out," Gavin O'Neil exclaimed in irritation. He certainly could handle this brewing fiasco. He sat down at his desk, penning the final touches on his notes for the monthly Board meeting, now just minutes away. He had to act fast to keep from losing the tremendous opportunity he had worked so diligently for two years to achieve. He'd strengthened ties between Downtown Los Angeles and the twin ports at Long Beach and L.A., and wasn't about to let it all go down the drain. Not now.

He muttered to himself, "MTA's improved marketing of light transit on the Blue and Green lines between LAX, Downtown, Long Beach and Gateway Cities communities increased usage and were icing on the cake." In addition, he'd helped develop a new holistic approach making trucking on the 710 Freeway run in concert with needs to speed revitalization of the Gateway Subregion. Everything had worked out as planned, except this unforeseen problem with Brownfields.

"No. I won't allow it." He grabbed the glass paperweight from his desk and smashed it against the wall. "No glitch in getting our rundown areas renewed is going to slow me down," he growled.

His irritation was caused by a call from Carla. She was furious about what had taken place with the Board. "The COG did all the work," she'd blurted. "Your Board of Directors are feeling their oats too much. They need to be taken down a notch. I thought you had things under control, Gavin." She inhaled, then continued without giving him a chance to respond. "How could they have engineered this behind your back? The COG got the Partnership started, underwrote its expenses and produced the EDA study–providing the money and research to make Brownfields important."

As she paused, Gavin jumped in, "Slow down, Carla. What 'behind my back'? I thought that we had everything in hand?" nervously passing a hand through his hair.

"Your Board of Directors voted to use some Brownfield sites for retailing. You know that. What are you going to do to correct this, Gavin?"

"I think there's some misunderstanding. I'll look into it right away. We have a highly qualified Board of Directors. I'm sure this can be straightened out, Carla."

Carla shot back, "I'm depending on you to do just that. Find out exactly what happened and why. Indicate that they have to back off or else."

"I'll take care of it, Carla." He thought, why am I being so devious? I didn't think making one or two sites retail would raise such a stink.

He must counterattack quickly! He summoned his young, but savvy executive assistant, Jenny Hope.

"Jenny, we ready for the Board ?"

"Of course," Jenny responded, "The charts and visuals are already in place. Anything else?"

She could change directions at a moment's notice–and relished the excitement of board meetings. She ran a hand through her short, blunt cut, almost as short as her dress, Gavin thought.

"What a mess! Keep me informed if anything changes. I need to prepare for the media blitz," Gavin talked as he walked toward the Boardroom with Jenny beside him. How the media covered this, he knew, would be key if he couldn't change the Board's mind.

The Board consisted of business, industry and educational representatives from the 26 cities in the subregion. Over half of the 31 members were assembled by the time Gavin entered and were seated at a circular table taking up much of the room. Moving around, Gavin made sure to greet each individual before taking a seat. The Chair, Don Morse, who ranked high at Boeing, quickly brought the meeting to order. Since this was an emergency meeting called by Gavin, he was immediately called on.

"Thanks for coming," Gavin said. "We're here today because of concerns that we aren't handling the Brownfields Program right. As you know, the original intent of bringing our toxic sites back to full productivity was to provide needed industrial sites for our out-of-work machinists. However, some of you felt that increasing our tax base through retail development of some of the sites was equally important. We have a dilemma. Gateway Cities COG, which got the original EDA grant, is rightfully upset. They feel that this board has betrayed their trust. We need to get this resolved soon. Any ideas."

There was an initial hesitation among the members to speak. "Our cities are broke. We've got to get more sales tax revenue to balance our municipal budgets," said Bob Finley, a small businessman on the Board. "Why do we have to use all the sites for industries which don't provide much tax revenue?"

"Because we need more jobs. I didn't vote for diversion of some sites to retail business in the first place," spoke up Gas Company rep, Jake Weir. "It's a mistake and we should re-vote with this issue in mind."

The meeting quickly turned into a heated discussion by those for and against a re-vote. Although there was some weakening of the position to include some sites for retail uses, there was no fresh thinking that could effectively resolve the problem.

Finally, Gavin interrupted: "We're not getting anywhere. The COG is ready to step in and request a new Board be formed. That won't solve our problem. It'll prolong the crisis and result in bad feelings and lousy press. We've got to work out a compromise satisfactory to everyone."

A university rep, Allan Bocker, spoke up, "How about returning to using all the sites for industry and appointing a committee to study how to generate more tax revenue by other means? There's no easy solution." He looked around, "Can we get both sides to agree on this approach?"

"That sounds like a good compromise. What does the board feel?" Gavin asked.

Gradually, there was agreement that this was probably the best solution to address both problems. The chair, after agreement on who would be on the committee to study and develop an approach to create more tax revenue for all cities, finally gaveled the meeting to a close.

It was also agreed that they had to go beyond a Board committee alone if they were going to get additional revenue. They must get their state representatives involved, since they had originally taken property tax revenues from the cities and created the dilemma. The tax committee agreed to meet again the next day to work on legislative contacts.

After the meeting, Gavin got back to Carla on the somewhat successful results. She wasn't totally happy but told him to keep working on the tax committee angle to see if it would help generate the additional taxes which all 26 cities so desperately needed.

* * *

Disheartened, Gavin ruminated on where he was in his career. Was this another situation where he was constantly going to be caught between two forces and end up as the fall guy? Like several other efforts over the past two years? He had been looking around for a challenge that might make better use of his many skills in economic development. Why? Was there something going on in his private life that left him unfulfilled?

An expert at turning around poorly run organizations, Gavin jumped at the opportunity to take over the floundering Gateway Cities Partnership over a year ago. The subregion hadn't yet recovered from the recession of the early 90's and despite the recent employment boom, continued to underperform. Strong, immediate action was needed to reverse the downward cycle.

Intrigued by the unique mix of cities, Gavin took the job. He disbanded the old board since he felt it did not fairly represent the business and non-profit leadership necessary to achieve needed change. The new board, including himself and three others at CSULB, constituted the new Partnership, with a mandate and board stressing more appropriate guidelines.

Within a year, they'd developed a series of strategies and initiatives designed to solve several key problems. Their plan had been simple; involve both private and public sectors in workforce development, recycling of dysfunctional real estate and Brownfield sites. Also important was creating a world class logistics system in the region's ports to encourage new technologies and make the region's businesses more competitive. He was proud of the Board's composition and loyalty to his program.

*　*　*

He also worried about the huge Alameda Corridor project's controversies. It was an important part of his strategy to revitalize the Gateway Cities region. It was hard to imagine digging a two track trench, 30 feet deep and over 100 feet wide for ten miles–half the length of the entire corridor–with thirty-nine bridges built to carry street traffic over the trench. With U.S.-Pacific Rim trade projected to double in the next 15 to 20 years, the Corridor would meet the Port's short- and long-term access needs.

He sometimes wondered what a small portion of the $2.4 billion funding package could do to enhance his own Gateway position. He possessed the knowhow to manipulate the complicated package in his favor. Would he, he thought jokingly? A lot depended on the Alameda Corridor and Pacific Rim trade projects.

Gavin snapped back to reality. The Board hadn't been as much help as he would have liked during the past year. But he had one other ace in the hole, Juan Rodriguez, who owed him big-time. Although he didn't want to play that card yet, he had attempted to touch base with Juan recently. His call had not been returned, not like Juan. Things change quickly in politics. Was Juan still a friend? Someone he could depend on if his back was to the wall?

So here he was, trying to make it all work. Why did he feel so bad? He felt the burning bile in the pit of his stomach. Did he have an ulcer? Did he have what it took to stick it out and make it work? He wanted to succeed so badly, but was it worth it?

He thought back fondly about his early days in Ireland when he had the whole world at his feet. It had been great when he had enjoyed rambling through the glades and vales of those wonderful years.

In the states for ten years now, he still couldn't forget the good years as a Gael. In fact, he still kept up with happenings there. He was especially fond of how they developed their job market, and felt he could use some of their good ideas in the Gateway Cities. A good Catholic, he still had an Irish lilt to his voice and adhered to the old traditions. Hopefully, the recent pledge by the IRA to allow inspections of weapons depots would lead to a shared government which would, over time, remove the bitter animosities now so ingrained in the psyche of the population. He hoped so because he wanted to go back to visit soon. He liked the Gateway Cities, but their struggles were hauntingly similar to Northern Ireland, especially when they tried to achieve environmental justice from Los Angeles. Such irony. It sent shivers down his spine.

He also hoped to visit Sacramento soon for talks with Juan Rodriguez and others about how to achieve the programs needed through Brownfields and Environmental Justice legislation. It needed to be soon. His patience was wearing thin. He would check with the others making the trip to see how quickly it might take place.

Gavin also wanted to learn more about the other 13 subregions in the Region. He had seen them shown on a map.* Of course, there was Los Angeles City itself which Gateway flanked. Then, those older cities to the west paralleling the Pacific Ocean including South Bay Cities, Westside Cities, and Las Virgenes/Malibu. Looking to the north, included were the more suburban Ventura County, North Los Angeles County and rugged Arroyo Verdugo Cities. Moving to the east, the wide range of San Gabriel Valley cities were next door, along with the huge expanses of San Bernardino County, Western Riverside County, the Coachella Valley and Imperial County further east. Last but not least, was rapidly expanding Orange County to the south. Such a variety of subregions with their fascinating topography, populations and cities which needed to be appropriately fit to the changing regional mosaic.

CHAPTER 3
TRANSPORTATION SHORTFALL

The possibility of up to a $50 billion shortfall was threatening to destroy the 2001-2025 Regional Transportation Plan that had already been postponed in 1998 due to the shortage of funds. The Long Range Transportation Finance Task Force needed to do something soon to resolve this problem. What could be done–and how soon?

_____

"Maybe computers never err. But humans put 'info' into the computer. Maybe the wrong information was put in or put in the wrong way. I'll be glad to show you my calculations. If we're going to be $50 billion short, we'd better know about it now so we can adjust our transportation programs to correct this problem. We don't want a 'garbage in, garbage out' fiasco aired in the L.A. Times."

Anonymous

"This above all: to thine own self be true."

Hamlet, Shakespeare

Harry Jacobson, the consultant for Transportation Finance, cornered Jim Robinson shortly before he was to open the monthly meeting of the Long Range Transportation Task Force. "We've got to talk,"he intoned with concern, running his hand through his thinning brown hair.

"What's up, Harry?" Jim looked up from the materials he had assembled to begin the Task Force's busy December 1999 agenda.

"It looks like we're going to have a $50 billion shortfall. That's what," replied Harry.

Jim whistled, "You're kidding? A $50 billion shortfall to make up? To meet our transportation needs between now and 2025? That's serious money."

"You're absolutely right, Jim," Harry said. "Did you have any inkling that SCAG would have such a serious problem in meeting its 2001 RTP transportation needs?"

"Well–no. I did wonder how we're going to buy all these highway improvements. But not this sort of trouble. What can we do about it now?" Jim queried urgently, since it was his job to find the money to ease the nearly gridlocked transportation system.

"Let's get the Task Force's advice," Harry suggested.

"It's going to take significant additional tax revenues and grants of some sort, and we better see what they think of the options."

Jim was concerned about doing this right to help him parlay a strong record as the chair of this prestigious task force into an opportunity to chair the Regional Council itself. Achieving that powerful position, he thought to himself, could lead to notable accomplishments and even higher office–perhaps in the state Senate or House. As a personal friend of Juan Rodriguez, he should be able to name his position if he could handle the Transportation Finance shortfall. Of course, he hoped that the Speaker could help him there too.

Although only the consultant, Harry knew the importance of doing a great job for SCAG on this, but was beginning to have second thoughts about what drove Jim as chair of this important committee. It was evident the man had ambitions. But if he was overly ambitious, he could do irreparable damage in his efforts to achieve career goals. He had the power and position to control the agenda and how decisions were made. Harry knew that he must be careful how he handled his role in this. Or he could get caught in the cross fire.

* * *

Jim gaveled the meeting to order and moved into the agenda as the last few members of a quorum straggled in. Better known as LRTF or "LAFF", it was one of SCAG's most important task forces. It held the "money bags" to keep the region going. Its leaders had clout with the king pins of the California legislature–and money ruled politics. Members always looked forward to visits from key Senate and House members from both sides of the aisle.

"LAFF" faced a quagmire of initiatives, laws and issues which made it increasingly difficult to get things done for local areas. Today's agenda held several crucial issues that had to be resolved successfully, one way or another, over the next 18 months. So Jim spelled them out to the Task Force as clearly and forcefully as he could.

"1. The state continues to get the lion's share of revenues at the expense of local areas and directs monies created for other purposes to its own politically important "pet" projects. What could be done in time to redress this?

2. Revenue increases are not keeping pace with needed improvements. This will require a major rework of state legislation. How could this be done in time?

3. We know now that improvements alone cannot solve transportation problems. What other solutions are available?"

Harry, the consultant added, "The Task Force must schedule meetings with the other nine SCAG task forces over the next six months. They all are going to need the money this task force brings in to meet their own needs. So, this task force's efforts to get more money from the state or Federal governments soon will be essential."

Jim knew that their plate was full. The real question was whether they would have the ability and time to handle what was on it.

An interesting mix of people made up the Task Force, and some of them had much to gain or lose by the results achieved. They represented transportation agencies, consultants, environmentalists, planners, and non-profits. A very titillating mix or, no pun intended, a "LAFFer". Jim took stock of those potentially most helpful in bridging the gap. The planners and environmentalists seemed to hold the most promise since they looked at the big picture in terms of land use. If limited funds were going to be available, then solutions must be reached through somehow controlling the location of new development to minimize the need to construct or widen freeways and add other infrastructure. He solicited their help by raising questions to get their responses and develop motions.

But the meeting dragged on with no unique thoughts being presented on any of the three issues listed on the agenda. Finally, when Jim had almost given up, a planner named Brad Gates, recently added to the group, spoke up. "I attended a conference on Smart Growth at the Biltmore Hotel last month. This group has been trying to get people out of their cars and into transit by encouraging links between job to housing locations. If these places could be mixed in a higher density setting, fewer people would need to commute long distances."

A freeway advocate, Joe Mason, piped up, "Yeah, we've heard that one before. Most people don't like to use transit or live in high density areas. It doesn't work," he said pessimistically.

Others felt that jobs-housing mixes didn't work because people wanted to live in nice areas generally located a good distance from where they worked. Historically, this had been the common practice.

Gates, the planner persisted, "I know those arguments. I've heard them all my working life, but this time it's different. Things are so bad, we can't afford to continue to build these freeways to provide short-term solutions. We don't have enough money and even if we did, the environment is going to hell in a hand-basket."

An environmentalist, Tom Mullin, added, "Brad's right. Freeways don't solve the problem. You build them and all they do is create more traffic and we're back to building more. It's never ending," he scowled. "Also, we're only fooling ourselves if we think that the environment is getting any better. You know its lousy. More children are getting asthma and other respiratory problems. Global warming is worsening, and America has become the biggest polluter. We've got to make a stand now?"

This was the discussion Jim had been seeking! Maybe there was a chance that these issues could be resolved some way soon. He asked the attendees if they needed more information.

Brad responded enthusiastically, "Shopping areas, even recreational and cultural facilities could be built into these land use clusters, doing away with many other auto trips. Needed transit lines should be added so that the car wouldn't be required for so many trips. This way, more residents could either walk or bike to their destinations–or use transit to get there."

Jim was even more intrigued. "Brad, could you get together several pages of information on land use-related approaches available to reduce the need for freeways for our next meeting. We can put it on the agenda if you can get it to me early. Also, those favoring freeways can do the same thing."

"No problem," Brad responded. "I'll provide some good examples."

"I'll get some examples together on problems with jobs-housing links," Joe Mason, the freeway advocate stated. With that, the meeting adjourned.

After some small talk with task force members, Jim left. It had been a long day. In fact, where had the years gone? Jim, a big, solidly built man of 40, once played football at USC. He'd been dubbed "Cat" by his teammates for his moves on the field.

Jim went back to his downtown office. He was a high-level executive with a public relations firm, Honack, Jones and Associates, as well as councilman for Beverly Hills. This involved a lot of meetings and cocktail parties, with his football prowess at USC helping him rise in the firm. Not only could he make some good moves on the field; he was known for his glad handing prowess too. Suddenly remembering that he had to attend a cocktail party at a Home Builders convention down the street, he quickly checked his messages at the office and set off to the party.

*   *   *

The CIG Convention always put on a good feed and attracted a great mix of people. The party was in full swing when he arrived. Grabbing some shrimp and carrot sticks to nimble on with his cocktail, he began a swing counter-clockwise around the floor pressing flesh. This was how he did his best work. After greeting some old friends and making new contacts, he felt ready to call it a night.

"Are you THE Cat Robinson I've heard so much about?" purred a low, throaty voice behind him. Stimulated by the sexy voice, Jim turned around to see a petite, blue-eyed blonde looking him over.

"Yes, I'm Cat. Who might you be. I've never seen you at CIG affairs before."

"I'm Lila Moore, a lobbyist with the Home Builders. I came on staff recently. I hope you're not leaving yet. I'd enjoy talking with you about your work."

Jim was taken aback by this saucy, attractive woman who had caught his attention. Intrigued by her head-on approach, he checked her out. "I've got plenty of time. Why don't we get comfortable with a drink at the watering hole down the street."

"I'd like that," Lila responded. They walked to Cactus Rose and found a table. He ordered a scotch and water and she a gin and tonic.

"You know, I've lived in L.A. all my life and heard a lot of football stories about you. I went to the other university–UCLA. You used to beat us while you were at SC. What're you doing now, Jim?" she asked.

"I'm with the public relations firm, Honack, Jones and Associates," Jim responded as he gazed into her beautiful, friendly face. "Heard of us? We focus mostly on public and non-profit clients and help them maximize their impact on the private sector."

"Yes, I've heard of your firm but didn't know you specialized. I might be able to provide some help at the Home Builders."

Jim was attracted by her directness. It was unusual in an industry where people had hidden agendas and could be devious. Was this a 'put on' by her or just how she approached life? He wondered. Obviously, she was ambitious and seized the moment. He decided he wanted to know more about her.

"Lila, would you like to take in an evening at the Hollywood Bowl this Sunday? " Jim asked hopefully, slowly sipping his drink. "The Boston Pops is playing and I could arrange a tasty picnic package to eat there before the concert."

"Hmm. This is short notice. Sure would like to hear the Boston Pops, though. They're among my favorites. Well...okay. You're on," she decided with a smile and a toss of her head. "Sounds like fun. I'm already looking forward to it. Call me with the details when you know more."

Saying he would, Jim left abuzz with strong feelings of attraction. She was so easy to talk to. She might even inspire him to dress better. She wore her business outfits in a way that were very feminine while still being all business. Clever. Maybe she could prove helpful in other ways.

* * *

The week passed quickly. With Pops tickets in hand, Jim picked up Lila Sunday afternoon in his blue Mercedes convertible. She was stunningly dressed in a chocolate cotton knit skirt which hugged her body. The tunic had ribbed mock turtleneck and pockets, highlighted by a slim, ribbed skirt. Jim couldn't take his eyes off her as she hiked her skirt and showed a lot of leg getting in the front seat. He knew he must work more on his attire even though he felt he had impressed her in his brown sport coat, light yellow sport shirt and light brown slacks.

Arriving at the Hollywood Bowl, they arranged their picnic materials and blanket on the overlook and got comfortable. He opened the champagne and poured two glasses, offering a toast: "Great times together in the coming weeks, Lila! May your job prove very rewarding." They drank to this, gazing deeply into each other's eyes.

Lila handed Jim a club sandwich, "What a great idea, Jim. I can't wait to hear the Pops. Such a beautiful setting and day," gazing around at the lush shrubbery and flowers.

"You're not from California originally, are you?" Jim asked.

"No, New Orleans. I miss the city, although I didn't like the hot, sultry weather. How did you pick up on it? Do I still have a trace of an accent?"

"A little... in a very charming way. You know, I've had wonderful times in New Orleans in years past–Pat O'Brien's, the French Market, to name a few."

"I'm curious now. What gave me away? An accent or colloquialisms ...?" she puzzled

"Well, you do keep a little of the south in your voice. Draw out some words. Use some quaint expressions native Californians don't say. I like how you say things. It's very refreshing. Don't try to change anything. It's a part of you that I especially like."

* * *

Driving back to her place, they chatted about their lives, happily learning a great deal about each other. Knowing of Jim's prominence in SCAG and that CIG encouraged their supporters to get their positions for more freeways and residential development supported by SCAG, Lila had seized the opportunity. Her involvement with Jim would really look good with her bosses.

"Jim, I'm glad you like to attend CIG affairs. What do you find most interesting about us?" she asked, trying to draw him out even more.

"You have important positions to understand," Jim responded. "CIG helps to provide desperately needed housing and is concerned about the increasing number of traffic tie-ups. SCAG must know your positions to respond as much as possible to them."

"I'm glad you feel that way, Jim," Lila went on. "Maybe a little inside information on how they're thinking would help."

"Sure, Lila. But I'm more interested in our relationship, in being with you."

Arriving at her condo, Lila invited him in. One thing led to another and suddenly they were kissing. Jim held her close, whispering in her ear, "Let's get together soon."

"Love to, Jim. You're so easy to be with," she purred.

Jim couldn't get over the attraction between them. He originally thought of her as only another interesting face and an entre into CIG office politics. He needed to probe her about housing positions at CIG which might help him with the RC. But he was in no hurry since he wanted to see her more–much more.

"Let's get together later this week. I'll give you a call," he said, giving her a kiss before leaving. Driving home, he couldn't get her out of his mind. Why did he find her so interesting–just another playmate or trophy? Who cares. He longed to have a relationship with her. Soon!

* * *

An opportunity came to see her again at another Home Builders party the following Wednesday afternoon. Arriving with great anticipation, Jim spied her talking with several guests. Sensing his arrival, she quickly detached herself and moved to his side. He felt the attraction radiating between them like the tides and moon. His heart beat a little faster.

He couldn't help noticing her cleavage. The black, off the shoulder, short cocktail dress showed off her white pearl necklace and matching earrings perfectly. She greeted him with a low laugh and eyes full of desire. He drank her in. "Let's get out of here, Lila."

They decided on her condo. They quickly fell into a deep embrace on the sofa upon entering.

* * *

Later, they relaxed in each other's arms, enjoying their feeling of intimacy. Wow, Jim thought. Where could this be going? How real could this be or was it just a plan to use him? She might be thinking the same thing. Both of them could have difficulty handling this. They would have to slow down—or this might get out-of-hand so they would both be hurt.

Lila snuggled closer to Jim, his warmth permeating her.

"Lila, this can't get better. But we need to talk about where we're going with this. Don't you think?"

"I don't want to think about it now. I'm enjoying being with you too much...But I understand what you're saying," Lila responded, her languid blue eyes feasting on him. "What do we do? I didn't think I would get so involved with you when I first met you."

He thought to himself. We're both professionals and our passion could get in the way of accomplishing our jobs effectively. Should I mention this?

"I agree, Jim. We've got to slow down some and let our ardor come back to earth," Lila said, backing off, looking at him and softly caressing his face with her hand. "You know neither of us wants to be hurt."

"Yeah, we're in professions which at times are in direct political conflict."

"What should we do, Jim? I can't stay away from you. I feel so safe in your arms." Lila glanced dreamily at him. "You're such a hunk. You also make me laugh with the 'little boy' faces that you throw at me. Quite the lover."

They bantered went back and forth, enjoying their closeness. Neither one wanted this to end. Playfully, they laughed and enjoyed their camaraderie.

Finally, they decided to face up to their dilemma. How should they handle this? Jim made the first move. "We've got to keep our distance for a while, don't you think? How we do it is another matter. Any ideas?"

"No. Let's think about it...We need to go to work. That would be the first step. Then we can talk over the phone in safer territory," she responded thoughtfully.

"Okay, let's do that," Jim said, ready to leave.

"I'll talk to you later, Lila," he said, walking out of her house without a backward look. He knew he had to do it that way.

* * *

Entering his office later, Jim struggled with his dilemma. He had to get his mind back on his work. It wasn't easy, her essence still with him. It had been awhile since he had been so close to a woman. He reflected on his failed marriage to Trudy over 15 years ago. They had been close for the first year and then drifted apart when they got caught up in the crazy 70's and work. Thankfully, they didn't have any children to complicate things. He still wanted children with the right woman.

The question surfaced—was Lila the right woman? He didn't know much about her other than the feeling he had. That, he knew, wasn't much to go on once the physical attraction wore off. Did they have anything in common? Did she have the ethics, morals and feelings about life in general which they would want to share with any kids they might have? Could they handle the give and take—part of any marriage? He didn't want to make the same mistake twice that he had with Trudy. They didn't know each other when they married young. He needed to back off. But the flesh was weak and he didn't know if he could. They would have to talk about it and chart a course. Until then, he needed to bury himself in his job.

* * *

The next day, the special sub-committee met on data regarding smart growth and freeways which Jim had requested at the last LAFF task force meeting. Jim looked forward to hearing the reports made by the planner, Gates, and freeway advocate, Mason. He wasn't disappointed.

Gates led off by providing information on smart growth and how it could reduce the need for freeways while minimizing congestion.

"Smart growth or livable communities involve a healthy mix of homes of all economic groups, along with shops, work places, parks and civic facilities. All need to be within walking distance of each other, linked with public transit and a center human in scale," he said.

"Are there many existing areas like this," asked Jim.

"Not enough. Mixing of uses is key along with a linkage with public transit and residents having a variety of incomes," Gates replied.

"What about our ability to reduce congestion through freeways?" asked Jake, another member.

"Two different national studies determined that congestion hasn't been reduced through the widening of freeways or building new freeways." Gates cited an analysis of the respected Texas Transportation Institute and studies by the Surface Transportation Policy Project (STPP) as verifying this.

"How can this be if more capacity is added?" asked Jim.

"The STPP report indicated that part of this was the phenomenon of 'induced traffic,' or the encouragement of more driving and auto trips by the same group of drivers. They went on to say: 'It's like trying to cure obesity by loosening your belt.'"

Jim chuckled at the analogy. He moved on to the freeway advocate.

"What did you discover, Mason, which refutes this?"

"The report, 'Preserving the American Dream' by Wells Fargo, maintains that the widely held perception of the negative effects of suburban housing are based on 'half-truths, poorly understood facts, and outright falsehoods,'" Mason said. "The report directly challenges two of the most potent criticisms of suburban housing: the loss of undeveloped land and the higher costs of providing infrastructure to low-density suburban areas." He went on, "The report rejects the inference that urban sprawl is bad. They feel that it actually contributes a great deal."

"I would challenge this study," Gates said. "An organization commissioned this which, in the past, has been dedicated to catering to a conclusion favored by its clientele. The two organizations I previously cited have been studying congestion for over 15 years. They even came in with a freeway bias prior to the results of their study. They couldn't dispute the findings since they also discovered separately that traffic congestion had been increasing ten percent annually in recent years. Just think," he emphasized, "ten percent!"

"But the Wells Fargo group's argument is that comprehensive planning won't make any more efficient use of land than the free market," Mason countered. "Also, housing development is an important source of economic growth that shouldn't be hurt by restrictive planning policies."

"That statement alone indicates the bias of this group," said Gates.

"Sounds like the two studies on smart growth have covered good ground," said Jim.

"Yes," said Gates, "The STPP study said communities which are investing in strategies giving people alternatives to driving, such as transit, bike lanes, and land use planning, are finding these techniques can be a popular and effective means of fighting traffic congestion."

"Well, what are the sub-committee's feelings on this subject? Should we go with the findings of the two foundations or that of Wells Fargo?" Jim asked the group.

"I propose that the findings of the two foundations be approved by LAFF," Gates said. There was a second and the motion passed with only two against or abstaining.

Jim had mixed emotions about all this. He knew the Wells Fargo study reflected what CIG, Lila's group wanted. Caught in a dilemma, he couldn't think of a way to have the preliminary vote reconsidered. He would think about it, and if possible, have it looked into further before the final vote was cast in two months by the full LAFF group.

With the vote, he adjourned the meeting.

* * *

The following week, Jim went to the monthly Transportation Finance

Task Force meeting ready to focus on how to begin to develop the state legislation needed to float the Region's transportation needs over the next five years–and hopefully through 2025.

Harry Jacobson, the staff consultant on finance, had prepared a series of memoranda on projected gas taxes and other revenues to help wipe out some of the $50 billion shortfall expected through 2025 to handle needed transportation infrastructure improvements. The objective now was to develop the "idea" or materials needed for state legislation. It would be sent to friendly lobbyists and state legislators to start what is called "the California legislative process."

The meeting began with great anticipation for finalization of this "idea." As Chair, Jim moved through the preliminary agenda quickly.

"Harry. Are you ready to report on your projections."

"Yes, Mr Chair," Harry replied. "Based on the various memoranda which we sent the members either with the agenda or by fax last week, we have developed, with the Task Force's direction, some possible alternatives. From these, you can vote on preliminary numbers and tax approaches so that some legislative possibilities can begin to be drafted for circulation to the legislative policy committee in Sacramento in the next few weeks."

"Please move ahead with your findings and options," Jim urged. Finally! He exulted. He needed this to justify his trip to Sacramento to meet with Juan. The timing couldn't be better.

He looked back on his life and career. It hadn't been the roller coaster some people went through. His had been steady in its upward movement. Born and raised in Beverly Hills of affluent parents, he had received the best preparation possible. His father, William Robinson, had been a well known lawyer, specializing in public sector clients; his mother, Jodie, a former singer who met his father at some Hollywood doings. Jim had received the best private education that money could buy, attending Edgewood Prep School and Wells High School. His football prowess wasn't well publicized, but USC had followed his limited football and track career, knowing he had the makings of a fine halfback along the lines of O.J. Simpson. He had the same speed and catlike qualities that had imprinted the nickname of "Cat" on his career.

Jim enrolled at USC and quickly became, over the 1979-82 period, one of the best halfbacks to ever attend SC. A consensus All-American in both 1981 and 82, he starred in defeating Notre Dame and getting USC to the Rose Bowl both years. He then got his law degree at Harvard before turning pro. Drafted by the Los Angeles Rams, he had a scintillating career through 1992, when he retired to practice public relations and law with his father through Honack, Jones and Associates.

He married his college sweetheart in 1983, but it didn't last. They were both pampered and unprepared to adapt to married life. Divorced in 1985, Jim wasn't interested in matrimony again soon. Never really tested by life, having received everything on a silver platter, Jim also wasn't prepared for the political ups and downs he experienced through the PR firm and involvement with SCAG. He had a colossal temper when denied. Although he tried to hide it, he was generally unsuccessful. Plus–he was just plain spoiled.

Like much of society, his fuse had become shorter, moral code more muddled, encounters cloaked in uncertainty, anger and fear. The rash of shootings in schools around the country were symptomatic of this, in Jim's judgment. Where anger used to be expressed through fights, pranks or words, now cowardice prevailed with the final act of destroying life through the use of a gun. As an athlete, Jim had been raised in an era where society considered sportsmanship to be important, embodying the idea of competition. Sports' value as a source of inspiration and example of character was often noted with pride. When the admirable qualities of honor, fair play and respect were reflected in sports, he felt we were uplifted and inspired. But when sports programs showcased the barbaric qualities of bullies and braggarts and were pervaded by cheating, society was demeaned. Surely, he felt, the growing incivility of society is a factor, but most people recognize that sports can exert a cause and effect on the decline of sportsmanship. Much of the problem, Jim felt, stemmed from confusion on what is "part of the game." The trend was to ignore rules and traditions of a sport in favor of anything that provides an advantage. Without thinking of the implications, many good people had bought into gamesmanship, the antithesis of sportsmanship. Sportsmanship, as Jim saw it, was about the honorable pursuit of victory. Gamesmanship focused just on victory, on winning by fooling the referee and considering that to be just as good as winning by outperforming a competitor.

Jim felt this trend had permeated society in general, whether in the courts, entertainment, the professions or elsewhere. Jim wasn't sure just what made him tick at times. He generally felt he passed as a good person but then, in some instances he wasn't quite so sure. He had a lot of anger and other shortcomings which concerned him. Could he work to keep them in check?

* * *

Returning to the present, Jim knew that he had to prepare for the Sacramento trip. Could he channel his anger and other problems in the right direction? He needed to impress Juan on his leadership abilities. His future success depended on it.

CHAPTER 4
COMMUNITIES
BUILDING AND COMING
TOGETHER

The new job retraining bill, Workforce Investment
Act (WIA), was the opportunity of a lifetime.
The current job training system, JTPA, was
based on the old traditional factory model geared
to a hierarchy of job responsibilities. The new
economy, directly opposite, encouraged people
to work for small companies–or themselves and
would work well within its more flexible boundaries.
Also, discussion of toll road ripoff problems.

"The fates of our region and its low-income communities are
inextricably intertwined, which means that attempts to address
poverty and neighborhood decline help all residents of the region."
<u>Growing Together</u>, Manual Pastor, Jr.

"Ann, can't we get these 'fraidy cats' interested in anything other than
contemplating their navels? The Regional Advisory Council's been in existence since '67 and needs to do more good things. They're non-elected's,
generally professionals, that get together to discuss regional affairs, keep
up-to-date about what SCAG is doing–or debating about policies already
in place."

Henry Ferrotte, Vice Chair of the Regional Advisory Council, sat at his
desk in his research firm office, struggling with how to get RAC moving.
A tall, lanky, middle-aged man, he hoped for some constructive change. It
was January 2000, and he was increasingly frustrated over seeing members
arrive at monthly meetings late or not at all, quibble about what they
should do, but lack any real interest or passion for doing something new
and different. Henry explored possibilities on the phone with Ann Philpot,
a long-time RAC member.

"Nothing really trail blazing,"Ann agreed. "That's for sure. No wonder
we have a reputation of 'Do Nothing' among RC'ers."

"Every time we talk about deviating from the status quo, some nervous Nellie gets upset and feels we're overstepping our boundaries. You know our bylaws mention the need for VISION. And I did get elected by proposing to improve things. They barely knew who I was at the time."

"Why don't you call Marcine and get her involved. She has some good ideas on community-building. What can you lose?" On that note she hung up, leaving Henry pondering his role.

Henry hoped Marcine Simpson, Executive Director of the Jobs Coalition, would be interested in brainstorming an approach that her agency and others might be able to coax into life.

Prior to calling Marcine, Henry ruminated about how he must link up with community-building efforts and strengthen anti-poverty programs at the neighborhood level. Traditionally, the RAC members of ten community-based service agencies tended to do their own thing and not work together to achieve what he thought they could. Much was due to a lack of time, staff, or fear of the risk involved, especially when reporting to their unpredictable and politically correct boards.

Greeting Marcine warmly on the phone, Henry got down to brass tacks.

"I'm sure you're familiar with such programs as Welfare to Work and the existing Job Training (JTPA) program. How about the new Workforce Investment Act (WIA) approved by Congress? The state legislature has been looking at seven bills to find the best one to implement this new act."

"I'm familiar with everything but WIA. But what can I or my agency do at this early stage?" she asked in resignation.

Henry laughed: "Not much now. But what I have in mind might take some work to put into action. Are you interested?"

"Of course I'm interested," Marcine answered. "Go on. Tell me about WIA."

"WIA offers the first major restructuring of our federal job training programs in 15 years. It tries to improve the system by consolidating programs to provide a complete continuum of services. This allows job seekers to use vouchers and strengthen accountability. It also ensures a strong leadership role for business. Still interested—or do you want to think about it?"

"I couldn't spend much time on it. I've got too much on my plate already. I've got six job training intake centers going now in South L.A. What more we can do to retrain these needy guys?"

"I know you're concerned. Wish I could help."

"You can," Marcine answered. "This program, if its half as good as it sounds, could be a big step forward. But how are we going to get all these

41

other social and anti-poverty programs onboard, up to snuff and cooperating on a bill that hasn't been approved yet?"

Henry laughed again. (He'd learned to laugh a lot to reduce stress.) "Can I call you Marce?"

"Sure."

"Great. Call me Hank. I can do most of the work setting it up as long as you'll let me use your name and agency to break down their resistance. I know they have the same problems as you do–in spades. I just want to see these agencies, the poverty-stricken and RAC, all succeed. I don't have much to lose based on RAC's record–but I don't plan to lose. I'm sure it'll work and plan on moving ahead on this right away. If I can get everything going, I want the various anti-poverty agencies to handle it."

"Okay, Hank! Keep me up-to-date on when you want the first meeting," Marce responded.

"I will. You don't know how much I appreciate your faith in me, Marce."

*   *   *

Several days later, homework done, Henry found interest in his program by most of the anti-poverty members on RAC, and moved ahead to effectuate it. One job bill cleared the legislature and was signed by the governor. Henry then asked for a meeting of the members.

He needed to see Juan in Sacramento to get his support. In turn, he would do everything possible to rally support for Juan's bill, now out of Committee and being circulated within the House; a great bill, but its chances of passing weren't good. Even if approved, there would probably be riders and language inserted to weaken it. But it was a bold step forward. Such bills generally took time to make their way through the House with enough support and deals made to see the light of day and win–or finally be buried. Then deals must be made with the Senate–or a companion bill floated and passed there. He hoped it would be approved. The L.A. Region needed this regional bill as soon as possible.

He looked forward to talking to Juan again. It had been a long time since all the events that had made them friends for life. That was a tough time period for both of them. How they survived was a miracle. They must do a little reminiscing when they got together again.

*   *   *

As Marcine wrapped up work and prepared to leave, she thought again about her earlier phone conversation with Henry. She had really enjoyed it.

She arrived home to her little condo in Compton, very convenient to her Watts office. As she opened the door, her twelve year old daughter,

Lucy, yelled out:

"Hi Mom. I wondered when you'd get home. I'm hungry as usual."

"Hi Honey. Sorry I'm late. How about spaghetti tonight?" she asked as she hugged all 70 pounds of an attractive, pig-tailed tomboy.

"Okay," Lucy made a face. "We'll be turning into Italians soon," she said, giggling.

"Silly, honey. But I like your sense of humor. How's school?"

"Super. More A's," she said, grinning from ear-to-ear.

"Oh, my brainy kid, you're at it again. Kidding. You know how proud I am of you," Marce said. "We've got to get you ready for a birthday party next week."

What a bright and outgoing child, she thought. Marcine felt fortunate that she could work without concern about Lucy, confident she was mature beyond her years. It hadn't always been that way, she remembered painfully. Her ex-husband Daryl had created a lot of problems. Into cocaine, he abused Lucy and her. They always seemed to have bruises, scratches, even a broken arm.

It took a long time to break off, but he finally moved out. A jealous and possessive man, even after he left and the divorce was final, he would come back and torment them with threats. It took two years for Lucy to get over the abuse and feel safe and happy.

Marcine had gone through a lot, operating in the survival mode. The one good thing her former marriage had provided was the move from Detroit to L.A. ten years ago. She worked hard to get degrees in Sociology and Social Work at UCLA and had, over time, been recommended for her current position with the Jobs Coalition. She began that from scratch, knowing of the need for counseling and job retraining for low income residents of the Alameda Corridor. She knew she still had a long way to go but maybe this WIA bill would open up possibilities for her.

* * *

Henry kept quite involved with the subregions–especially Gateway Cities and its economic development arm, Gateway Cities Partnership. In this way he knew Mike, Gavin and Carla well. He would have to make sure that Marce met and worked with these people since her agency served most of the Gateway communities.

He reflected back on the new job retraining bill, WIA, which he recently talked to Marce about. One thing he knew, the current job training system wasn't working well. Based on the traditional old factory model, it focused on everyone working within a hierarchy and having job responsibilities which never changed. The new economy, directly opposite, encour-

43

aged people to work for small companies–or for themselves, quickly moving from job to job using independence and creativity to survive. WIA would work well within its flexible boundaries, if handled right.

Henry wondered how he could get more information on the bill? Maybe Gavin with the Partnership would be a good possibility with his involvement in retraining efforts at Gateway Cities.

* * *

Gavin was hard at work when Henry called the next day. They had met briefly at a Gateway Cities COG meeting several months ago. Gavin remembered he was with that spineless RAC organization at SCAG? Oh, well, hopefully this call could be handled quickly.

"Gavin, sorry to bother you but I'm trying to get RAC involved in a worthwhile project. Since we have a lot of community-based service organization reps, I think I've got them interested in collaborating on a WIA project. I'm sure you're familiar with WIA?"

"Sure am. In fact, I was thinking about how to introduce WIA to the Partnership. Go on, I'm interested," Gavin said, quickly sensing that RAC might be useful after all.

"Great. Maybe we can help each other. It seems . . ." After talking about some of the components of the bill, they agreed to meet the next morning to draft an approach.

* * *

They met at Gavin's Paramount office near the 91 Freeway. Both Henry and Gavin had done some thinking overnight and were more than ready to develop an effective approach.

"Our biggest challenge will be SCAG's staff since they want to ramrod some aspects of the pilot project due to their access to regional organizations, data and staff," Henry commented. "Of course, their RC members are elected officials who can also more easily attract the business and education leaders needed to make it all work."

"I see SCAG finally recognized that the educational system was in bad shape and gave it a 'D' in their State of the Region Report," Gavin said.

"Right," Henry replied. "In fact, many wanted to give Education a 'B' until several of us spoke up to suggest it really should get an 'F' due to school system problems at L.A. Unified and other districts. They finally compromised with a 'D', a big breakthrough."

"Plus, SCAG has five years experience with its Regional Economic Strategies Consortium that brings together employers, educators and training experts in key industries." Henry realized their importance in being there to help SCAG make it happen.

"We both have reservations on SCAG's providing the necessary leadership," Gavin acknowledged. "The six county regional approach is key since it involves half of California's population. A lot can be achieved if this is handled right."

"Sure can," Henry stated. "The key is getting these ten community-based organizations in on the ground floor. As I mentioned yesterday, Marce has agreed to get things going. The next thing to do, now that we're in agreement, is arrange a meeting of these agency reps as soon as possible. Then we can move ahead with SCAG's blessing."

"Okay," Gavin said. "I'll wait to hear from you about the meeting time. I plan to meet with the Partnership sub-committee on this tomorrow. I should be able to get several of their technical people to come to the meeting. Just give us a few days notice, Henry."

* * *

The meeting took place the following Tuesday at 10 AM with 14 participants. Six of the community-based organization reps were able to attend. Even those missing would be provided with all the materials and minutes from the proceedings.

The office location was in a tough neighborhood–located in Watts, the heart of South-Central L.A. The area looked like a war zone with its barred entrances and windows, graffiti-pocked walls and lack of signs advertising businesses located there. It reminded Henry of some areas in downtown Washington, D.C. where the CIA had offices in back rooms with no identification. Parking was strictly on-street at the driver's risk.

He parked as close as possible. Locking his car, he walked to a building he thought housed the Job Coalition office. He pushed a buzzer on the wall flanking the gated entry:

"Your name please," a friendly female voice responded.

"Henry Ferrotte to see Marce Simpson."

The entrance gate began to slide open along with directions indicating where to go. Henry walked down a dark, gloomy hall until he spied a door labeled "Jobs Coalition." Entering a small office holding several beat-up chairs, battle-worn desks and battered wood filing cabinets, Henry greeted Marce with a smile.

"Thanks for coming, Henry. Welcome to our swank offices," she said, grinning impishly. "Hope you weren't mugged getting here."

"No sweat, Marce. I've been in worse slums on urban redevelopment studies. But this neighborhood does look tough," he conceded.

"I wanted to test your resolve on working with us. We're on the front lines. Some friends are watching your cars to make sure they aren't cannibalized or stolen while you're here."

Momentarily startled, Henry then grinned. "That takes care of that concern. Show me around your luxurious offices, will you."

While they were talking, the other attendees arrived.

Marce gave them a quick tour. Battered desks, scarred and nicked wood file cabinets of all types, decrepit typewriters and computers, and other thrown away office furniture and equipment were displayed. No fax machine or fancy phone system existed, Marce indicated, even though they went to great lengths to lock down every evening. There was no assurance that gangs wouldn't find some way to break in. The staff did much of their work out of their homes and took important papers and work home with them in the evening. They never left alone if they had to work late. Their cars were old, beat up and not worth stealing. Henry was impressed by her courage.

Without the luxury of a meeting room, they crowded into her office. Some were fortunate to find a chair or stool, while others sat on the floor or on corners of desks. They quickly got down to business. Meeting results included discussion of the industry clusters involved composed of wealth-creating complementary firms. Clusters also drove the vitality of support- and local-serving industries. Examples were construction, retail, and restaurants.

Focus was on precision machinists being targeted by Gateway Cities. The growing entertainment, multimedia and transportation sectors were also emphasized. Industry skill standards would be developed, including occupational, academic and technical skills. All information needed would be provided the various community colleges developing the curricula for retraining students involved. Since work had been done previously by the Partnership through the four area community colleges, this would be no problem. They had been able to get two educators to attend.

The workshop moved along well, with Marce, Henry and Gavin outlining what they hoped to achieve over the next few weeks. Assignments were made as everyone agreed to meet again in thirty days with concrete results expected.

* * *

Marcine struggled getting "reverse commuting" going for residents of the Alameda Corridor. She didn't know what to do next to get MTA involved in the construction trade so her organization could achieve the various goals established to allow the Alameda Corridor to reach its potential. Otherwise, reverse commute transportation of low-income people seeking the skilled, living wage construction jobs within the Alameda

Corridor project couldn't occur.

Talking about this dilemma with Sheryl, her compadre in this venture, Marcine said: "Why can't MTA be more cooperative? Lack of teamwork and organization."

"Right. They won't listen to reason or cooperate on the goal of making transit more available for their core market, the minorities and poor."

"Just think what the availability of shuttles and vanpools would do, especially tied to child care for trainees of construction jobs," Marcine said. "They need a way through reverse commuting to get to child care centers, training locations and their new jobs on time. Until they begin earning enough to buy cars, they won't break out of their transportation dilemma."

"Yeah, the next step before auto purchase would be the use of self-taxis available at one of our program hubs. They need to be employed or in a training program that requires a car to be eligible. A good driving record and valid driver's license are also needed," Sheryl said.

"Hopefully, SCAG will be able to help us, if not now, sometime soon."

"Do you think that Henry can assist in breaking through this log jam?" Sheryl asked. "I hope so. He's trying but bureaucracy works so darn slow, as you know. I get so frustrated," Marcine replied.

* * *

Henry continued his efforts to help through his SCAG contacts and even through some connections he had at MTA. But SCAG was slow to change due to its size, inertia and cronyism. This was built-in over the years as its top echelon got comfortable in its ways. They had little desire to change with the times–unless forced on them. This would be their first major crisis. Henry wouldn't be deterred in his efforts to press for change. He decided to circumvent the problem by going public on it through Bea. He called Bea and asked if she could help.

"I can't get MTA to work with the community-based groups on improving the job situation for the minorities, unemployed, low income and unskilled. Do you have any ideas how you might, if you felt moved, develop an article to put them on the spot to get something done?" he asked.

"I don't know, Henry. I'd like to do an article on this–but I'm not sure how to handle it. Give me some more details and I'll put on my thinking cap while you're talking."

"All these big agencies develop a bureaucratic numbness to change. They don't want to take chances. Be careful and don't risk anything, their superiors keep preaching. So they muddle along doing as little as possible to survive. Although lots of people who get involved with them come away frustrated, they don't themselves want to rock the boat to pressure them to change. So the situation continues to worsen. My feeling is that SCAG, facing its first real crisis, won't be forced to face up to it until public opinion forces them to change. The MTA issue is another where a huge bureaucracy involved holds similar feelings."

"Well put, Henry. I think we can accomplish a lot through this interaction. I've been aware and concerned about SCAG's problems for some time. Your bringing it up the way you have provides just the logic I need to develop another of my investigative journalism articles."

"Thanks, Bea, for your support. I was beginning to think that I'd been over-reacting to this since I like organization. I guess I feel everyone else should also be so inclined."

"Tell me about what you've been attempting with these community-based agencies, Henry. That could be key to everything else."

"You're somewhat familiar with the new job retraining bill, Workforce Investment Act, aren't you? The current job training system, JTPA, was based on the old traditional factory model geared to a hierarchy of job responsibilities. The new economy, directly opposite, encourages people to work for small companies–or themselves."

"Right. It makes a lot of sense."

"Well, I've been meeting with Marcine Simpson and members of the community-based agencies with RAC. We've held several workshop sessions. They've been trying to get MTA to hire them to carry out some of their job retraining contracts–with no success. We've tried to put a little pressure on them through SCAG, with no response. They always come out politically correct in their concern but don't follow through on action. We're really fed up. I think both agencies need to have a little dynamite exploded under them."

"And I take it, the dynamite you're referring to would be through an article exposing both agencies inadequacies?"

"Hopefully–if you agree, Bea."

"I'll do it! Assemble all your background materials and give me a copy. Also, have Marcine call me for a meeting. I've met with her before and am impressed with her abilities and drive. Thanks, Henry, for bringing this to my attention. I think we can do some good here by applying a little 'dynamite' to get these agencies to stop wallowing in their bureaucracy," Bea said.

"You're welcome, Bea. If I can help you any time, please let me know. Many thanks."

* * *

Bea got to work and several days later, on January 20, 2000, came out with another of her investigative journalism articles captioned:

SCAG/MTA BUREAUCRACIES
NEED CHANGE !

A great deal of change occurred as audits and investigations took place that rattled SCAG from stem to stern. Even MTA moved to include the social service agencies in their job retraining programs. Bea and her expose's continued to press for needed change. Hopefully, this was only the start of a fresh effort to reinvigorate regional cooperation. Only time would tell. Another successful effort at community-building and coming together accomplished.

* * *

Charlie Bates, CIG Legislative Policy Analyst, began sitting in on LAFF proceedings in late 1999, knowing that CIG must somehow be instrumental in drafting the proposed transportation legislative package–using some member to its advantage. He also wanted to be sure that strong policy was formulated on toll roads in Orange County and Southern California which would greatly increase housing starts. Here again, the Task Force would be in a strong position to get this done. The key, Jim Robinson, chaired the Task Force. Charlie had gone to great lengths to have Lila meet and get involved with Jim. Everything seemed in place to accomplish good things for CIG but so far it hadn't happened. He was irked, to say the least.

"Do you think you can contact him and keep things going?" Charlie asked impatiently.

"I think I can. We have an Open House Saturday evening. I'll call and invite him to it."

"Thanks. You know, Lila, you've done such great work for us," Charlie indicated.

"I feel bad about doing some of these things, " Lila responded. "But I'll move ahead."

"Let me know how it works out. I'm depending on you," he said cool-ly, as he left.

* * *

Jim was working on the toll road issue for the next Transportation Task Force meeting. Deeply, involved, the shrill phone startled him but Lila's voice made him push the paper aside.

"Listen, Jim. I thought of you when I heard about the CIG Open House this Saturday evening." She paused. "Could you come? I'd like to see you."

Jim grinned. "I'd like to see you too. Where has time gone? I've been too busy."

Lila seemed upset at this statement. "Okay," she said, trying to keep a cheerful tone. "Lets plan on eight Saturday evening at CIG. We can do something afterwards."

"Fine, Lila. See you there."

Jim stirred around uneasily after their short conversation. He knew he had to push the toll road issue more with the Task Force to help fill the money gap. The 1998 RTP had identified toll road financing as a way to add highway capacity. Several private roads were built, two operating through a public sector Toll Road Authority, and one by the private sector through a special bill ramrod through the legislature. He knew that some on the Task Force were uneasy about these roads since they were being built either to ease excess congestion or to open areas to development.

Some members of the legislature also resisted because of private sector involvement in passing the bill and the big private profit margin permitted. Environmentalist and planner concerns voiced that urban sprawl had to stop somewhere and the toll roads only helped perpetuate sprawl.

Still, Jim felt he had no choice but to continue using these roads to make up for insufficient public funds. He knew he couldn't be faulted for taking this approach, but it still bothered him.

*   *   *

Jim arrived at the Open House at 8:30 with mixed emotions. He tried to play it down by dressing casual. Lila, dressed to kill in a form-fitting midnight blue stretch velvet dress, which accentuated her sexy long legs and body, made his pulse beat faster. They nodded hello when he entered, but she didn't detach herself from her group. Finally, what seemed like hours to him, she came over and greeted him coolly. They chatted awhile and then left for his pad on the edge of downtown L.A., which was a very masculine converted loft with overhead timbers and open layout He gave her a tour and then they settled in to chat on the comfortable sofa.

They were more reserved tonight, possibly because they both had time to think about things. The other night had been different since neither thought about a relationship then. Before, it had started out as just another amorous encounter. It was different now. This could go places if they so desired, Lila thought. But she wasn't happy with the way Jim had treated her.

"Did you know about our efforts to get highways and other things through the state legislature?" Lila asked.

"Not directly. Are you involved in that too?" he queried. Things were getting interesting.

"No. But I do touch base with others. We're also trying to develop a toll road program."

"Yeah. I'm tinkering in that area too. What does CIG want to happen? Public control through Toll Road Authorities? Or private control through private firms and non-profits?"

"I'm not the best person to talk to. I think it's private control though. Like that for the 91 Toll Lane extension. I can give you a name or two, if you're interested."

"I'll think about it and let you know, Lila. Say, lets get away from business, shall we?" He slipped his arms around her and they briefly hugged, but she still seemed distant. She kept that small "I have a headache space" between them.

"We're both reticent about getting too involved right now, aren't we?" Jim joked. "It doesn't mean that we have to be afraid of each other though, does it?"

"Definitely not," but Lila pulled away. "Let's take it slow though and get to know each other better. I think we ought to call it a night," she said coolly. She was tempted to go further but his responses tonight concerned her. CIG was a very dangerous group to deal with if his agenda differed from theirs. Plus, she needed to report this conversation with Jim to Charlie tomorrow.

* * *

Then an article on a toll road sale hit the front page of the L.A. Times. Reportedly, a non-profit group of local businessmen were prepared to buy the 91 toll lane franchise for $225 million. Reports stated the toll road wasn't as successful as originally reported and they wanted out. The Times kept the matter on the front page for the next week as indications were that the 91 extension wasn't the only toll road involved. All of them had non-competition clauses which barred improvements on public freeways which in any way cut down on toll road volumes and, thus, revenues. There seemed little doubt these pacts put public freeways at a disadvantage and the pacts written and passed in the state legislature favored private builders over the public.

Jim continued to research the toll road legislation issue and discovered: 1) The right of private investors to make a return exceeding 21 percent the same time Caltrans was required to use its "best efforts" to ensure the project's success; 2) The fact that the developer need only pay a $10-a-year franchise fee to Caltrans for the duration of the 35-year lease; 3) Full liability for the toll road rested with Caltrans which had no right to money damages for defects in the road. The condition leaves taxpayers responsible for defending lawsuits and compensating the injured; and 4) the right of the developer to sue the state for damages if the state's action damaged the toll road's business.

In discussing these points further with Harry, the consultant for SCAG's Transportation Finance Task Force, Harry pointed out: "It could destroy the public freeway system. Private enterprise could take over and charge what they wanted in tolls and the public would be held hostage to this."

Jim went on: "These defects in the agreement meant that the more affluent toll road users would have a quality highway–better maintained, less congestion–and the ordinary citizen would get the potholes and the gridlock. What a ripoff!"

He called Bea and told her about the four points he had developed on the toll road fiasco. She agreed to put an article together summarizing these points for publication in the paper.

* * *

Jim and Harry discussed the toll road issue further before the next Task Force meeting, with Jim asking: "Are toll roads inherently bad!"

"No. But it's almost impossible to craft a bill that would protect the public interest while at the same time allowing the private sector a guaranteed profit," Harry responded. "It's too complicated when you're involved with peoples fickle habits, the ups and downs of the economy and the political process which attaches all sorts of riders to bills to get them passed."

"I see what you mean, Harry. Any thoughts on strategies to get rid of the shortfall?"

"Yes, we need to get the Task Force to craft and adopt several bills to be presented to both houses in Sacramento. I think the following could go a long way to reduce the shortfall:

1. Concentrate on funding transit instead of new highways.

2. Discourage private funding of toll roads.

3. Emphasize O & M (Operations and Maintenance) to get existing facilities up-to-date."

"Okay, let's do it."

* * *

These three principles were presented at the next Task Force meeting and adopted. However, at the following TCC policy meeting, they met strong resistance from several quarters. Jim, faced by mounting pressure from groups like CIG, defended this approach against sprawl.

"I'm committed to making this region stronger. Based on all the give-and-take we've had in the Transportation Finance Task Force on this, I'm convinced that the sooner we 'bite the bullet the better,'" he urged, looking for strong TCC support.

Unfortunately, some of Jim's normally strongest supporters came out against such policy and it was defeated. Jim took it hard. He felt he had been betrayed and lashed out strongly.

"I'm surprised that some of you, who normally back my position, have buckled. Why?"

An embarrassing silence followed until finally, George, who normally backed him, replied: "You know it's a sticky issue, Jim? All of us have to play the political game and this is one issue which could lose us votes."

"Not if you go to your constituents and explain what's involved, George. We've got to start facing up to our problems and looking at them more from a regional standpoint. We're not doing enough to educate our citizenry. Until we do, we'll all feel exposed. I feel strongly on this."

"That's easy to say–but hard to accomplish, Jim," George replied.

"Does this mean that the RC is going to continue thinking local control on everything? If so, it means that our participation in SCAG is meaningless. We've got to have 'balls' or we're going to continue accomplishing nothing. We're going to continue to 'fiddle while Rome burns', so to speak," Jim retorted.

This outburst was met with silence. Jim sat down and the meeting continued on another issue. Jim finally got up and walked out, seething.

* * *

Later at his condo, Jim ruminated about what took place. He felt betrayed by those he thought were his friends and supporters. He had learned a lot about regionalism and felt ready to totally embrace it. Now, he had second thoughts. Self-interest seemed to be the way to go, based on what he witnessed today. No one seemed willing to go the extra mile to get his voters involved in and understand the regional process. He wouldn't expose himself again this way in a public body. It wasn't worth it.

What should he do? How else could he benefit? he would have to wait and see what came up. This betrayal had hurt his psyche deeply. He knew himself too well. He wouldn't forget about how he had been humiliated today when standing up for regionalism. He would get the last laugh on this. Time would be on his side in vindicating him.

As he thought about how he would get revenge, excitement gripped him. He felt an adrenaline "rush" and enjoyed it. Being in control by fooling others as to where he stood on things. Being unpredictable and difficult to handle. This power really did give that adrenaline "rush" which he enjoyed. It was like a drug high he had in his college days. Very enjoyable–and needed in politics when everything else failed. He smiled in anticipation of the days ahead.

CHAPTER 5
STATE LEGISLATURE
POLITICAL INTRIGUE

*Discussions begin on Regional Planning bill and
Non-Profit Alliance to stop polarization of our
cities and regions by non-equity issues.
Meetings in state offices to work out some
deals on legislative support. Results in stormy
two days at the state capitol.*

---

*"All truth passes through three stages. First,
it is ridiculed. Second, it is violently opposed.
Third, it is accepted as being self-evident."*
                                    Arthur Schopenhauer

"Wow! Things happen fast some times–hopefully with a happy ending for us. It's hard to know in politics. We'll just have to wait and see," Juan Rodriguez addressed his two assistants, Otto and Joe, as he sat at his State Capitol desk. Already near the end of February 2000, time whizzed by with only a few bills being approved.

"I got calls from Robinson, O'Neil, Ferrotte and Nelson last week saying they're ready to meet me in Sacramento," he said, getting up and pacing back and forth. "I've scheduled a joint meeting Thursday morning, followed by one-on-one's with each."

"They all have personal agendas, some polar opposites of ours which will have to be handled individually," Juan explained. "But all four know each other and have had similar problems–and maybe if they all put their heads together, the results could benefit us."

"It's a great idea, Juan," Otto replied, enjoying the moment. "With the right ground work, everyone comes out ahead."

"You bet," Joe piped in. "We need to put issues together that will benefit all. It'll let our regional bill move ahead with even stronger support."

"Okay, then, let's do it," Juan said. "We've got all the bills and paperwork. How should we view the objectives of the four?"

"Robinson is the most assertive and ambitious politically," Otto exclaimed, narrowing his slanted eyes. "He represents the entire L.A.

Region and badly needs help getting a multi-billion dollar Transportation Finance bill passed for the Association of Governments."

"Yeah, he's going to be hard to handle," Joe emphasized. "He's arrogant and wants too much. He must deliver more for us. We should lean on him for help."

"I hear he expects to be the next chair of SCAG's Regional Council (RC)," added Juan. "He won't take no for an answer."

"He also wants a House seat eventually like so many of those RC cats," said Otto.

"Well, he should be willing to help our legislative package." Juan came back to his desk and sat down. "It's to his advantage since it will provide him needed resources."

"I bet O'Neil of the Gateway Cities Partnership wants assistance too," Joe said. "Passage of the right WIA job retraining bill in the legislature is high on his list.

"Plus, California's toxic soil legislation on liability is poor compared with other states," Otto said. "Oh, yeah. Equal treatment for poverty areas and more affordable housing."

"He'll be strong for our legislative package," added Juan.

"Ferrotte has similar interests." Joe glanced at Juan. "He must provide support for our legislation."

"Nelson should be counted on to help develop our legislative package since he's chair of the Subregion Coordinators–all 14 subregions could be funneled through him," Juan said, shifting around in his seat while eyeing the clock. "What does he want–besides the world on a platter?"

"A lot," Otto stated. "Major funds for broad brush improvements on Gateway Cities 710 Freeway corridor, as well as major corrections in transit service. Completion of the Alameda Corridor and fixing groundwater problems are high on his list. He's really involved."

Joe took off his glasses, polishing them as he spoke. "Toxic soil correction, poverty area equality for funding and job retraining programs are key. He has a full agenda for his impoverished district–hard to fill."

"The beauty–and conflict–of democracy in action," Juan groused. "Lots of discussion and compromise to get some parts of what's needed. We all want the world, but generally 'it ain't there'–at least right now. Some need more than others. We've got to get them something to equalize things. That's the excitement of our bill if we can get it passed without losing its intent."

"I agree," said Otto. "Does this provide what you need for the various agendas? Combined, of course, with support of your legislative package."

"Definitely!" Juan rubbed his hands together as he got to his feet, a satisfied smile creasing his face. "Lets get it together. I have another meeting scheduled. Great work, you two. We're really cruising now. I'm getting excited about things. We need to talk soon on the investigation about the leak and track our enemies. Let's get together on this before meeting with the L.A. Four–and later, the three women–Carla, Marcine and Bea–in L.A ."

* * *

Later that day, Otto and Joe met with other staff members investigating the office leaks hampering Juan's legislative campaign for his bill. Progress had slowed in getting Amy Fuller to pass on information to Jake Posse and others who might be in her pipeline of deceit.

They had a breakthrough yesterday, though. Amy received a bite on the planted disinformation they were feeding her. Those shadowing listened in on a meeting she had last night at the Highlights Club. Hank, in charge of the investigation, provided a progress report.

Otto and Joe received Hank's report, followed by a Q and A session. Hank produced some interesting news.

"Amy met with Jake Posse all right. But the real surprise–get this–she met later, after Jake left, with one of Juan's old friends, considered an insider for his past meetings," said Hank. "A real breakthrough, although this will stun Juan. An old pal, Evon Morales, got this planted information. Once he passes it on, we'll find out where it surfaces. Then we can determine how to handle both leaks."

"What a breakthrough," said Otto. "I'm glad we were patient in handling it. Who knows where this will lead. There could be other leaks too."

"How do we handle this, Otto?" asked Joe, who, at first, couldn't believe the information received. "It's scary info and we must be careful how it's handled. When do we let Juan know about it?"

"Right away! The political consequences could be devastating. Where it surfaces will tell. I'll pull him out of a meeting now," Otto said.

* * *

"There's no doubt about this?" Juan exclaimed dubiously when presented with the facts. "Hank, you're positive Amy met with Evon?"

"Positive! We even checked the license plates and video-taped the conversation," Hank stated. "You can view the tape so you're sure. We're waiting for the planted information to surface so we can trace it further."

"I'm stunned! Why would he be doing this?" Juan exclaimed. "Our friendship goes back to childhood. We've drifted apart in recent years since Evon lost his bid for re-election to the House from East L.A. But he's been in to see me several times and supported my efforts in the house in recent years. Why would he do this?"

Juan's thoughts drifted back to his youth when the two had been inseparable.

*   *   *

Juan's home turf in 1960 was L.A.'s rough Eastside. He lived in a
tough neighborhood and belonged to a gang. He felt he had no choice,
although he shielded it from his mother. He had just completed serving two
years in Juvenile Hall for an auto-theft conviction as a teenager. He had
gone to school with Evon and both had been convicted on the same
escapade. They completed their sentences before returning to their East
L.A. neighborhood.

Their childhoods were similar, important at the time. Born in 1945 to
Hector and Rosa Rodriguez, Juan was the oldest of seven children. His parents worked hard to keep a roof over their children, although they had
problems helping their children grow up on L.A.'s Eastside. Since his
father suffered from asthma, Juan felt pressured to act as the "man of the
house." Although he partially succeeded, he couldn't stay out of the street
gangs who offered him a feeling of belonging as a part of their "family."
Peer pressure was so great that two of the seven children got into trouble
with the law and experimented with hard drugs. In fact, one currently was
in prison, while the other died of a heroin overdose.

Inseparable growing up, Juan and Evon dropped out of school in the
ninth grade when both were convicted of auto theft. This messy situation
changed their lives forever. Feeling their oats one day, Juan challenged
Evon to swipe his shop teacher's car. Evon took the dare, brazenly snitched
his teacher's car keys when he wasn't looking. Juan joined him in the joy
ride and they drove up to the teacher, laughed in his face and took off again
on the streets reaching speeds of over 100 miles per hour. Cops chased them
and finally caught them when they ran out of gas. Juan claimed that he had
nothing to do with Evon's stealing the car–just along for the ride. Other students supported Evon in saying that Juan egged Evon into stealing the car.
Both were sentenced to two years in juvenile hall.

Evon probably never forgave Juan for getting him in trouble and lying
about it. He may have felt that Juan didn't stand by him when needed and
exposed him to police action for things Juan caused. Although they continued to be friends, the relationship was damaged by Juan's lies and dis-
loyalty. The feeling that Juan was smarter and better than Evon always
seemed to be there.

They both returned to school and graduated. They also had a common
interest–becoming lawyers. Several years and numerous jobs later, Juan

began his quest toward a law degree by attending two community colleges and eventually, Hastings Law School. Evon joined him at Hastings.

Juan caught the political bug, and assisted by Evon, worked on numerous campaigns for several years and became acquainted with political activists who helped him to enter politics. Evon was swept along. They entered and won races for the House from adjacent districts. But Evon didn't fare well in the House, being defeated for re-election. Their career paths veered apart.

* * *

Returning to the present, Juan knew now Evon blamed him for his re-election defeat. He felt Juan helped rob him of his glory. He did well while Evon's future withered. He should have been more sensitive. Could he have done more to help Evon? Looking back, Juan realized he hadn't assisted Evon with his re-election campaign. Juan rationalized by feeling that his hands were full getting re-elected himself. Could this be considered a cop-out?

Thinking further, he hadn't liked some of the positions Evon took on bills submitted during their first term. Juan didn't think Evon did his homework on the issues. Several lobbyists influenced Evon and others to back their bills without looking into all sides of the issue. Juan had become disenchanted with Evon's lack of clear thinking. Possibly he should have advised Evon more. But he felt it would be considered interference. He realized now he'd gone his own way and left Evon to fend for himself. He knew Evon didn't have his background and preparation for politics and the constant need for moralizing that Juan fortunately received.

Maybe Juan should have been "his brother's keeper," since he'd encouraged Evon to run for election. Evon must have felt lost and "easy" to manipulate by the lobbyists since Juan no longer took time to help him cope with his new life. However, Evon could, at times, be such a difficult person to deal with when crossed. Juan remembered some situations growing up where Evon was his own worst enemy. It looked like just such a situation took place again. How does one handle such an unlikable person? He had helped him out many times in the past. Should he do it again for old times sake?

Evon could do him a lot of harm by surfacing his past. He needed to leak some of this to the press before Evon or someone else broke it at the wrong time. It would hurt him initially, but he should have been more circumspect about his youth earlier in his career. Impossible to keep anything a secret in this day and age.

* * *

"I'm going to tell you about events I'm not proud of which took place when I was young, some of which could hurt me politically," he said to Joe and Otto, as he paced nervously about the room, his hands waving in the air. "You may want to change jobs as a result. I'll understand."

"No! No!" Otto said, committed by the look on Joe's face. "No matter what, we'll see you through. We believe in what you're doing and will back you one hundred percent."

"I haven't done anything wrong since I began my career. I had a tough youth and I made some mistakes which I've paid for. I learned. It was wrong. Evon was part of my hidden past and could get back at me. He could blow the whistle to bring me down."

His loyal assistants were concerned as he disclosed sordid details of his childhood. Understanding the problem, they backed him. They put together a scenario to follow in leaking key information to the press that had not been known before. Bea Johnson, the investigative reporter, was part of the friendly media included in the leak.

As often happens, the quickest response to leaks comes from enemies. Evon was the first to accost Juan, arriving at his office after hours. Juan was alone, deep in his work when he came.

"You haven't changed—still manipulating people!" Evon thundered.

Startled, Juan glared up at him, blurting: "What do you want?"

He couldn't categorize his look but his intent was obvious. Evon lunged around the desk at him. He knew Juan had wised up to him and his political game. He grabbed again and succeeded in jarring Juan off-balance. The chair toppled. Grunting, he moved in and began hammering Juan with his fists, a wild, savage glint on his face.

Juan thought he'd outgrown the rage he grew up with as a Latino outsider, but found it still there. He must not succumb to it though. No fist fighting in the legislature! How should he handle this? He blocked more blows, finally able to get Evon in a bear hug and wrestle him to the floor. Pinning Evon's arms and legs and keeping astraddle, Juan cautioned:

"Let's stop this nonsense and talk it out, Evon. This is no way to act." He gasped for breath, angry, but also saddened.

"You're not going to get away with this, you idiot" Evon yelled. "I'm going to get you for what you've done. You ruined my political life. People will know where you came from and what you're really like, " he yelled.

"I lost big due to lack of support by you in the last election. You even set me up and lied to the cops about the 'joy ride' we took when we were just kids. You're so sanctimonious. Now people will question your so-called 'integrity' bit. It's time you're exposed!"

"So you're the one who's been spreading all those rumors." Juan said, holding him down. Emotions tore Evon apart with their ferocity, as he continued to shake with rage. All this anger had been bottled up as he played his cat and mouse game with Juan over the past months.

Finally spent, Evon calmed down. Although still leary, Juan let him up. They sat across from each other for several moments, both too tired and upset to say anything. Juan wracked his brain on how to handle this, deciding now was the time to begin the process of forgiveness.

"I didn't realize how you felt. Your posturing and sweet talk on how we worked together so well in the past and you owed me everything fooled me," Juan stated. "You should've let me know how you felt, mentioned your problems and asked for help."

"Wasn't it obvious that I needed you? Have all my life. How can you be so blind?" Evon sputtered with frustration. "Never easy for me. Knew I was losing you–especially recently, as you continued to increase in popularity. Hated you so much for rubbing it in about being smarter. Couldn't stomach you. Was too proud to ask for help," Evon responded angrily. "You–I guess–too busy in being 'politically correct' to see through me."

"That's past. We can work something out," Juan said, although not sure how. "Too late to start over, Evon? Providing my enemies information for a long time?" he probed.

"I didn't. There's certainly been interest. I used the leak for personal revenge, thinking two wrongs made a right."

"Then who's been spreading this crap about me?" Juan exploded in anger.

"I know Amy was meeting someone else later. I'm not sure who other than it's a skirt," Evon said, thinking frantically about how to mend fences.

"A woman?" Juan queried, a puzzled look on his face. "You know more? A name, where she's from, why Amy was meeting her?"

"Oh, let's see. What did she say?" Evon puzzled, a frown on his face as he scratched his head. "She's from L.A.. I know she attended your Long Beach meeting. Oh, yeah! I know. She's upset about your proposed legislation which might eliminate a new freeway planned for the 'burbs' and fowl up some 'rich cats' financially. Fancy dresser, a looker, gray hair, middle-aged. Any help, Juan?" he asked desperately.

Floored by Evon's effort to get back in his good graces, Juan wondered if this could be a trap? How sincere could he be? It was difficult to gauge Evon's response. He did remember a woman matching his description dressed to kill in a red outfit, whipping up the crowd at the Long Beach meeting.

"Possibly. I'll check with my assistants. Step back from this awhile, Evon. Don't know, maybe we can work out something–if you're interested. Let's go slow."

"I'm interested, Juan. What you say about our problems makes sense." Evon said, a pleading tone entering his voice. "I'm a unknown quantity now, I know. Hope we can get back together."

"Okay, then. Check back with me in a week or so," Juan said, moving to leave.

* * *

"Otto, check on this woman through your L.A. contacts? She sounds like she's involved in some 'sprawl' group. Call the guy who was at my meeting in Long Beach," Juan directed after recounting his encounter with Evon.

"You bet. Shouldn't be difficult. I'll get back ASAP."

* * *

"Stuck out like a sore thumb at the meeting. Judith Stru___ __ ___ of Keep Our Population Expanding (KOPE), which loves urban sprawl and more freeways," Otto reported later in the day. "You're #1 on her hit list. KOPE has money and shadowy figures behind it. She must get instructions from someone in Sacramento. We're checking the people behind it and how to handle their hate and distortion bit."

"Look into Evon Morales and see who he's working with. Hope no one, but who knows. I can't go on his word. If we're going to use him in the future, I want to know where he's at."

"Okay. Should your probe of Jake Posse continue?" asked Otto. "How about Amy? Three meetings in one evening–a bit much."

"Yeah, continue the probe of Jake Posse. Also, we've got to be careful with Amy. Minimize her use by others wanting to exploit her connections," Juan ordered. "Are we ready for the meetings with the 'L.A. Four' tomorrow? Can we get them all in?"

"All set. Big meeting at 8 AM followed by afternoon meetings. Plenty of time."

"Fine. Eight tomorrow then."

* * *

"Great to get you together. Just like old times. How long's it been?" Juan asked as he shook hands with his four L.A. friends.

"Two years for me, Juan" responded Robinson. "Awhile for all of us. You look great. Politics sure works wonders on you."

"Highs and lows in politics. Some days it sucks. Good to get together.

A lot of things to bring you up-to-date on. Where you need help, we'll cover this afternoon. Now, let's get down to business."

"Most metropolitan areas are going through a pattern of inner city decline, as well as older suburb decay. This is made worse by the growth of regional polarization. There has been denial by some politicians that a substantial proportion of the infrastructure financing occurs in the newer, better-off areas. However, I can prove there is little equity in improvements made throughout any metro-region, including L.A. This may surprise you but it shouldn't."

"Yeah, it does surprise me" replied Jim. "I know there's clamor among some L.A. area communities that they're not getting their fair share. But we're pouring a lot of money into these areas–and I know we're doing a good job. You know I'm chair of the Transportation Finance Task Force at SCAG. We haven't added all the financial needs up yet, but I'm sure there's equity in our region."

"I have figures concerning the L.A. area which will surprise you," Juan countered. "There are extreme inequities currently existing. We can talk about that later. What I want to discuss today is how we must build coalitions to permit all citizens to share equally in the good life."

"You see before you," pointing to the screen, "a list of seven principles which I feel need to be adhered to so we can prevent polarization from spreading in our metropolitan areas. I'm in the process of forming a non-profit Alliance to make this happen. Let me briefly cover these seven principles which will guide us in our deliberations this morning."

"1. Ensure government has power to achieve community, stability, equity and renewal. We can accomplish this at the state level through my regional planning bill," Juan explained.

"2. Reduce barriers to affordable housing available to diverse racial and income groups. This is a ticking time bomb which must be turned off. The RHNA Housing approach is not working in terms of getting cities to share their affordable housing requirements."

"3. Target economic development to low-income people and communities. Two and three are key to achieving equity and environmental justice. Again, poverty areas are not getting the financial help from banks and others. They're being red-lined too often."

"4. Promote land use planning for balanced growth, equality and social justice. Land use is not being used as an important part of the equation in achieving balanced growth and social justice. This has got to change to stop polarization from growing."

"5. Develop/fund balanced transportation systems, promoting access to jobs and housing. This boils down to more and better mass transit for low income families–and help in reverse commuting."

"6. Promote high-quality, fully-funded, integrated schools throughout region. Educational improvements must take place targeted for low income children if we're going to have any hope in turning things around. Principles four, five and six are important to achieving a better life for all families," Juan explained.

"7. Modify financing and tax structure, creating greater tax base equity. This will be the toughest nut to crack since it goes against local control but is needed to help break the 'have/have not' community syndrome. Here again, my bill will be instrumental in achieving this."

Juan continued: "Our first three reforms are the most significant in terms of the socio-economic stability of the urban center: fair housing, property tax-base sharing, and reinvestment in important urban services. They break down poverty so that lower income households are spread throughout the metropolitan area near their jobs, not concentrated just in the inner city. This stabilizes poor neighborhoods over time by surrounding them with good housing. By providing equal use of limited resources, as a variety of housing and other uses permit, all areas will share in the tax revenues generated."

"Great," Mike broke in. "Your bill will keep some communities from hogging all the tax revenues while others less fortunate can't even provide the minimum urban services for an adequate quality of life."

"You're absolutely right, Mike." Juan answered, enjoying their camaraderie. "Finally, all this permits rebuilding housing and other land uses needed to attract the middle classes back to the inner city. Industry, businesses and other private land uses can be restored through reinvestment in run-down areas, completing the re-investment cycle."

"Right, Juan. Do we have some companion bills which can help make this happen?" Jim asked.

Juan paced back and forth, his eyes thoughtful. "Yes, Jim. There are several other bills being considered now which can help, once property tax-base sharing is passed. It'll attract a lot of legislation since it promises what in American politics almost never can be delivered-immediate lower taxes and better services to residential areas."

"Going on, my second three reforms reinforce and permit the first three to operate efficiently and sustainably. These reforms encourage better land planning so as to place jobs closer to where the workers live, combined with effective management of community growth to improve the environment. In addition, a new form of welfare reform must take place, mixed with needed public works projects; and finally, a wide range of highway programs and well-managed and coordinated bus, light rail and rail-transit projects. I'm excited that they can be successfully developed. They should produce balanced growth so as to mix all income groups and be accessible by transit. They will also minimize needed governmental expenditures and ensure the environment is adequately protected," he concluded. "Any thoughts?"

"I would imagine that the various legislative committees have key bills in process which will help your bill along," Henry encouraged.

"You're right," replied Juan. "However, we do have a big problem with one element. These reforms can only be effectively administered and sustained by those elected to coordinate this for the entire region. We know that this element goes beyond what the Regional Council's elected members currently do and isn't possible in the L.A. area at this time. We can't hold an election until people understand these issues and realize how important it is to vote on them. We need to start the education process through discussion with possible allies. It won't be easy."

"You're absolutely right, it won't be easy," Henry agreed. "But we're prepared to help make it happen."

"Great." Juan said. He went on to outline the remaining key elements of his proposed bill. "Finally, a broad mix of tax and public finance reforms are needed to overturn the reckless incentives created by generations of erratic tinkering with a highly fragmented, over-regulated local marketplace." He fumed as he thought of the rampant waste over the past several decades.

"I'm not going to go into these in any greater detail today," he concluded. "You can see that these principles, if used correctly, can stop polarization and achieve effective land use planning for the entire region. My proposed bill, HB150 focuses on these simple principles. Any thoughts you have would be appreciated."

"I think they cover the essential points,"said Mike enthusiastically. "It's just what we need for the Gateway Cities area. We're missing out on funds needed to eradicate the area's pervasive poverty."

"Definitely. We have little money and it must be spent wisely. It isn't now," Henry added..

"If we can get this bill passed, we'll make great strides straightening out our poverty-stricken areas. Just what we need," Gavin agreed.

"Generally, I support your principles," Jim interjected. "However, if we go too far, we'll paralyze the region's growth process."

"How so, Jim?" asked Juan, rubbing his ear, preparing for conflict.

"We have limited funds to use. Right now, the L.A. Region's up to $50 billion short of meeting its transportation needs through 2025. If too much money is siphoned off for the inner cities and inner suburbs, we'll gridlock the region."

"Ah, ha. I'm not surprised at your statement," Juan responded. "You haven't had the opportunity to think through these seven principles and apply them to the L.A. area. These approaches generally aren't being applied now! When applied, most of the expensive freeways, trunk sewers, new schools, water lines and other infrastructure considered necessary wouldn't be needed if sprawl were curbed. Much of the proposed growth could be achieved through infill. Do you see this?"

"Not to the extent that you're talking about, Juan. You'd need to increase densities significantly to do what you're suggesting. The politicians won't allow it," rejoined Jim.

"What do the rest of you think about what's being said? " Juan asked, his eyes sweeping the room. "Am I really whistling Dixie or what?"

"I don't think so," said Gavin. "They've already paved over L.A. Why make it worse?"

"We're virtually gridlocked now and more freeways won't help," Mike emphasized.

"What you're advocating would change the way cities are put together. They would make people's lives more meaningful." Henry noted. "Jim, which principles create a problem?"

"I guess the fifth and seventh principles on tax base equity and significant changes in the transportation system," Jim said, preparing for a battle since the others were against his thinking. "A little on land use planning too. I'm visualizing the impact on my city, Beverly Hills."

"We're getting to the key issues which divide the 'have' cities from the 'have not's'," Juan noted with concern. "You don't think the well-to-do communities have been subsidized for years at the expense of the poorer and politically weaker communities, do you, Jim?"

"No, I don't, Juan. We may get more revenues per capita for improvements but we also pay more taxes. We can't be responsible for helping others by giving them what they haven't earned . You won't be able to sell this to our tax payers. There would be a political revolt," emphasized Jim, scowling at the thought.

"But you want poorer cities to take the industrial and commercial uses that created our Brownfields," Juan retorted. "Also, the less affordable housing units that cost more in services than they return in tax revenues.

Plus all the extra services involved. There must be better ways to balance the books so all citizens can benefit equally from the opportunities provided those able to exploit the system," Juan continued. "Otherwise, the system breaks down and society pays anyway–at least the middle class."

"Jim, give it more thought. Juan is right," Henry said. "Our cities and region are breaking down by continuing to do this."

"I don't know. You're asking me to buy into something that the region's leaders won't agree to," Jim exclaimed! "Why pick on me to support this?"

"Let's back off," Juan cautioned. "One step at a time. I'm not expecting you to buy into this today. The legislature itself probably isn't ready yet. But we've got to begin thinking of ways to make our urban areas work better before we're paralyzed by these problems."

"I agree, Juan," said Gavin. "I'm willing to help generate support for your bill, with possible modifications, so all our cities can flourish again."

"You're right. I'd like to establish a citizen's committee to study the bill," said Henry. "In fact, our RAC group in L.A. could develop support through its Regional Citizenry."

"The Gateway Cities Subregion would also be willing to study the merits of the bill–along with help from other subregions," Mike enthused.

"Don't get me wrong, Juan. The RC and its policy committees–especially the Community Human Development (CEHD) Policy Committee–would want to study it through one of their sub-committees," Jim countered. "We need to look at all the possibilities."

"Great! Than we're in agreement that this bill should be studied through a variety of venues in L.A.? That's the best way to educate people from all walks of life on the regional process–and what needs to be done at the state and federal levels to improve things. Let's move on to other matters we need to discuss," Juan enthused.

The remainder of the morning was spent on less weighty issues. They broke for lunch after agreeing to go into their one-on-one meetings, beginning with Henry, followed by Gavin, Mike and Jim.

*　*　*

"Henry, I marvel time and time again how we survived those two incidents in East L.A. so many years ago. They were scary. I owe you a great deal for saving my life."

"Juan, it goes both ways. Your assistance saved my life in an earlier incident."

"Henry, I know you have needs. Joe and Otto of my staff have kept me up-to-date on things taking place in L.A. We're here to help. What's on

66

your mind?" Juan asked, moving around his office, as they began their afternoon session.

"I've got some requests, some of which will be covered in more detail by Mike and Gavin later. I need help on getting the right WIA job retraining bill through the legislature. My compadre, Marcine with the Alameda Corridor job training group, needs help on this too. I understand that your staff has zeroed in on one bill which fits our needs best. We would appreciate your help in shepherding it through committee with some modifications which I will outline," Henry said.

"We'd be glad to help. I'll be contacting Marcine during my L.A. visit in a few weeks. What else?" Juan asked.

"We have an affordable housing problem, including extreme over-crowding, the highest in the nation, if not the world. We need a bill to provide funds for developing more housing soon. Otto can help with the details on this. Also, we desperately need equal treatment in funding for our poverty areas. This fits directly into your regional bill on needs. Can we get help here too?"

"Certainly. Otto will handle this problem. The WIA job training bill, affordable housing and equal treatment for poverty areas are vital to our bill too. Anything else?"

"That's it in terms of my major thrusts, Juan. I'm thrilled that you are focusing on getting your bill the support it needs. I'll do everything I can to provide the assistance it needs and deserves in the L.A. area," Henry pledged.

"Thanks, Henry, for your support. I'll be glad to appear before your group when I'm in L.A. later this month. See Otto on these needs on the way out. Keep up the good work."

* * *

"Mike, thanks again for spending some time with us while in Sacramento. I've enjoyed your support over the years. What help can we provide?"

"The Alameda Corridor has problems getting its 30 foot deep, ten mile long trench built. Ground-water problems are killing us. The Metropolitan Water Agency won't approve continued construction until certain standards are met. Could you help move this along? The whole project could be ruined if this isn't corrected soon. The State Water Board is the key agency to break the bottleneck. A special bill may also be needed to move things along. We need help desperately."

"Certainly, Joe will work with you to resolve this problem. The Corridor is vital to the success of my bill since economic development is its cornerstone. Anything else?"

"Yes. Its crucial that our 710 Freeway Corridor be revitalized in a holistic way, combining auto, truck and transit travel, plus an effective plan for adjoining land uses. Can you work with Caltrans to get the needed funds–up to $2 billion? This is vital to our future."

"Definitely, Mike. This is one of our most important spurs to regional economic development, second only to the Alameda Corridor. We'll get right on it," responded Juan with a smile. "Anything else?"

"No. You've got my support. Hopefully, I can get the other 13 subregions to back your bill. Good luck. Call me any time for help," Mike replied.

"Thanks again, Mike. See Joe on these needs. Have a good trip back."

* * *

"Gavin, I still remember fondly our discussions when I visited you last in Ireland. I'm glad you could come to work with Gateway Cities. How's the Partnership doing? How can we help?"

"We're doing better," Gavin replied, "but progress is still slow because of the Brownfields issue on toxic soils. The cities are slowly buying into it. But the big difficulty is California doesn't provide the liability protection needed like most other states. Can you swing your support to getting the proposed bill out of committee and passed? We'd move ahead rapidly with liability resolved."

"You bet. We've been watching this bill and think we have the support to get it passed."

"Great! Also, the WIA job retraining bill is crucial to get unemployed workers retrained to fill the machinists jobs vacated as workers retire. Plus, help on getting more equality in funding to meet the needs of our poverty area residents. These are my most crucial needs. By the way, thanks again for your support in getting me the Gateway Partnership job."

"You're welcome. You've done a great job. Consider it done on my help on your needs. They fit directly into my bill and we're excited we can help meet your needs. I also appreciate your support on my bill. See Joe and Otto on these needs. Have a good trip back and I'll stop by and see you when I'm in L.A. next," Juan said, shaking Gavin's hand.

* * *

"Well, Jim, it's been a long time since we last talked. It seems like years since our great college days at SC. What wonderful times. How're things going with the RC?"

"Fine. Yeah, there were great times at SC. Hard to believe how fast time flies. Getting down to my needs, I hope you can help. If I can get some adequate funding for transportation projects and other needs, I think I have a good chance of becoming RC chair soon."

"That's great," Juan responded as he sized Jim up. Jim exuded arrogance, as Otto had stated. Maybe I need to cut him down a peg, he thought. I'll hammer him on critical funding..

"How can we help you?" he asked as he moved his effort into first gear.

"Well, Juan, as I said this morning, we could have up to a $50 billion shortfall on transportation which we need to cover to meet our 2025 needs. We just completed putting together a finance bill for SCAG which will hit your committees next week. We need your support behind this bill. Also, we're working on a bill for housing and community development similar to TEA Z1, and we need your support on it."

"Well! You know how to ask for the world, don't you?" Juan replied with sarcasm. "Why should I support you when you don't seem ready to help me on my proposed bill? Especially since my bill provides the basis for meeting your needs in transportation and housing/community development at a lower cost to the taxpayer. This doesn't add up."

"Come on, Juan," Jim said, growing flushed. "You know there's no comparison between our bills, particularly the small chance your bill has in passing this year. We need this money now, not several years from now. Come on, you owe me. Help me out," he said heatedly.

"Since when do I owe you, Jim? It's the other way around. What gives with you. You've become so taken up with yourself–and arrogant. You used to be so much fun to be around–and down to earth."

Juan had hit home. He completely deflated Jim's ego. Red faced and scowling, Jim was stunned by Juan's remarks. He thought that it would be easy to get his support based on their great camaraderie of the past. What should he do now?

Otto disappeared from the room when this exchange began. He knew that the discussion would be brutal and embarrassing for Jim. It was best that he not witness it as a staff member.

"Come on, Jim," Juan said, back pedaling. "Let's sit down and work things out in a way that benefits both of us. We're in politics. I've got something you want. You've got something I want. Okay?"

Jim was frozen-faced and unseeing!

"How can we compromise, Jim? Come on, sit down and let's talk it through."

Instead of sitting down, Jim cursed Juan, abruptly picked up his attache case and walked out, slamming the door behind him. He walked past the three waiting–and out the outer door. Everyone was transfixed by this stormy exit.

* * *

A little later, Jim entered the House chapel on the spur of the moment. He was distraught, desperate to receive some solace to handle the problem he faced. A simple place framed by a raised altar with a white cross as a backdrop. In this quiet setting, Jim struggled to come to grips with what had happened.

Although Jim had never been very religious, he knew he must seek spiritual help. The chapel had been there throughout his years of visiting the Capitol, but he had never before considered using it. Now, when he needed help, it was there. Although he found it awkward, he knelt humbly to pray.

"Dear Lord, I know I've strayed from you in my lust for political power. All the things I learned as a youngster about helping others, being humble and keeping you in my thoughts have passed me by. Help me to face my problems and work them out honorably," he whispered in a broken moment. This place had already done wonders for him. He began to receive some peace for the first time in years. Caught up in his career, he had become selfish and self-centered.

He continued to kneel as he struggled with his emotions. He asked God for direction in facing up to his dilemma. He knew he had a long way to go to change his deeply ingrained attitude. Juan had been right. He was arrogantly obsessed with power. Could he humble himself and apologize to Juan for his behavior? He'd never been able to do this in the past. Always his way or the highway. His parents had doted on him and given him everything he wanted. This had continued as he received all the breaks in his education, as well as movement up the ladder politically. He never had to earn his way. It just happened as political favors earned by others were used to advance his career.

Time stood still as he struggled internally. It was a shock to discover others around him where he knelt. Henry had his arm around him praying. A feeling of love came from this contact, filling him with wonder. He looked up and found his three friends clustered around him in support. They had been disturbed by his abrupt departure from Juan's office and had followed him. Juan had asked them to keep him in sight and assist.

Jim brokenly asked them for help in mending his rift with Juan. He got up and sat with them in a front pew. They considered what he might do to patch things up. Then they together went back to Juan's office in support. They waited around until Juan could be located and then left.

"Juan, thanks for seeing me again," he began haltingly. "I want to apol — apologize for my rude behavior." He struggled with the effort, since he felt uncomfortable doing it. "I'd be willing to try" again he found it difficult to say the words, "to work out some sort of compromise so we can support each other. I know I have been remiss in considering the needs of all the people. Can we try again?" he asked contritely.

"Okay, Jim," Juan said, cautiously eyeing him to see how serious and contrite he really was. "Let's sit down and try to work something out. This won't be an easy process...but I'm willing to try. I'm not sure you're really ready to follow through on this. It definitely will take some time and effort on our parts due to our differences, but let's take the first step. We won't be able to solve much tonight and we'll always look at some things differently. That's the nature of politics."

With that, they hammered out a means by which Jim would support Juan's programs at this time. They left the meeting realizing that much still needed to be done if they were to work effectively together. Juan, in particular, felt the future would be rocky between them on programs coming up–both in Sacramento and L.A. It disturbed him a great deal. He must be careful not to expect much from Jim, especially regarding his legislation.

CHAPTER 6
REGION IN TUMULT

*Title VI of the 1964 Civil Rights Act states that no
person will be denied the benefits of programs receiving
Federal financial assistance. The President's Order on
Environmental Justice states that minority populations and
low-income populations must not be exposed to high and
adverse human health or environmental effects from its
policies or programs. The L.A. Region hasn't been
sufficiently complying with this. This must be changed soon
or Federal Tea 21 Program funds could be withdrawn.*

"It is not because things are difficult that we do not
dare; it is because we do not dare that they are difficult."

Seneca

Juan was met by his harried L.A. office administrator, Fred Fuentes, on his arrival at LAX from Sacramento on Southwest Airlines. Chaos reigned around the terminal, with people, cars, buses, taxis scurrying every which way. The irritating noise and smells of toxins permeated the scene, with aircraft passengers and visitors wending their way through the tumult.

"I'm glad you could meet me, Fred," Juan said, shaking his hand gratefully as he got into the waiting double-parked car. "This isn't my favorite airport to fly into–not by a long shot."

"It's really bad on 405–virtually gridlocked 5-9 AM and 3-7 PM," Fred said as they managed to bluff their way out through cars double- and triple-parked at the curb. "True also of traffic in the skies, aircraft landing and taking off, passengers scurrying around the terminal area, cars and cabs coming and going."

"Hey, this is bad. Is total gridlock just around the corner?" Juan observed. "What are regional leaders doing about it? It's definitely not going to get better by itself."

"I'll need to focus on this while I'm here," he thought to himself.

Fred briefed him on his schedule as they drove to his office for the meeting. Marcine Simpson, Carla Perez and Bea Johnson were concerned about

Environmental Justice issues which they felt SCAG hadn't addressed sufficiently. They represented poverty areas covering Gateway Cities, although Bea's principal job was L.A. Times investigative journalist and TV host. Juan felt they would feel more comfortable meeting jointly with him on this issue.

Reaching his L.A. office early, Juan spent some time making local calls, going through mail, fax and phone messages. The women arrived half an hour later and Juan greeted them in the conference room.

"I understand your concern about Gateway Cities communities not having the tools to adequately address their problems," Juan opened the meeting. "Can you give me some specifics?"

"Look how long it took to get SCAG behind a complete redo of the 710 freeway. It's over fifty years old and completely out-of-date," Carla responded. "Its lanes have been patched so many times it's dangerous to travel from Long Beach to Downtown L.A. There have been several tragic multi-vehicle crashes. And the high truck volumes take up two lanes. The interchanges can't handle the volume, there's no room for transit, and the bordering land uses are marginal."

"The Air Quality Management District's (AQMD) track record is even worse in handling air pollution which affects the poverty stricken masses packed into the area," Marcine interjected. "In 1994, their staff recommended that facilities be required to cut risks when emissions exceeded ten cancer cases per million nearby residents. Yet the AQMD board proceeded to set the standard at 100 cases per million, ten times the recommended level."

"Such gripping problems," Juan exclaimed, "and I bet you can add many other examples of lapses in affordable housing, schools, transit, and airport approaches. But can you say that your subregion has been ignored while other higher income areas have received preferential treatment? That's what Environmental Justice is all about."

"I've got all sorts of examples on that," Bea quickly responded. "I've culled the L.A. Times news files over several years. Examples include Cerritos in the Gateway Cities Subregion, as well as Orange County; especially L.A. City, Ventura County–even the Inland Empire."

"That's what we need. Human interest stories telling the tale of public monies being used to the disadvantage of the poor and downtrodden," Juan agreed. "Bea, can you put together a series and run it in the Times? Or some video tapes for TV?"

"Both, Juan! I'm excited about this. This is my way to payback–as an Inner City resident, I've witnessed it all my life. Now I'm finally in a position to do some good."

"Outstanding. I owed you one from the Long Beach debacle and this will make it two. Hope you win an award on this. You deserve one. Let me give it some thought and write up something on it."

"Just what I've needed, Juan. Carla and Marcine can really help too," Bea responded, smiling at them. "We've been having 'woman talk' all week about the changes that are needed."

"Yeah, Marcine and I have put together some people from lists for Bea to interview for the big story," Carla said, her black face beaming.

"Plus, I've got this great quote by Doris Block, Director of the L.A. Food Bank, who I met recently while visiting her agency," Marcine added. "She said, 'I can remember when Los Angeles wasn't a third-world city, there wasn't this huge pool of abysmally poor people separated from an excess of incredibly rich people, by a shrinking middle-class just hanging on by its fingernails.' She would be a good one to video-tape regarding her clientele"

"I'm impressed," Juan replied. "You've been doing your homework. What else needs to be covered?"

"The real issues are education, jobs, retraining and getting people to and from work–especially at early and late hours. If people can't get to jobs in the suburbs, then a reverse commute will be required from the inner city," Marcine said. "This requires some form of cheap and convenient transportation so they can keep those jobs."

"Yeah, I know," Juan added. "You and your organization have been doing excellent work getting MTA humping on this, Marcine. We want to make sure you get enough help. Let us know if SCAG or MTA are not providing enough assistance," Juan added.

"We're still plodding along until the Workforce Investment Act is implemented statewide and SCAG handles some of the regional organizing for job training," Marcine said disappointedly. "We need help there but it's still too early to act."

"I don't know how to phrase this, Juan, since it's such a touchy subject," Bea frowned. "We're often at wits end on how to get SCAG focused to do more effective planning, particularly for poor and minority areas such as Gateway Cities. It should be a no-brainer, but it isn't. They're afraid to stick their necks out. They play it safe politically, not only by giving L.A. City everything they want, but also any suburb with a lot of political clout. That is, all but Long Beach which L.A. wants kept down. How're we to get our fair share in this climate?"

"I'm glad you brought this up, Bea," Juan mused. "It's difficult to come up with a fair solution here, but if SCAG doesn't treat the poor and minority areas right, they're in danger of losing their TEA-21 money. You can hold the Environmental Justice issue over their heads now."

"That's true but it's still tricky to handle. Our cities don't like to take chances. Local leaders still remember how L.A. screwed them over the years and got away with it. L.A. has subtle ways of getting back later through other projects we need their support for."

"You're right, of course. It has to be handled adroitly and as a group so that no one city is singled out," Juan said, getting up to pace the room. "The politics of greed ensures that cities with the most clout and money win these political tussles. Poor people and minority neighborhoods don't usually have the clout it takes. But that's beginning to change. If I can get my regional bill through the legislature, you'd be surprised what could happen."

"Give us the details and tell us how we can help," Bea said.

Juan gave them key aspects of his regional bill and how they could help to get it passed. They agreed to spread the word and help out.

* * *

All the political corruption which took place in Sacramento worried Juan. Where did it end? He flashed back several years when, active in city government, he came in close contact with people from every persuasion as he pressed the flesh before and after meetings. He remembered Andre Phillippe vividly. Such a unique individual. Andre, a huge, balding Latino, had brooding black eyes and drooping mustache. His shoulders tended to slump forward as he stood in his baggy black pants and dark sweater. He spoke in a squeaky, tenor voice and used wire rim glasses on occasion. On first impression, you thought you were talking to another weirdo frequenting public meetings, getting attention for one of his causes.

Andre was different. He grew on you with his tales of corruption in L.A. city and county government. Sometimes you couldn't decide whether to avoid him–or try to draw him out on an issue. Many politicians ignored him–didn't want to be seen talking to him. But Juan became fascinated. Why was he drawn to him and repulsed at the same time? His tales were both riveting and disturbing. He attended all the big L.A. meetings–city council, planning, police, schools, parks, housing, county supervisors.

One of Andre's tales centered on kick backs reputedly being received by a planning commissioner and city councilman for voting to approve a real estate project. It involved a swing vote with $100,000 under the table. Andre supposedly got wind of it by nosing around meetings, reading the minutes and talking with knowledgeable people about the latest happenings. He had a nose for following the money and innately knowing the people who might be on the "make." Juan didn't pick up on it for six months, but invariably found what Andre said proved out, even if it seemed preposterous at the time.

Juan remembered vividly one conversation which recounted Andre's efforts to get officials to put much needed schools, parks and recreation programs in crime-ridden areas of East L.A.

"What does it take to get facilities and services to East L.A., Bob? Why won't you do what's needed?" Andre had asked in disgust.

"We don't have the money, Andre," replied Bob, the head of Recreation Services, glaring at Andre. "Our budget won't permit it."

"You know that's not true. Many of the surrounding neighborhoods get preferential treatment due to the councilman's influence. And this neighborhood has been ignored for years– and you wonder why gangs develop."

"Well...we do the best we can," Bob replied defensively. "We have to work within the political system, and it's not perfect."

"Yeah, you got that right," Andre pounded the table with his fists. " It's who strokes who, who greases the palm, who promises or threatens the most–that gets the dole." Andre raised his hands in frustration. "I hope some day that the Feds get smart and require all neighborhoods and cities to be treated equally no matter what influence is brought to bear. These poor, downtrodden neighborhoods need help–much more than those that end up getting help. I could document easily how unfairly things get done in L.A."

"You're not going to be successful, Andre," Bob emphasized. "Promises have been made in order to ensure the votes are there at the next election. And it's all legal."

"The time will come when I'm going to have the last laugh on this," Andre lashed out. "I'm going to press for change and nobody is going to stop me–you hear?" he added as he left the room.

Andre had been right. Several years later, TEA-21 included a provision to enforce Environmental Justice. But it took continued pressure by Andre and other activists to get this provision added. Even then, it was too generally interpreted to have effect.

He got weird when threats on his life were discussed. He claimed that he'd been promised a new house, car and money if he'd just get lost. Looking back now, these alleged threats and bribes didn't seem so far fetched. Lots of money changed hands between developers, realtors and politicians on projects involving millions of dollars. After all, people don't always get rich just by making smart use of money and contacts in the good old fashioned way–earning it honestly.

Juan hoped to have Bea interview Andre, assuming that he would be willing to go public on corruption. He might feel threatened and uneasy about exposing himself. The interview would have to be more general in coverage without naming specific persons on the "make."

* * *

Talking further to Bea after the meeting, Juan learned more of her background. It was fun to interview an attractive reporter like Bea, even better than being interviewed.

"Bea, I can't keep up with you," he said. "You always seem on the move, finding out what makes people tick. Tell me a little about yourself."

"Fair enough, Juan. I'm always asking others to give away their secrets. Why not me?" she went on. "I'm separated from my husband, Leo, who I guess could be called a 'dead-beat dad' since his disappearance two years ago."

"That's tough. Still married? Any children?"

"Yeah, still married. It makes things tough in terms of relationships. I just keep busy, especially since I have an eight year old son, Seth, who's dyslexic," she said.

"Can you spend enough time with him?" Juan said sympathetically.

"I'm focused on Seth's educational development. This requires tutoring and special counseling which is expensive and time consuming. But it's worth it."

"You're certainly very talented. What else keeps you going?" Juan probed further.

"I love to paint still life from my downtown art studio loft. It's so relaxing and rewarding to be painting urban and nature scenes. Seth and I enjoy doing it together."

"That's wonderful. You both have the same talent. How'd you discover Seth's artistic abilities?" Juan asked.

"Seth's being dyslexic and always wanting to be with me when I went painting. I discovered that painting exercises can help those with dyslexia due to the use of the left to right motion while painting. It allows the eye and brain to work through the reading problem which dyslexics must overcome. From that, his artistic talent took off and flourished."

"I want to get to know you better, Bea. You've overcome some difficult situations. I trust things will work out well for you. I'll be back in touch," Juan said with emotion as they parted.

* * *

Leaving Juan's meeting, Bea arrived late with Marcine at the Aviation Task Force hearing at SCAG. One of the most political and explosive task forces she could remember covering, it also involved environmental justice for the poor and minority population. This issue didn't get much coverage until LAX expansion got serious.

Marcine saw Bea as a live wire when reporting politics and human interest stories for the L.A. Times. She knew a lot of people and was well liked. Very colorful, zany in some ways and a joy to watch in action. About forty, 5 feet 5 inches, 120 pounds, she was a pepperpot of slender build. Men considered her attractive, especially since she had upgraded her wardrobe and hair styling to complement her black hair and brown eyes. Some people would call her a little flakey due to her free spirit desire to live life to the hilt. Marcine knew Bea enjoyed dancing at the clubs around downtown and the westside when she found time. Although she dated some, she had no steady guy.

Marcine encouraged Bea to cover Environmental Justice as its importance in regional transportation planning grew under the new TEA-21 provision and controversy developed on the need for more attention to noise and congestion problems around LAX and the jurisdictions under the flight path of the nation's second busiest airport. Bea blocked out a story as the meeting unfolded:

NEIGHBORHOODS AROUND LAX UP IN ARMS

Tempers got short and nerves were frayed as a policy hearing regarding L.A. regional airports dragged on for two hours at SCAG's TCC Committee hearing June 1. After 18 months of work, the Aviation Task Force seemed no closer to resolving the controversy surrounding L.A.'s future regional airport system.

Passionate speeches from several Regional Council members were sandwiched in among pleas by representatives of several cities surrounding LAX that its expansion be limited or stopped completely due to Environmental Justice issues (noise, congestion, air quality) adversely affecting poor and minority families concentrated under flight paths.

Ten scenarios on regional airport development through 2025 had finally been reduced to four Efforts to reduce these further to two caused heated debate. Costs and time became the critical factors to resolving this issue.

Whether to spend $500,000, $800,000 or $1,100,000 for further environmental impact studies for two to four scenarios were considered along with time factors which ranged from meeting the June 30, 2001 RTP deadline to extending it up to four months beyond the deadline, creating a crisis with the Feds.

Finally, crucial votes approved moving ahead to complete environmental impact studies on all four scenarios.

TEA-21 studies require measuring the impact of aviation noise and congestion on minority and poor neighborhoods. Measurement was based on comparing total 2020 projected noise impacts as mapped for each scenario with the RTP baseline. Each of the scenarios would impose noise impacts greater than 65 decibels, a reasonable noise level, on more people overall–and more non-white people–than the alternative in the 1998 RTP. For example, Scenario Nine (airport improvements without El Toro as a regional airport) would affect 80 percent of total non-whites while the SCAG Region 2020 Plan (RTP) would only affect 69 percent–a difference of 11 percent.

At a recent hearing on the various scenarios, the audience was filled with LAX Airport neighbors speaking against expansion:

"I can't sleep anymore with the increased volume of airport traffic and the noisier aircraft using the airport," complained a young black woman among the protestors testifying. "My babies are becoming more irritable and impossible to handle. I'm at wit's end and I'm about to lose my job due to stress."

"Congestion is so bad I won't fly out of LAX anymore," said a businessman among the hearing's protestors. "My business connections in other cities dread coming to L.A. due to the airport congestion. In fact, I've just recently been warned that if I planned to continue to work with them, I must fly to their city or make other arrangements."

This was the general tenor of feelings of over 25 protestors who participated in the LAX expansion hearings

* * *

SCAG was busily working on a study of Environmental Justice issues dealing with how Federal monies were being used in minority and poor neighborhoods compared with white areas. When such facilities (sewer, water, transit, streets and highways, airports, schools, housing) were plotted, it was expected to show needs of non-whites had been ignored for many years. This study was expected to be presented to SCAG's Environment and Energy Policy Committee within two months.

Regional Advisory Council (RAC) members were intrigued when they heard of the study. The minority, poor community was finally being heard, but it took the fear of losing Federal money to make it happen. They also believed that the study would show the favoritism being shown the City of Los Angeles.

The South Bay city of Inglewood had waged a lonely war with Los Angeles for many years over LAX expansion. The mayor expressed it well in his statement to the Task Force:

"It began in 1978 when this low income, minority dominated city identified short-term actions that LAX and FAA could take to reduce the number of people exposed to high levels of aircraft noise. Although some improvements were made over the years (primarily home insulation), the latest effort to expand the airport further was met with anger. In three 1999 actions by the Inglewood City Council, efforts were made to divert 20 percent of air traffic away from Inglewood airspace, lower the noise threshold level from 65 to 55 decibels, and challenge environmental impact findings adverse to the city's interests. City representatives had appeared before the Regional Council and Aviation Task Force on several occasions to get environmental justice. The battle continued as LAX moved forward with its efforts to expand.

"Inglewood Environmental Justice concerns ranged from property value reduction to increased traffic, noise monitoring systems, avigation easement development and FAA match requirements. Restricted also was use of mitigation monies–excluding roads, public safety, infrastructure needs–along with health and safety hazards, soot and debris, and jet fuel emission and dumping. The noise abatement chronology began in 1978 when the city prepared an Airport Land Use Planning Study, moved through noise policy studies in the 80's, and on into noise mitigation plans (land recycling and residential sound insulation) in the 90's. Battling to get recognition for airport-impacted problems as aircraft noise increased and operations expanded several fold, Inglewood, through land recycling had relocated 1,100 families from noise incompatible areas, making way for development of airport compatible industrial and commercial uses. When completed, insulation of over 1,450 homes will also have taken place.

"Inglewood didn't get this done easily, fighting the City of L.A. and LAX Airport for many years when Environmental Justice possibilities for minority and low income communities were non-existent."

"This is the completion of my statement to the Task Force. Thank you for your patience."

The Task Force chair thanked the mayor for his coverage. Perhaps when areas such as Watts and Gateway Cities also begin to flex their muscle, progress will become easier, thought the chairperson. After a few more statements, the meeting was adjourned.

* * *

Almost two months had passed since the altercation between Juan and Evon in Juan's office. One day while "kicking around" with Otto and Joe, Juan asked whether they had any luck in their surveillance of Evon and Judith Struthers, head of Keep Our Population Expanding (KOPE). Otto indicated they had been getting information back on both for some time and Evon had been very quiet on the political front. He had a part time job as a taxi driver. Judith, on the other hand, continued to press for more urban sprawl and freeways across the state but kept a low profile. However, Otto felt more things were happening than met the eye.

"Juan," Otto asked, "do you think that Evon would be willing to go undercover for us, join KOPE and get us some inside information on their plans?"

"Let's find out. I'd like to get him involved again. It doesn't sound like he's doing well financially driving a taxi part-time. Why don't you call and have him come in later this week?"

"Okay, I will." He looked at Juan's calendar and asked: "How about tomorrow at 6 PM? It's late in the day and we can keep his coming low profile."

"Fine. Let's do it."

* * *

"Evon, glad to see you again. Sorry we weren't able to get back with you sooner," Juan said as they sat in Jim's office the next day.

"Good to see you too, Juan. The extra time to think about things worked out well. I've been driving taxi part-time and considering things. I totally agree now with your view of how we went our separate ways, and I'm willing to start over–if you are, of course." He seemed to be relaxed and in a much better mental state.

"That's great. I've also been giving it some thought and realize how much I took you for granted. I thought we might talk a little more today. Would you be interested in working for me as a sort of consultant who can help out on the political front? I'm still working on the mechanics of how it might work, but I think you would enjoy it. I remember how you liked politics and could be very creative. What do you think? Do you want to explore such a relationship?"

"I'd like that. Depending on what's involved, of course," Evon said. "I've learned so much from you over the years, I'd like to help out any way I can. After all, I really look on you as my mentor and feel bad about how I handled the recent situation. It's a part of growing, I guess. The real question, I think is do you feel comfortable having me work with you?"

"Yes, I do, Evon. The nature of the assignment I have in mind for you reflects this. Remember that well-dressed, middle-aged, gray-haired lady that you saw involved with Amy of our office?"

"Yeah. How could I forget," he said, rolling his eyes, as he thought of the painful episode.

"Well, her name is Judith Struthers, head of KOPE, or Keep Our

Population Expanding, an urban sprawl group headquartered in Sacramento. They act as lobbyists for a number of large corporations interested in keeping America's dream of suburban growth going to maximize their profitability. Another example of greed taking over. They're very active in trying to destroy planning–particularly regional planning–in California. Their major interest is Southern California, and my regional planning bill in the legislature is a threat to them."

"Wow, they sound dangerous. So, what would I have to do, Juan?"

"Well, we need to find out all we can about them. I know you would be good at this. It would also be good training for future work in the political arena. What do you say?"

"Sounds interesting. Just what would I have to do to get this information for you?"

"Go over to KOPE and indicate your interest in working for them. I understand they're currently looking for someone who's good at following the legislative process. Your background as a former assemblyman would be perfect."

"Yeah, Juan, but they know we've been friends," said Evon.

"But the word's out about our falling out. Just continue what you were doing, stating your discontent, and all that. Can you play that game?"

"I think so, although it wouldn't be easy after understanding your side of the situation."

"I understand your reticence, Evon. Just look at it as a way to get back at the people who are trying to destroy our way of life. We'll give you some background and training."

"I trust your judgment, Juan. I'll do it."

* * *

Later, Evon underwent some training and arranged to meet with KOPE officials on the job. He passed all their tests, especially after their finding out how deep-seated Evon's feelings were against Juan. He joined their team, learned the ins and outs of their organization and received assignments. Once a week, he met with Otto to pass on what he learned. Although little was learned initially, his position allowed him to follow their agenda. At the appropriate time, he would be ready to pass on critical information. He felt good about his role.

* * *

Marcine sat with her daughter, Lucy, thinking about her recent conversation with Juan, Bea and Carla. She had mentioned Doris Block's characterization of L.A. as a third world city in the way it was currently developing. Even worse than poverty, she thought, had to be violence, TV shows children were watching, pornography on the Internet and the decline of the family. Poverty and the lack of medical care for poor families not being able to get medical insurance certainly ranked high, but these other issues held even higher priorities with her.

"Lucy, do you think I'm too hard on you by limiting your TV viewing, Internet chatting, and exposure to violence?"

"At first, I thought so, but after talking with my friends at school, I have to agree with you. I really appreciate how we've come together as a family."

"What do your friends say or do that makes you appreciate our talking things through?" asked Marcine, proud of her daughter's ability to see things as they were, not what she hoped they would be.

"My friends do what they want to do since their parents don't influence them much. They watch any of the TV shows they want to, see R rated movies and even pornography on the Internet. They think you're too tough on me, although secretly, I think they wish they had a little more structure in their lives."

"Yeah, it's hard growing up in an R-rated world, isn't it. I didn't have that problem since most of these things weren't there to tempt me when I was young." Marcine reflected on it. "Well, that's not really true. Every generation has their temptations. We thought it was cool to smoke, lie about our age to get drinks, and sniff glue. But nothing like you face with drugs and violence."

"Gee, I didn't know you had big temptations too. Why do we tempt fate? Is it a part of growing up?"

" I think it is. We're always trying to push the envelope a little. Create some excitement in what we consider to be dull lives. Kids think their parents are so out of it and don't realize that they went through similar temptations themselves."

"This talk we're having is great, Mom. When we relate like this, I begin to understand more how difficult it is being a parent. Let's do it more often."

"Okay, Lucy, you're on. We used to do a lot of this sitting around the dinner table or listening to the radio. Now there doesn't seem to be time for that. I think that's why violence has become such a force."

"What do you mean by that, Mom?"

"You kids are exposed to so much information and experience from others than anyone had before. So the parents aren't really in charge any more. Kids learn about sex, violent behavior and other ways to do things from outside sources, not always the best to copy. Movies, rap, TV, Internet and all sorts of entertainment compete for your attention and kids want to be in with their peers. So they don't listen to their parents who they often consider to be squares."

"Yeah, that's true," Lucy said. "I've sometimes thought you were out-of-line with your rules. It's tough growing up with all these things being thrown at you. No wonder some kids go bad, get into drugs, gangs or groups with violence on their minds."

"The other thing I worry about as a parent is how technology has taken over. This era of mobile communications has created a new breed of digital nomad. Along with all the other things happening, it seems to be eroding the sense of belonging or community. So many go around with a cell telephone stuck in their face, ear phones in their ears, living in another world. Lots of kids don't exercise and get fat as a result. Or they don't do their homework since it's more fun to do video games or 'chat' on the Internet. Others don't get enough sleep and doze in class, missing their lessens which don't seem important to them."

"Mom, you're really turned on–but making sense."

"Sorry, Lucy. You wanted to talk and it all tumbled out. Do you still want to have these chats every so often?"

"Definitely. You make so much sense. I guess I'm lucky I've got a mother who's really interested in me who I can relate to. My friends don't feel that way."

"Okay, we'll have more discussions. Think about things you want my opinion on, and I'll try to give you my two cents worth."

"Okay, Mom, it's a deal. Thanks."

Later, Marcine reflected on their discussion. She felt good that it took place and allowed them to interact. So natural between parent and child.

* * *

Marcine met with Bea the next day to talk further about needed Environmental Justice strategies. What had been happening in the days since they met with Juan on EJ had really made them more conscious of the issue and how all-encompassing it was for everyone.

"You know, Bea, I talked with my daughter Lucy last night about the need to communicate better on issues facing youth today, along with the problems we're having with TV. I realized that Environmental Justice didn't just involve cleaner air, better housing, improved jobs and improved education for low income families. It cut across the boards regarding an improved quality of life for all families, no matter their income level. Of course, even here low income families are more likely to be adversely affected due to more limited options and less time available for parents to talk to their children. What do you think about this?"

"You're absolutely right, Marcine. Improving the quality of life crosses over into better police security, quality recreation programs, good schools and parks, smutless television, and improved opportunities for our families and children, no matter their background. We've got to look at the total picture or we'll miss our opportunity to improve our overall environment."

"Do you think that things are getting worse or better over the range of quality of life issues, Bea?" asked Marcine, concern on her face.

Bea without pause, answered: "Worse!"

"Yeah, I thought you would say that. I agree with you. We've got to do something about this too. We can't continue to bury our heads in the sand and say that we're powerless to do any thing about it either. We've got to stick our necks out and start to collectively work for change," Marcine stated.

"In the next few months, we need to talk with others about this–and work collectively to achieve change. We're just standing around, shaking our heads, but doing nothing constructive about it," Bea said. "Let's get involved and make a difference."

"Yes, let's begin today–through the regional organization, our subregions and local areas," emphasized Marcine. "We can make a difference."

CHAPTER 7
CONTINUING TRANSIT
DILEMMA

L.A. REGION FACED WITH GRIDLOCK!
"Virtual gridlock is almost here. Area citizens are faced
with driving alternate days to work, a doubling and
tripling of parking lot fees and prohibition of free
employee parking. These measures will be required due to
the unwillingness of local leaders to focus on significant
expansion of transit now as necessary to solving our
regional transportation problems. No leader has stepped
forward and stated that building more freeways will not
reduce traffic congestion. Further, a worsening of air
pollution will force the L.A. Region to adopt stricter
standards–including at least doubling of transit per capita
–to meet Federal dictates." Statement of Ned Logan, well
known transportation expert, at the Commonwealth Club,
Tuesday, April 11, 2000.

"We're at a crossroads as a region on how to handle our overall regional transportation problems. "We can't continue to ignore what's happening
on our freeways and in the air," said Rudy So, L.A. councilman, at a meeting of the Transit and Transportation Finance Task Force, "As Ned Logan,
national transportation expert, said last week at the Commonwealth Club,
'Unless we get our act together soon–and I do mean soon–we'll be forced
to institute alternate day driving, high parking charges and no more free
employee parking.' To keep from being stuck with these requirements, we
have to adopt a major transit plan which will get more people out of their
cars into a wide range of transit options."

"Political suicide," exclaimed Ty Smith, Chamber president. "Such
things don't make sense. It'll never fly with the voters."

"Do you have a better solution?" Rudy defended angrily. "If we don't
have an effective solution, Federal money for expressways and other
improvements will dry up. L.A. will die."

"No," Ty answered, defending the status quo. "It's just not the right
solution for L.A."

What brought this to a head had been earlier discussions at the joint meeting of the task force. Dissension flared when transportation trips, transit trends and needs, and monies available for 2000-2025 highway and transit improvements were outlined.

*   *   *

Jim Robinson chaired the joint meeting in tandem with the L.A. councilman, Rudy So. He appeared glad to have Rudy, with his clout, handling this difficult meeting. Normally, he might have resented Rudy's help, but not today. Rudy had been through all the political wars over the past thirty years in terms of gas shortages, smog alerts and fights for transit dollars.

The meeting began innocently as transportation-funding options had been paraded before the assemblage. People's eyes glazed over as billions of dollars were discussed, time periods of 25 years into the future considered, and the implications of various bills proposed in the state legislature glossed over. Few questions were raised as the audience was virtually put to sleep by the coverage.

What produced a wake up call for the group came with the discussion of what had happened to transit regionally, added to the black hole sucking up transportation monies with no improvement in traffic conditions. Suddenly, people realized that something had to be done–at long last. There was no turning back or ducking the issue. A definite action plan must be developed–if not at this meeting–at least very soon. Very, very soon!

Rudy paced back and forth as he began the discussion, forcefully outlining the history of solving L.A. transportation problems–do nothing until it's almost too late. "This approach won't work since to make transit palatable to citizens, it must be in place and working effectively. Lead times of five to ten years will be required to build rail and/or introduce separate bus lanes to speed traffic along major routes."

He went on: "SCAG must develop and adopt a Corrective Action Program (CAP) which will prescribe what needs to be done or we'll have gridlock. I can't spell it out any clearer. GRIDLOCK! In addition, SCAG must develop a scenario showing how bad it's expected to get if the public doesn't accept the Plan." He emphasized strongly: "It must pull no punches. People have been led astray too long by a lack of guts in describing and handling our perilous situation."

"You're absolutely right, Rudy," Marvin Potts, SCAG Executive Director, broke in. "Even with legislative approval of the SCAG Transportation Funding Proposal, we still won't have enough money to develop transportation programs needed over the next 25 years."

"Sixty-two percent of the RTP budget will be used by various forms of transit in the future," stated Gerald, a SCAG participant. "This should be enough to provide the transit needed to supplement a more limited highway system as five more million people are added. However, struggles between transit and transportation agencies, cities and counties must be minimized to make sure it's used wisely."

"We've got to get people out of their cars and shorten trips dramatically," interjected Jim Robinson, the co-chair. "Just think. We've got to more than double the transit trips per capita– 72 trips–over the 34.9 trips now being provided. Everyone must make a major contribution. We've got to suck it up and–DO IT."

They passed a resolution–with dissent–to accomplish this on paper, beginning with another meeting to develop programs to sell transit and marshall the necessary support.

*   *   *

After the meeting, Jim took Henry aside in the hall to discuss strategy. It was the first time they'd talked since the Sacramento trip. Jim was defensive because of the discussions and unsure how the wind was blowing politically. He also knew he must see Lila again soon to get her pulse on things personally and politically.

"Henry. How'd you think things went?" Jim asked.

"Not too well, Jim. I've heard this before–then nothing happens. We've somehow got to send the message to the people loud and clear. Even if there is the danger of 'the messenger' being the victim and losing politically. Any suggestions?"

"I'm not about to commit political suicide on this controversy," Jim said. "I've got too much to lose. Do you have any contacts within SCAG who could leak a story which would hit the Times and stun the public? Possibly through Bea?"

"I'll speak with Gerald and Rudy about just such an approach. SCAG won't take a chance directly but maybe if something were leaked, it would take the heat off," Henry said.

"We need to get agreement on doubling transit ridership per capita or force commuters to absorb triple their current parking fees or lose free employee parking privileges. That should get everybody's attention. We've got to get people out of their cars." Impatiently, Jim said, " I've gotta go. Keep me in the loop, Henry. Thanks," shaking his hand on the way to the elevator.

*   *   *

Jim hurried to pick up Lila. He'd called earlier to arrange to meet her that evening. She seemed cool after not hearing from him for two weeks–but agreed to see him. That was a break through. He wasn't sure where he was going in general, much less with her. He needed a little R and R and hoped that she would rev his batteries tonight.

Lila was stunning as usual, decked out in a long, deep purple polo dress of rich stretch velvet, opened at the front and highlighted by her diamond earrings and diamond ring. Her cleavage was obvious and Jim hugged her in greeting, relishing the moment.

"You know I've been wanting to see you, Lila," he said. "Busy schedule lately. Both in and out of town. Please forgive me," handing her a dozen red roses.

"Jim, you know what red roses mean–passion!"

Although still put out with his nonchalance, she said with a devilish grin, "I might accept if the evening goes well."

"Dinner and dancing at that nice spot you recommended near your place, for openers?" he questioned.

"Oh, Mindy's. A great place. You hear what I say at times, don't you," she joshed. "Let's go," she said with a fleeting hug.

They had a great time at Mindy's, where the fare was Italian, the decor cosmopolitan, and the ambiance of Rome. A lot of dark red lamps with glass shades, wallpaper, music. Nothing dynamic but a comfortable place. They danced until midnight. They brought each other up-to-date on some of their political doings and CIG events. She seemed especially interested in his meetings with the Speaker in Sacramento and the transit/finance task force meeting in L.A.

"Jim," she asked, how did your meetings in Sacramento go last week on Juan's regional bill? I understand that it's going forward soon, through both houses?" .

"It's still in committee. Has a long way to go. Why your interest?" he asked.

"I try to keep up with state legislation in my job at CIG. What you do fascinates me."

"Well, it isn't always so interesting when we need to put it in lawyer terms," he replied.

"How do you feel about the bill?" she asked, explaining CIG's reservations about some specific details of the bill that had never been covered completely. She needed to know about what was in the bill for CIG, particularly Jim's feelings on it. Her boss was getting impatient.

"I'm not sure where I stand now," he replied. "I have some reservations but the details of the bill are being worked out in committee and will likely undergo more amendments as it goes forward." Being evasive without arousing her suspicions was difficult.

"Do you feel it has a chance of being defeated?" she asked.

"It'll be difficult to pass this year, like most complicated new bills. I doubt if it will go anywhere. Don't worry your pretty head about it," Jim replied.

Jim changed the subject and chatted about his childhood in Beverly Hills. Lila brought up more details about her New Orleans background, then shifted back with more questions.

"I'm concerned about emphasizing transit over freeways. Do you think they'll go ahead with that? People aren't going to stop using their cars. Why should they?" she asked.

"Fear of gridlock," he replied. "Haven't you been caught in one of those massive traffic jams that go on for hours?"

"For thirty minutes or so. But that doesn't happen that often, does it?"

"More and more!" he replied "Many people are getting trapped in their cars for up to four hours, Lila, and you'll understand when you get stuck like that. People are getting frustrated with spending more on gas and cars without being able to move on the freeways," he emphasized.

She subtly continued to probe. "But if they stop building freeways and make more people take transit, the home builders won't be able to build as many homes."

"They still could build apartments and condos," Jim answered, quizzically wondering where this was going. He tried not to be evasive but it was difficult to avoid her questions. "You're sure asking a lot of questions, Lila. I guess you like me only for my mind," he jested.

"I know I can be a pest asking so many questions," she exclaimed in retreat.

"You know how to live dangerously, don't you. You've got me thinking though. I'm not too thrilled about tons of apartments either. I'm not sure that I'd vote for transit myself."

Conversation lagged as their differences continued to cool relations. They decided to call it an evening as they left the restaurant. They made plans to see each other later in the week. As Jim left, he puzzled over the dangerous game of "political talk" he played with Lila. It could come back to haunt him, he realized, but he was falling in love with her. Still, he had no idea how serious she was about him.

His differences with Juan also had not gone away–and he didn't know what to expect on that score either. Too many unresolved issues faced him. Could he handle all this and come through unscathed., he wondered? Only time would tell.

* * *

On his way home, Jim noted the L.A. Times headlines screaming at him from the newsstand:

L. A. GRIDLOCK SOLUTION: DOUBLING TRANSIT
TRIPLE PARKING FEES, NO MORE
FREE EMPLOYEE PARKING

Grabbing a paper, he rushed home and called Henry for more details.

"Quick response, hey? They jumped at leaking the news from the task force. It's so sensational it got front page headlines. Going to be interesting how the public reacts to it," Henry volunteered.

"It's Bea's byline. She sure gets around–and gets results. That takes talent and connections," Jim mused.

He quickly scanned the lead-in:

> Joint Finance/Transit Task Force considers major policy changes in effort to get public to use mass transit more. Only drastic actions including tripling parking rates and elimination of free employee parking can provide solutions to looming gridlock for the L.A. Basin.

Jim judged Bea's article outstanding, and decided to have lunch with her tomorrow.

* * *

After Jim left, Lila called CIG and let them know she would be in later and then go on to an evening meeting. She moped around the apartment, unsure of where her relationship with Jim was going and how it would affect her work with the Home Builders. She mulled over her past and its impact on her current feelings regarding Jim.

Despite some lucky career moves, her life hadn't been easy. Born of gifted entertainer parents on the edge of the French Quarter in New Orleans in 1965, she learned a great deal about singing and acting as she grew up. She enjoyed some minor parts in high school musicals like *Mame* and *Oklahoma,* but wasn't considered gifted. Later, attending Louisiana State, she found her niche, performing leading roles in such campus productions as *South Pacific* and *Cat on a Hot Tin Roof.* Upon graduating from LSU in 1986, she entered the Miss America contest and became Miss Louisiana on the strength of her dancing and acting. She fared poorly at Atlantic City, though, being eliminated early in the Miss America pageant. Following a brief, unhappy marriage, Lila divorced and left to try her luck in Hollywood.

Like most attractive young women drawn to Hollywood, she found it difficult to get a break without used her body to attract celebrities. Working as an extra to see if her face would attract some attention, she found lots

91

of other young women with even more beautiful faces and bodies doing the same thing. Dancing in *The Wedding Singer*, she got good coverage in a night club table scene. But "extra" work was too iffy and unlikely to get her a break.

Not wanting to be get trapped in the flesh business, she took work with several housing developers as an attractive spokesperson with sex appeal. She saw an opportunity there to meet rich, well-known people and other celebrities. She ran into Jake Posse at a CIG event and they hit it off well. He asked her to represent CIG to key people they wanted in their corner politically. She was leary of the sexual innuendos that sometimes came with the job, but agreed to do it while she continued to explore better ways to penetrate the entertainment business.

Jim was one of her first assignments. She was unprepared to handle the duel role when she found herself attracted to him. Things were moving too fast for her, torn between her desire for a career, having a permanent relationship with a man she respected, and keeping her commitment to CIG. It was not her style be a "shady lady" and court the heartache she knew was possible. What should she do? She could tell that Jim was beginning to wonder about this relationship too.

*　*　*

Later, as Lila updated Jake Posse on her progress with Jim, she felt Jake's unhappiness.

"Lila, I'm getting tired of hearing about your political talk with Robinson without any real results. Let's try a new tactic. He obviously needs some competition. How about dating someone else after telling him you've given up on him due to his dalliance. He's obviously taking you for granted or feels your working for CIG causes a problem. The threat of losing you might get him out of his rut if he really does love you as he says."

"Okay, I'll call him and let him know that I'm going to date other men, that he's all talk, no action. It might work. Worth a try," she agreed, with trepidation, suddenly realizing that both her job and her relationship with Jim were at risk

*　*　*

Jim was surprised to get a phone call from Lila so soon. He wasn't happy to hear she had given up on him but realized it was his fault due to his fear of entanglement with CIG and Lila's fuzzy intentions. They decided to cool it for a few weeks and let events take their course.

Concerned about the abrupt break off, Jim buried himself in his work.

*　*　*

Jim had lunch with Bea at the Beachcombers Restaurant the following day as planned. He was surprised but pleased by the new Bea. This dowdy dresser of the past, that he had never got to know in earlier meetings, had changed. Bea was attractjvely dressed in a slim white cotton knit skirt with matching mock turtleneck. She looked fetching with silver earrings and bracelet, complemented by previously hidden assets–her stunning, petite figure, high cheek bones, nicely coiffed brunette hair, and dark brown eyes.

Jim had assumed that seeing her would be just another business interview. She greeted him with a warm smile, flirting briefly with her eyes. He was totally unprepared for this change.

"Jim, it's been awhile since we last chatted. Always one of those encounters involving a quick turnaround on a story. Its nice to have some time to get acquainted, isn't it?"

"Definitely, Bea. I've been following your stories in the Times. It's a joy to read them," he blurted as he looked her over, "You look great."

"So you noticed. Yeah, I got tired of not enjoying life more, although I've always been a little zany. I decided that I wanted to look nice and be more appreciated."

"Well, you've done that–in spades." Jim said, with a broad smile. "Say, tell me more about your job. Based on how you write, I know you've had great experience."

"You're very observant. Yes, I'm what you would call an investigative journalist. Do you know what that is?" Bea asked.

"Not really."

"Let me illustrate. When I was 16, attending high school in Denver, a shocking event took place. It changed my life. I can still remember that day in Phoenix in June 1976. I read about it in a Denver newspaper and followed it on TV. It seems a Arizona Republic reporter named Don Bolles had been asked to meet in a downtown hotel by a source promising him information about land fraud involving organized crime. When the source didn't show, Bolles returned to his car. Turning on the ignition, a powerful bomb ripped through the car, leaving him mortally wounded."

"What a shock, Bea. Did you know him?"

"I met him once through my dad. He did some investigative work for him."

"What happened to Bolles?"

"Doctors amputated both legs and an arm, but couldn't save him. My dad, also a reporter, was distraught, being by his side in the hospital for ten days."

"I can imagine his feelings."

"Dad took it very hard. He called on 37 colleagues he knew to investigate. You see, Bolles was known as one of the first investigative journalists, a new and evolving profession."

"What a story. Did they find the killers?"

"First they set out to find, not Bolles' killer, but the sources of corruption so deep that a reporter could be killed in broad daylight in the middle of a big city. They were out to show organized crime leaders that killing a journalist would not stop reporting about them; it would increase 100-fold. By the way, they did track down the people behind it and put them away."

"So that's why you're so dedicated today to changing things in L.A. and improving the city?"

"Yes. It's my calling."

"I'm impressed. Thanks for telling me about it."

"Thanks. Changing the subject, I heard you recently developed an attractive loft unit downtown with rafters and fancy wood arrangements. I have a loft condo downtown too. I've had it for several years." Bea said.

"Oh! I didn't know. I'd like to see it some time, Bea," Jim enthused. "I guess we're two of only a few who live downtown. I love my loft."

Jim couldn't believe how much she'd changed. He had taken her so much for granted that he hadn't seen her as a full person. Suddenly he "discovered" her. It was like growing up around a teenage girl and suddenly discovering in a flash one day that she had blossomed out and no longer fit the kid sister role.

"What's new with SCAG, Jim?" she inquired. "Are you making any headway with financing all the transportation improvements needed over the next few years.? I'm enthusiastic about all the plans for light rail to the east side, Pasadena, Santa Monica and the Valley."

"Yeah, getting those new projects completed in the next few years will be great for L.A.– especially downtown. I'm working hard on it through the Finance Task Force. You know, I think we located in the right area for housing, Bea", said Jim enjoying the repartee with a woman who knew what he was talking about. He couldn't take his eyes off her, but wondered whether his attraction might be over-compensation for his recent breakup with Lila. He also saw the potential conflicts with being involved at the same time with two attractive women covering regional affairs. A potential triangle like this should be avoided, he knew. He would have to be very careful.

Time passed quickly as they got to know each other over Alaskan salmon, tossed salad, and red wine. They were so enthralled that they never got around to talking "shop." The Beachcomber was one of those trendy L. A. restaurants built around a nautical theme with a selection of pictures on the walls highlighting the restaurant's ties to the nearby ocean and celebrities. However, today it made no difference whether they talked here or in some greasy spoon. The setting quickly faded into irrelevancy.

They parted after planning to get together for a drink later in the week.

* * *

The days whizzed by for Jim as his work and SCAG committees took up his time. He and Bea met again at the Foundry, a popular drinking spot for the business crowd downtown.

"Jim, I love this place. It has all the architecture of the turn of the century. It even looks like a foundry occupied it at one time, based on the stone masonry and water works."

"Yeah," Jim replied, enjoying her attractive features and sexy red dress with a low-cut neckline. "The Foundry is one of my favorites too."

"Why don't I show you my loft this evening? I'd like your reaction. It has a big studio, for painting is my hobby. That and my son, Seth," Bea stated. She was curious about how he would react to these revelations. Having been through a few relationships in the past which had scared her off other men, she wanted to make sure that Jim wasn't out for one-night stands.

"Sounds great, Bea. With an art studio involved, it should offer a lot of color."

Finishing their drinks, they left for her loft a short walk away. It was in a old, recently renovated three story industrial building in an area of shops, restaurants and antique bazaars with considerable pazazz. Through a side entrance, they walked up to the second floor where Bea unlocked one of three doors facing out, and entered.

Jim was impressed by the unit's ambience. Its open layout and exquisite view of the downtown scene exuded a lived-in feel along with a riot of colors.

"Bea, this is outstanding. I can't believe what you've done with it." he exclaimed.

"Wait til you see my studio. That's my pride and joy," Bea enthused.

They passed through the neat and colorful living area and kitchen, to a huge room with cathedral ceiling at the rear. The loud colors and busy clutter of the art studio leapt out at Jim. Before them lay an art bench with palette, a collage of art brushes, paints, easels and frames. Along one wall stretched containers of linseed oil and turpentine, and a rack full of wet paintings.

Another wall held completed paintings, many of hers but also some by other artists. The studio provided a wide range of art objects that showed an artist's versatility–especially with urban scenes, people and buildings of every type.

"You know, Jim, art is supposed to be an expression of the heart and soul," Bea said.

"I believe it is, Bea. Your setup here is simply awesome," he exclaimed.

"That's why I get such a boost from sitting down and losing myself painting," Bea said, a satisfied smile brightening her face. "Let me show you around some more. I love this condo. Also, you must meet my son, Seth, who is the light of my life."

Jim winced, unable to keep up with the events unfolding before his eyes. He was used to an one-on-one relationship, such as with Lila. Here he was confronted with a woman who had so many things going. He didn't know how to compete for her attention. It almost overwhelmed him.

She paused, pointing out: "See the view of Downtown L.A. and the mountains in the background. I really enjoy it even though it's not the real dominating view you probably have from your loft at a higher elevation."

He reflected, looking out: "Yes, I do have a view of the coastline and some other areas that you don't. But your view is outstanding, with its human scale of the surrounding neighborhood. This is great, Bea."

"Thanks. Now let's meet my son, Seth. He's eight years old," she said, walking Jim to the next room where Seth was doing school work. "Seth, this is Jim Robinson, who I work with."

Seth got up and shook Jim's hand. "Hi, Mr. Robinson. Nice to meet you."

"Hi, Seth. You have quite a mother. Do you like her painting?"

"Yeah. Mom takes me everywhere she paints. She's the greatest," Seth said, grinning broadly.

"Now, Seth. Don't get carried away," she said, smiling fondly. "Get on back to your school work. Keep practicing your reading and spelling. I'll be with you in awhile, okay."

"Okay, Mom. Bye, Mr. Robinson."

"Goodby, Seth. See you around," Jim answered as they walked on toward the living area.

"Well, you've really got the cook's tour without getting fed, Jim. How about a little snack before you leave? A club sandwich and iced tea?"

"That'll be fine, Bea. I'll perch on one of your bar stools and oogle your great view. Next time I'll show you my loft."

"It's a deal."

After the sandwich, Jim and Bea exchanged a few more words before he left. They shook hands as he departed.

* * *

Later, upon arriving home to his loft, Jim puzzled over his new friend. Quite a difference compared with Lila. Bea had her act together and wasn't about to move quickly into a relationship without exploring what was involved for both of them. A very wise lady.

Should he chance dating both Lila and Bea? He didn't feel right about it since Lila was a very jealous and possessive person, plus the chance of a nasty triangle was something he didn't need. Still, he wanted to keep seeing Bea. Maybe riding horses together was a safe way to handle the situation. It would have to do for now. Bea seemed agreeable to this approach anyway.

He admired Bea and the style in which she handled her jobs and her son. She had been through a lot in her former marriage and didn't feel that she needed to be married to be happy. She probably could be very passionate too with the right person at the right time. But, he certainly didn't want to get on the wrong side of her, especially with the journalistic type of job she held. She, on the other hand, could do him a lot of good. A good ally as a friend.

In the meantime, he needed to get his life straightened out. So far, he'd been successful in keeping his problems with gambling, finances and women out of the news. But, unless he got his finances in line, things could get out-of-hand quickly. He wasn't happy with his precarious situation and needed to start cleaning up his act.

His problem revolved around his need to live dangerously. He had been that way ever since his football prowess at SC. Being the center of attention seemed to be required. He thought he could do anything and get away with it. So far he had and he felt he could continue to do so, no matter the consequences. Besides, who could stop him? That question was no longer academic!

CHAPTER 8
CITIZEN BONDING

*Mis-communications had plagued both RC and
RAC for several years. Particularly since the RC
grew from 15 to 71 members. Also, representation
increased from just L.A. City/County to six counties
and 14 subregions. RAC got lost in the shuffle,
especially since they hadn't stepped to the plate
asking for more. The turnaround began with rebellion
among key RAC members and RAC Retreat results. The
new Chair also knew many RC members, had knowledge
of what needed to be done, and was willing to gamble to
make things happen in a non-threatening manner. The
timing was also right since the RC was faced with a 2001
RTP deadline, key controversial issues and a struggling,
evolving SCAG staff. Hopefully, the Joint RC/RAC Task
Force about to be convened would be able to get them
working together again. They needed each other.*

"Man's reach should exceed his grasp."
                                    Robert Browning

"Walk softly, but carry a big stick."
                                    Theodore Roosevelt

One of the big problems facing the SCAG region involved developing
a strong Regional Citizenry which could create the needed backbone to
jumpstart the Regional Process. To achieve this, the elected officials needed to cooperate fully in carrying out needed planning without always feeling that the non-electeds were going to steal their thunder.

"Henry, ready with your July RAC report?"

"Yes, Mr Chair," Henry replied. "I'm Henry Ferrotte, new RAC Chair,"
he said, nervously looking out at the rapidly emptying RC chambers
arranged in a horseshoe of two rows of attractive oak desks for 70 representatives. An audience of about 200 could view the proceedings.

"I know some of the RC members from my involvement with a wide
range of SCAG committees, task forces and subregion meetings," he said,
looking around at the RC members remaining near the end of a busy RC

Agenda. It had been highlighted by the unusual presence of six L.A. City Council members–clustered around him–to vote on the regional airport issue.

"We had a very successful retreat on May 24 at the Southern California Edison Center–complete with facilitator," Henry continued.

"Last month I had my RAC presentation tabled due to the small number of RC members remaining. It appears that we have a similar situation today. It's difficult for the RAC to communicate effectively at the end of a long agenda. Especially since any policy we recommend has already been acted on earlier." Henry hoped he hadn't over-stepped his rights, even though he'd carefully reworked his talk, knowing what had happened.

"Mr. Chair," one member spoke from her RC position. "Could the RC move the RAC Report up in the agenda–possibly before the information section earlier in the meeting? It might solve this problem."

"Yes, that's a great idea. Let's make that change," the Chair directed the Secretary..

The RC Vice President, curious about what was taking place at RAC meetings, then spoke up. "Could you give us a summary of what happened at your recent retreat?"

"Yes, Madam Vice President." Henry proceeded to give her some of the retreat highlights.

"Was a RC observer there?"

"No. We want to include an observer, based on our retreat findings, but we've never had a RC observer or been able to send a RAC observer to the RC Retreat," Henry responded.

"We'll have to work on that. I suggest that RAC provide one page summaries of their monthly meetings for our agenda packet," she replied.

"We'd be glad to." Wow, he thought, the two things he wanted most to happen were handed to him on a silver platter. Henry breathed a sigh of relief after this rapid exchange. The Chair followed with an invitation for his participation in RC deliberations at any time. This also was a first.

Two victories in one day, but at what price! Henry knew that he would pay a price for this. He sighed. The RC expected well thought-out policy recommendations. It would be his job to ensure that this happened–even if it took extra effort on his part to develop final RAC findings. Henry now felt RAC could enter the Joint Task Force meetings on a more level playing field with the RC representatives, but only time would tell.

So went another day in the life of getting RAC more involved. Elected Chair at the April RAC meeting, he had to wait until May to have a Vice Chair selected; two being finally elected since neither candidate could find time to be at all monthly meetings. So many adjustments.

* * *

Henry posed some concerns through his discussions with several members before the monthly meeting of the Regional Advisory Council:

"Hey, guys. We've got to do something soon to force things to turn around for this region."

"I agree, Henry. But what can we do? The RC and SCAG won't listen to us," replied Marcine Simpson.

"Let me tell you two stories illustrating what we're facing," Henry continued. "One involves the use of a 'Black Box'. To get SCAG's attention, just mention the 'Black Box' and they get uptight. Everything moved along great last year toward completion of the 2000 Regional Transportation Plan (RTP). All bases had been covered and it seemed that every new highway project in the Regional Plan had been justified. Proponents were jubilant."

"Then Tony, a subregional coordinator, raised a question. 'I've checked manually through the various projects listed. For the life of me, I can't understand where all the money will come from to justify a huge $50 billion—not million—of projects. How could this be?'"

"The policy committee chair exploded: 'Don't you trust our numbers, Tony? They're very reliable. After all, they're from SCAG's technical staff.'"

"Tony wasn't deterred. 'Where did they get their numbers?'"

"'From the Black Box ,' the Chair blurted impatiently."

"'Where did the Black Box get its numbers?' responded Tony testily."

"'I don't know,' came the caustic reply. 'But you know, Tony, the Black Box is always right. It always comes up with the numbers we need and want.'"

"'Maybe we should look into how these numbers were developed then. My manual review of the projects show a deficit of $50 billion. How can I be that far off going through it manually? I even double and triple-checked my figures,' Tony responded. 'Plus, I had my staff check it out and they came up with the same results.'"

"'Let's get our staff to explain it to you then.' The chair's concern now ranged between anger and alarm. 'Hank, please explain the Black Box to Tony. We need to get this approved and close the meeting.'"

"Reluctantly, Hank took over the podium. 'The Black Box data comes from mobile sources, SCAG projections, and credits given Southern California for technology yet to be created,' he said. 'It's a little controversial. We've gone over this with a fine tooth comb and it checks out.'"

"'Have you ever checked things manually by project, Hank, to make sure that it's right?'"

"'No! No! That's never necessary. The Black Box never lies. After all, it's computerized. So how could it be wrong? Computers never screw up,' Hank stated brashly."

"'Maybe computers never err,' Tony responded in a concerned tone. 'But humans put information into the computer. Maybe the wrong information was entered or put in the wrong way based on your formulas. I'd be glad to show you my calculations. If we're going to be up to $50 billion short, we'd better know about it now so we can make adjustments. We don't need a 'garbage in, garbage out' situation aired in the L.A. Times.'"

"'You're right, of course. But we won't be able to do it, Mr Chair, so you can make a decision today,' Hank cautioned."

"'Can you get us an answer by tomorrow? Just call me, Hank, get it done and let me know. I'm tired of this,' the Chair exclaimed, his concern rising since Tony never went off on a wild goose chase. He realized this could become a political football if Tony was right and corrections weren't made now."

"That's one of the stories. What do you think resulted upon a recheck?" Henry asked.

"I'm afraid to ask, considering the stories I've heard about SCAG," Marcine replied.

"Tony was right. The Black Box screwed up. Garbage in, garbage out. The data was incomplete. It really shook up SCAG. They had to postpone their RTP to this year. They still have a nervous reaction when the 'Black Box" is mentioned."

"That's scary. Now, I'm really intrigued. What's the other story of a screwup, Henry?" Marcine asked.

"We call it 'the Toll Road fiasco,'" Henry said. It's more recent but RC and SCAG still don't like it mentioned. It even gave the California legislature and Caltrans a blackeye."

"How? Tell us about it," several chimed in.

"Well, it seems some at SCAG got an idea that whenever they needed more money for freeways, private enterprise could provide it. So, without checking it out sufficiently, they proposed and adopted it as one of their action policies. With that, they didn't have to worry if sufficient public money wouldn't be available over the planning period."

"What's wrong with that?" Marcine asked.

"Several things. It perpetuates urban sprawl for one thing. It also assumes private enterprise won't want to get their money plus built-in profit back if things go wrong. To make a long story short, such an attempt almost took place recently. In fact, its still being debated back and forth—the 91 Toll Road controversy where all connecting freeway widenings were prohibited to avoid adverse effects on toll road profits. The legislature and Caltrans both got caught with their pants down on this. SCAG kept quiet about it, but they were in violation too, if ever pressed for improvements."

"Wow! You're right. We need to make sure things don't get screwed up this year," Marcine exclaimed.

* * *

Henry mused about the major changes in SCAG's organizational structure over the past several years. They still had a lot of problems, but were beginning to evolve into a more efficient and vital organization. Originally a top-down group controlled completely by the City of Los Angeles, it now represented all six counties as a regional body.

The Regional Council originally had 15 members, all from L.A. County. It operated as a caretaker organization, developing plans and reports reflecting a limited viewpoint. As such, local planners, legislators, and politicians didn't take them seriously. Their expertise was in developing paper plans. Little was accomplished since the regional leaders held little authority in terms of money to carry out the plans.

In 1988, when the movement for stronger regional planning began in Sacramento, SCAG reorganized to represent all six counties. The Regional Council grew from 15 to its current 71 members. Fourteen subregions were finally carved out of the huge region of 16 million people. The air pollution problem brought in the Air Quality Management District (AQMD), and the Metropolitan Transit Authority (MTA). In addition, money for freeways poured in and SCAG began to carve out an empire of its own, working with these other agencies. The process was not pretty or efficient, but changes began to be made to reduce air pollution, expand bus service, establish subways, and expand the increasingly overrun freeway and surface street systems. Along the way, SCAG opened itself up to corruption and inefficiency due to its poor organization.

Henry remembered it all—even the corrupt and inefficient parts—as the region continued its haphazard growth in all directions. It also brought back unpleasant memories of his near death in East L.A. in the early 1980's. How he survived that episode he still didn't understand. That was the day Juan Rodriguiz and he met for the first time; how their lives became intertwined from that point forward.

* * *

As a young economic development consultant, Henry focused on renewing slum areas through urban revitalization. Awarded a contract through the Community Redevelopment Agency (CRA), Henry became involved with a 200 acre slum in El Monte, also the breeding grounds of some of the most infamous East L.A. gangs–especially Latino ones.

Henry's style involved walking the renewal site to get a feel of its current characteristics, problems, needs and potentials. He also looked at adjacent areas since their uses and condition could eventually impact the project area's future–either for better or worse. As he reconnoitered the area that day in early May 1982, a Latino gang accosted him. Apparently, they became suspicious of him as he checked out the area, like he represented a rival gang or an enforcement agency threatening their territory.

In reality, Henry was just moving down one of many streets in this ugly, decrepit housing project, checking out what had caused the blight. Composed of a collection of old, beat-up apartment buildings, battered, crowded and narrow one- to three-family homes, scattered liquor stores and other retail outlets, the area looked like a war zone. All its buildings had declined to the point nothing more could be done to fix them up. No parks or open space, no trees–with streets going in all directions. The residents either shuffled around or stayed inside out of harms way. Junked cars were everywhere, along with garbage and weeds where lawns should be. Housing had gone through several generations of disrepair, with pealing, chipped paint the norm. Roofs were barren and leaky with makeshift patching.

That's when five Latino gang members accosted him. Dressed in beat-up blue jeans, a baseball cap and mountain hiking boots, unprepared for confrontation, Henry believed he had done nothing to irritate them. He was shocked when the leader, dressed in baggy black pants and sporting visible gang tattoos, challenged him.

"Hey, gringo, whatcha think yur doing?"

Realizing the danger, Henry immediately tried to defuse the situation, "I'm studying this area–the City of El Monte requested it," he said smiling, brazenly masking his fear.

"What for?" one stepped closer to Henry. "You plan to rip things down and ruin our area, whitey?"

"No. Improve the area, put up decent housing, parks. Do you guys wanta help?" Henry realized he treaded on dangerous ground no matter what he said.

"No way! We don't want none of yur fancee planning. We like the place the way it is," the gang member exclaimed, punctuating his words with a finger to Henry's chest.

Henry stepped back. He wasn't sure how to get out of this situation whole. He could see tomorrow's headlines, "PLANNER SLAIN BY GANG MEMBERS ON EL MONTE STREET".

"Wait a minute, you can help. Just tell me what improvements you need?" Henry blurted nervously.

"You wanna know what we want–while filling yur pockets? Guys. Let's blast the balls off this mis'able SOB. We need be rid of this trash an' his promises to make things better. He's nothin' but trouble fo' our area," the leader said. He pulled a gun and aimed it at Henry's mid-section. The boy's arm stiffened, his finger closing on the trigger.

"Right, Whiz. Let's take him down," said his sidekick.

Out of nowhere came a shouted command: "Drop it, all of you, and get your hands on your heads, NOW."

Henry, frozen with fear, was caught in the middle between hostile forces. He looked around hesitantly.

Whiz's eyes shifted quickly from Henry, glancing around toward where the voice came from. It didn't scare him at all. He'd been through things like this.

"Guess you didn't hear me." Several shots rang out–the bullets aimed at the feet of the gang members, forcing them back.

"Which of you wants to lose your cajones? Come on, drop your guns and get your hands on your heads, NOW!"

Whiz turned around boldly and fired several shots although he could-n't see anyone to shoot.

"You think I'm kidding, don't you? I'm not." Two more shots were fired, with one nicking a gang member in the arm and another passing through a sleeve.

Whiz finally got the message. His gun hit the ground. He wanted to live for another day. The others followed suit, thinking they were surrounded. They put their hands on their heads apprehensively.

"Get moving–NOW. Don't stop running or you'll regret it. M-O-V-E!"

The gang split in all directions. Since they had nothing to shoot at, they wanted nothing to do with this. Whiz figured–another gang out to get scalps–and he'd get revenge another time.

After making sure they were gone, Juan gestured for Henry, from his new location on the roof of a nearby abandoned building, to come to him.

Not knowing what to make of this, Henry warily walked into the build-ing and up the stairs to the roof. Concerned about this man who had a gun, he couldn't figure why the guy wanted to get involved in helping a complete stranger. Who was this guy dressed in a sweater and gray pants quizzically looking him over?

"You saved my life," he said, finally breathing a sigh of relief. "Who are you anyway?"

"I'm Juan Rodriguez, Boyle Heights councilman. You're going to have to be more careful in the heart of gangland. You're lucky."

"I know," Henry shuddered as he replied. "Those punks meant business. You knew how to get their attention." He reached out his hand, "Henry Ferrotte, renewal consultant. I've tramped a lot of slums without this type of reception."

"Learn from this and you'll live longer," Juan said with a grin. "Let's go have a cup of java, Henry, if you've got time."

"All the time in the world–thanks to you."

Finding a fast food place on a nearby major street, they sat down to talk. Juan revealed he just happened to be working his way through his district to touch base with his voters. He told Henry how, due to his familiarity with gangs, he worked with the local police in an effort to reduce gang control over the El Monte area. The upsurge in their activity worried him. It pitted gangs against each other to establish territorial control at the expense of residents. Today, he felt some bad things might take place. As usual, he brought along his nickel plated Walther PPK 9mm snapped over his belt inside his pants. He felt safer carrying it and said that Henry should do the same in the future. Things had changed for the worse in this neighborhood.

* * *

From that terrifying beginning, the two became fast friends and helped each other achieve their goals. Juan was fascinated by what Henry did. Knowledge of the needs of the people in the slums, and the ability to fashion plans which made sense. Henry, in turn, used this know how to help Juan get elected as L.A. County Supervisor.

Two years later, Henry, attended a political rally for Juan, now running for the state legislature. Sitting on the dais, he looked out over the audience and noticed an intense young man in the front row nervously following Juan's every move. Short and pudgy, with a swarthy complexion and long black hair, he wore a brown sport coat, open at the neck. He was acting very strangely and ill at ease, with his hands in his pockets.

Suddenly, the man flashed a .38 revolver. Without thinking, Henry flung himself from the dais at the man, hitting him from the side as the gun went off–reverberating painfully in his ears. This quick move ruined the gunman's aim as he pulled the trigger, the shot going over Juan's head into the ceiling. Henry, chest bruised and aching, grappled with the man and finally subdued him with help from several in the audience just as the police arrived.

It'd been a wild scene as people screamed and dove for cover. Shaken by what happened, some of the audience began to reassemble, assisting the shaken Henry and Juan. The man's revolver, a 2 inch, Smith & Wesson .38 MP, remained in a cordoned off area where it had fallen. A tired, worn gun with gouges on the barrel, it had the wood broken on one grip. Scary to look at, considering what it could have done to Juan's future career .

Finally, when the man had been taken away, order restored, a grateful Juan clapped Henry on the back and thanked him for his fearlessness. "You saved my life. How'd you know what to do so quickly? To size him up so well. I'll always be grateful for your fearlessness ."

"I guess we're even, Juan. We must have joined destinies," Henry said, shaking his head and painfully clasping his chest, still not believing what had taken place. They clung to each other, marveling at their good fortune.

* * *

Reflecting now on the close calls he and Juan had years earlier, Henry knew God had been watching over him. Raised in a poor family struggling to put enough food on the table and a roof over their heads during the 1930's depression, Henry attended a fundamentalist church in a small Michigan town. It was a unique experience that shaped his life toward volunteering to help others less fortunate. Although he outgrew the Bible thumping and the long testimonies involving screaming and "blessing the Lord," Henry still attended church regularly and prayed about his decisions. He was concerned about gangs, the drugs that ruined lives, the growing violence, the lack of family ties, and lagging religious foundations among many in the younger generation.

He still remembered his father talking about the Japs bombing Pearl Harbor–listening to the radio when it was announced and being shocked by it. The forties was a simpler time, when ordinary people were more sharing than competitive. A time when American society, for all its inequities and injustices, involved less loneliness, alienation, self-absorption and cynicism. A time when we paid for victory with an inevitable loss of innocence.

Henry credited his formative years for how he turned out. People now faced with problems became frustrated with life and often resorted to violence to air their feelings of inadequacy and powerlessness. He had worked with gang members who had been shaped by this feeling of hopelessness.

They lashed out at those who got in their way, making things worse. He felt that God was very important and often saw how lives were changed dramatically when he became involved.

Regional planning offered a means by which people could improve their lives by living in a better environment, becoming better educated, getting and holding a job, and advancing. That along with ridding cities of congestion and pollution. This is why Henry joined the regional movement, making the most of his planning background, teaching career and religious upbringing. His rise to RAC chair reflected this desire to make life better for people. He was pleased with the results, even though it involved a frustratingly slow process.

Henry had become used to the frustrations of changing and improving city life during his years as an urban planner. Extending this process to the region—especially the larger than life L.A.Region—was just another challenge to meet and improve on. Just another frustration to break down to size and resolve.

* * *

Preparing for the Joint Task Force meeting, Henry set up a three-way conference call with fellow members Karen and Mary.

"You ready for the Task Force meeting with the RC members?" he began. "We were successful in getting moved up on the RC Agenda, plus we get a page monthly on RAC policy in the agenda. Any thoughts?"

"That's great, Henry," said Karen. "I'm wondering about the best way to select our strategic partners to work with in the RC? I'm in tune with the representative from my subregion. Do we have a final say on this?"

"You bet," replied Henry. "We need people we're comfortable with who'll keep our interests in mind. Mary, what's your thinking on this?"

"I have reservations," Mary replied. "I know my RC rep but I'm not sure she'd be in my corner if we needed her. What about you, Henry?"

"I guess when we get to know more RC members and where they stand, we'll feel more comfortable about working with them. I've worked well with several Gateway Cities and Orange County subregion members, and Bob Long, of Riverside. So I have more contacts to select from. The same goes for liaisons to both subregion boards. Have either of you worked closely with other subregions?"

"No, not like you. Do you agree, Karen?" Mary asked.

"Right. I see what you mean, Henry," said Karen. "Maybe these meetings with the RC members will begin the process of helping the RC and RAC communicate better with each other," said Karen.

"How about developing a budget, either through SCAG, or preferably from corporate sponsors? No strings attached, of course. Any ideas who we could get to contribute?" asked Henry, throwing a dart at a board in his office.

"Maybe the utilities and banks would help," said Mary. "It's a tough call since we don't have much visibility or clout now. How about developing a Web Page and offering advertising through it? I guess we could call several firms and see how they might help. One or two of them might show some interest. We wouldn't need much to start, and then we could grow it as we begin to show results."

"We also need to be mentioned in key meetings the RC leadership has with the media," said Henry. "This is going to be a hard sell, as staffer Adam Ferris is already checking to see if we have any more big issues to raise. I guess he didn't read our Retreat Notes closely–or at all. He's also very mysterious when asked to elaborate on the five models of how a new RAC might operate that he included in his original proposal to the RC. He sure knows how to be elusive. A real politician. How was he with you when you were Chair, Karen?"

"Not too helpful. I finally did my thing, knowing he would let me know when I strayed too far from the SCAG line," she said. "We've got to press our advantage to get as much as we can. Right, Mary?"

"In spades. I've probably been with RAC longer than anyone–over 20 years. I've seen SCAG and RC participants come and go. We've got to be tough, but not too tough. We'll have to feel our way on this. Our priorities must be laid out clearly to show them only one issue at a time. Hopefully, we can get several meetings out of this and keep them guessing a little on how much change we want. It's going to be tough though, with two wily politicians like Jane and Kate involved, true county commissioners at heart."

"Okay, then. Let's put our ideas together. I'll also solicit some from other RAC members. The RC needs us more than we need them. They've got a tough 2001 RTP to put together and not enough transportation money to go around. The Regional Airport issue could haunt them too," Henry said, rising to his feet and strolling around his office to stimulate his thinking.

"That's true, Henry," said Karen. " Well, I guess that's all I have at this time."

"Same here," said Mary.

Henry thanks them both and signed off, saying, "these should prove to be interesting meetings if we play our cards right. I'll talk to you both soon."

* * *

The 2000 RC Retreat, on October 4, 2000 at the Raddison Resort in Knott's Berry Farm, focused on SCAG's fiscal structure. The agency had been through a serious fiscal crisis, resulting in a major audit, and internal financial, accounting and contracting reviews in 2000.

After several hours of discussion of a wide range of items, the retreat adjourned, with the feeling that SCAG had moved back into a healthy financial situation, although some were not sure.

* * *

Five members of both the RC and RAC scheduled a series of important meetings to determine RAC's long range future. The RC had been significantly reorganized several years ago, but the RAC hadn't changed over twenty years, except to expand its number of members. Coverage in the first three meetings taking place focused on providing more diverse representation, achieving greater participation in meetings, providing leadership on topics which the RC needed RAC input, encouraging greater policy committee participation by RAC members, and adequate SCAG staffing and budget.

They continued to debate. The jury was still out on this. RAC had different groups (specializations, different portions of the Region) which could be subdivided into working groups, which in turn would be part of a larger RAC. They worked to develop an outline of how the RAC might be structured. Such things as adding several non-electeds to each subregion board without voting rights, as well as "mini-RAC's" for each subregion were debated with no firm conclusions reached. The RC was to be advised and the final approach presented to the RC's General Assembly which would be meeting some time in May 2001. However, nothing took place on this matter.

* * *

Henry couldn't shake the feeling that something drastic needed to be done soon if RAC was ever to achieve its destiny for supplying an alternate opinion on important matters facing the region. Once he left as chair, he knew that whoever replaced him probably would permit RAC to slide back into its role as a SCAG vassal. Or the RAC could very well be disbanded as was being hinted. It looked like all he had attempted to do was in naught. Reflecting back on his military service and the term used when everything possible that could go wrong, did, he muttered to himself: "I feel like we're being screwed, glued and tattooed–and can't do anything about it. Unless...?!!

CHAPTER 9
TRANSPORTATION FINANCE CRISIS

*Transportation Finance Task Force
moves ahead to get financing for 2001
RTP through state legislature. Meets
with RTP Technical Advisory Committee
in effort to fund its transportation needs.
Problems with MTA and its approach to
making transit more viable.*

---

*"Bull markets are born on pessimism, grow
on skepticism, mature on optimism, and die
on euphoria."*
-Financier John Marks Templeton-

"Jim, your broker, Kent."

"How much money did I make today?" Jim asked, awaiting the tale his broker would spin on how he had made another killing in the "dot-com" market. He loved boasting about it.

"We've got to talk," Kent said cautiously. "Nasdaq bottomed-out–big! You lost a bunch. You need to sell now while you're still ahead."

"Whataya mean?" Jim asked, stunned. "I thought you, with your expertise, had this all figured out. You know that one down market day in July 2000 doesn't mean a thing. I'm a gambler as you know. I do well at everything Vegas offers."

"This is different. My gut feel, which is seldom wrong, says the market has turned around. The Dow is up, with shifts back to the real economy–not speculation."

"I thought you had guts when I asked you to represent me. Why chicken out now?" Jim asked, scowling at his broker's change in posture.

"You know I've had a great deal of experience in the market," Kent continued, "anticipating when to get in and out. Dot-com stocks have had their run. It's past time to shift back to blue chips. Most of the tech stocks haven't made a dime since they started. It's been all spec. Trust me, it's time to get out."

"No, stay in. I'm a gambler and willing to take a chance."

"Jim, It's your decision but please, think it over carefully. You've known my position on this since you asked me to get you some dot-com stocks."

"No. Stay in," he repeated. "Call me tomorrow."

Jim inherited Kent from his father and they seemed to hit it off well working with blue chips. But since the high risk dot-coms and junk bonds became a part of his investment strategy, friction occurred. Maybe he should look around for a more gutsy guy–like Cy Peck, since he considered Kent's safe approach as "chicken." This run by dot-com stocks seemed to be a once in a lifetime chance to make it big.

He'd been making ten percent annually on blue chip stocks; then he noticed dot-com stocks were appreciating over 100 percent almost weekly. It'd been a great move by him to shift some of his stock holdings of $5 million over near the beginning of Nasdaq's run up from under 2000 to over 5000. It was smart to jump in when a number of dot-com's were $2 stocks. Some were over $100 now and still rising. Wishing he'd moved more of his holdings over at the start, it still angered him that Kent had advised against it.

Kent's stock motto, "operate the opposite of what people believe about stocks and the marketplace," seemed to work for blue chips. But his rules on when to let a stock go didn't seem right for dot-coms. Such as "let a stock go when it drops by ten percent from the purchase price or when you've made a profit"; or new highs on lower volume (signs of weaker demand); or stock moving fast and going nowhere (full swing of its price during day). Dot-coms or junk bonds were higher risk but more his style.

Gradually, he wore Kent down and switched more of his blue chips–but only after the dot-coms had shot up to $50 or more a share. Still angry at Kent's squeamishness, Jim's blood pressure rose. He decided Kent had to go.

* * *

The next morning he contacted Cy, who agreed to handle his stocks when he was ready to switch. Jim waited to hear from Kent so he could make the change.

Finally, Kent called and gave him the bad news before Jim could discharge him.

"The dot-coms have dropped over 1,000 points since yesterday. Most of your stocks are below 40. You're going to lose big but you still should sell."

Jim exploded. "Whaddaya mean below 40 and sell?" he yelled over the phone. "I'd lose over a million if I did, you idiot. I bought too many of them at 50 since you were so chicken when I couldda got 'em at 2. You're out. Cy Peck is taking over. Contact him and transfer my account." He slammed down the phone, fuming and red faced.

Agitatedly pacing around his study, he cursed to himself: "It can't be! That broker screwed up. I wouldn't make such an idiotic blunder. I've always been good at making my inheritance grow. Kent really gave me bad advice. The stockbrokers only look out for their fees." He kicked some SCAG reports stacked on the floor, sending them sprawling.

Gradually cooling down, he grudgingly admitted that his own stubbornness created some of the difficulties. He must face up to the problem.

He lamented: "Why'd I go on margin to buy those stupid dot-com stocks? I shoudda known they couldn't go up forever. I was just too greedy." At home in his loft study, he shuddered at his plight.

"You dumbbell, you knew you shouldn't take such a chance over the advice of your broker–and everyone you asked. Those tech stocks were way over-priced when you bought in later–you knew it but you thought you'd luck out, you greedy idiot."

Jim Robinson knew he faced ruin unless he acted fast. He'd financed many of his stock market escapades with money he didn't have–buying on margin. But he hadn't gone through his brokerage house. Sweating profusely, he continued to shake at his dilemma. Fear gripped him as he crumpled into his chair, hands on his face, oblivious to everything around him. A beautiful day outside, but he felt as if he were in hell.

Somehow, he must right this sinking ship. But how? He'd told Kent to get lost, and Cy knew nothing about his account. Another stupid reaction without thinking things through. His anger overtaking him again.

He must keep his losses quiet. It wouldn't look good for the chair of SCAG's Transportation Finance Task Force to be seen with his personal finances in shambles.

* * *

Deciding he must apologize for his angry outburst, he called Kent back.

"Sorry, Kent, for my anger and hanging up on you. That was uncalled for. Please forgive me. I hope you haven't made any changes on my account?

"No, although I had made the initial move to transfer it. But it might be best if you did change brokers if you don't approve of my advice," Kent said.

"I've thought it over and realize you're right. I need to dump all my tech stocks. Can you sell now and let me know ASAP how bad my losses will be?'

"Okay. But think about it, Jim. I don't want an unhappy client. Life's too short."

"Sell and get back to me. Also, I hope this will remain just between us. Can you keep it quiet?"

"Don't worry. As your broker, I'm required to keep all client actions quiet. I'll call back as soon as I can"

"Thanks, Kent," Jim replied, realizing how close he came to really screwing things up.

* * *

Kent called back about an hour later. By then, Jim was so paralyzed with fear, he could hardly stand the suspense.

"Jim, it's not good but I've sold all your tech stocks. The money is back in safe blue chips. When you have time, we need to reassess your overall stock portfolio based on recent market trends."

"Okay, Kent, but what's the damage?" he asked with trepidation.

"Unfortunately, you're out about $500,000. I hope you weren't doing this on borrowed money?" Kent stated, concerned about how Jim had been acting.

Jim gasped but kept his emotions in hand. "No, I stayed away from that," he lied.

He'd borrowed several hundred thousand to finance his dot-com escapade. In addition, to ease the burden, he'd put together another $200,000 by hocking some family jewelry, selling a car and a boat, and some property. Now he had a better idea of the extent of his debt. Thanking Kent, he hung up pondering his dilemma. He couldn't tell anyone who he had borrowed from either due to its sensitive nature. How could he get out of this hole? He must quickly develop some strategies to defuse the bad situation.

* * *

Within two days, rumors began circulating of his losses. It was impossible in this information age to keep such things quiet. The rumors, of course, exaggerated his difficulty, listing his losses much higher and citing the reasons as everything from income tax fraud to money laundering–even including selling votes in Sacramento, extortion, and gambling debts in Vegas.

Jim didn't know what to do. He wanted to see Lila again, and go to Sacramento to see what he could do there. At this low point, Lila called.

"Jim, this is Lila. What's all this I've been hearing about your financial problems," she demanded? "I'm really concerned."

"Thanks for calling. There are a lot of untrue rumors going around. I'd like to see you again and explain–say tonight?"

"Alright, about eight. Take care of yourself."

"I'll be there dressed casual," Jim said, concerned–but not sur-prised–by her response. He would have his hands full tonight.

* * *

When he arrived just before eight, she let him in, receiving his kiss coolly, and moving quickly to the family room.

"Thanks for seeing me, Lila. I don't blame you for being wary about seeing me."

Non-committally, she waited to hear what he had to say.

"Lila, I probably shouldn't be bothering you again. Especially with my financial troubles."

"What sort of financial troubles?" she asked. "Are the rumors true? I always thought that you were independently wealthy, with not a care in the world about money."

"There's no such animal. You can overreach yourself no matter how much money you have–or had. You heard the rumors?" Jim asked with great embarrassment.

"I heard you were laundering money and got in trouble. I paid no atten-tion, it was so far fetched–and certainly not true," Lila declared.

"That's one of the weirdest rumors out there," Jim replied. "Not true, of course. I'm certainly not into narcotics."

"You want to talk about it, Jim?" she asked, gently touching him. "I'm concerned about you. How can I help?"

"I got greedy, borrowed money in the stock market and lost it on some high flying tech stocks. My broker urged me to get out, but I thought the market would rebound. Instead, it really bottomed and I'm out over $100,000," he said, lying about the amount and circumstances to minimize the problem. "That's money I don't have. So I'm looking around for ways to pay it off–legally of course."

"Why come to me, Jim? You know how little I have. Zilch resources?" she said, puzzled by his need to talk to her about his financial problems.

"Yeah, I know. But I trust you and thought that just talking about it might help me. You know as well as I, there aren't many friends I can talk to about something like this. I feel safe with you. Plus, I feel bad about leading you on in our relationship," he said, with a sad, concerned look in his eyes. He used that puppy dog look that prompt's women to mother their man.

She went over to him, wanting to take him in her arms, but knowing she couldn't. She'd learned a lot from him, she thought. A lot about greed and gullibility, about facades and consequences–and the transience of love. She could write a book on that!

"What can we do on this, Jim? I have some contacts at CIG who might help, but I'm sure they would have some conditions you wouldn't like."

"You're right. I can't go there. I'm going to Sacramento in the next few days, encourage legislation needed for the region and convince people I'm doing it for them. Let's leave it at that, Lila. I'll be back in touch as soon as I can," he said, firmly committed to this path of working things out. "Thanks for your support when I needed it," he added, with a light kiss.

As Lila closed the door behind him, she couldn't shake the premonition that things were going to get worse before they got better–both for his financial troubles and their relationship. He was all wrapped up in himself. She just happened to be available as a port in a storm to soothe his ego. Seeing her gave him a safe alternative to really facing the truth about himself–and ducking the consequences at least temporarily. She knew she had to protect herself better in the future–or get badly hurt by him emotionally.

* * *

The Transportation Task Force met with the RTP Technical Advisory Committee (TAC) to continue its process of getting input from SCAG task forces. Multiple funding problems had been outlined in both the 1998 RTP (which was not approved), and had been magnified in the 2001 RTP.

Harry, the finance consultant, dramatized the desperate problems which SCAG faced in financing many of the improvements, realizing that some weren't achievable.

"Ladies and gentlemen: The 1998 RTP contained over \$9 billion in highway improvement projects in addition to those already committed. In addition, the 2001 RTP identifies arterial improvement needs totaling more than \$50 billion. So, you see the problem. These don't include all the toll lanes (HOT Lanes) on a number of highways which would be funded privately, assuming that the toll road fiasco will be resolved. The Finance Task Force has been working to find funds to handle all these improvements. We need your help and guidance."

"Harry's done a yeoman's job in figuring out how to do this through a variety of sources," Jim added. "This unconstrained list of projects far exceeds the available public funds in the region over the plan's 2001-2025 time frame. The amounts are staggering. We need to figure out other ways to reduce the need for more highways–including transit, higher housing densities, closer ties between jobs and housing, and other approaches."

"During the last several months," Harry said, "the Task Force has developed a revenue forecast for the 2001 RTP. Fifteen revenue sources have been approved and two forecasts produced. But, two factors work against increasing the revenue stream: policies regarding zero emission vehicles, low emission vehicles, and alternative fuels; and current California Air Resource Board policies which will reduce the consumption of gasoline (and gas taxes) over the planning period." Pointing to the chart, "The first yields a revenue forecast of $110 billion while the second reduces the estimate to $99.8 billion."

"So we're in deep trouble matching revenues with proposed facility expenditures?" asked Rudy, a RTP member in the audience.

"Absolutely," responded Jim, "we're about to push the panic button to get everyone's attention."

"Let me emphasize several figures on the power point." Harry added, pointing to the chart. "A 'Regional Checkbook' has been created to show revenues matched against forecast expenditures. The first forecast shows a shortfall of $0.6 billion and the second, a shortfall of $10.8 billion."

"And I take it the second forecast is the most realistic?" asked Luke, another member

"Right," Harry continued. "But that doesn't cover everything either."

"What do you mean?" Luke shot back.

"Just that we feel that we'll probably have a $50 billion shortfall if we continue to build highways like we have in the past," Harry said, to drive the point home.

"You've got my attention!" Luke exclaimed. "What can we do to make sure we will have adequate revenues?"

"We need a financial strategy to close the gap with additional taxes and/or raising the rates on existing ones," Harry explained.

"We need ideas for ensuring that revenues will keep pace with growing population and travel demands over the next quarter century," added Jim. "We must also economize by using what we have better. Think of ways you can help us meet this need."

"Why do we need to introduce these ideas to ensure adequate revenues for key facilities?" asked Luke.

"If we don't, the average speed on our highways could drop from 32 miles per hour today to less than 16 mph by the year 2025 during peak periods. We're approaching gridlock."

This admission stunned the audience–really getting their attention. Harry again gestured at the chart. "Clearly, traditional revenue sources for constructing, equipping, maintaining, and operating the region's transportation systems are inadequate to meet projected needs. Even using the

Governor's Traffic Congestion and Relief Plan to its fullest, we will experience deficits."

"Does this mean we'll be out of conformity, subjecting SCAG and its programs to takeover by the state?" Rudy interrupted.

"Right. Unless we further limit our congestion and air quality problems," Jim answered.

Harry continued: "Based on this chart, the funding strategy must meet at least two objectives:

1. Provide sufficient revenues to fund the program of projects in the adopted 1998 Regional Transportation Plan as well as the deficits in the baseline cost. This totals approximately $33 billion.

2. Provide sufficient revenue to fund high priority projects needed to ensure that the Region will remain in compliance with air quality requirements."

Jim broke in pointing to the chart: "To address this revenue shortfall, we will need an alternative funding strategy based on these four principles."

Aware of his own revenue shortfall, the irony shook Jim. Maybe he should pay attention to these principles himself, he thought. His problems weren't in billions but were more than enough to get him in trouble.

"1. Ensure that local/regional control is maintained over the decision-making associated with expending the revenues."

"This would require close attention to selecting improvements and that would get the most 'bang for the buck."

"2. Build on the existing practice of ensuring that the system's users pay."

"The importance here is that those who use the system most should pay their share of the costs."

Maybe, Jim mused, this second principle could be used to resolve his financial difficulties. He needed to think things through before he went to Sacramento. "Build on the existing...to defray substantial portions of the cost," sounded intriguing. It could be applied to his situation if he sucked up the danger and consequences. But–was it worth the trouble involved?

He went on with the principles on the chart:

"3. Provide flexibility to ensure that the most cost-effective projects will be constructed first.

"This means making sure that those projects that would return benefits most quickly (possibly transit) were built first."

"4. Design and build projects needed to ensure air quality conformity requirements using debt financing to avoid delays that could cut off future federal funding."

"Since transit generally improves air quality the most, this principle would favor better transit."

Again, the emphasis on prudent use of debt financing in Principle Four rang Jim's bell. Why not try it? He had to take chances now, and that's what he had always done before. Now, as never before, was the time to take the plunge back into the thrills and chills involved in working the system, he thought, lapsing momentarily into his own private world.

Snapping back to the moment, Jim heard Harry saying, "This won't be easy, but we've got to bite the bullet, admit our problems and take concrete steps to solve them."

The stunned audience sat silently trying to figure some way out of this dilemma without success.

Harry continued listing some alternative revenue sources. Possibilities included a local sales tax addition of one-half of one percent for the next 20 years. Another was to index the state gas tax to inflation. A third emphasized highway user fees applied to vehicle miles traveled (VMT tax) which penalized those who commuted long distances to work. Elected officials from the Inland Empire were against it, as expected.

Two other approaches involved tolls on highways during peak periods and privatizing many of the proposed toll road facilities. Both were regressive, funding transportation more heavily by those with more limited incomes. Privatizing toll roads also wouldn't be popular, as proved in the toll road scandal that erupted in the newspapers about six months ago.

A sixth approach brought the private sector into the funding of transit facility development and operation through developer contributions, benefit assessment districts, joint development, and value capture techniques. This approach would be covered in greater detail at a later meeting.

The final possibility was to explore federal funding programs more fully. Geared again mostly to mass transportation projects, bonds would be involved, in this case GARVEE bonds, to fund transportation projects with future federal highway funds. Or funding major transportation projects of national importance through a five-year pilot program in the Transportation Finance and Innovation Act of 1998.

The options outlined an ambitious approach meeting the needs of a transportation system being overwhelmed by gridlock. But, nothing less would do. The committee members shook their heads about how to handle these issues in a quality way in the short time available. They would need to work quickly to flesh out reasonable approaches to all these issues.

The meeting adjourned after agreeing to meet within thirty days to begin to reach some decisions.

*   *   *

Evon continued to report regularly on how he was doing as an "insider" in the KOPE organization. He met Judith Struthers, finding her fanatically opposed to planning. She crossed swords a few years back with a planning agency whose Zoning Board wouldn't allow her to rezone her property on the edge of a residential neighborhood for heavy commercial and industrial development. This embittered her against planning in general. Any chance she got, she worked to destroy or screw up the planning process. Urban sprawl offered the best opportunity, so KOPE was born and allied with big money interests.

Evon found KOPE close to making a big move, but wasn't sure yet what was involved. He also found a close tie with CIG behind the scenes. They included efforts to kill needed affordable housing projects for low and moderate income residents. This proved fairly easy to do since liability insurance (guaranteeing builders wouldn't be subject to suits for shoddy construction) had been held up in the legislature with help from CIG. Other similar actions involving higher density housing had resulted in a number of unpassed bills in both houses in the past several years.

*   *   *

With their common interests in helping the poor and minority residents of the region, Marcine and Bea met regularly for lunch to keep each other informed of emerging problems and opportunities. Their coverage converged on frustrations with MTA's slow-moving bureaucracy that seldom seemed to get things done. The new general manager was beginning to improve this, but even then, built-in high costs from union and management difficulties continued to plague bus and transit operations. The bus strike added to this futility.

Marcine and Bea met today at a little restaurant, Lolita's, in South-Central L.A. which offered a variety of ethnic foods. Enjoying the latest offerings, they observed the street scene from their canopied sidewalk table.

"Just think, Bea, no matter whether SCAG allocates 62 percent of its total funding to transit, it won't increase transit patronage unless something drastic is done to restructure the entire system. It's just not convenient enough and cheap enough to get most people out of their cars."

"Yeah, I know. It's a tough nut to crack. Everything's so out of whack that it seems futile to break the log jam. People in the know say transit is the single most important component in the success or failure of the RTP. So what happens if it's a big failure?" Bea asked.

"I don't know whether the L.A. area, like Atlanta, has the political and financial 'will' to make the dramatic changes needed to make it happen," Marcine said. "Everyone still wants to drive their car everywhere. It's so engrained in their psyche."

"I went to a Regional Transit Task Force meeting the other day and they were struggling bravely with ways to restructure the whole system, even trying to align all the transit lines throughout the region into a coherent, interlinked system. It's an ungodly mess, with jurisdictional and managerial rivalries infesting any decisions. A few 'convenient' deaths might be the only way to resolve some of the petty issues that keep things from happening. It reminds me of John Randolph's description of a corrupt but gifted politician: Someone who 'shines and stinks like rotten mackerel by moonlight.'"

"Yeah, there are too many of those, unfortunately," said Bea, wrinkling her nose.

"What were some of the approaches being batted around, Bea?" Marcine asked.

"Transit operators must be able to develop and maintain services that attract users," Bea began. "The Task Force said at a minimum, services must be much more available when the riders need them."

"But, wouldn't that be a tall order, especially in L.A?" wondered Marcine. "It would require reliable, on-time service, easy transfers even to different bus lines–so more people can get from origin to destination quickly. And a reasonable, single fare that is honored by all bus or transit providers.

"Yes, all of these are crucial to success," Bea acknowledged. "Services also would have to be accessible to riders without physical, institutional or informational obstacles."

"I imagine that would require bus stops with adequate passenger access and egress, as well as regional transit and municipal operators able to coordinate services that cross jurisdictional lines." interjected Marcine. "It could also call for more information on schedules, traffic tie-up locations and other smart street technology."

"Right. All these and more are critical requirements," Bea said. "The system absolutely must meet the customer's needs."

"Wouldn't this also require routes that easily serve shopping, employment, entertainment and other popular destinations?" Marcine wondered. "And lower fares off-peak, or even free service in certain circumstances?"

"Right, Marcine. Absence of these key capabilities are why bus and transit services are poorly utilized now."

"Why does MTA have such a poor record even with its high subsidies?" Marcine asked, watching a blue bird light on an adjacent table to peck at crumbs.

"High cost is one reason." replied Bea. "MTA operates some of the nation's most costly bus lines. Because it's a monopoly, its wages, benefits and work rules are out of line with the market."

"Other reforms needed include encouraging more competition with other bus lines, and repeal of the city's ancient anti-jitney law, which would permit alternatives to MTA bus service," Marcine volunteered. "Also, I think they should shift the basis for transit subsidies away from providers like MTA and give the money to riders, instead, to spend as they choose. We need to get more competition into the system to squeeze out some of the waste."

"Of course," Bea added, "they're also looking at using many sizes of vehicles–such as jitneys, taxis, and small buses–that could save money and serve people's needs in areas where regular buses can't penetrate."

"Now, that's using their heads," Marcine agreed. "But one thing really perplexes me about L.A. attitudes. As an affordable-housing developer said recently, 'We used to have communism to be against. Now we just have density.' This probably overstates the intensity of residents' opposition to further density in their neighborhoods. But we know that increased density around transit stops benefits everyone. It gets people out of their cars, improves quality of life, and connects people to the larger region. Why can't more people see these potentials?"

"You're on the right track, Marcine. I hope people will wake up to what they're missing. Our discussion sure will help me assemble my material on affordable housing."

"Great. We need you to light a fire under us to start solving our housing problems. All we have now are lousy excuses. Don't give up, Bea."

"I plan to keep this and other regional problems under the microscope," Bea replied. "There's a big audience out there hoping we find ways to make the Region a better place to live. I'm convinced that if enough leaders believed we could find solutions, we could whip this regional problem. I'm going to use my columns to get more people's attention. We can lick this if I can get more people like you involved."

"Any other angles you can use, Bea?"

"Well, MTA is crafting a new long-range plan that envisions spending tens of billions on highway, street, subway, light rail and busway projects over the next 25 years. It could keep L.A. County moving by constructing busways across the San Fernando Valley and along Wilshire Boulevard, and by building light rail lines from Union Station to Pasadena, as well as the Westside and Eastside, with extensions possible in later years."

"That's promising–if it happens. Any other new wrinkles?" Marcine asked hopefully.

"Oh, yes," Bea remembered, "an extension of the Red Line subway beneath Wilshire Boulevard from Western Avenue to Century City, perhaps as far as Westwood. Depending on politics and construction obstacles, even extending the Green Line to LAX."

"Hey, if most of this occurs, it could help make transit work for the average person."

"Yeah, they said that by 2025, transit trips would increase to 9.9 percent, as compared with 17.2 percent by carpools. Even with 72.9 percent of motorists still traveling alone," Bea said, "that would be a big improvement. Let's hope that works. Otherwise, we're going to have total gridlock."

"You've got a lot to write about, Bea. Why don't you make this into a series?"

"I plan to–reinforced by interviews with key politicians, professionals and citizens. I want to open people's eyes, especially with such stunning projections as the average speed on most area freeways during the peak morning commute dropping from 34 mph to 20 mph–or less. Zeroing in on what this would mean in the life of the ordinary citizen."

"That's scary, Bea. A few statistics with some shocking examples could turn things around. Well, I've got to go. Thanks for taking time to discuss your investigative journalism work with me."

"My pleasure, Marcine. Keep the faith."

CHAPTER 10
INNER-CITY REINVESTMENT

*Efforts made to remove toxic wastes from
some Gateway City Brownfield sites.
LAEDC moves ahead to back site assembly,
and state subsidies to finance toxic waste
removal. Gateway Cities Partnership
guides plan to remove toxic wastes and
help retrain workers to meet growing
shortage of machine tools specialists.
Black churches get involved in
economic development and school
improvements.*

"We live in a world of no boundaries."
Source unknown

"Such a frustrating situation! This Brownfield challenge could be excit-ing if we had more to work with," exclaimed Gavin O'Neil as he talked with Carla and Mike at their COG Paramount offices.

"An under-statement," Mike Nelson said. "The state limits liability, the local population's limited education stymies effective job retraining for needed machinists positions, and many of the cities won't admit they have toxic soils. This slows site assessments and classification."

"We've got to move quickly—or any momentum we've built-up will disappear," Carla Hawks said. "Can you imagine, we're already in August, over halfway through 2000."

"I know," Gavin said, with a scowl. "If the poor cities in Gateway's northwest quadrant feel things aren't going to happen soon, they feel like they're wasting their time and limited resources." He paced back and forth, glancing at his partners for signs of encouragement.

"We've got ten cities with 87 sites involved, which is quite a break-through. But what're they doing with their sites?" Carla asked.

"Toxic waste technicians are measuring the contamination first. Then they'll classify the sites for industrial re-use and timing of development. Finally, they'll market them, and each city will get ten percent of the expected $200,000 involved to help pay for cleanup," Gavin said in his lilting Irish tone.

"Most importantly, we've got to have concrete results on this," Carla replied.

"The six Hub cities, where many of the sites are located, have been ignored for years by other Gateway cities. They need to feel there's hope for them," Mike added. "They're the poorest communities with the most immigrants and highest housing densities. They even lack the basic services–water, recreation, education and power–due to lack of public investment."

"We must also diversify our retraining efforts so the unemployed and under-utilized can receive the training and education they need to be part of this effort," Carla reminded them.

"Also, get them temporary jobs with Alameda Corridor construction work, upcoming 710 Freeway upgrading or local service jobs created," Gavin said. "We can manage that much."

"Lack of city money available gets in the way. Let's make sure the project managers know this and accelerate their funding efforts. That'll be essential to make it happen," Mike said, getting up and moving around to stimulate his circulation.

"Now, on education, the big problem we've got to resolve with the community colleges and local schools is how to maximize job opportunities for their students. Lots of residents speak only Spanish and lack even elementary school education from Mexican schools, making it difficult to train them due to poor communication," Carla said, shaking her head in frustration.

"We've got to somehow make this a sustainable subregion. Right now it isn't," Gavin said, pounding the table. "You know its educational level is so low, we can't train all the machinists and other skilled workers needed without bringing them in from outside. Look at Huntington Park. Sixty-nine percent of its high school students don't graduate. The educational system must be reworked to prevent going back to two unequal school systems–one for minorities as in the past."

"We must get our educators and job training specialists together this week to get things moving," Gavin concluded as he stood and closed his briefcase, bringing the conversation to a close. "That's my first priority–along with focusing on the Sustainable Communities Conference scheduled for February in Long Beach."

* * *

In Sacramento, the state legislative committee worked on breaking the log jam over limiting liability for developers of Brownfields. Otto and Joe from Juan's office fought to move the Brownfield legislation out of committee, so it could be voted on by both houses.

"Nationally, the Environmental Protection Agency has been awarding large grants to assess environmental conditions at Brownfield sites," Igor Popinovich said to his committee. "In Congress, more than 19 bills have been introduced which would clarify critical liability issues and offer financial incentives for Brownfield cleanup."

Otto's Asian eyes narrowed. "Here in California, a different situation entirely. The legislature in August 1998 failed to extend the state Superfund law that vastly curtailed the state's authority when the law expired January 1, 1999."

"California's Brownfield program doesn't function as smoothly as it should," Chairman Igor responded. "What we've got seems more like a patchwork of solutions than an adaptable, coordinated program that adequately meets developers' needs."

"You're right. Our laws tackle only narrow aspects of the Brownfield process on a limited number of sites," Joe said.

Igor emphasized: "To effectively promote reuse of Brownfield sites in California, lawmakers must implement a comprehensive policy package, one which provides limited liability relief for prospective purchasers. It must also establish the regulations needed in order to attract urban redevelopment, minimize costs, and reduce the time needed to complete projects. Any questions so far?"he asked, intensifying the debate.

The committee members shook their heads as they scanned the material.

"One added point. It must create public financial incentives to leverage private sector dollars. Also, provide clear, achievable guidelines for determining how 'clean is clean' regarding soils."

"Can we get the bill out of committee with those provisions?" asked a worried Otto.

"I hope so. Let's vote the draft we've developed so far. Are there any objections?" asked Igor.

"Hearing none, the bill is reported out for house floor consideration."

Afterwards over coffee, Otto and Joe discussed how they'd present the successful committee action to Juan. Also, how best to package it for presentation to both houses.

* * *

Jim Robinson hadn't been directly involved with Gateway Cities' Brownfield program, but he wanted to be included because this area was second only to L.A. in population, and would prove crucial to the future of the whole L.A. Region. So many things were happening which must be nursed along including Brownfields, 710 Corridor upgrading, the Alameda

Corridor, the vital two ports and the light rail transit system. Each one involved a lot of bucks, and they could help him politically in many ways.

He knew Alan Stoneham, chairman of the Center Housing Corporation, had $100 million available for affordable housing, much of which should be spent in the Gateway Cities area. Several years ago, Jim had been involved in that area when the high-tech Century Freeway construction removed existing housing and displaced 25,500 residents. This 17.3 mile east/west stretch from LAX to Norwalk ended up costing more per mile than any other highway project in America.

Jim jotted some figures on his notepad. The 105 Freeway cost $2.2 billion to build, plus another billion for its mass transit line. The Green Line, a 23-mile 10-station light rail line running down its median, opened in 1998.

He then called Alan and asked, " I understand your nonprofit group still has some money left over after reaching the original goals on relocating Century Freeway displacees?"

"Right, Jim. We've built nearly 4,300 apartments and houses within 12 miles of the freeway–and we still have $100 million left. Most of it will go into an endowment so we can continue to help nonprofit developers build affordable housing in the Gateway Cities area."

"Great job! But I know there's still a tremendous need for more housing. Anything I can do?"

"Glad you asked. We need to float bonds to cover the balance of the housing cost plus necessary public facilities. Can you help that along?"

"You bet. I think I can entice the state to match your funds. How does that sound?"

"Wonderful! This will permit us to increase the amount of affordable housing available to Gateway. When you have time, let's get together to discuss the details. Thanks a million, Jim."

"Glad to help, Alan. I'll be in touch soon."

* * *

Jim gave Mike Nelson of Gateway a call to notify him of this arrangement.

"That sure helps," Mike said. "It'll help meet the new construction need called for by the RHNA affordable housing program."

"You bet. Keep me in mind if you need anything else, Mike."

As Mike got off the phone, he couldn't shake the feeling that Jim had a hand in every pot. He'd heard rumors of Jim's stock losses and wondered what he was up to in financing housing for Gateway Cities. Stoneham was a personal friend of Mike's, but he wasn't audacious enough to call him on something like this. But it needed looking into. Jim had never been interested in Gateway Cities before. A little beneath him with all its poverty and problems.

* * *

Brownfield efforts on industrial sites for Gateway and other areas were underway through Leo Pastor, the business development rep of the L.A. Economic Development Corporation. Enticing local communities to better utilize their toxic sites consumed much of his time and his staff had recently been in touch with a key developer to revitalize Brownfield land in Gateway.

"Ken, we're facing a dilemma. From a tax perspective, retail redevelopment helps both city and state. In contrast, manufacturing operations primarily add to state revenues," Leo said.

"Yeah, I know the problem. The cities want uses which bring in the most tax revenue," the developer replied.

"We need to make them understand we're trying to provide them with better paying jobs which manufacturing offers–paying more than retail jobs."

"But retail space brings a higher rate of return to me and is easier to market," Ken responded.

"But there's greater demand for industrial space. Retail is overbuilt."

"Your sites have all sorts of problems. First, developers like me are wary of acquiring land which has liability for contamination. Second, cleanup standards may be prohibitive even if the extent of the problem is clear," Ken said. "Until the state addresses these issues, this potentially valuable industrial land will remain underutilized or used for retail purposes when possible. We can't afford to operate any other way."

"You're right. We're working with the state to provide the legislation and incentives to make it happen," Leo said. "Don't give up on us. We're going to break the log jam soon."

* * *

Meanwhile, Marcine and her associate Laurie Monarch were deeply into an effort to get additional funds for desperately needed revitalization in Southwest L.A.'s ghetto areas. Her umbrella group, Alamada Corridor Jobs, had utilized all possible Federal and private funding, and might not be able to sustain further economic development efforts. Yesterday, Laurie had been talking with her minister, Charles Manning, at the powerhouse AME Methodist Church which had 17,000 members. He lamented the lack of involvement by black churches in economic development, compared to the great strides being made in Houston, New York City, and other major cities. Laurie decided to discuss this further with Marcine, especially after reading a Times article by Bea on the inaction of L.A. black churches in achieving either political power or economic development.

"Marce, can we push some buttons to get something going? AME and several other black churches are asset rich, have celebrities and boast some great nonprofit organizations among their ministries. Yet, they aren't actively involved in economic development. How come?"

"They don't wield any political power in L.A., Laurie. No black leader has emerged to tap this power base probably due to the Region's fragmented nature and history of riots and segregation. I like your idea to funnel some of these assets into the programs we're promoting."

"What can we do to make this happen?" Laurie asked.

"The problem is that's black church leaders haven't been forces for political change–and without political power, economic power is beyond them. Historically, moral protest and resistance have been their prime activities. A few efforts to change things have been made on school vouchers and police brutality, but there's been no follow through to translate that into the political power needed to make things happen on the economic development front," Marcine said.

"So, what's next?"

"We need a meeting to mobilize this support and bring these black leaders forward. Maybe we can piggy back black church involvement in revitalizing neglected neighborhoods. They need to do this to confront current urgent needs, since many churches are located in communities that are financially on their knees. Despite an improved economy, poverty, homelessness and unemployment remain at crisis levels in these neighborhoods. Also, we've got to impress on them that the AME church has historically been the one institution where black people took care of their own in the face of persecution and neglect. Finally, more AME religious leaders recognize that economic parity is essential to the evolution of the black freedom movement."

"Wow. You've been thinking about this for a long time, haven't you, Marc?"

"All my life. That's why I got into this business. Maybe our time has come, Laurie. Do you think you can get something organized and work through your minister to marshall support for a meeting. We've got a great opportunity here. Let's not let it get away from us."

"You bet. He seems interested in doing something–if we can point the way and attract the leadership to make it happen."

* * *

Jim pondered how his problems had mushroomed. He needed a change of pace from his SCAG, gambling and women problems. Depression virtually had him whipped.

He needed to take a break, riding his horses. They were his first love, ever since his father purchased a little Arabian pony for him on his tenth birthday. He loved stroking and talking to them. They understood him.

By boarding his two black stallions, L.A. Traffic and L.A. Smog, at the L.A. Fairgrounds stables near downtown, he was generally able to ride them several times a week. People got a big kick of their names which reminded him of his commitment to reduce the Region's two biggest problems. He got the idea from friends who used similar names for their horses raced at Hollywood Racetrack.

"I wonder if Bea would be interested in riding with me tomorrow morning?" he mused. "She lives close by. I'll give her a call. That should ease my depression. Beautiful horses and fast women, as they say in Kentucky. Of course, that would apply to Lila, not Bea, but so what."

He gave Bea a call.

"Do you like horseback riding? If so, I'd like to get you to ride with me."

"I never thought you'd be into horses, Jim. I love horses and used to ride all the time when I lived in Denver. I can't wait to ride with you. When?"

"Is tomorrow morning about six at the Fairgrounds stables too soon?" Jim asked.

"No. I'll be there. I can get my sitter to handle Seth while I'm gone. Give me directions."

* * *

The next morning, Bea arrived in her jodspurs outfit complete with fancy boots, bright red blouse and snappy cowgirl hat. Happily, she followed Jim to the stalls where they gave each stallion cubes of sugar, and hearty stroking to their manes.

"L.A. Traffic, meet your rider, Bea," Jim said to the beautiful black stallion who nuzzled him. Bea reached over, stroked and talked to him like they'd known each other forever.

"Aren't you a doll, L.A. Traffic? He told me why he named you that, but I think you'd be happier with a name like Black Beauty," she said, stroking his head as she swung into the saddle.

"Let's go, Bea. Hey, you really look right at home on him," he said, reining L.A. Smog toward the path. "There's a nice riding path nearby which you'll enjoy. Let's enjoy the wide open spaces, guys." They cantered down the trail, lost in their love of horses and the joy of being alive on this beautiful morning.

"Enjoying your job, Bea?" Jim inquired.

"Yes, I am. It's a great challenge being a journalist both in print and on TV," she answered, her horse wending down a dip in the trail.

"I can imagine. I admire what you do and how you challenge people to improve the world, even if its only doing something unimportant."

"Actually, Jim, I feel that everything's important. Little improvements add up in the long run to breakthroughs, whether it's less crime, better education or approval of a critical bill in the legislature," Bea said. She looked around, enjoying the beautiful trees and shrubs, the brilliance of the wild flowers, and the birds and bees doing their parts to keep nature harmonious.

"You're right, of course. Speaking of major bills, is there a chance that you might be able to write about the importance of our transportation bill in the state legislature?"

"Certainly. It's really needed. I only hope you're considering a total approach to this funding–priorities for the inner city, jobs closer to housing, more affordable housing in all portions of the region and more transit?"

"As much as we can, Bea. Rome wasn't built in a day," he said as he ducked under an intruding branch.

"But Rome's development included common people," Bea replied as she urged her horse, L.A. Traffic, to a trot.

"Are you saying that you'd like to see changes in the bill?" Jim asked, spurring L.A. Smog to match her horse's moves.

"Yes. I think it's too slanted to the suburbs and higher income person. L.A. is going to suffer if the inner cities and lower income families don't receive equal treatment," she said, as she admired God's handiwork.

"Go ahead and write your column to reflect that. We need this money badly. Amendments in committee or the legislative process are expected and your thoughts may be just what's needed to put the bill over the hump in top form."

"Okay, Jim. I'll do it. Get me your material and I'll write something up. By the way,"she said, "I've been hearing rumors about your having financial difficulties."

"Only rumors, Bea. You know what they say, politics is ninety percent rumors. I had to adjust my finances a little but otherwise I'm fine."

"Glad to hear it, Jim," Bea responded, although not convinced by his glib response.

"Well, Bea. I guess we'd better get back to the stables. I've got a long day ahead," Jim said, reining his horse toward the stable, not wanting to parry any more questions.

They cantered back to the stables and on to busy days. Both Jim and Bea had enjoyed this chance to commune with nature on the backs of such beautiful animals. Bea wondered why his answer to possible financial problems didn't seem to match the details she'd heard, but hoped she was wrong. She knew he relished danger and controversy. Although she enjoyed being with him, she wasn't sure it was wise to continue seeing him. Maybe riding with him weekly would be a safe way to explore any possible relationship. Time would tell.

* * *

As he walked to a meeting with CHARO from a East L.A. bus stop, Gavin puzzled over how to make more small Gateway businesses succeed. Also, how to make interested young people computer-literate and able to become professionals in the computer firms he hoped might be attracted to the area if trained or trainable employees were available.

Jim Robinson had arranged this meeting with Jake Allison, an old family friend, who headed CHARO Community Development Corporation, and agreed to provide entrepreneur training, computer classes, child care and loan-processing assistance to unemployed Gateway workers. Jim would also provide a rent-free building in South Gate as a base for the Gateway Cities' incubator program.

Arriving at CHARO's office, Jake greeted him.

"We appreciate your interest in expanding your involvement from the East Side to Gateway. We feel the new building which will soon be available will allow you to develop a permanent incubator program to house your many options," Gavin said as their meeting began.

"I welcome the offer, Gavin, and especially look forward to introducing our incubator support services which distinguish our program from others. It's been quite a challenge to put this together–and there's such a need for it, especially in your area."

"Could you describe your program a little? What will it provide to a new business?"

"Certainly," Jake replied. "If you're starting a small business or industry, you're going to have to buy a computer, pay for telephones and other office equipment. But when you use this incubator, the only thing you will need to have are the tools of your trade."

"Could you be more specific?"

"You'll have four walls, with phone and computer lines put in. We'll have a business services room where you can share computers, copier, fax and other types of office equipment. Your phone will be answered when you're out, and conference room space for meetings will be available. The only space you'll be paying for is what you need to do your work.

"But there's more to starting a business than that?" Gavin said.

"You bet. That's where my program really kicks in. We'll have a resource library that has information on preparing business plans, marketing strategies, handle billable hours and others."

"What about economic data?" asked Gavin, becoming more intrigued.

"We'll have information on different types of industries, employment data, economic data, and import/export data. And you'll only have to pay for our computers and copiers as you use them."

"So many new businesses have difficulty surviving. How do you handle that aspect?"

"The new entrepreneur must agree to go through work-related seminars, because 75 percent of all new businesses die within three years. They go down the tube because they don't have a business plan or know how to manage their business," Jake said. "The key to a business incubator is their technical assistance and support geared to moving new businesses out on their own within three years.

"That's just what we need. It gives them a chance to spread their wings without having to save a lot of money and then experiment in a constantly changing market place."

"Plus our support services are outstanding–centers for entrepreneur training, careers and business assistance, along with a business incubator," Jake continued. "We've also added a business financial center where we help people find loans. To top it off, we are also opening a contract procurement center. With these facilities and services, we're confident that Gateway businessmen will be successful."

"Wow. I wish I'd had all that support available when I got into business. I could have saved a lot of time, money and heartache," Gavin said.

"I think it's the only way to go, especially with the education, language and training problems this area's facing. We even hold classes covering language problems. And, our GED programs will allow many of the new employees to eventually graduate from high school."

"One last question. How much do you think this incubator will help the local economy?"

"It's going to bring business contract opportunities to the community along with new industry and business. For example, there are ten hospitals within an eight-mile radius of us that buy more than $500 million a year in products and services. Little of that work can be garnered by our existing small businesses due to the way contracts are awarded. Big corporations get that business now since they can use the block bidding process," Jake said. "But if the incubator clients and graduates of our programs collaborate in bidding on these jobs, we'll get our fair share of the business through our own form of block bidding."

"That's encouraging. Thanks, Jake, for your great coverage," Gavin said, rising to shake his hand. "Let's get started. We've got a lot of work to do–but I know we're in good hands now. I think we can get it done"

"Thanks, Gavin. Before you leave, let me show you through our facility so you can visualize how we operate and how our services tie together."

* * *

"You know, this Sustainable Communities Conference in February 2001 in Long Beach couldn't happen at a better time for our program," Gavin told Dion, his land recycling assistant. "Eventually, we'll be able to market our services to the various cities due to all the benefits they'll be getting. They'll realize that they should 'pay to play' once they see the value-added they'll get."

"Yeah. If the cities don't pay, they won't get the benefits. It goes with the territory," Dion said. "Right now, they're too poor to be able to pay."

"You know, the COG already looks on the economic development arm as its most important partner–and the Partnership feels the same way about the COG."

"That's the whole idea of the Sustainable Communities Conference. Focusing on transportation and land use-related issues are the keys to creating a better community," Dion said. "You've convinced me by what's been happening. The San Gabriel Valley Partnership has led the way by demonstrating their success.

"Yeah, they now have a $500,000 budget and a staff of five. Depending on the size of the city involved, they're charging up to $10,000 per year for services which their Partnership provides," Gavin said. "And the cities are pleased with what's offered."

"You know," Gavin continued, "this all came together when the COG was awarded a $250,000 Brownfields Assessment Demonstration Pilot. The study identified thousands of acres of Brownfield sites that weren't being used because of contamination."

"Now that we've expanded the focus of our alliance between business, labor, education and the public sector, we're able to bring everything together–working not only on Brownfields, but workforce development, port-related traffic issues, and marketing the subregion to attract higher wage jobs to the area," Dion said.

* * *

Marcine pondered an entirely different issue. Her job development group must figure out how to get families earning less than $13,000, jobs in the Alameda Corridor. A family of three with an income below $13,000 a year is poor. But if all poor, able-bodied family heads worked full-time, the poverty rate could be cut by more than half. Also, a higher minimum wage would be a powerful incentive for those poor whose income from minimum wage jobs can't match what they could receive on welfare. A proposed income tax credit program might create the needed incentive for them to take jobs–along with a higher minimum wage. This kind of work could provide a great antidote to poverty, one far superior to welfare.

Moreover, measuring the impact of some of these proposals on the poverty rate alone misses their importance to those who aren't poor but are still struggling to make ends meet. Marcine figured that roughly one-third of the population had incomes below twice the poverty level (about $26,000 for a typical family). These proposals would help this bottom one-third to experience some of the prosperity in the rest of the nation.

* * *

Picking up the cause of this 'bottom one-third,' Bea broke this story in her weekly Undercover News column in the Times,

"Recently, a shadowy state agency convened under court order to fix a school construction-funding scheme flagrantly biased against California's most overcrowded, poor urban districts. That it took a civil rights lawsuit to force the State Allocation Board (SAB) to reform is appalling. Even more disturbing, the growing conflict between wealthy and inner-city districts may prevent a just remedy.

"At the root of the problem is the board's practice of handing out school construction money, including $3 billion that voters approved through Proposition 1A in 1998, on a first-come, first-served basis. Each of California's 1,000 school districts must complete a detailed application process, including architectural and construction planning and extensive environmental review of proposed sites. Unfortunately, those districts that fill out the forms fastest, not those with the greatest demonstrated need for new facilities, get most of the money. The question becomes, how can this state agency's approach be overridden?

"As a result, inner-city districts, where students are crammed into year-round facilities with broken toilets and playgrounds buried beneath portable classrooms, receive little support. Richer districts serving suburban and exurban regions–pocket funds for Olympic-sized pools, band-practice rooms and even soccer fields."

Bea's article went on, "The Los Angeles Unified School District, for example, contains 12 percent of the state's K-12 student body. One-third of its mostly inner-city pupils receive substandard, multi-track year-round instruction. Yet, under the SAB's formula, the district would   be paid just one percent of all Proposition 1A funds. Thankfully, this was successfully challenged by a coalition of LAUSD students."

"One irony is that the more detailed reform processes with their complicated formulas and time lines requires results which the poor districts have great difficulty meeting. So, at this time when educational opportunity is championed by most, SAB is disproportionately funding politically well-connected, wealthier districts at the expense of inner-city areas. In politics, the odds always favor the privileged and powerful. This has been proved over and over in civil action suits involving toxic waste, ironically caused by deep pocket corporations."

As usual, Bea's hard-hitting article indicated the difficulties still encountered by the low income and minority groups even in good times. Much still needed to be done to effectively harness the state legislature to right many of these wrongs.

"Could this be done soon enough in this increasingly "have/have not" society?" Bea asked in concluding her article. Only time and action by those able to make things happen would change things for the better.

CHAPTER 11
EMERGING REGIONAL TRANSIT

*Red Line opens to San Fernando Valley,
bringing much needed boost to region's transit
system. If accomplished speedily and as part
of a strong plan, transit can help to reverse
the gridlock. Some coverage given to
subway corruption and mismanagement. A
balance of effective subway, metrolink, light
rail, rapid bus, bus corridor, para-transit
and linkage of bus routes needed to effectively
get people where they need to go quickly and
cheaply. This requires an innovative,
imaginative and well-managed approach.*

---

*"Nearly all men can stand adversity, but if
you want to test a man's character,
give him power."*

Abraham Lincoln

"Hey, buddy, this is great. I haven't seen such a crush of people since I rode the subway   in the 'Big Apple' 10 years ago," Lonnie, a fellow passenger, said to Henry, as their Red Line train sped deep underneath the Santa Monica Mountains to the San Fernando Valley during rush hour traffic in late September 2000. Lonnie and his wife were enjoying the trip, particularly the mass of people so characteristic of NYC subways.

Great excitement reigned on the opening of L.A.'s Red Line all the way to North Hollywood after the epic tunneling it required.

Lonnie, in his element, waxed eloquent about all the big city features he missed, plus how the rich were taking over the country, half the people were poor, Russia and the Cold War hoax, and Star Wars waste. He couldn't stop his enthusiastic thoughts long enough for Henry to break in but the humor in Lonnie's remarks saved them.

Such is the excitement of riding subway and light rail. Henry mused about the importance of subways, as he stood hanging on the support jos-

136

tled by the people around him–from every strata of life. Mass transit's importance obviously focused on getting lots of people from point A to point B cheaply, efficiently, and in an environmentally sound manner. But it had also altered neighborhoods by changing established patterns of human living. The urban organism got reorganized, as stations altered the cluster of service shops and activities that sprang up around them, and as individual mobility widened. New activities were knit into the city's fabric.

Most of all, Henry felt, the train functioned as an urban Mixmaster. Metro Rail as a critical cog in the larger social engine of the city, ratcheted up the sense of cosmopolitan living that made cities something special. That feeling of being at home and alive amid the dizzying diversity he considered essential to a vibrant civic life. Even if the transit station's architecture might not be the best, the station's importance in establishing the focus for neighborhood activities was essential.

"Say, Lonnie, have you been following MTA's corruption and mismanagement?"

"Yeah, it's a crime how it's almost ruined L.A.'s efforts to achieve a subway system," Lonnie said in disgust.

"I've lived here awhile and the history of the internal struggles go way back to the days of the RTD in the 1960's when Downtown L.A. was reeling from business losses and championed subways as the way to make downtown the heart of the region again," Henry said. "By 1978, the Red Line proposal had been unveiled to spend the billions of dollars available. Threatened by the likelihood that the outlying counties would be ignored, the L.A. County Transportation Commission was formed in early 1980, with efforts to produce revenues primarily for suburban light rail lines. This touched off a decade-long feud between the RTD and Transportation Commission on how money would be spent from Proposition A, which gave the Commission tremendous financial control over L.A. transit investments."

"Yeah, we came to L.A. in 1990," Lonnie said. "Although the feud was eventually won by the Transportation Commission, it virtually destroyed the credibility of public transportation, especially the idea of a rail system. It became a battle between the two agencies in Sacramento and Washington. RTD bus ridership rose dramatically initially but the desire for a Wilshire Corridor subway reduced the number of busses available, raised fares and restricted headways between busses to connecting points."

"MTA finally evolved when the two agencies merged," Henry continued. "But the feud went on internally between surface and subway advocates. Ground was broken on light rail's Blue Line to Long Beach in 1985 and the Red Line Subway in 1986. Mis-management, excessive union demands and corruption continued through the years as General Managers came and went due to difficulties in working with an unwieldy, political Board. In late 1992, the Blue Line began operating, followed soon by the first leg of the Red Line in early 1993," Henry said.

"I hope they get their act together and make transit an important part of the Region," Lonnie said. "This will never be a great city like the Big Apple until they do."

* * *

Andre Phillippe attended many meetings of the MTA Board over the years. An outspoken critic of their inability to manage their billions, he spoke out in a public comment opportunity at one of their meetings.

"How can this Board ignore the sinkhole boondoogle which virtually crippled downtown Hollywood as construction of the subway passed through it?" he asked heatedly. " It hurt so many small businesses. What's being done to prevent this from happening again?"

"Also, contractors had an open season with inflated costs which wasted billions of dollars," he continued, punching the air in anger. "These huge cost overruns were compounded by lax safety efforts that resulted in several construction workers losing their lives deep underground while drilling through the Santa Monica Mountains. These things have got to stop," he exhorted.

"We're doing all we can to correct those problems, sir." the chair responded with resignation from the rostrum in the plush Board Room of the lavish 27 story MTA headquarters. It had been built at a cost of over $480 million in 1995. "Unfortunately, these things do happen, but we deplore them as much as you do. Thanks for your comments."

Andre continued pressing them about their $7 billion debt, and the interest payments that now demanded over 30 percent of MTA's annual budget, as he had at previous meetings. He and other activists also voiced many other concerns about problems which plagued the MTA's subway endeavors all through the 1990's. But to no avail.

* * *

Jim and Lila, hand in hand, entered the upper reaches of the Grandstand at Hollywood Racetrack on a hot, late summer afternoon. They were mesmerized by the emerald green setting for the golden brown oval below. This beautiful sight would soon be enhanced by some of the most beautiful race horses in the world.

"Jim, this setting is almost too beautiful for words," Lila said in awe. The newly watered track glowed, with the oval connected by a track and starting gates.

"It has everything, doesn't it? I never stop marveling when you add the pulsating horses and jockeys strutting their brilliant colors," Jim remarked.

They were standing at the top of the Grandstand next to the Jockey Club. Lila, her long blonde hair rippling lightly in the wind, wore a white halter sun dress, which highlighted the golden tan of her shoulders, her cleavage accentuating her figure. She knew men noticed her–and enjoyed the moment. Jim, sensing this, possessively slipped his arm around her waist.

"You obviously like the racing scene. I thought you might," he said, grinning as he looked into her eyes. "This is the perfect setting for you to stand out in a crowd," he added with a chuckle.

"Well, a little, I guess, Jim," she said, trying to be demure. "What do we do now?" she asked, quickly changing the subject.

"Let's get a table in the club and order lunch. Then, we'll go down and place some bets on the first race before it begins in an hour."

Proceeding to the Club, they were seated at a swank table with the best view. They ordered sandwiches and drinks to be delivered just prior to the first race, and went to place their bets.

"Where do I place a bet?" Lila asked. She'd been to races before but felt it best not to let on knowing too much.

"I'll do it for you if you like–which horse, how much?"

"I'm not sure," she said. She looked around, then pointed to a horse being mounted by a jockey in scarlet and yellow stripes. "That one. Twenty."

"Okay, let's go to that window," he said pointing across the room, " and we'll place your bet. Later, we'll wager on other races by going through copies of the *Daily Racing Form* and the track's program," Jim said.

They walked to the betting window. Jim put $20 on a horse named Camelot to win for Lila and $250 on his favorite, Prince, with 5-1 odds to win.

Jim escorted Lila down below to view the horses being walked around the parade ring. They could see all nine entries.

Lila's eyes sparkled. "They're so beautiful, Jim. I never realized how magnificent well groomed race horses could be, decked out in their colors. There's Camelot and Prince. What odds does my horse have?"

"You have 20-1 odds, not good, but if you win, you get back $400. Not bad, eh?"

"Not bad. What are your odds?" she asked.

"5-1," he said.

"That means your horse has a better chance of winning. How much would you get?"

"$1250, if I win. There are three other horses more likely to win according to the handicappers, but I feel Prince will win. I've studied entrants in all twelve races and plan to place bets in each one. I'll help you place your bets once we get settled," Jim said, a gleam of anticipation on his face.

They got back to their table just in time for the first race. Soon, their drinks arrived and they settled in.

The first race entrants entered the track with bugle fanfare and cheers from the stands. Ponies escorted them to the starting gates.

Camelot, Lila's bet in scarlet and yellow, entered the outermost gate. Prince's pale blue and dark green, stood innermost among the racers. September Song, carrying orange and black, started dead center of the nine runners and came out of the stalls first, heading an arrow-like formation.

Watching from their table, Jim focused his binoculars, and glowingly described how their chosen mounts were doing.

"Prince is second on the rail at the mid-point with Camelot still on the out-side, several lengths behind. Going past the stands, September Song, the favorite, led by two lengths. Lila, look," Jim pointed. "Camelot passed Prince–second behind September Song. Coming into the stretch, it's nip and tuck, as Camelot makes his stretch run."

The crowd screamed as they got behind the long shot Lila had bet on. Prince had faded, falling back to eighth. At the end, Camelot surged past September Song to win by a head.

Ecstatic, Lila jumped up and down. She couldn't believe she won on a longshot with her first bet. Jim was at a loss for words. He'd expected to be explaining the difficulties of picking a winner.

"You've just won $400. What's your secret?" he asked, once she stopped jumping and squealing with glee.

"Beginners luck, Jim. Can I collect now?"

"Sure, we'll take your ticket to the winners window. We also need to bet on the second race. Based on your luck, I'm not about to suggest which horse," he kidded.

Back at their table, Jim told Lila about the Jockey Club. His firm held a $5,000 corporate membership which included a four seat box, parking stickers and guaranteed table in the dining room. He often brought clients to the races–and she'd been his client today.

Although Lila didn't win again, by betting only $20 per race, she still netted $180 for the afternoon. Jim, in contrast, betting $250 to win each race, lost $3,000. No winners.

Through each race, Lila noticed how his mood swung from wild enthu-siasm when his horse was ahead to deep gloom when he lost. His picks ranged from one close second and a few thirds, to mostly back in the pack finishes after good starts.

Afterwards, Jim defended his approach to Lila. "As you can see, my system didn't work today. But I've had days when I've made over $2,000," he said.

"Do you bet often?" Lila asked, inquisitively.

"Off and on," he replied evasively. "Mostly through my bookmaker. I don't often have time to come out to the races."

"Racing really turns you on, doesn't it?" she stated.

"You bet. Winning races gives me the excitement I crave. It's more than a hobby or sport. I like to beat the odds," he replied, gazing at her.

"What's your system?" she asked.

"Well, its not handicapping–more like statistical probabilities based on knowledge of horses, jockeys, racing history, tracks, races won, odds and other factors. I've computerized it into a program but it still has a lot of bugs in it, as demonstrated by my losses today."

Lila sauntered over to the grandstand railing. Turning and tapping her foot in frustration, she inquired, "Aren't you getting in over your head. You already lost a bundle on stocks. Hardly anyone makes money gam-bling. 'Gambling's like drugs. Once you're addicted, you're likely to go down the drain.'"

"I'm not going that far. "I know what I'm doing, Lila. Anyway, it's my money," he said heatedly. "It's none of your business."

Again, his eyes gleamed expectantly and Lila wondered uneasily about his compulsion.

"Just be careful, Jim," she pleaded soothingly, placing her hand gently on his arm to calm him.

"I will," he mumbled defensively. "But I've got to keep trying. I'm so close, don't you think?"

"I think I've had enough racing for one day," she said with concern etching her forehead. "All I can do is tell you, as a friend, you're addict-ed. Let's go," she said, irritated by it all.

"Okay, if that's the way you want to end the day," Jim said, not under-standing why Lila was so put out.

As they left, Jim knew he must keep Lila in the dark about the simulcast racing, lotteries, Las Vegas excursions and internet betting which he pursued, along with the stock market. So far, his debt grew. But he would turn this around–soon. He knew his understanding of the system was only a heart beat away from success. Just hang in there a little longer. Then they would appreciate his brilliance.

* * *

Andre Phillippe continued his advocacy of transit as an effective force in reducing L.A.'s monumental traffic tie-ups. He knew that many types of transit had to be used if transit was to solve the transportation problem. It wasn't just a rail vs. bus issue. He met his friend, Seth Abrams, a MTA bus driver and a loyal union member, for lunch. They always had great debates about what to do to straighten out MTA. No one ever won, but the sparring helped them hone their arguments.

After ordering at Rusty's, their downtown favorite, they settled down to their current topic–how diversified should MTA get in meeting the Region's transit needs? Andre led off.

"The more I see MTA trying to meet Federal requirements through the courts by providing more busses and better service, the more I feel they're on the right track."

"How can you say that?" Seth responded. "Riders get very frustrated when they're constantly tied up in traffic and late to work."

"That's because they have to compete for space with the auto." Andre replied. "If they could have a corridor of their own like rail, they could do better with less money."

"Prove it!" Seth demanded.

"MTA researchers recently came up with figures that indicated that the public subsidy that supports 100 bus trips will support only 40 light-rail trips, 10 heavy-rail trips or six commuter-rail trips. How does that grab you, coming from MTA itself."

"There must be some weird reason to make it work out that way," Seth said. "Length of trip, age of transit vehicle, rider volume, percent of capacity or other reasons. It doesn't make sense."

"It's got you wondering, hasn't it? It did me too," Andre said, chuckling at his friend's disbelief of these statistics.

"Yeah. There are so many variables, it's hard to figure out transit," Seth said.

"Granted. But I still feel that the solution's a mixture of all forms of transit used opportunistically to fit the need. A real holistic approach. How does that grab you?"

"Come off it, Andre. Don't give me that crap. If you're serious, explain it to me in layman's terms, will ya?"

"I'll try, Seth, ol' buddy. I'll try."

"What's this so-called 'holistic' jazz, my fine, well-educated friend."

"It's just a way of saying that if you took transit as a total, it might add up to more than all its parts–bus, rail, jitney, and others."

"How's that possible?"

"I guess because if they work effectively together, they might create more business and achieve higher capacities. I'm not sure why, but it happens in many other things."

"Okay, then explain further what you're talking about," Seth said, still not understanding or believing what his friend talked about. Used to being thrown for a loop by Andre, Seth found it good to keep him talking.

"Well, bus corridors may be the answer. MTA bought up several such corridors (including Burbank-Chandler in the Valley) for rail use. Using statistics from the busways created for lanes on the San Bernardino Freeway, this research suggests that busways can provide more than three times the passenger miles per hour than the Long Beach-Los Angeles Blue Line at more than twice the Blue Line's average speed (52 mph versus 21 mph)."

"Yeah, but one's in a highly congested urban area and has a lot of stops, while the other's in a high speed, rural area with no stops. One operates at all hours, while the other probably operates only certain hours of the day. It doesn't sound right," Seth said, puzzled by all the different situations.

"Okay, then let's consider using the other forms of transit for only certain purposes. That's the logic of a total (holistic) approach–tie it all together so each is being used for its best purpose," Andre said, biting into his sandwich.

"I'm beginning to see what you're talking about, Andre. This total approach is what we need. Let's work together to make it happen, even if it takes a transit strike."

"I've got to go," Seth said, looking at his watch as he rose. "My shift's about to start. This should take care of my part of the meal," handing Andre a five. "Let's do it again soon."

* * *

The transit strike they were talking about came only a few days later. On September 16, it paralyzed the Los Angeles area as 400,000 riders were forced to find other forms of transportation to get around. Already jammed freeways and streets strained under the increased load of cars, bringing the system close to its breaking point. The strike hit the lower income workers hardest. Some were forced to walk up to six miles to work, others had to develop a sort of taxi system, sharing rides with others to defray the cost of the trip and parking. Many were hours late to work, causing some to lose their jobs. After 32 days, it hurt the poor and minorities badly, and this strike that 'no one noticed' took around the clock bargaining by Jesse Jackson over the last week to end.

One reason was the scale of the metropolis, and its ability to hide entire cultures and populations within its ever-expanding boundaries. Los Angeles is so vast it just absorbs things that would paralyze other cities. Olympics, national political conventions–they come and go largely unnoticed by the general public. So it was with the month-long transit strike. Many people were hurt by it, but most hardly noticed.

* * *

Soon after the strike, Phillippe and Seth attended a Regional Transit Task Force meeting at SCAG to tie transit and land use more closely together. This intrigued them. Transit Oriented Development (TOD), a speaker claimed., may be one of the least understood and most underused forms of development in the U.S. Even less understood is Transit Oriented Joint Development (TOJD), which are TOD's done under some form of joint public/private venture.

After the meeting, the two went out for a fast food lunch.

"Just think what this could do for L.A.," Phillippe said. "Assuming MTA doesn't screw up, this could be the answer to providing higher density housing along transit lines."

"Yeah, and other areas like New York, Atlanta, Portland, the Bay area and Washington, D.C. have already proved that TOJD's really work," Seth said. "I understand that MTA owns or controls land near most of the Red Line and Blue Line stations, and is seeking to team up with developers to turn empty fields into attractive multi-use developments."

"Do you think they can achieve that without screwing up royally, Seth? I hope so."

"Hope so, too. Lots of people are looking over their shoulder now. That's encouraging. Do you remember how they defined a TOJD?"

"Yes, a TOD is a development area within 1/4 to ½ mile of a transit station where mixed-use development can concentrate. Joint development of this area would be TOJD," Phillippe answered.

"They said mixed-use development involved higher density residential, office, hotel, retail, entertainment and public facilities in a compact and fairly dense pattern."

"Wow! By this means, more people could live and work in the same area, reducing their need to travel. It sounds great, doesn't it," Phillippe said, excited by the possibilities. "Many people in these areas would hardly need cars."

144

"It's almost too good to be true. Even locals should buy into it. Plus it will increase transit ridership significantly."

"You know, it could be used in many situations, not just along the Red, Blue and Green Lines. In suburban areas, at major street intersections; in the inner city where there already is a high population density; and in developing areas, for new downtowns," Phillippe added.

"I see that over 28 million square feet of downtown office space was built in San Francisco as a result of BART, their rapid transit system. Just think what this could do to Downtown L.A. and other area downtowns."

"The big thing is that all this took place without federal-aid policies encouraging TOJD development. They required local agencies to pay back federal funds from preplanned TOJD's as a first priority."

"Yeah, fortunately during the 1990's the Federal Transit Administration (FTA) recognized the problems with their TOJD policies, and passed legislation that enables local transit agencies to retain all of their joint development revenues on TOJD projects as long as they meet certain conditions," Seth said.

"That will really speed up development of these mixed-use developments and affordable housing in these areas. That's a real breakthrough," Phillippe agreed, as he looked around at others wolfing down their lunch. These were the people who could benefit the most from this new development if things went right.

* * *

Timing appears to be right for the development of "Transit Villages," with all forms of subsidies, financing and plans for light transit surfacing in L.A. Developers–a group of builders and architects with deep pockets who were being attracted to sites around transit stations which MTA had held on to, surprisingly. This could provide a way out of MTA's huge public debt.

MTA's director of finance, Harley Graham, in conversations with several developers, planners and architects in his office, encouraged them to go the transit village route by explaining their basic ingredients.

"Yeah, but it must be done using good design principles and land planning," Roger Ebert, a knowledgable L.A. architect reminded them. "Noise and vibration are minimal with modern trains. The noisiest thing about light rail is the bell that announces trains approaching the station."

"If you introduce higher density housing, it can pose problems, though." said developer Ellery Noblock. "How do you handle that?"

"You're right. The real challenge is to separate the public nature of a train station with the private nature of housing. Security and privacy for residents are issues that you can't ignore."

"Also, you've got to build community, not just housing units, especially when you're dealing with higher density apartments, parking and recreational amenities," Walter Steep, the planner involved stated. "The key is to introduce urbanity into a neighborhood without destroying it. It takes an effective team of professionals working together to achieve this."

"Plus there must be adequate off-street parking for residents, shoppers and light rail 'Park and Ride' commuters," MTA's Graham emphasized.

"We've got to build on the successful projects accomplished in Washington, Baltimore, Portland, Dallas and other cities. Definitely another animal, you've got to do more than just build units willy-nilly, like some do," Noblock said.

"Just think about the opportunities for young families, singles and others who want to live close to their jobs. Some of these mixed use developments will also hold office and industry. This is a great opportunity for proving that jobs/housing can work," Steep said, as the planning session ended.

*   *   *

Henry formerly lived in Dallas and shuddered at memories of the horrible traffic jams on the North Central Expressway in the early '80's. In his consulting business, he often wished that he could have had an efficient rapid transit system to use. But Dallas, like L.A., was thought to be the last place on earth where people would use transit.

Recently, visiting Dallas, he was astounded by the changes taking place. An old friend, Bill Harrick, wanted to meet him at a transit station instead of his home. So he drove to the station near his old home off the North Central Expressway. Enjoying the opportunity to see Bill again after all these years, he asked about this change in attitude.

"What made this happen, Bill? Everyone wanted to use their car when I lived here."

"It's mostly good design and attractive mixed-uses like you see in this station that made the difference. Texas in general and Dallas in particular are not where you'd think this could work," he said, "but we couldn't build our way out with concrete."

Looking around at all the young people rushing to activities, Henry said, "The young people here have really taken to it. How do you explain it?"

"Light rail benefitted from a shift in demographics, the young seeking a livelier lifestyle and the older, more mature seeking an alternative to the auto."

"I'm still puzzled why the young consider this the 'in thing.' In my younger days here, I never considered the bus as a way to have fun," Henry mused.

"Let me show you around Mockingbird Lane. That's the name of this transit station, named for Highland Park's major street," Bill said as they strolled through a fascinating mix of well-designed buildings grouped around the transit stop.

"See the mix of fine restaurants, nightclubs, entertainment areas, with garden and high rise apartments and condos connected to office buildings and other work places. It's the most livable area for many young and old people who don't really have to go far to accomplish all their daily tasks."

As they walked along, sometimes changing levels and using outdoor and indoor passageways to thwart Dallas' famous heat and humidity problems, Henry was struck by the exciting mixture of uses and crowds.

"Wow! I'm impressed. Who would've thought that savvy young Dallasites would be attracted to this? I wish L.A. would try something like this."

"Why can't they?" Bill asked. "Both cities are private enterprise-oriented, unlike Portland, where they used state legislation and a lot more public investment to get their transit system. L.A. could do it too with the right leadership—plus good architecture and design. You can also protect the old, historical buildings by building residential lofts like the one coming up on the right," he gestured as they continued their walk through the station.

"It's beautiful and it fits right in with the design of the whole station area," Henry remarked as they passed a two story red brick building which had once been a school. Now it was a very attractive apartment complex arranged around a public square.

"You know," Bill continued, "studies have proved its value. $800 million in development has taken place within walking distance of the DART line; as compared to $860 million to build the transit line."

"Why is this station so crowded? Aren't they all designed like this?"

"No, they're not. Each station is unique. Each has a sense of place," Bill said. "We went to great lengths to ensure it. Different architects, different design firms, and a well thought-out relationship to local history to make it all fit together."

"What about land values? Have they jumped as a result?"

"You bet. A local economist recently cited a rise of 25 percent in property values around the stations in the five years since they opened. That's a telling argument all by itself for mass transit compared with the sprawl generated by freeways."

"Thanks for the tour, Bill. I appreciate the time you took to squire me around. If Dallas can do this with its lousy climate, it should be a walk in the park for L.A.," Henry remarked, stopping again to savor the busy scene around him. It had been worth the trip just to see this.

* * *

Henry returned to L.A. from Dallas more enthused about the significant opportunities for making the Region a much better place to live. He puzzled about what needed to be done to change it from a "Region in Turmoil" into possibly a "Region Aroused".

He decided to call Juan and Mike to discuss this issue. Since Juan would be in L.A. that weekend visiting his family, the three made a date to get together Saturday to discuss possible solutions. As chair of the Subregional Coordinators group, Mike would be an important barometer for "turmoil" issues.

* * *

They sat talking over coffee after breakfast at Juan's home reviewing all the things that might have influenced the growing turmoil over the years. They decided to list them with no particular order of importance.

Juan led off: "The failure to create a balanced transportation system certainly has created a lot of havoc to the region. A balanced transit system must be achieved."

Mike countered by mentioning the still unresolved worker retraining problem: "We're in a period of great change with the new economy still evolving. A large percentage of our workers must be retrained with today's skills allowing them to make a livable wage."

"Right," Henry exclaimed, shifting in his chair. "To make things worse, too much of the inner city area's soils are toxic, making them unusable to build on for industrial and residential purposes without renewal. I've heard that between five and ten percent of the nation's built-up area is of this character—having toxic soils. The Brownfields program must be expanded quickly if we are to head off further turmoil."

"This is made still worse by our continuing problems with air pollution. Things are improving but the lack of a balanced transportation system just makes things worse," Juan stated.

"Yeah, what you say makes sense, Juan," Mike stated. "But there must be a balance of area renewal stressing economic development tied closely to the new economy. Things must be in concert if we are to effectively turn things around."

"Plus needed affordable housing is not being provided, especially in relationship to the location of jobs throughout the region. This is creating a lot of unnecessary stress on our young families," Henry said.

"That's six key problems. Quite a few more exist, unfortunately," Mike replied. "I'm thinking of some that other subregional coordinators have been mentioning at our monthly meetings, such as the growing problem with our regional airport system–or the lack of one since LAX is the only one catered to. This dangerous situation has got to change–and soon."

"That's closely tied to our problem of assuring all our citizens receive effective Environmental Justice, involving aviation, highways, residential areas, or others," Henry broke in.

"Plus we can't begin to fund our growing transportation needs even with continued significant federal assistance," Juan replied. "We just aren't using our limited resources right."

"We also have these 14 subregions–all with unique needs–which must be allowed to participate more meaningfully in the regional planning process," Mike responded with lines of concern etched on his face. "I don't think we're even beginning to utilize them right."

"Plus we're not effective in guiding growth and improving our land use system synergistically," Henry replied. "We need to finally achieve Growth Visioning to get away from continued sprawl."

"What about tax base sharing?" asked Juan. "Are we ever going to fig- *Fiscalization of Land-use* ure out ways to equalize how we spend our money, or are we going to continue to perpetuate the 'Have/Have Not' fiasco in our cities?"

"Wow! Twelve issues which create turmoil. Let's get to work to correct these in the last year of the 2001 RTP. A major effort toward achieving A REGION AROUSED should be our primary goal!"

CHAPTER 12
VISIONING
RESHAPED GROWTH

The CEHD Policy Committee formed a sub-committee on "Growth Vision Project". It would develop alternative livable region scenarios involving the entire region and each subregion, and focusing on: 1) transportation/land use strategies to reduce auto travel; 2) neighborhood smart growth and transit/pedestrian-friendly development; 3) land use/transportation impacts of livable community strategies; and 4) transportation access and investment analysis linking communities with schools and job training centers.

"Go confidently in the direction of your dreams. Live the life you have imagined."
Henry David Thoreau

"To .... imagine the possible visions is the art of visioning; to formulate an implementable, preferred vision is the politics of visioning!"
Alvin Toffler

"I'm tired of seeing the region go through a continuous process that produces no real planning. Just extending the freeways, ad finitum. That's planning?" Henry exclaimed. "No wonder we'll eventually add Bakersfield as a suburb–and San Diego as just an extension of L.A. Thanks to toll roads and sprawl. Why can't we try–just once–to do something that represents the latest in good regional land use planning?"

"I agree, Henry,"Mike responded. "No guts from SCAG's staff–or the RC. I'm not sure who's more chicken? A lack of leadership in both cases!"

"What're we going to do? Give up and strangle in our vomit? What's worse–congestion or crippling air quality? I'm fed up to here," Henry said, putting his hand to his throat.

"Keep on making things more painful for the RC through your 'hot button' editorials every month at RC meetings," Mike encouraged.

"Definitely. I'm going to keep doing it even if I alienate more of them. It's for their own good. Enough of their country club atmosphere and preparing for a house seat in Sacramento," said Henry.

"Maybe SCAG will realize that they need to try something else. Maybe Growth Visioning again," Henry said.

"Yeah, so it didn't fly last time. They shouldn't give up."

* * *

SCAG finally got the message, especially with their lack of money to extend freeways, plus the need to improve air quality to meet tightening Federal standards. At the next CEHD Policy Committee meeting, SCAG staff proposed the establishment of a Growth Visioning Subcommittee. Henry wasn't thrilled initially. Just a small group of electeds to envision something or other. But after thinking about the possibilities that Growth Visioning might spark new directions for the region, Henry changed his mind.

He asked to be appointed to the sub-committee? The committee leaders initially didn't buy it. They thought only elected officials should be on the sub-committee since they were politically involved. Some SCAG staff were against his involvement, probably due to such factors as his being a planner, and making them nervous with all his "hot button" issues.

Eventually, though, he got support from several of the leaders who wanted change. He was appointed as the only non-elected official initially on the committee. Of course, he couldn't vote but who cared. Maybe he'd provide some influence just being there.

* * *

Opening the first meeting of the Growth Visioning Subcommittee on October 26, 2000, SCAG's Planning Director Javier Aguilar said, "We must do more to improve our neighborhoods through livable community and smart growth efforts at the subregion level. We also must apply the approach to the entire region and its subregions. How it's done is up to you and the RC. But before we get questions, let's try to define Growth Visioning. Here's what the staff suggests as a starting point."

"Growth Visioning involves the development of a regional plan which creates the best in a livable environment taking into account growth pressures, and the constraints of air quality standards, financial resources, transit, aviation and environmental justice. These forces would explore urban forms that could meet to the needs of the L.A. Region over the 2001-25 period."

"As we move along, you probably will amend that significantly."Javier continued. "To start things off, several scenarios should be developed as to how the region and subregions could look and function as the 2001-2025 planning period evolves."

"That's great to provide a framework for the effort," Sophia said, asking others around the table, "but what elements should be in each scenario?"

"Focus should be on forms of transportation and land use strategies to reduce auto travel," Janelle from Orange County, answered.

"Also, provide a safe environment for growth through transit and other pedestrian-friendly development," chimed in Wilbur Gant, from the South Bay Subregion, looking for approval from the other committee members.

"Great. Any other requirements?" Javier asked.

"How about the impact of land use and transportation in developing our livable community strategies," Sophia added.

"Good thinking," Javier responded. "Shouldn't we also consider schools and job training centers as a community nucleus?" he added, looking ahead to the task. "I'll explain later on how we need to have transportation access and investment analyses done on ways to best use them."

"That's a great start, unless someone has better ideas?" Sophia said, nervously patting her hair as she glanced around the room.

"I see a problem with all this," interjected Wilbur Gant, who was often outspoken at Community/Human Development (CEHD) meetings. Clearing his throat to launch into one of his patented complaints, he continued. "This is another sneaky effort to usurp local control. I'm not about to vote to permit the region and state to tell my city what land uses it's allowed to have. They've taken our property tax dollars already so my city is continually broke. Where will it stop?"

"We can't do anything about the property tax take-away, Wilbur" Sophia said. "You may be right, but in some instances the cities need to pool their resources so, say, one transit stop is established representing several cities. Sometimes, land uses should be regional in their impact, not local."

"You'll need to do a better job of convincing me," Wilbur replied. "If we give in here, they'll still want more changes–it never ends."

"Why don't we develop a scenario that lists what's needed, how it can be achieved, and the benefits each city could receive? Then we all can make up our minds," she said. "An actual test."

"I'm willing to try that. But if it doesn't look good, I'm voting it down," Wilbur said with a scowl.

* * *

The subcommittee struggled in its early phases as its members didn't really understand its function and how it differed from "growth in general." Since he was the only non-elected official on the committee, Henry had been keeping his mouth shut. But he finally spoke in frustration:

"I'm excited about this SCAG effort in Growth Visioning. I've been involved in similar programs in other parts of the country and they've been very successful. However, this is going to take several years to accomplish. This won't help the 2001 RTP but should make the 2004 RTP very meaningful. It requires getting involved in physical planning as an integral part of land use planning. It offers opportunities for growth in a variety of ways. We'll need patience and a strong staff commitment–along with consultant involvement."

This moved the committee off the thought that they could get things done in several months in time to be included in the 2001 RTP. They finally realized that it would fit better in the schedule for the upcoming 2004 RTP. The SCAG staff moved ahead to develop a budget, time table and consultant contracts to cover initial coverage in February and March 2001.

* * *

Juan Rodriguez was relieved that he would be going home to Long Beach for several months. The legislative session had been long and painful. It involved a lot of work getting all the bills passed during the final furious days. He often wished he could go back to being just a simple legislator. Being Speaker of the House required so much additional work. But it had been worth it. Some effective bills were passed which would help all of California.

Now he couldn't wait to see his wife, Marie, and their three children, Roslyn, Jose and Juan, Jr. He tried to get home weekly during the January to June sessions. Lucky twice a month to get away for a weekend, but that wasn't enough. Not for a young, growing family like his.

Juan reflected on his rapidly approaching re-election campaign, and the need for time to prepare for it. But finally, he could devote more time to his family. He hoped and prayed that the nastiness of Sacramento politics wouldn't spill over into his home life. Otto, Joe and the rest of his office crew would keep things going and alert him on any political shenanigans he should know about. Hurrying off, he thanked his staff for their efforts.

* * *

Henry attended another meeting of the Growth Visioning Subcommittee. Even with an interesting agenda on tap, only five of the twenty members showed up. Members listened to speakers on several different growth guidance systems they might consider, and other matters.

153

Afterwards, Henry met with Javier in his office to discuss his physical planning approach.

"I think by going to mapping and participation, you'll get more members attending. They can't visualize the problems or possible solutions through use of just numbers and concepts–especially for an area as large as the L.A. Region."

"Let me show you an example of the maps we're considering," Javier said, rising and going to a wall stand with maps shown. "This large map has the detail you want."

"Perfect, Javier. It has the detail that RC members need to visualize their city."

"We also intend to use a model that creates a reuse of existing land, not focusing on growth alone. You suggested this approach a year ago in our Forecasting Task Force."

"Wonderful. Then you can create scenarios to keep the urban area's boundaries constant, even with continued growth?"

"Definitely. Plus, we're working on a 'status-quo' scenario showing what the continuation of urban sprawl outward will do to the region. Whether growth by 2025 might extend as far north as Bakersfield if we continue current densities, lack of redevelopment, and freeway extensions continue unabated."

"I'm glad these proposals are getting some attention. It's frustrating. I've thought of giving up and walking away."

"Yeah, I've been watching. We must make things happen and we're running out of time. The new planners we hired are excited by the possibilities."

"Great. But how are you going to handle your consultants on this? Will these big, high-flying firms go along with this thinking?" Henry asked, a frown etching his forehead.

"We've thought about that and decided to go with RFP's of less than $25,000 for the initial studies and firms grounded in successful growth guidance programs for the big one."

"Sounds great."

Javier rose and extended his hand, "Okay, we're ready to rip. Thanks for your help, Henry. Let's stay in touch."

*   *   *

SCAG, now desperate to develop a strong plan, was prepared to pour a couple million dollars into Growth Visioning. Javier moved ahead with his request for proposals to meet the 2001 RTP time constraints.

"This signals our willingness finally, to use land use planning to edu-

154

cate both the RC and the public on possibilities beyond continued sprawl to reshape the region's future through 2025," he said.

"Yeah, this is ten times the budget we originally had," Tim Henson, his assistant planner said. "We can do a lot with that, especially since we're firmly committed to make it happen."

"If we don't make this work, we're in deep trouble," Javier reminded him.

"No sweat. I've seen what other regions did on something like this. Henry is right. The RC needs to consider better ways to plan the region's future–besides just building more freeways."

"How much time do you need to develop these alternative futures, Tim?"

"About two months, unfortunately. Plus we can't advertise something we don't have and RC'ers won't understand until it's visually displayed."

"Right. We can't afford to go off half-cocked on this. We'll go ahead with our proposal though to get ready."

* * *

Problems continued to occur as committee members struggled to understand the Growth Visioning process. It remained difficult to get enough members to attend due to the size of the region and the feeling that this was just another committee–not one of the most important committees. Some problems involved focusing on all the numbers and getting the right maps in use. But the most difficult issue to overcome was local control of land use. Local officials had no desire to share land use authority regionally to control sprawl.

Fortunately, a crisis intervened to provide a great opportunity to demonstrate how several communities could benefit fiscally by working together on regional development.

Activity along the 710 Corridor had been sporadic and disappointing in many ways. In efforts to upgrade and revitalize the Corridor, Gateway Cities would need some interchanges redesigned. But several cities had land within the Slauson interchange, and prior decisions had allowed each city to permit commercial activities in its portion of the interchange without thought of their impact on lands elsewhere. The Corridor sub-committee brought this issue to a head at a Gateway Cities meeting. Each city thought that it should be able to do whatever it wanted on their land.

"We've got to consider a better approach to this," the sub-committee chair, Kent, said.

"Otherwise, we'll end up with the same dysfunctional arrangement we had before–resulting in continued chaos in congestion and parking problems."

"You're right–but I don't want my city elbowed out of needed sales tax revenue in the process," remarked Carla.

"I think we have a solution to that. It won't come easy but this interchange is perfect for what is called Transit Oriented Joint Development (TOJD). We've been thinking of low density Transit Villages with housing, retail and community services within a quarter to one-half mile of a transit station. This was recently aired at the Regional Transit Task Force meeting but never pursued for lack of State legislation providing subsidies to help make it happen."

"Yeah, I heard about that. But it just didn't attract any interest."

"The reason is it takes citizen commitment rather than government support to happen. In each joint development, you need a champion who is able to push it from plan to reality. No one has stepped forward yet, especially after state legislation failed."

"So what are you proposing?" asked Carla.

"Concentrating it in mixed development, combining retail, work activities, housing and some community facilities in a high density transit station area covering the three blocks in the interchange area. With the right developer and plan, we could strengthen the economies of all three Gateway communities and make life more livable for all."

"It's a great idea, but I'm not sure it'd work, Kent. Look at the poor history of transit development in the L.A. area."

"It could work if we coordinate land-use policies in the three cities through you, Carla, as the coordinator. Plus a real effort by Gateway Cities and SCAG to finance it and attract a developer knowledgeable about joint development. Without these things, increased transit investments will only lead to underutilized facilities as in the past. A recent survey of six Chicago suburbs confirmed that commuters will walk or bicycle to the train station if getting there is a pleasant experience. Just think what people would do if a mixed use station were put there with all the activities it would provide?"

"I see you included me as the coordinator of this. Do you think I could rally people around this? It would take a lot of effort and preparation of architectural and market studies to convince me. But if I could see that it made sense, I'd work hard to make it happen, Kent."

"People would rally around you. That I know," replied Kent. "Okay, do we have agreement by the sub-committee to move ahead with this proposal, and convince the Gateway Board, Growth Visioning, CEHD and RC of its need? I think it's an exciting idea."

It was passed by the 710 Freeway Sub-committee and submitted to the Gateway Board for approval. Although it took two months to navigate all the committees, it passed all the way through the RC, and became the first real test of Growth Visioning's ability to change the Region's makeup. Despite moving quickly this time, there was fear that the normal process of getting needed approvals would take a year and the opportunity would be lost. So a short cut was introduced to permit planning, architecture and engineering to move forward together while Carla began gathering the interest and support of neighborhood groups from the three cities involved. These efforts could make or break the success of 710 Corridor revitalization and go a long way to spearhead Gateway's regeneration.

* * *

Growth Visioning by SCAG continued to struggle for support from the sub-committee. They were only beginning to understand how Growth Visioning could look at alternative futures (2001-2025) and reshape growth in the region and its subregions. Committee members–for the first time–would have the opportunity to help develop what the region might look like many years from now.

Some CEHD committee members began to realize that they must help change things as the threat of open warfare between the two societies–the haves and have nots–became more pronounced, threatening their good life.

"I'm just beginning to realize the danger we're in if we continue to ignore the needs of those less fortunate," said Rod Higgins, a member from Orange County.

"All of our communities have areas that need improvement and people unable to afford decent housing even when two family members are employed," responded Ventura County's Anne Golden.

"I'm excited about Visioning's opportunities to help us and other Regional Citizens learn what needs to be done to avoid the dangers of inaction. Plus the potentials we could achieve with commitment to the process," continued Rod, while recognizing the enormity of the need.

"I went out to a low-income neighborhood in my city the other day and talked with some of the residents," Anne continued. "They impressed me with their willingness to work, get retraining and better education. But they're getting disillusioned as they get further behind each year while others with breaks and connections succeed. We've got to help them turn the corner so they can get a small but important piece of the American dream too."

"Another resident outlined the problems he and his wife faced each day. It's too much of a 'dog eat dog' type of existence. No one seems to care whether they survive or not. There's little help for low income people who want a job but don't know how to go about getting one that offers them hope and possible advancement. They feel that the only jobs available are beginning level with no chance for job training for a new career. Also, there often are no health, vacation, or retirement benefits offered. They're afraid they're being passed over as others get the breaks."

"Companies used to provide a feeling of belonging, but no longer, especially for those at the bottom of the scale. Unions no longer have the clout to help them achieve their potentials. Helping each other is so important. Why is this no longer available?" Anne asked.

Rod agreed: "It's too much of a struggle for them, especially if they have language and education problems–and a family to feed. I was talking to a young fellow, Felipe, the other day who was really down. He holds three jobs, gets up to deliver papers at 3:00 a.m., works in an apparel factory during the day, and finishes things off by doing yard work in the evening. For all this, he only makes $800 a week with 18 hour days. He uses transit but spends over two hours just getting around from job to job. With a wife and four children which he rarely sees, he's worn down by these never-ending problems."

"However, his worst problems involve getting adequate housing and education for his children. This is the American dream which they aspire to. We've got to give them more help."

* * *

After discussions with Rod about how some people were having difficulties making ends meet currently, Anne decided to find out how some of her young friends were doing. While shopping, she bumped into her neighbors, Sarah and Joyce, and asked if they found the economy good for them.

Sarah responded: "It seems most people are doing well currently. But I have a hard time making ends meet. This is the first time I've had a little money to buy some clothes. Generally, we can barely meet our bills without over-using our credit cards."

"Yeah, I know what you mean, Sarah," replied Joyce. "As a young family with two children, we are always in debt, even though we earn $70,000 together."

"Why?" asked Anne.

"Well, first of all, housing is so expensive," said Sarah. "I'm trying to save to buy a home, but have difficulty paying the rent, even though I earn $45,000. Rents increased $500 per month in the last year to $1,400. I'm lucky as a single mother, since I've friends who have been forced out on the streets who earn $40,000 a year."

"We have similar problems," said Joyce. "We've saved enough for a down payment on a $200,000 house but can't find one. It's such a sellers

158

market that even if we found something we liked, it would be bid out of our reach."

"What other problems do you have in today's market?" asked Anne.

"Finding time to spend with my children after a two-hour commute to and from my job. Also, paying for child care and keeping up with my children's schooling." replied Sarah. "They're real young, a boy and girl, ages 4 and 3. There's never enough time in the day for them."

"Likewise here. My husband and I both work and find it hard to keep the family together. We've tried to take transit or bus to work but find it difficult due to poor connections and reliability in using them. So we're forced to drive and pay the parking fees and increased gas expenses. I wish we lived closer to our jobs. We're also concerned about the quality of the schools and day care for our two daughters, ages 7 and 6. It's such a hassle."

"I didn't realize the problems you were having. Thanks for your comments."

"That's only the tip of the iceberg, unfortunately," replied Joyce. "Let's talk more some time. There are other concerns such as fringe benefits, lack of possibilities for advancement, lack of opportunity to build retirement benefits, medical coverage limitations and inflation fears, to name a few. It's tough to do it all when the 'dog eat dog' corporate world seems so unconcerned about their employees problems. They seem to feel any employee can be easily replaced, so why be concerned."

"Yes, I get the drift. Let's talk some more. Hopefully, there are ways out. I want to discuss what we're doing on the regional level in growth guidance which might address some of your problems. Let's get together next week to talk more about this. I'll call you on the time and place," Anne said, realizing the opportunity she had to test what they were talking about.

* * *

Anne met with Sarah and Joyce the following Thursday for lunch to explore some thoughts she had which might help solve their problems. She'd called Tim, the SCAG planner, and got him to send some materials on the type of neighborhood proposed by Growth Visioning.

They showed how the old idea of a neighborhood school in the center of the neighborhood could be buttressed by the adjoining job training center for adults. Also, the potentials for housing near jobs so their families could have more time to spend together and incomes wouldn't be stretched as thin as their hours.

Although current neighborhood schools were generally located on major streets, efforts would be made to put them and adjacent parks in the center of the neighborhood. Sometimes they might be K-6 grade, but in some instances, smaller K-3 schools might be required to handle over-crowding. The job training center adjoining the school would permit joint use of some activities, or might be located on a major street to serve several neighborhoods. The approach would vary depending on the needs of the area.

They were excited about this. They hoped all this could be done–soon.

* * *

Carla, meanwhile worked on making the 710 interchange affecting three Gateway cities operational by talking to a lot of community leaders and residents. She felt this was also an opportunity to get the Growth Visioning effort going for the Subregion. SCAG wanted them to develop a possible scenario which would meet the Subregion's needs over the 2001-2025 planning period.

The transit station at Firestone offered opportunities for mixed commercial and residential development around it. Close proximity to the developing Alameda Corridor at Firestone should also offer significant opportunities for industrial and commercial activities. Plus, the anticipated redesign of the 710 Corridor interchange would provide even more opportunities for commercial development. These three different activities would provide Gateway Cities with opportunities, if handled well in their development. Their central location would also be a plus for the future of Gateway Cities. Their Growth Visioning efforts at the subregion level could boost these possibilities.

* * *

Growth Visioning continued to develop its program as the three consultants completed their programs covering Urban Form Implications and Possible Visions – 2025. These studies helped the committee move ahead.

Wilbur Clements of Civil Tech gave the first report on urban form implications of the 2001 Regional Transportation Program (RTP), while the second came from Chuck Deming of Regional Possibilities exploring alternative vision scenarios for the region through 2025.

Civil Tech crunched the data for each subregion based on 2001 estimates of future growth through 2025 for residential, job and transit development. The Growth Visioning Subcommittee realized the impacts of population and employment growth on traffic congestion, housing needs, transportation investment choices, and air quality on their areas would have significant long range planning implications. Analyzing the effects of the 2001 RTP update on future subregion urban growth patterns would be an important first step in the process of developing a sustainable regional

160

future. Thus, land utilization–existing and proposed–was for the first time looked at from a subregion and location standpoint by the members with interest–and concern. This approach was long overdue and potentially very meaningful. What did it mean and what should the subcommittee do to make the land utilization process more effective for the communities and subregions represented on the group?

In turn, the Regional Possibilities consultant study provided a look at various strategies the region might implement if certain "what if" approaches were used. Chuck Deming focused on such things as "compaction" versus "dispersal" of land development in both coastal and inland areas of the huge mega-region. He looked at this also for different degrees of vehicular and transit movement which might be involved. Likewise, "conservation" and "preservation" of the region's natural eco-systems considered impacts of continued sprawl on the region's various watersheds and rivers–as well as how growth guidance might protect the environment.

Committee members differed in their thoughts on what needed to be done to guide future growth. They were fascinated by the land use configurations shown within their subregions and communities and wanted to learn more. Gateway Cities efforts were mentioned regarding cooperative efforts by three different cities to create a better mixed use commercial layout for the redesigned Slauson interchange along the 710 Corridor. The committee asked for more details on this to consider at the next meeting. Mention was made that less land would be used commercially generating greater retail sales potential, while traffic congestion and accident possibilities would be reduced at the same time.

They marveled at this cooperative effort to coordinate between communities and wanted to see more of it in other subregions. Regional land use planning suddenly made much more sense to them. They could see increased profitability, less traffic congestion, and increased safety. Maybe local control wasn't always the best way to go.

CHAPTER 13
REGIONAL OUTREACH

SCAG strove to improve efforts to attract more people (called Regional Citizens) who could help educate others on the need for regional cooperation and action. The RC and RAC began to make SCAG's Outreach more effective. Problems with Outreach in poverty areas and Inland Empire threatened to set back the Regional Citizen movement.

"I've never met a person I didn't like."

Will Rogers

"Thanks for seeing me about Outreach, Bea."

"My pleasure, Marcine. A crucial issue like Outreach needs more attention and understanding if this huge region is to achieve its potentials."

"I'm glad you feel that way. Unfortunately, too many SCAG-types don't seem to feel it's important. I don't see any creative new approach by SCAG's leaders being developed to satisfactorily reach new Regional Citizens."

"Why isn't this happening? I agree we're missing out–from my more limited perspective."

"Outreach just isn't taking place to the degree needed throughout the entire L.A. Region," Marcine said. "Maybe it's because we haven't defined what Outreach is. It should involve 'reaching out' to new people all the time, along with strengthening ties to already involved Regional Citizens. How can it grow when we use the same old dull approaches. We aren't even effectively reaching out to the minorities–in their own neighborhoods."

"What do you mean by that, Marcine?"

"Ironically, most people I meet in the minority neighborhoods I 'work' have never heard of SCAG–much less know what it does."

"I'm flabbergasted! They've never heard of SCAG?" Bea exclaimed.

"Right. This indicates how insular SCAG has become–as well as how poorly the Outreach Program has done over the past few years."

"Well, what can we do to ensure that this improves–as soon as possible?" Bea asked.

"We need to develop an Outreach process that permits selecting not one but several Outreach consultants familiar with the needs and actions of people in their parts of the metroplex. It doesn't matter who their constituency is–whether poor, minority, ethnic, professional, well-off or whatever background."

"Do you think this can be done?" Bea asked with a perplexed expression.

"Yes, but only if we get away from how we've selected our Outreach consultants in the past. No hint of the possibility of a political payoff should exist."

"How can I help? Can a story about Outreach problems help?"

"Definitely. Most citizens in the region don't even know the importance of 'thinking regionally', much less how they could help improve their areas by becoming involved. An article by you–or better yet, a series of articles–well placed in the Times would really help."

"Okay," Bea said, pacing back and forth with nervous energy. "I'll write some articles on Outreach and Regionalism then. Would you be willing to help me on this, Marcine?"

"I'd be glad to help in any way I can. Just give me the word and tell me how."

"I'll see what I can do and will be back to you soon with an approach, Marcine."

* * *

"If we're going to curb our traffic congestion and air quality problems, we'll need more regionally-motivated people in each county," Mike Nelson said. "Currently, L.A. County seems to provide most of the representation."

"Right," Henry replied. "I think RAC can help if we get adequate funding and staff support. We already have an Outreach consultant to coordinate things."

"True. But we need greater participation by the subregions and involvement by Regional Citizens from all walks of life. Otherwise, we're only touching the tip of the iceberg. We've got to do better."

"That's why people need to know just who a Regional Citizen is. We know it's a person who understands and is dedicated to the Regional Process, but even more important, they must be ready to interact effectively with others interested in making the region work," said Henry.

"Also, how do we achieve a strong, diverse regional citizenry base?"

said Mike. "Get the business and professional people involved to help elected officials. They provide important viewpoints from all walks of life, including the business community, professionals like engineers, social workers, doctors, teachers and planners, and community-based groups representing the common citizen."

* * *

Four people deeply involved with kick-starting the Gateway Cities Subregion initiative were sitting around a table at the Cerritos Senior Center after the December 2000 COG meeting. Carla, Marcine, Mike and Gavin were discussing approaches to increase the number of Regional Citizens in the area. Their subregion didn't take kindly to expanding the regional process since local control seemed to be the best and safest way to make their cities more livable. The cities could cite examples of being burned in the past when they worked with adjoining cities. The four racked their brains to come up with ideas to stimulate other area citizens to join them in the larger regional process.

"We should develop a pool of people who have recently benefitted from actions of our Gateway organization. Encourage them to join. I'll bet each of us can come up with at least one name to start the process going. What do you think, guys?" Marcine asked.

Carla cited Anne, an acquaintance of hers who had mentioned her problems with the Los Angeles River near Long Beach. "She told me that every time it rained hard, the concrete-bottomed Los Angeles River sent torrents of water cascading down to Long Beach, creating havoc on her property, depositing debris and dirty water before it ran off. It proved very depressing as it happened several times a year, keeping her from protecting her investment or build on it. Upset and very emotional, she wondered what could be done to correct the problem. Her contact at the City of Long Beach said there wasn't anything the city could do about it since the problem began upstream. She realized then the importance of working with other cities to resolve such problems. Recently, Long Beach worked with Gateway Cities to get a Conservancy Bill through the state legislature to protect lands bordering the L.A. River from one end to the other. Anne now feels there's hope for her."

"We must send a letter inviting her to join the Regional Citizenry to work on similar efforts in the greater L.A. Region," Marcine said. "Appreciating what's been done through this organization and other regional bodies, I'm sure she would happily help us work on other regional improvements. She could pass on her experience so others might, as Regional Citizens, cooperate to improve things beyond the boundaries of their own communities."

"That's a great example, Carla," Mike said. "It reminds me of Jed, one of my acquaintances, who also benefitted from subregion action. In his case, the 710 Freeway improvement efforts now underway, extending from Long Beach north to Downtown L.A., were involved.. Jed has a restaurant at the Slauson interchange with the 710 surrounded by dilapidated uses which hurt his business. He also needed to expand his parking and create a more attractive and safe entry to his business. The 710 upgrade did the trick. He's indebted to Gateway for exerting pressure to get the 710 upgrade going. Certainly, he's another prime candidate for Regional Citizenry and, I feel, will be glad to help out."

"It's great to hear these success stories," Carla said. "We all get tired of being called Socialists, or even worse, Communists. Some of these people, afraid of these regional improvements, talk about how terrible we are for trying to help others be successful. They feel the people we're helping haven't worked hard enough to deserve it. But they really have no idea what we do or how we're really helping them. That goes with the territory, I guess."

"Yes, I'm afraid so, Carla," Marcine said. "Your stories of people who've really been helped by the regional process remind me of Sara, a friend of mine, totally wiped out by the system, as she called it. She'd dropped out of high school with no job skills, because she had two children as a result of some one nighters with men on the prowl. She felt trapped by it all and was a candidate to go on drugs–or rob a bank. Desperate and depressed, she went to the Job Coalition as a last resort. We worked with her to turn things around. So beaten down, with no self esteem left, it took a long time for her to regain hope. But she finally got her high school GED certificate, became interested in training for one of the Alameda Corridor jobs, and gradually turned her life around. The Alameda Corridor effort spurred by Gateway efforts, got her in touch with the opportunities she needed. I don't know if she's ready to reach out to others to become Regional Citizens, but she would be an ideal example of someone who's reached bottom and found a way back. Only a regional program like this could have helped her."

"Wow! Such a great example, Marcine," Gavin said. "We take so many things for granted that we forget how many fall through the cracks. I've thought of a person that might fit the Regional Citizen category based on an entirely different situation that Gateway helped. It involved Sue, who lived in housing located in a Brownfield area in the process of redevelopment. Her house was surrounded by decaying industry and toxic soils which threatened to wipe her out due to the difficulty of turning things around. No one wanted to buy her unit; it couldn't be fixed up since no loans were available, and her safety was threatened by the marauding gangs that had taken over the area. But our program, financed and backed by Gateway and the Feds, gave her hope. Now she's able to sell her home and relocate to a much safer, more desirable area within her community. I'm sure she would be glad to give a testimonial on her turnaround. I think we have some great Regional Citizen possibilities."

"I agree," Marcine said. "I'm sure we can add others to these possibilities. Let's get moving on it. It'll be great for Gateway."

* * *

In its monthly meeting, this time devoted to Outreach, RAC members listened to the SCAG consultant cover Outreach programs currently underway. Using a Power Point presentation, Elena Malesi described how her Outreach program for SCAG focused on its Regional Planning mission for the six counties and 14 subregions.

Elena outlined their efforts to reach the 16 million residents of the region and looked forward to RAC participation in its many programs.

She went on to indicate the improvements made in Outreach over those achieved previously for the 1998 RTP.

"For example, by signing up 8 out of the 14 subregions for Outreach programs, we've penetrated a greater portion of the region. No subregions signed up for the 1998 RTP. We expect to sign up 11 of the 14 next year, all but L.A. City, North L.A. and the Westside Cities."

She went on to mention the multiple program needs now facing Outreach for 2001 compared with the single-purpose 1998 RTP, and mentioned the challenges presented by the $40 billion funding shortfall expected..

After her presentation, questions were asked from the floor.

"Elena, how can we help you the most?" asked Karen.

"There are lots of ways, depending on how much time you have, your background, interest and access to people. The subregions are key both to developing Regional Citizens and strengthening the overall Outreach Program."

"Well, I'm trained to handle workshops, forums, one-on-one dialogues and even involvement in electronic town halls," Karen said.

"You will be a valuable member of our team."

"What database do you have?" Mary asked.

"We have all sorts of demographic and transportation-related data available by area, both for regionwide outreach as well as for each subregion and city."

"How can organizations like unions and other non-profits get involved?" asked Hugh.

"By offering your services and understanding the nature of the subregion's needs."

"What are your methods of developing activities for a subregion?" asked Betty.

"Developing community surveys, a newsletter, public workshops, and organizational presentations. Also, participating in one-on-one stakeholder meetings with community leaders, website promotion and developing a cable program."

"What do public workshops involve?" asked Mary.

"The workshops can be on the Regional Transportation Plan (RTP) or a part of a public forum for the subregion. Emphasis should be placed on explaining the highlights of the RTP to as many groups and individuals as possible, including those groups and individuals who haven't traditionally been a part of the RTP planning process. They must have a feedback mechanism the audience can use to provide public comment on the RTP."

"What about the stakeholder meetings?" asked Karen.

"We obtain important one-on-one feedback from key community leaders and officials on the RTP update process, Task Forces' preliminary work and relevant subregional transportation issues and projects."

"I don't understand how the website promotion is handled?" asked Mary.

"We coordinate the inclusion of SCAG RTP documentation on the subregional website as well as cover the RTP planning process on SCAG's website."

"You are involved in video conferencing for each subregion too?"

"Yes. We can participate in a subregional video conference to link the region internally or with other cities to discuss RTP issues, programs and topics."

"That sounds like a big agenda," Karen said. "We'll do everything we can to help you."

* * *

An Electronic Town Hall workshop was held at Cerritos College which linked the Gateway subregion to a site in the adjoining South Bay Subregion and a Transportation Department site in Washington, D.C. Although there were sound and picture problems initially, the workshop was a big success. Glitches like this could be expected in the initial meeting. Microphones were positioned on the dais and throughout the audience so there could be maximum interaction between the participants at the three locations. Even more locations could be involved if needed. The screen showed the people involved at several locations through insets, along with those at the main site. All sorts of situations could be televised and the audiences at each site could be kept apprized of everything. They were able to get knowledgable people from several locations to speak and interact on this important subject without taking a lot of time from their regular jobs. In this case, the issue was goods movement from the Port of Long Beach.

Through their questions and answers, attendees learned that a number of things needed to be done to ensure that gridlock didn't take place on the 710 and other freeways inundated by more and more 18 wheelers making necessary deliveries throughout the metroplex. This could be done by scheduling deliveries around the clock instead of just during business hours. Also, by working to eliminate the movement of empty containers back and forth, doubling trips and costs involved. These and other suggestions were proposed and adopted to ensure that the L.A. economy didn't grind to a halt.

Business leaders, elected officials and professionals attended this meeting, the first of many planned electronically. The interaction of these leaders taking a few minutes away from their busy schedules indicated the potentials of events like this

Those in attendance were eager to schedule more events since this approach attracted more regionally-oriented people who ordinarily would be too busy to attend. And it promised to reward them for their attendance with influence on important matters.

* * *

Effective outreach in such a huge region (roughly 150 miles by 200 miles) is exceedingly difficult to develop. Every part of the region is important to the economic future of this metropolis of 16 million residents as it emerges in the coming decade as the most vital economy in the world, measured in jobs, global linkages, and technological edge.

Bea devoted one of her "Undercover News"columns in the Times to the future of L.A.'s economy. As she indicated in her column, there were pluses and minuses:

"It could blow these opportunities if its outreach efforts are unsuccessful. Its weaknesses are an undereducated work force, inadequate schools, housing and transportation, and sluggish industries threatened by changing technologies. But it's much less vulnerable than it was in the late 1980's. Then it was still powered by government contracts for the defense-aerospace industry, as well as by major banks and large companies that disdained and crowded out the smaller firms."

Her article went on: "The economy has been transformed. Small to medium-size companies populate its industries; more than 95 percent of the region's firms employ fewer than 50 people. Unlike a decade ago, the region today relies on no single industry for more than three percent of its total employment. This region has so much more diversity now that its key industries are: movies and television; tourism and entertainment; international trade; technology; warehousing; and health and biomedicine."

"Such diversity is unparalleled. However, its difficulties are significant. Business moves at a quickened pace; competition is global and demanding. There are a lot of rich people–but many more poor people. The region must train its low-wage, undereducated work force to qualify for better jobs. Failure would mean a vast, permanent underclass for the region and the loss of industries to other places with better workers."

The c[...]tinued: "Already, employers are begging for workers who can d[...]line work, not to mention workers with special skills, even as h[...]ousands of people labor at low-paying menial jobs. Southern California still is the largest manufacturing center in the U.S. But it has a different character than before. Some 643,000 of its four million workers are in manufacturing. It offers some of the highest-paid jobs on earth, but also has almost 800,000 workers earning wages that place their families below the Federal poverty levels of $16,700 a year. Involved are workers in the garment trades, warehouses, retail stores and restaurants.

"However, there are significant improvements taking place which must be continued. Studies in four of the most depressed poverty areas show a significant turnaround. Areas included are: the Compton and Florence-Firestone areas in Gateway Cities; South-Central L.A.; and Santa Ana in Orange County. Not only has unemployment declined in these areas, but more people are buying homes (even as home prices climb). Even retail sales have risen as more stores have been added in these store-poor areas."

Bea's column concluded: "On the other hand, Southern California is one of the top five U.S. regions in high-tech employment and production–more multipolar, more dispersed and more diverse than Silicon Valley. Southern California is the largest of these technopolises, surpassing Silicon Valley when Orange County is included. Like other activities formed over time, a wide range of smaller high-tech hubs have mushroomed here. These included the hardware-oriented hotbeds of telecommunications and biomedical technology, led by Irvine, home to roughly 2,000 high-tech firms."

* * *

SCAG and its committees wrestled with little success to effectively include the Inland Empire (Riverside, San Bernardino and Imperial counties) and their four subregions in the regional planning process. Outreach efforts were made attempting to link these areas to the remainder of the huge SCAG Region.

One recent effort involved linking education, jobs, economic growth, regional airports and balanced housing together to overcome the time/distance problem for participants. This is a killer for Outreach efforts. It erodes participation by outlying citizens and thwarts the regional process. Slowly, efforts began to come together through better airing of SCAG committee meetings in Inland Empire satellite centers, plus focusing more Outreach monies on needed development of Regional Citizen development efforts (surveys and other educational efforts).

Mike and Carla were discussing the Outreach situation.

"It's a tough sell considering the huge region we have. You can understand why the outlying areas are complaining."

"Yes, Mike. The subregions must provide the basis for achieving better Outreach. Unless Outreach efforts have strong subregion bases, we're never going to achieve our objectives."

"Plus the Regional Advisory Council has never been able to expand its Regional Citizenry base which it has a mission to do, unless it gets the money, staffing and adequate ties to the subregions," replied Mike, shaking his head.

"I think we're just beginning to become effective in making Outreach work. We can't just throw money at it and expect it to function effectively."

"No wonder we have seven lawsuits currently within SCAG. People are getting tired of being ignored. Plus the state doesn't help any with its top-down dictates regarding RHNA Housing (Housing and Community Development) and transportation (Caltrans). Or being frustrated by the lack of understanding of subregion problems by such big organizations as MTA, Air Quality Management District (AQMD) and Metro Water District (MWD)." Mike shook his head in frustration about how 'organizational bigness' had frustrated the Outreach process.

"No wonder the learning curve for new RC/RAC members is so long and difficult. That alone discourages retaining Regional Citizens. We tend to encourage more people to be against the regional process than for it. Or so it seems to me at times," exclaimed Carla, rolling her eyes in disgust.

"Yeah, we're beginning to inherit regional dysfunctionalism as a result. Good people are burning out and leaving just when they could begin to really be effective."

"Let's really work through the subregions and RAC to make Outreach work more effectively. Money and staff have got to be put in the right places at the right time to make this work," Mike emphasized. "That's why I'm spending so much time as chair of the Subregional Coordinators."

"And we need to figure out how to get out to the Inland Empire and other outlying locations more often. That's a toughie."

"It sure is–but I still believe it can be solved through a concerted effort by everyone."

"How so?" asked Carla.

"Possibly have split sessions of RAC where some members work on regional projects agreed on, while the remainder have a meeting of members in its own area (like the Inland Empire). Then rotate so meetings are held for Orange County and south L.A. County in an accessible location, and the remainder of the members work on some research project prompted by its review of regional problems. Move it around so all parts of the region participate."

"Not a bad idea. Do you think it would pass inspection, Mike?"

"Something of this type has been suggested. It's worth a try."

* * *

In addition, a south-central group, Clear The Air, headed by Amber Golar worked to get low income groups involved with a voice regarding Metro Planning Organization (MPO) re-certification issues concerning SCAG. Some of the materials received from the Federal Highway Administration (FHWA) on MPO re-certification were passed out to the group for question and comment. Such questions on public involvement as: "If SCAG has a public involvement process or a subsequent revision, is there at least a 45 day public comment period before the process or revision is adopted?" Or on Environmental Justice: "What does SCAG do to ensure that their services are accessible to persons with disabilities?" Also, regarding RTP review, "Does the RTP include design concepts and scope descriptions of all existing and future transit facilities with neighborhood-by-neighborhood air quality analysis and cost estimates?" For planning studies, "Does the public involvement process for the studies differ from public involvement process used for other SCAG activities?" Some members felt that not all of the questions could be answered affirmatively, but that could put SCAG in violation. If considered serious enough, this violation could result in denial of re-certification and loss of federal funds for the whole region. They discussed such questions and decided they should attend the public hearing on MPO re-certification in May to register their grievances.

* * *

Bea followed Outreach closely and wrote several articles on its problems and the opportunities that were being lost. Indirectly, her articles helped fan increased interest in Regional Citizen development. She planned to write about other important planning topics in the weeks ahead.

Her concern about SCAG and its many missed opportunities grew. SCAG certainly had the money and staff with which to achieve much more. Ingrown bureaucracy and lethergy seemed to threaten its continued existence. Of course, she thought, there are enough other huge bureaucracies involved with some of the same problems which just made things worse. What could she do to help turn things around? Too many excuses existed, and they muddied the waters still more.

CHAPTER 14
REGIONAL AIRPORT DILEMMA

*Two SCAG aviation policies offer the
opportunity to resolve an exceedingly
political dilemma. One is finding a way
to provide an effective regional airport
system, complementing a strong LAX
regional airport with others to be added
in timely fashion. This would result in
the L.A. Region being on a par with other
regions with three or more regional airports
with populations of less than half that of
this region's. Proposed Maglev system also
becomes part of this issue.*

---

*"Airports have historically been run for the
benefit of the airlines, but we're starting to look
at service from the customer's point of view."*
V. Buckingham, Massport (Logan Airport
Regional Authority), 2001

*" Life is a race. You run it as long as
you can and as fast as you can."*
St. Paul

"How can a Task Force justify spending two years debating regional
airport needs!" Clark Ford, Ventura County member, heatedly exclaimed,
"and still be fighting factions wanting only LAX expansion? I strongly
object to this travesty, Mr. Chair. It doesn't make any sense. Metro areas
less than one-half our size–Dallas/Fort Worth and Washington,
D.C./Baltimore–have three regional airports. The Aviation Task Force
(ATF) must realize this before it's too late." As a task force member, at the
committee meeting held at SCAG, he felt deeply involved.

"I understand your frustration on the slowness of our deliberations,
Clark," the Chair said, "but we need help from the Feds on aviation ground
rules and SCAG on getting the traffic models developed for each alterna-

tive. It's a slow process, especially when the L.A. city council insists that LAX be expanded before considering potentials for expanding other facilities into regional airports." His job as ATF chair seemed full of snags.

"We'll never be able to get a good Regional Transportation Plan (RTP) done on time at the pace we're going. We'll be out of conformity–or have such a bad plan that we'll wish we were," Clark said, continuing to pace the floor in frustration. He glared at some of the L.A. city council members in attendance who were succeeding in slowing the process.

"We want SCAG and ATF to agree to expand LAX to its proposed limits. It's the heart and soul of the region and it's a mockery that the rest of you can't understand," Greg Gagne, L.A. councilman from the Valley said, gesturing to the task force.

"I agree. We've gone out of our way to legislate environmental improvements for cities surrounding the airport, including Inglewood," Robin Gather, from the L.A.'s westside said.

"Plus, we're going to tie up any possibilities that your Maglev rapid train system will get approved by the Feds. It's not going to work. Just wait and see," said Rudy von Tomovich, representing L.A.'s Eastside.

Clark felt they were a distraction on all motions, coming to all ATF meetings en masse in a 15-strong bloc. Prior to this, only one councilman came to the meetings. He and other members used to criticize L.A. for not being interested in regional affairs; now he wished they would stay away and stop disrupting effective regional interaction with their political maneuvering.

"We've spent over two years debating the issue of regional airport needs and we're no closer to a solution today," the chair said. "Obviously, we need more than one regional airport serving 16 million people–especially considering that the Dallas/Fort Worth region holding five-plus million has three, including huge D/FW Airport."

"You're absolutely right," said Clark. "Look at the Washington, D.C./Baltimore area. They have Dulles International, Baltimore / Washington International and Reagan National Airport handling less than 8 million population."

"How're we going to get our Task Force, the FAA, and the various airlines together to resolve this issue?" Robin Gather asked.

"Don't forget the L.A. city council members we have to contend with. They want the world's biggest airport which, if expanded, will be inaccessible to surface transportation and passengers– and where will they park? But LAX w-i-l-l be the biggest," Clark said facetiously.

"Yeah, the freeway system serving it won't be able to absorb the traffic no matter how many improvements we make. Plus the communities surrounding it will wither away due to the increased noise and air pollution," said the Chair.

"Yeah, look at the noise problems faced daily by families in Inglewood," Clark said. "Does anyone ever think of the impacts on the families and children living in the areas around LAX?"

"The key, I believe, rests with adhering to those two SCAG airport policies," Robin replied. "Policy No.18 calls for each county to provide environmentally-acceptable airport capacity within its own market to meet local, domestic air passenger demand. While Policy No. 19 asks that airports be expanded and added to the system in a way that reinforces regional growth patterns and makes communities more livable. Those two policies together make so much sense."

"I believe the RTP and Transportation/Communications Committee (TCC) will render the right final solution to this. Let's hope so," Clark said. They left the meeting still arguing.

* * *

The regional airport issue, focused on the expansion of LAX to make it the sole regional airport, guaranteed the 1998 RTP wouldn't be completed on time. The 2001 RTP was considered the economic engine by which regional airport issues would be totally resolved. The Aviation Task Force (ATF), formed to evaluate additional scenarios, also provided further policy direction to the Regional Council. The ATF defined and evaluated nine new aviation system scenarios over a two-year period. During the first two months of 2000, the group selected four of these for further analysis, including the previously adopted 1998 RTP Baseline Scenario, which served as the foundation of the airport study.

The baseline scenario did not include high speed rail or consider any capacity limits on airports studied. For example, LAX could serve 94.2 million annual passengers (MAP). The other three scenarios put existing constraints on airport capacities, as well as being tied to high speed rail, which if adopted would not be operational until 2008. They were developed to permit all portions of the region to share in regional airports if termed feasible. One scenario focused on Ontario and other Inland Empire airports' ability to meet future demand with LAX 's limits set at 70 MAP. Another scenario covered El Toro and its ability to handle aviation demand with LAX constrained to 78 MAP. Finally, the last scenario focused on how LAX expansion, based on its master plan, would affect the regional airport system without the development of El Toro.

SCAG planners had to consider such issues as ground access, air quality, aircraft emissions, sensitive land uses in noise areas, impacts on minority populations, and economic impacts. When these impacts were estimated, no clear winner emerged. The planners realized that the complexities of these issues created enormous political pressures and concerns difficult to resolve. The Transportation and Communications Committee (TCC) met October 1, 2000 at SCAG to consider these scenarios and further steps to be taken. Both Jim and Juan attended the meeting due to its importance to the region and the RTP. Juan made a special trip down from Sacramento.

The chair of the TCC, Lloyd Deer, called the meeting to order, citing its objective. He then asked for questions from the general public.

"You know the issues. Do we need any further discussion on this topic which has been covered in depth over the past two years by the Aviation Task Force?"

"Mr. Chair, I have a question," Jim said, rising to speak..

"All right, Jim Robinson, chair of the Transportation Finance Task Force. Go ahead, Jim."

Jim went to the microphone and laid out his concern: "I'm a booster for expanding LAX which, I think most of us agree, should take place. I can't for the life of me understand why we're spending all this money and time to study locations that won't ever attract enough passengers to justify their existence?" Looking around at the audience, he continued, "I know you all want to be located near a regional airport, but planned expressway improvements will help speed things up."

"Mr. Chair, I'd like to answer that question," Juan Rodriguez said, rising to speak.

"House Speaker Rodriguez, how nice that you could come down from Sacramento to attend this meeting. Go ahead, Mr. Speaker," the chair motioning him to the microphone.

"I've been closely following your deliberations on the regional airport issue. Since I go through a lot of airports nationwide, including LAX, I'm concerned about the congestion problems occurring all over–Denver, Dallas, Washington, New York–to mention a few. While other major metropolitan areas have planned ahead to meet their regional airport needs, I feel L.A. is years behind on this. I respect Jim Robinson's trying to protect LAX's turf, but I firmly believe we must move on now to create a network of airports which will meet our passenger and cargo needs over the next 25 years. In Sacramento, we're working on a long range regional planning bill which also covers aviation plans for all California regions, including L.A. You must not duck this opportunity to add these needed airports. Thank you."

"Mr. Chair, could I provide a little more detail on my remarks since I wasn't able to complete my thoughts when the Speaker asked for time?" Jim asked.

"Go ahead, Jim."

"The infrastructure built into LAX is significant and plans for future improvements include the area around LAX. These cover parking, MTA expansion efforts and other private endeavors. If LAX isn't allowed to expand according to its master plan, many of these needed improvements won't take place. Please take these proposed efforts into consideration. Thank you."

The TCC moved ahead and approved the plan to test all four scenarios.

* * *

RAC scheduled a discussion of the Regional Airport issue as one of its hot button issues. Representatives from SCAG and the Inland Empire were included as speakers. The Inland Empire speaker, Emory Smith, who was involved with the March Air Force Base property and another tract, used a Power Point presentation to outline the importance of providing the eastern portion of the region with a large regional airport to supplement the smaller Ontario facility that was rapidly reaching its capacity.

"We need to assemble a huge tract of land now and push ahead to develop a large airport, somewhat like how Dulles International in the Washington, D.C. area came into being in the 60's. It could be done cheaply now with little problem with airport noise due to its size," he said.

After both presentations, RAC debated the regional airport issue and adopted a policy recommending agreement with the TCC position, while adding a proposal that other regional airports be developed to serve the Inland Empire and Orange County.

* * *

"We're at loggerheads with the RC on both LAX expansion and the Maglev project. I bet they really love us, Rudy. Do you see us winning out on either or both?" said Greg Gagne, L.A. councilman from the Valley.

"Maybe both, since some of them agree with our viewpoints. Of course, Robin Gather opposes LAX expansion since many of her constituents are airport neighbors who hate the noise," replied Rudy von Tomovich, representing the East Side.

"Yeah, but she's the only one. She's definitely against Maglev because she feels that a high- speed train that uses magnetic levitation and propulsion to carry passengers and freight along a guideway at speeds over 200 miles per hour is ludicrous."

"The thing that bugs me is they feel that the private sector can build this 92 mile system for $7 billion and charge fares of $13.50 one way, even without federal help. I believe that more funding from SCAG sources will result. They say it won't, but I doubt that. Even so, the private interests are going to want something in return," Rudy said disgustedly, rolling his eyes.

"Can you imagine Maglev connecting LAX to downtown, the San Gabriel Valley, and three other airports in the Inland Empire and north L.A. Six stops at the most for $7 billion. Give me a break," Greg said.

"Plus, the developers in both Germany and Japan have failed to get their systems funded in their countries. I think Southern California should study a wide range of alternatives to meet its transportation needs. Then they should lobby hard for Federal, state and private investment to build them."

"LAX expansion wouldn't happen if Maglev were put in place. Of course, many RC members feel that Maglev is too fast, too expensive and has too few stops to meet everyday needs. We might have to change our thinking if a high speed transit system averaging say 80 miles per hour, with more stops and tied to connecting local light transit were constructed, Rudy."

"Maybe, but I don't see it happening. They're in love with technology and the desire to be first in the world," Rudy replied, concerned about the way things were going on Maglev.

"Oh, here comes Robin now. Maybe she can fill us in on the latest about LAX."

"Hi Greg, Rudy. What's new?" Robin Gather asked as she breezed up to them. She wanted desperately to bust their LAX expansion balloon.

"We've just been talking about LAX expansion. We know you're against it but–"

"Well, the latest info I have is that expansion will cost $12 billion. Just think, we could probably completely outfit both Palmdale and an eastside regional airport for that."

"But they don't have the location LAX has. What are they proposing for $12 billion?" Rudy asked, thinking about how that would help expand the demand for parking.

"Construction of a new terminal for growth, along with an expressway to the airport off 405," Robin replied. "Also, construction of a road ringing the airport to improve access. The environmental report is virtually complete. Just think of the neighborhoods and housing that would be destroyed to achieve that–along with increased noise and congestion?"

"You're way off base on those statements, Robin. You know that, don't you?"

"What I'm concerned about right now," Robin said, dodging the issue for the moment, "are the reports circulating that the parking and billboard interests are financing our campaigns and make us comply. I'm upset about that. All this talk about corrupt L.A. politicians is driving me batty. I'm tired of it." She stared at them, waiting to get their reaction. Robin, well known for speaking her mind on things, had done it again.

"We've got to finance our campaigns and LAX won't expand unless there's adequate parking nearby. I know you don't agree but your voters want totally different things than ours," Rudy said.

"And your voters are more apt to use transit than ours," Gregg added. "In fact, you probably would like to see MTA's Green Line go all the way to LAX. That would hurt the parking interests' big payday. I'm not sure how they made sure that the Green Line didn't deadhead at LAX when it was built. I'm sure it's a pain using the shuttle bus to transfer. In addition, the taxi and shuttle services provided wouldn't produce as much income if more direct light rail service were provided."

"We feel we can get the Green Line to deadend at LAX now with the new transit funds available. Let's see you stop that. You can see why so many residents around LAX are upset, especially considering further expansion. You guys aren't representing L.A. You're only representing special interests. How can you sleep nights?" Robin asked, looking them in the eye.

"Come on, Robin, don't be so hard on us. We've got to survive," Rudy said.

"You'd be able to survive just as well if you thought more of the city's interests–and the region's future. You know they're tied together more and more, don't you?"

"You believe that hogwash, Robin? I'm surprised," Greg said. "You know that the Valley is trying to secede from L.A. It's a dog-eat-dog situation. We've got to get back to local control, not go regional. Get a life, won't you?"

"I sometimes wonder what this world is coming to," Robin replied. "So much greed, pride and selfishness."

"There you go again. When are you going to give up trying to reform the human race?"

"With you guys around, not tomorrow," she said, walking away disgusted.. "You're hopeless."

*   *   *

LAX continued its campaign to expand its limits and add needed runways and access roads to make it happen. To counter this, El Segundo led a coalition of 83 cities objecting to LAX expansion. Included in the coalition were neighboring cities objecting to traffic congestion and aircraft noise. In addition, a number of Inland Empire cities eager to attract air cargo business from LAX joined the coalition.

Bea saw an opportunity to move things along through her interest in good regional planning and desire to break down the LAX-L.A.City coalition blocking resolution of the regional airport problem. Some investigative reporting was needed on how added airports had been handled in other major regions. Also, possible locations for new airports in the metroplex. She began planning a series, making calls to contacts in Dallas, Washington, D.C., and Atlanta.

An old friend in Dallas who had been with the Dallas News gave her a start on the Dallas-Fort Worth Metroplex solution.

"Hi, Bea. Long time no see. Still enjoying crazy L.A.?" he chuckled.

"You bet, George! This place is no crazier than Big D. You guys take the prize with your Texas politics. Say, can you help give me some perspective on how you ended up with three regional airports in your area? We can't get beyond one and we have three times your population."

"Sure. I'll send you some material on it. Cutting to the chase, we had a simpler problem than you have. If you'd nipped your LAX expansion earlier, you wouldn't have the problem you have now."

"Yeah, I know. Plus, Burbank, Ontario and Long Beach were built on small sites preventing expansion. And Palmdale has plenty of room but it's too far out," Bea acknowledged, as she reflected on how things happened historically in a huge area sprawled over what would cover several states back East.

"You've got it. Dallas Love Field and Fort Worth's airport evolved as they represented their growing cities in an aviation era. Fortunately, Love Field was small like Burbank's airport with surrounding neighbors–whose high income residents wouldn't allow expansion. Your LAX was able to expand by cramming its noise problems down the throats of poorer neighborhoods around it. Now it's spent far too much and is close to so many people, it's hard to break the cycle. But its got to be done. There's no other way."

"What did you do to break the cycle, George?" Bea asked.

"Our leadership could envision what both Dallas and Fort Worth would become. They also saw that the 60 miles distance between the two cities could be an asset. So they began looking on the quiet for around 10,000 acres of cheap land between the two cities which could be assembled easily and got an option to buy the land for a specified price. They worked with the FAA and other Federal agencies to get the go-ahead to develop the D-FW Regional Airport they have today. Finally, they assembled the highways and other infrastructure and made it happen. Luckily, no one wanted to see Love Field expand since it was surrounded by Highland Park and other fancy, ritzy neighborhoods. Plus, they had the city leadership which wasn't blinded by short term profits for the city, or ignoring the region's needs like Los Angeles has."

"But D-FW 's way out and almost unreachable at first. How did it evolve into the successful airport it is now?" Bea asked.

"The population grew that way, just as it is in the Inland Empire now–and would, even more, if a big regional airport was plopped down there. Plus, a big airport like that would generate a lot of high-paying jobs. So the industry needed would evolve there naturally if given half a chance."

"Yeah, they already have the land there at the deactivated George and March Air Bases.   I don't know what they're waiting for. Highways are somewhat in place and some of the other infrastructure. It's a natural, espe-cially since the big outcry is how to get more industry into the Inland Empire to balance out the overage of housing. Planners call it jobs/housing balance."

"You've got the idea, Bea. Get the right leadership, and the FAA and airlines will fall in line. It happens that way. Go get 'em!" George said.

"That's terrific, George. I couldn't have said it better. Thanks for your comments. I look forward to getting the backup materials you mentioned," Bea said. "I'll come see you sometime, hear."

Next, Bea called another colleague at the Washington Post, who she enjoyed talking with about national politics from time to time.

"Minnie, this is Bea. It's been a long time, hasn't it? I bet you're sick of the elections by now? I know I am"

"Bea, I thought you might be in town. No such luck," Minnie replied melodiously. "I'm doing fine. What can I help you with–besides votes? Couldn't resist that the way the election keeps going on and on in Florida."

"We've got this regional airport problem which also won't go away. I know that D.C. and Baltimore had a similar problem at one time. How did you finally resolve it?"

"With Congress, we had the same problem that LAX provides in col-lusion with City Hall. They were located just across the Potomac from National Airport which wanted to be their regional airport. No one was going to take that away from them, come hell or high water. Of course, Baltimore is only 20 miles away and Baltimore-Washington Airport evolved as Baltimore's airport and grew into a regional airport."

"But how did Dulles International come into being? That was, what, forty miles out in the Virginia countryside in the middle of nowhere when the site was considered?"

"You could call it a hard sell," Minnie replied. "People knew National–or what is now called Reagan National–was so tiny that they couldn't expand it much more. In fact, they had some fatal crashes with planes landing in the river, while at the same time, they kept filling in the Potomac to lengthen the runways needed by the big jets."

"Yeah, I remember the plane crashes and the human interest stories. A motorist rescued a passenger from a plane in one instance in the wintertime, I believe."

"Right. Well, they needed 14,000 acres of cheap land way out in Virginia, and the only place they could find it was out in the Hunt Country. So, on the sly, they got this acreage assembled, with an option to buy at a ridiculously low price. They just made it happen, again with FAA, DC, and Virginia's approval. Congress certainly helped so they could continue to have their so-called fancy 'private' airport across the Potomac to use. Again, it took leadership–and quick action on the quiet."

"I go into Dulles all the time now and things have built up on all sides. But I can remember when it was so far out that it seemed like a foreign country, and people didn't like to be routed there rather than National," Bea said. "What happened?"

"The population grew out to Dulles–plus an airport of that size creates jobs and industry of its own. Then other industries are attracted and it just multiplies. An airport of that size just makes things happen."

"Thanks, Minnie. Great information! Could you send me backup info out of your archives? I'm beholden to you on this."

Bea did the same on Atlanta by calling a friend with the Atlanta Constitution to learn how Atlanta's Hartsfield regional airport evolved. She stressed leadership and the feeling that the central city and region needed to work together more on issues like this.

* * *

"I see the new administration in Washington supports more jet runways and airports around the U.S. to ease delays at existing airports. They understand surface transportation and airport congestion is alarming to the public health, safety and general welfare," Marcine exclaimed to Bea.

"I'm not sure that their approach is right though. They want to cut corners on environmental reviews to expedite the process. It might hurt the inner city more, like around LAX."

"Possibly. However, these environmental reviews take too long. They should at least have the state and Federal reviews going on at the same time. Some reviews take up to four years and that's way too long."

"Right," Bea exclaimed. "We've got to plan more effectively for a regional system of airports for all metropolitan regions. Too often, we're shooting ourselves in the foot by making progress so complicated. But the airlines need to cooperate more by realizing they must diversify by slating more flights at competitive prices at two or more airports in each metropolitan area. This will improve air safety, reduce impacts on neighborhoods surrounding airports, and reduce both air and surface congestion by allowing passengers to use the airport closest to their home."

* * *

The March 22, 2001 meeting of the TCC on Regional Airports was a frenzied affair, taking over four hours to reach a decision. After a number of scenarios were voted down, Scenario 8 was finally approved. It focuses on minimal expansion at LAX, with El Toro, Ontario and several other Inland Empire airports spreading the passenger and cargo load through 2025.

The regional airport issue had divided people considerably since so many issues came into play. NIMBYism, noise, toxic air, economic development, congested highways and nearness to a regional airport were all complex issues that had to be resolved. Plus, the region had ducked this issue too long and it had become a political football between L.A. City and the surrounding cities and counties.

* * *

Bea saw a major article coming out of this latest meeting on regional airports. It would be helpful to highlight such an article in the <u>Times</u> to help frame, and perhaps even influence the coming months of political intrigue on LAX expansion and the alternatives to it.

The outline began forming in Bea's mind:

"Upcoming was a passionate struggle between warring forces characterized by L.A.'s forceful feeling that they would not be denied their inalienable right to achieve the growth needed to keep LAX the premier airport in the U.S.–even the world. Arrayed against them were many leaders representing the many smaller, surrounding communities not willing to bend to the dictates of the central city's traditional dominance.

"How they would be able to survive and win this struggle with this entrenched bureaucracy was difficult to perceive. But win they must–or the L.A. Region would lose its way. Why? Because there would be gridlock, both on the ground and in the air. The region could not afford to have this happen. Strong efforts must be made in the next few months as the final 2001 RTP was completed to ensure that a strong regional airport system emerged–with LAX still its jewel but buttressed by other strategically located, growing regional airports."

She hoped it could take place and would do everything in her power to make it happen. She knew it could occur with the right leadership. But it would take– A REGION AROUSED.

CHAPTER 15
AFFORDABLE
HOUSING CONTROVERSY

*The RHNA Housing issue has created a
difficult dilemma with efforts to provide
all portions of the L.A. Region with a
wide range of affordable housing. This
would create a better balance of jobs to
housing. New programs must provide more
reasonably priced affordable housing for
sale and rent.*

"Okie use'ta mean you was from Oklahoma.
Now it means you're scum. Don't mean nothing itself,
it's the way they say it."

John Steinbeck

The problem of high housing cost
disproportionately falls on low and
very-low income renters. Californians
not only pay more for housing than
residents of other states; housing costs
also account for a greater share of
Californian incomes.

Raising the Roof

Whenever Bea thought about the affordable housing problem, she couldn't shake the memory of how the Lee family came into her life. Sing Lee was a homeless man. With his family, he had slipped into California off a freighter from China a year ago while docked at the Port of Long Beach.

Homeless and destitute, knowing no English, Sing had an indomitable, happy spirit. He turned up at L.A. City Hall one day looking for work–any kind. With a wife, Song and two little two year old twin girls, Sue and Lou, they burled their way into her heart through their interest and spirit. They were hired at minimum wage to handle some of the growing janitorial duties.

184

Bea discovered that they lived in an old abandoned Cadillac parked on the street near city hall. How they were able to live happily in such a tiny space was a tale in itself. But they appreciated having the space since they had no money for housing.

City hall workers quickly adopted them, hiring them to keep their facilities clean, in exchange for clothes and kitchenware. His wife, Song, was a bundle of energy less than five feet tall. The two little girls, their pigtails flying, were inseparable twins. City hall never was the same after the Lees arrived. However, as Bea knew, most homeless and house less families weren't so fortunate.

*   *   *

"Madam Chair, this housing policy committee must focus on solving the housing problem. To require the Western Riverside Subregion to absorb additional housing units on top of the foreclosed units lying vacant in the area is ludicrous. Especially when these affordable units are desperately needed elsewhere in the region. How ironic!" This declaration came from Al Deerfield, Executive Director of the Western Riverside Subregion, as he addressed the chair of SCAG's Community, Economic and Human Development Policy Committee (CEHD) on November 5, 2000.

"I realize your frustration, Al, but we agreed 18 months ago to the SCAG staff's proposal to gradually close the gap on differences in mix of housing between subregions."

"By majority vote only. That's easy to do if enough subregions are satisfied with their housing—and want to protect it. Now, you have a 'catch 22' situation. You're requiring us to absorb over 20,000 additional units on top of an existing 10,000 vacant foreclosed units. I want some action to redress this wrong."

"So, if nothing is done soon, your Inland Empire superiors will take action to correct it. Right, Al?"

"Right—in spades! We're tired of messing around with an impossible situation that will destroy our economy and diminish the entire region," Al thundered.

"Okay, we'll go into closed session, including legal counsel, to make a decision," the chair declared. "Let's clear the room."

Once the room cleared, the closed session proceeded rapidly. Two factions—one involving those subregions who wanted change since they would have to absorb most of the affordable housing units versus those who wanted things to remain the way they were with few or no additional affordable units. After minor scrimmaging, a vote was taken. Al's threats had shifted some safe districts who felt threatened by the possibility that if Al didn't get his way, they might end up in worse shape. These shifts gave Al's group a majority and a victory of sorts. Those waiting patiently outside were readmitted.

The Affordable Housing (RHNA) hearings then were reopened to test a Western Riverside model on affordable housing allocations based on income equity throughout the region.

* * *

Henry checked in by phone with Betty Atwater, Director of the L.A. Non-Profit Association. "I'm shocked by how we as a society can't provide decent housing for our low income and minority families, especially considering we're going through one of the most prosperous periods in our nation's history. I understand some desperate workers pay $200 per month to rent sleeping space on a living room floor from 11 PM to 6 AM, with no bathroom privileges."

"Yes. Others sleep on buses because they can't find an apartment they can afford. Some crowd into homeless shelters, where up to 20 percent of occupants currently hold full-time jobs,"

Betty responded. "To sum it up, we're experiencing housing problems that require workers to live farther out, double up, rent unimproved garages or spend too much of their take-home pay for a roof over their heads. What can we do to turn this around?"

"Everyone must demand action including citizens, developers, elected officials and state legislators. I thought the RAC meeting on affordable housing went well. RAC members were stunned by the magnitude of the housing problem. How did your summary on affordable housing go when presented to the RC yesterday?"

"Okay, I guess. Based on their facial expressions, some RC members liked it, but I sensed others felt threatened–possibly guilt. Hard to tell," Henry said. "The chair hastened to say that they planned to develop a regionwide housing program and would be convening a Housing Summit soon. I think our program proposing regional education and planning programs hit the mark."

"Yeah, I think your concern that all cities would be hurt economically unless they develop adequate affordable housing raised some eyebrows. Also, your statement that some workers, faced with rent increases of up to $500 a month, just leave the state. There's no doubt that high housing costs are hurting corporate recruiting, while longer commutes adversely affect productivity."

"Right. Well, work calls, Betty. Thanks for your help. We'll see what the Housing Summit produces. We need SCAG leadership on this and RHNA I not just lip service."

* * *

The Affordable Housing (RHNA) process created a real dilemma for SCAG, the subregions and the Community and Human Development Department (HCD). Lack of understanding the housing market and the need to spread affordable housing throughout the region were limiting what could be done. Although SCAG proposed a much more gradual shift toward equalization of the stock of affordable housing units in the region, the unforeseen concentration of growth in the lower cost Inland Empire created an obvious problem and potential law suit.

"To think that SCAG would stupidly develop housing policies creating this situation," Kathleen Dewitt, San Bernardino County supervisor exclaimed. "I'm going to Sacramento to get this straightened out," anger and frustration etching her face.

"I could see this coming over a year ago, ever since the planners decided to implement a program preventing *equitable* regional distribution of affordable housing," Al Deerfield, Executive Director of the Western Riverside Subregion, stated. Al flashed back to events over the past year that chronicled the growing frustrations taking place. The Affordable Housing meetings started taking place in late 1998 but the hearings began in early 2000, bouncing back and forth as city and subregions fought about handling their housing allocations.

Only recently had the Fair Share issue emerged as Al, fed up with the politics of regional housing policy, developed this approach. The price of an affordable house based on income varied by county, ranging from over $170,000 in Orange or Ventura County to $118,000 in the Inland Empire. This forced lower-income households to move to where the most "affordable" housing was, penalizing the Inland Empire the most since the greatest growth had been there.

Other criticism showed that existing RHNA 'Fair Share methodology' would fail to ever reach the regional average distribution of homes. But it could be adjusted to achieve the regional average distribution of housing units in each income category within 25 years–allowing a true shift in the distribution of housing across the region to be achieved quickly.

If a RHNA approach based on both of these factors were adopted, all of the subregions would share equally in the new affordable housing units. Even more important, this would be more in line with the jobs available to these families.

* * *

Several weeks later, the Housing Summit convened at SCAG. Speakers and attendees included elected officials, developers, housing analysts, bankers, state and Federal officials. Henry and Marcine attended, to voice their views. Bea Johnson was also there, representing the Times as a investigative reporter prepared to do a series on regionwide housing problems.

Bea's column later summarized the early December 2000 meeting. "Data presented by SCAG showed the skew toward lower incomes in Southern California, much different from the rest of California. Along with the dominance of low pay jobs in the region, this produced the following policy dilemmas for the region's housing market:

-Almost all current housing production is aimed at higher income households seeking single family homes.

-A growing need to provide workers earning between $35,000 and $50,000 with new affordable housing options.

-Addressing housing needs to low wage and low skilled workers now forced to live in substandard housing or on the street.

-Solving the jobs/housing imbalance through infill, mixed use and multi-family development in job-rich areas."

The Urban Land Institute's Ward Brokaw discussed the barriers and obstacles presented.

-The lack of support for diverse types of housing. In order to resolve housing problems, cities, businesses and the general public must reach consensus on their housing needs.

-For many jurisdictions, zoning codes are obsolete, particularly for infill projects.

-Lenders adept at underwriting infill housing, mixed uses, and other such options, were in short supply.

-Infrastructure improvements–schools, streets, sewers–were needed in the urban core to spur these markets.

-The jobs/housing imbalance must be corrected."

In addition, the building industry representative, Jake Posse, indicated "that construction defect litigation contributed to the lack of multi-family housing construction. Under state law, builders must warrant construction of multi-family units for ten years, substantially adding to insurance premiums, and the overall cost of any given project. Legislation was needed to provide relief to builders from these costs without weakening protections for the consumer." Bea found the findings alarming and planned to focus future columns on the difficulties SCAG and the region faced in resolving this critical problem.

Discussion of the expected loss of up to 150,000 units of Federally-assisted affordable housing followed. The contracts supporting these units were due to expire soon, putting them back on the open market and evicting the current residents for lack of income to pay the higher rents. These mostly involve California's expiring Section 8 rent subsidy contracts.

"What a dilemma. We've got to find some way to protect the people in these Federally-assisted units. Any ideas?" Felix asked.

"Opt-out (or discontinuation) projects are most likely to be in racially and economically integrated neighborhoods, while renewing projects are located in more segregated areas," Henry chimed in. "Also, not all displaced families will be able to get enhanced vouchers from the Feds to help pay part of the rent. This is still iffy."

"We've got to educate them now so they won't fall through the cracks. Officials must assist them to hold onto their lodging. We don't want them forced out by their lack of action," Marcine said.

"Yeah, but those were signed agreements for a specified period of time–usually 20 years– between the developer and the Federal government," Ernie Elsworth, a developer, reminded the group. "Developers took a chance back in 1980 when they built these units. It seems to me, there should be some proposal for creating a new arrangement now. What do you think?" he asked, glancing around at the people assembled.

"Yes, it makes sense," said Ted Jones, a Federal Housing official. "Developers must be approached early by elected officials to work out some arrangement. Many of them may be willing to compromise if it seems in their best interest."

"Good points. Let's work to make it happen, guys," Felix said. "We've got to move along faster due to our full agenda. The next topic involves regulations that delay the development of affordable housing. Any thoughts?"

"Yeah, zoning and general plan requirements often prevent the higher housing densities needed to justify development of new affordable housing," Henry said. "They may also inhibit needed innovations in design. We need to do something about this."

"Another issue is streamlining the review process. It takes 11 months, on average, to approve all the permits for construction and occupancy," Marcine reported.

"Plus there are significant costs beyond construction, such as building permit, school district and processing fees. These need to be reduced when possible," Ted stated. "Another problem is that existing infrastructure's often inadequate for future construction. The community should invest in upgrading the sewer and water infrastructure at no direct cost to the new user."

"Excellent ideas. To cap this off, opportunities exist for housing to be developed through the use of underutilized commercially zoned areas. We also must encourage the development of infill housing and adaptive reuse of buildings," Felix said, looking at the clock. "Let's move on and talk about how to finance infill housing."

"Urban Infill Housing (UIH) is an innovative tool which the Fed's old Section 608 program used to provide housing for returning veterans after World War II," Ted remarked. "The same type of program could be created by FHA with a large revolving insurance fund backed by private enterprise. Only persons needing affordable housing would be eligible for these units."

"Can this be accomplished soon?" Felix asked.

"Congress is expected to approve it early next year," Ted reported.

"This brings up possibilities at the state level," Felix said. "What have you available from the state, Hillary?"

"I've been itching to mention some of the new programs the legislature approved recently," Hillary Jacobs said. "To allow housing subsidies to be put to their highest and best use, we need to prioritize the housing fund to meet the greatest need. We have opportunities to use state subsidies for affordable housing if each city complies with the Regional Housing Needs Assessment (RHNA) and approved housing element approval."

"What programs do you offer?" asked Felix.

"The California Tax Credit Allocation Committee (TCAC) allocates tax credits to affordable housing. Last year, TCAC funded approximately one in five applications for credits, reserving over $95 million in credits for projects around the state. In addition, the California Debt Limit Advisory Committee (CDLAC) awards allocations of tax exempt bond activity to qualified local agencies."

"Any other housing programs coming down the pike?" Marcine asked.

"The legislature created several new housing programs last year, which I'll outline. There's a great opportunity for cities to be rewarded for aggressively addressing housing needs as identified through the regional planning process."

"Excellent. It's lunch time and I'm sure people are hungry. All this is 'good food for thought.' No pun intended," Felix said with a chuckle. "Let's break now, and return later for more discussion after lunch."

When the Summit reconvened, Hillary continued outlining state sources of monies for affordable housing. Other topics were also explored, including jobs/housing balance.

Felix opened that issue by raising the oft-stated belief that job/housing balance won't work since people seem to prefer to live some distance from where they work. "Any thoughts?"

"I think a lot of people would welcome the opportunity to live near work if such improvements as transit, higher density housing, shopping, good schools and recreation were available close by," Henry said. "Many service jobs require workers who need affordable housing. But a balance of good housing for all income groups is needed to make it work."

"Yeah, but there's a big difference between people's ability and desire to live and work in the same area. They often don't seem to coincide," said Marcine.

"If gas prices double and congestion on the streets and in the air gets worse, we could see a change in attitude," Henry observed.

"We also need to provide good jobs to residents. This means job retraining centers and quality education," Marcine offered. "A job retraining center strategically located in the neighborhood would be important."

"All these plus new, adequately subsidized housing programs could provide the housing and neighborhood infrastructure to make it work," Henry added. "For example, if the AB 2048 bill were approved at the state level, I'm sure it would encourage jobs/housing balance."

"What does AB 2048 propose to do?" asked Marcine.

"Its primary objective is to help the balance between jobs and housing by providing a return of more state property tax revenue to cities. It would be done here to develop housing in high-growth urban and older suburban job centers where we currently lack housing for the workforce," Henry replied.

"Can you clarify how it might work for a city?"

"The bill would authorize cities located in metropolitan areas with an imbalance in housing and jobs, to create a housing opportunity district. Once the district has been established, the city would ask the state to refund the city a portion of property tax revenues resulting from increases in assessed value of new home construction within the district."

"That's a great idea. Let's look into it," Polly suggested.

"Any other thoughts before we adjourn?" Felix asked. None were forthcoming.

The first Housing Summit adjourned.

* * *

After the Housing Summit, Henry and Marcine planned to take in the sixth annual Leimert Park Jazz Festival in South Central Los Angeles. They both loved jazz, eagerly anticipated the wide assortment of jazz musicians assembled each year on this occasion. Some 300 artists performed pieces ranging from Ragtime to Dixieland, swing, West Coast, soul, Latin, pop, and contemporary.

They also enjoyed dinner at the adjacent Five Spot Jazz Café. It offered jazz along with a range of appetizing meals. As they entered, they 'dug' the jam session in progress, and were soon seated. Both ordered lobster tails, one of the house specialties.

"Isn't this a neat place?" Henry said, enjoying the flickering candles and colorful table cloths against a backdrop of rustic timbers. "How did you hear about this place, Marce?"

"From friends. It's always been a great place for kicking off your shoes," Marcine said. Their lobster tails arrived and they dug in with gusto. Then they danced and had another margarita before moving on to the Festival in a nearby shopping center plaza. Local radio station KRMG hosted it, and the MC highlighted the various eras and artists as the performers illuminated the greatest pieces of the last 100 years.

"Jazz began in 1906 with Buddy Bolden," the MC began. "It gradually blossomed into an authentic art influenced by a mixture of cultures possible only in America at the beginning of the 20th Century. Called Ragtime and Blues initially, it emerged as Jazz in New Orleans as Creoles and Blacks were forced to play together as second class citizens. They improvised to fill out notes available. As it evolved into 'hot music', it encouraged soloists to improvise and invent blues and swing music."

"Who was your favorite growing up, Marce?"

"I loved Dave Brubeck."

"He was great," Henry agreed, "but Satchmo Armstrong caught my fancy with his music, singing and showboating. Whenever I think of jazz, I think of him."

"As I got into jazz, I discovered Artie Shaw, Benny Goodman and others. Their music will live forever."

"Sure will. Billy Holiday, Duke Ellington and Charlie Parker come to mind too. What great artists."

"So relaxing too. I've forgotten about the housing problems we have. I'm reserving that for tomorrow, not tonight," Marcine said with a satisfied smile. Feeling that the evening had been perfect, they parted at their cars.

* * *

The Construction Industry Group (CIG) and KOPE continued to pressure the legislature to resolve the freeway construction and housing issues fueling continued urban sprawl. They not only went to the legislature directly, but also used the public comment, newspaper, and other opportunities available throughout the state, particularly in Southern California.

Jake Posse worked hard to keep CIG fully engaged in its struggle for more freeways, improved traffic conditions, and building more single family housing in new areas. He asked Lila Moore to meet with him on this. Lila had become a specialist on lobbying at the local and regional levels, and she knew the key deal makers well.

"Lila, how are you coming with your efforts to minimize the extension of low and moderate income apartment agreements in Southern California? Are the developers cooperating to assure a minimum of extensions of these agreements?"

"Yes, we've been quite successful, primarily because city elected officials haven't been doing their homework in providing incentives to developers to extend leases."

"The more we can get these developments to raise their rents to market levels, the more we can expand the market for single family units. It doesn't on the surface seem to make sense but it often works out that way," Jake added.

"Yeah, it's weird but true. More apartment renters with sufficient income reach a fork in the road on housing and decide to enter the market to purchase new single family homes. But this step often isn't taken unless market forces are right."

"Can you continue to force this issue?" Jake asked. "Or do we need to develop new strategies to make it happen?"

"SCAG's Housing Summit may force us to change directions since they've targeted this as a high priority item with their elected officials."

"Okay. Let's develop a public relations program to provide information on why these developments should go private. Can we put something together on this?"

"I think so, Jake," Lila said cautiously. "But first, I need to find out what help I can get from people like Jim Robinson."

"Do it. Don't worry about the cost," he said, pressing the issue. "If you need help, let me know. I can exert some pressure from my side too. We need to push ahead on this as quickly as possible"

"I'll contact Jim and others today about these needs, and see how they can help."

Lila had her marching orders. In recent weeks, her basic outlook had changed. With a substantial increase in pay and new job title, she became a hard core CIG advocate willing to do almost anything to achieve her goals.

She hadn't talked to Jim in several weeks. They were still going through a period of personal assessment as to whether they should enter into a closer and more committed relationship. Her call today would test whether they could get back together. Although she didn't reach Jim at his office, she left a message for him to call as soon as possible.

* * *

Much later that day, Jim did call back.

"Hi, Lila. Good to hear from you. I've wanted to call but felt that we both needed more time and space. What's new with you?"

"Very busy. My role has changed with my promotion to Manager of Consumer Affairs in CIG's Southern California office."

"Congratulations. Does this mean I don't see you as often?" Jim asked.

"No. Just my focus has changed. That's the reason for the call. I need your help."

"Okay, shoot," he said, wondering what she wanted now.

"I need your support for our efforts to increase single family housing development throughout the region. I remember your statement against apartments and higher density housing."

"Yeah, but that doesn't mean that I can convince others. How could I support you?" Jim asked, puzzled.

"I don't know how. You must have some ideas based on your RC role?"

"I'll have to think about it. It's not going to be simple. The region's in a difficult position and there's a lot riding on finding the right solutions," Jim said, a frown creasing his face.

"Well, Jim, I'm depending on you. Can you call back tomorrow morning?"

"No, the best I can do is late tomorrow, Lila. Things are busy around here, and your request will take some time to think through. Is there something you're not telling me that I should know?" he asked, feeling uneasy about her request.

"What do you mean?" she asked, defensively.

"Do I just support you–period. Or do I have to see people, make speeches, go places, whatever? It's never that simple in politics."

"I'm not sure myself," she said, noting a coolness in his voice.

"I can't agree based on a vague request. This is very political," he said with irritation creeping into his voice. "You know that, I'm sure?"

"Yes, I know it wouldn't be easy." Lila said. "It would involve giving CIG help to get more toll roads so additional lower density housing can be built. And we need to sell more single family housing to residents of all income groups."

"Wow! That's a tricky issue. I don't know if I can–or should–get involved. I'll think about it and call you late tomorrow afternoon. Okay, Lila?"

"If that's the best you can do, okay. I'm depending on you, Jim," she said forcefully, as she hung up. Jim sensed that she was out of sorts.

Jim debated with himself on whether to get involved. He previously had probed toll roads and found problems there. How could he reverse himself on this now with his position with the Finance Task Force? He wanted to help Lila but knew this would get him in more trouble. He didn't need that right now. He wasn't sure he should call her back.

* * *

The Keep Our Population Expanding (KOPE) group continued its fight to control housing development, especially in inner city areas–and around the Staples Center. Several non-profits concerned about Environmental Justice came out fighting. Marcine led this fight against KOPE with support from Carla. The Staples Center wanted to displace the renters of the units in the surrounding neighborhood so parking and commercial uses tied to the center's future could be built. Little money would be provided for relocation costs either, aggravating the problem of finding adequate housing nearby. It was the classic problem faced by long-time neighborhood residents who lived in dilapidated housing there and built many memories and close friends. Could KOPE get some concessions from them, or would it have to force them out?

* * *

SCAG saw more of the 15 L.A. councilmen as they sought to keep the city's affordable housing (RHNA) requirements low at the region's expense. This was a fight that would continue for a long time, and other cities in the region would also face this issue. Until resolved, the region's housing problems couldn't be effectively handled. The NIMBY issue would play over and over on this problem alone.

* * *

Political infighting continued. These housing problems wouldn't go away. The Inland Empire counties –Riverside, San Bernardino and Imperial–ratcheted up their battle with the state's HCD. Even SCAG got involved, but felt it should not have responsibility for affordable housing units.

The RC and policy committees devoted a portion of their generally open sessions to closed hearings where all but elected officials and legal counsel were excluded. One of these closed sessions included the following:

Warren, SCAG's legal counsel stated that "some meeting of the minds must take place soon or there would be one or more law suits filed by HCD, SCAG and/or the Inland Empire. No one wants to budge on low cost housing (RHNA)–especially HCD and the Inland Empire. What should we do? Time is running out."

"We won't budge," replied Wally from Western Riverside COG. "As you know, we still continue to have a significant number of foreclosed and vacant units which weren't taken into consideration by HCD or SCAG."

"San Bernardino, Imperial and Coachella Valley COG's are united with Western Riverside on this issue. We would become the low cost housing mecca of the region if we agreed to add this huge number of housing units," stated Jodie from San Bernardino County. "This is ridiculous–67,000 more low cost housing units?"

"Then how are we to resolve this issue if HCD won't reduce our requirements from around 504,000 down to 437,000 or 439,000 units?" asked Warren, the counsel.

"They're got to be reallocated to the rest of the region who should have received larger shares in the first place. L.A. City, particularly, has gotten off easy. Their inner city areas could absorb these units putting their residents closer to their jobs, solving much of the jobs/housing balance problem," said Jodie.

"L.A. City won't agree, just as they won't handle the LAX Airport expansion problem rationally," Wally responded.

"They're going to have to based on their population. Long Beach is doing their part, helping absorb overages for the rest of the Gateway Cities Subregion. They have the second biggest population concentration in the region."

"I live in Los Angeles and I understand your concerns," said Shelly. "Let me talk this over with the mayor to see what can be done. There must be some compromise that we can reach"

"Okay. Otherwise, we sue SCAG unless there is an reallocation of units satisfying HCD."

* * *

Bea, excluded from the meeting, had a lot of second thoughts on all the suits occurring. SCAG had become a party to several legal suits–numbering seven before the smoke cleared. Their budget, to handle the growing legal costs, had to be increased by over one million dollars. Where was all this legal fuss going? The weird part, she felt, was that SCAG became embroiled in issues which they could have avoided with adequate foresight.

At the same time, she thought, they had no guts to pursue issues which would protect their citizens–especially low and moderate income citizens. There would be no legal cost involved by going this route either. She saw another human interest article on this mushrooming problem. She couldn't wait to begin putting it together, to push SCAG to represent all the people.

CHAPTER 16
PROBLEMATIC 2001
REGIONAL PLAN

Preparations for 2001 Regional Transportation Plan (RTP) draft focus on determining gaps and linkage problems when joining together various plan components. Chair of the Subregion Coordinators is concerned about the RTP's relationship to proposed Regional Planning bill being developed in Sacramento. Trips to Sacramento in effort to influence bills needed for RTP and financing.

"You may delay, but time will not."
Benjamin Franklin

"The greatest risk is not taking one."
Anonymous

"We don't learn from history, do we?" Al Deerfield, Executive Director of the Western Riverside COG, bluntly began his address to the CEHD Policy Committee assembled in the San Bernardino Room at SCAG on Thursday, December 14, 2000. "Many of us were here when the 1998 Regional Transportation Plan (RTP) was approved under protest, with promises of a quick revision to address critical issues in 1999. Did we do it?" he gestured emphatically. "No! ... Don't we ever learn? ... I guess not."

"Let me summarize what's happened since. After a six month delay, a series of task forces moved to develop a 1999 revision to the 1998 RTP. It became apparent by early 1999 that a meaningful amendment to the 1998 RTP wasn't feasible as time ran out. However, SCAG felt that the work of the task forces would provide a running start for the 2001 RTP. Almost two years later, we're facing another last minute rush to generate a conforming RTP. Can you believe this?" he asked resignedly. "The incomplete state of the document presented recently illustrates how far we are from a draft

RTP, only a short time before it's to be adopted. This is after the Draft RTP was delayed from an original June 2000 target date," he stated disgustedly.

"There'll be no time for debate or discussion of alternatives! No time to bring new ideas or hybrids into the environmental process! Plus, our elected representatives will be handcuffed by the limited time, requirements of process, and a necessity to adopt a RTP," he emphasized harshly.

"We must ask why this process hasn't been better managed over the past three years? The Regional Transportation Plan is SCAG's largest project and major reason for existence. The importance of the problem and time line for resolution were surely apparent. Yet, the key issues remain open. Task forces have only identified issues and proposed some initial ideas for investigation. The heavy lifting of analysis and decision making remains to be performed," he went on. "Given the time frame, many of the detailed decisions will be made by staff, late at night, working feverishly to create a product to meet Federal requirements. They'll never see the light of committee discussion again. Indeed," he emphasized, "as we saw in 1998, capable, competent staff have now been assigned, and will need to work incredible hours to create a document in the remaining time. Are we to have a repeat of 1998?" he asked, his hands raised high overhead in frustration. "If not, let's roll–and get it done!"

* * *

The subregional coordinators adopted a motion at their July 27 meeting to attempt to have additional information presented on August 3:

"Request that the RTP Decision Document clearly identify strategies to address the issues raised in the Document, and that a detailed schedule of steps, products, and decisions be provided to the TCC at the August meeting. Further, subregional technical involvement in the analytical process in preparing the RTP is essential."

"You can see that this issue hasn't been satisfactorily resolved even though several months have passed. Why have we managed the process of creating the 2001 RTP so badly, and who is in charge of the process?" Mike Nelson, Executive Director asked key Gateway COG members.

"Well, it's clear that no one's in charge of resolving it." one member replied.

"We're getting closer and closer to the moment of truth," Mike said as they puzzled over what the preliminary 2001 RTP held for the Gateway Cities.

"Too close, Mike. We haven't plugged all the holes in it for the Gateway area. The Brownfields, affordable housing and 710 Corridor planning efforts aren't taken care of. And the 13 other subregions have similar problems."

"Yeah," Mike agreed. "I need to talk to the subregion coordinators and Jim Robinson about financing and other problems. I'll see what I can do," Mike said, closing the meeting.

*   *   *

The Transportation Finance Task Force's final meeting on the 2001 RTP took place on March 6, 2001. As Chair, Jim Robinson opened the meeting by outlining the problems of getting bills passed to fund the needed projects over the 2001 to 2025 period. He asked for members' thoughts.

One member responded: "There's a lot of guessing currently going on as to how to produce necessary revenues to achieve needed projects. There's a 'shell game' being played since I don't feel that proposing additional taxes will be bought by the region's cities' and counties' reps."

Another reflected: "There's a feeling the so-called Black Box is being utilized too much when policy makers aren't sure how to show the mechanics of justifying things. In addition, the financial accounts 'are being cooked' too often. How much will the growth of alternative fuel vehicles take away needed tax revenues? Can the region achieve air quality conformity and, if so, how much will personal behaviors need to be modified (9-10 percent of current practices versus up to 55 percent–or more) to achieve those objectives?"

Still another concern: "Roles of COG's and the Transportation Policy Committee (TCC) must be more closely examined. COGs approve projects while TCCs build them. Wordsmithing becomes crucial and, hopefully, isn't an effort to 'cook the books' to achieve conformity. Too often in the past, what's proposed wasn't put together right. I'm not saying there was a conscious effort made to deceive," he quickly added. "But incentives to achieve objectives are desperately needed." He added: "Hybrid vehicles–gas and alternative fuel in combination–are probably what will become popular in the next few years for achieving these objectives."

Everyone was uncertain about whether SCAG's bill, when crafted, would pass in the legislature. Also, whether they should use a regional gas tax approach to generate additional money for regional projects, even though it would require a two-thirds approval by the legislature.

The consultant, Harry, wondered aloud to Jim: "Still more changes in financing proposed. When will it end? I sense SCAG's really in trouble in getting the $25 to $50 billion needed. Fuzzy accounting procedures are being used to make the results look good–even if they're only cosmetic treatment. It's the thing to do in today's world to justify things and prevent red ink.

Putting 'future dollars' in with 'baseline dollars' (dollars actually approved and/or real) is one effort to 'hide' what's being done. But there's lots of other doubtful accounting approaches being used to make things look good."

He thought that they're getting a little desperate to "look good on paper" to achieve the 2001-2025 paper plan–realizing that an entirely new three year cycle (2004 RTP) would be coming up which would allow them to continue to make needed adjustments and get them out of   trouble. Wasn't that the SCAG way? This was one of the consequences of not opening the process to more parties and risking criticism to help make progress. "The greatest risk is not taking one?"

*   *   *

"Jim, we need to take this rough draft of the Regional Transportation Plan (RTP) to Sacramento to see how it relates to Juan's Regional Planning bill that's still in committee," Mike said. "Otherwise, we'll definitely be out-of-step with what's needed. The other subregion coordinators feel a lot of fine-tuning's needed too."

"I agree," Jim replied. "Can we go next week–say Wednesday or Thursday?"

"I'll call to make an appointment–and let you know the day and time."

*   *   *

They arrived in Sacramento late Wednesday afternoon and taxied to their downtown hotel. Plans changed quickly. They originally planned to grab a meal at the hotel and discuss their Thursday agenda over dinner. But, their hotel turned out to be a popular place for old friends. Mike and Jim were checking in when Mike received a big surprise.

"Mike Nelson, Is that you?" an attractive woman, finishing her check-in, called to him across the lobby. As she came toward him, she said, "How are you? It's been a long time."

"Why, Becky Sanchez, I'm fine," Mike responded, completely surprised at her presence. "I haven't seen you since 'DC'. Where have the years gone?"

"They've certainly flown by, Mike. You free this evening? I'm going out to dinner with old friends but would love to have you come along to reminisce about old times?" she said.

"I'll check with my partner here," Mike looking over at Jim. "Jim, this is Becky Sanchez, an old friend from Washington days some 20 years ago. Could we shift our business session to breakfast tomorrow? A lot of time has passed and we need to catch up on things."

"Hi, Becky. Yeah, I bet you've got some reminiscing to do," he said. "Sure, no problem. I'll see you in the morning."

Region Aroused

* * *

Mike flashed back to times in 'DC' some 20 years ago as he prepared for dinner with Becky. He remembered her from his five years in Washington urban affairs work at the U.S. Department of Housing and Urban Development (HUD) when he was fresh out of the University of Texas. He had majored in Government and got this great opportunity for national experience. Those were difficult days in the late '70's'. Carter was President and things were still happening nationally in urban affairs before all the budget cuts dramatically shifted so many activities to the state and local levels–closer to the action.

Becky had worked with him at HUD until a budget cut cost him his job and relocated him to Downey in the L.A. area. She hadn't changed much, still very attractive with her coal black hair and dark brown eyes. He looked forward to some reminiscing over dinner with Becky and her friends.

* * *

Meanwhile, Jim realized he had an opportunity now to see some sights and possibly gamble a little. He was familiar with Sacramento, having lived here for two years while a page in the State Senate. He'd developed some of his political connections while working here in the early 80's. Deeply engrossed in thinking of those times, he heard a familiar cultured female voice call his name, bringing him quickly out of his reverie in the lobby.

"Jim," Bea said, walking up to him. "Imagine meeting you here. I didn't realize you might be in Sacramento this week?"

"Bea, what a pleasant surprise. I'm here on business. Say, it's been awhile since we last went horseback riding, " he said, looking across at her beautiful, smiling face.

"Yes, I've missed riding with you. Hopefully, we can do it again soon. If you're going to be in town overnight, maybe we could have dinner. Are you available?" she asked.

"You bet. I'd planned having dinner with Mike Nelson, but he met a friend from Washington days and–now I'm free as a bird. Could you be ready in two hours?"

"Easily. See you at seven."

* * *

Jim enjoyed seeing Bea dressed up, especially since she'd dropped the dowdy librarian look. When he picked her up in the lobby, she wore a double breasted blue blazer over a light blue tunic sweater accentuating a long gray skirt, with flares. Her brown hair, piled on top, gave her a sophisticated, slightly sexy look. He liked her style, much different from Lila's, but totally suiting her personality.

"Bea. You look great," he said, enjoying the moment

"You say the nicest things, Jim," Bea replied, noting Jim's flattering reaction to her outfit.

"I enjoy dressing up for dinner," she went on. "Thanks for being available on such short notice. Where shall we go?"

"How about Trudy's down the street. It's quite the in-place, according to my legislative sources. We can walk there, if you don't mind," he added.

"Lead on, Sir Gallahad."

Walking to Trudy's, they caught up on the latest political happenings. Trudy's was one of those intimate dining spots made up of a number of small rooms which created a relaxed atmosphere important to any political or social occasion in the way they flowed naturally together–yet were uniquely different. Seated, they ordered drinks and a meal. They had barely begun small talk about their lives when they were loudly interrupted.

"Jim, what are you doing here?" fumed an agitated Lila, who in a loud, accusatory voice, glared down at them. "You told me you were coming to Sacramento for political meetings and didn't have time for fun."

Momentarily caught off-guard, Jim didn't know what to say as Lila stared angrily down at him and Bea. Red-faced and embarrassed, he stumbled to his feet, stammering:

"Lila, how are you? Mike and I planned to talk about our scheduled appointment tomorrow when an old friend he hadn't seen in years popped up, changing our plans. Bea and I just happened to bump into each other here. You've met Bea, the Times reporter, haven't you?" he said, attempting to smooth things over.

"Of course. Bea, you look o-u-t-s-t-a-n-d-i-n-g in that trashy little outfit that you're poured into," she cuttingly remarked, spitefully looking her up and down.

"Lila, stop this nonsense," Bea shot back, realizing too late the touchy situation she was caught in. "I didn't know having dinner with Jim would create such a fuss. I didn't know you two had a relationship. I'll leave if it'll help?"

People at tables around them gapped, enjoying the action. This wasn't unusual in Sacramento where such situations routinely occurred in the political process. Two attractive, well-dressed women willfully eying each other with strong distaste–ready for battle. Obviously, the diners wouldn't trade places with Jim's perilous position between two angry women.

Jim warily surveyed the situation, knowing little could be done unless they backed off.

"Bea, you've said some nasty things about CIG and me. I haven't forgotten what you've written about us," Lila continued.

"Never anything about you. Only that CIG hasn't been forthcoming on ways to house the less fortunate. What's that got to do with you?" Bea stated, getting her ire up.

"Lots. I work for them and feel I must stick up for their interests. All you do is dig up dirt and spread it in the news. I resent that."

"That's not true. I'm tired of your dragging my name through the mud, Lila. So stop!" Bea retorted.

"I won't. Turning to Jim, she said, "You never learn from your mistakes, do you?" She glared daggers at him. "After all my protecting you from the rumors–and continuing to believe in you. You haven't even gotten back to me on what we discussed two days ago. That's gratitude?"

"Lila, watch what you say. This'll be all over the papers and on the news," Jim warned, realizing too late that it wouldn't do any good.

"I don't care. I'll say what I like!" Lila stubbornly glared at Bea, and cattily remarked: "Bea, why are you decked out in that fancy outfit? Are you out to catch a man?"

"You should talk!" Bea said heatedly. "You strut around getting men all worked up," she said, getting more aggravated by the minute.

"What a sex pot you are. Think being a big reporter allows you to grab any man you want. I'm wise to you," Lila said, reaching out at Bea.

"Ladies, Ladies. Let's stop this name-calling," Jim said, trying to keep them away from each other. "If this continues, I'm leaving."

"No. I'm leaving," Bea said, rising from the table. "Lila, don't expect me to apologize to you for any of this," she said, whirling and stalking toward the entrance, asking the doorman to call a taxi.

Lila continued to glare at Jim. "What're you going to do about this mess, lover boy," she screeched, a slur in her voice.

"Lila, sit down and compose yourself," Jim said, desperately hoping she would cool off.

"I will not, Jim Robinson. Who do you think you are–ordering me around? To think we both were going to be in Sacramento on business and you didn't consider contacting or spending some time with me. I guess I know now who my friends are."

"Lila, please sit down so people around us can enjoy their meals," Jim pleaded.

Finally coming to grips with her anger and looking around, Lila realized what a spectacle this had become. She collapsed into a seat across from Jim, befuddled but still defiant.

Noting a slur in her voice and the smell of liquor on her breath, Jim asked her: "Have you been out partying?"

"Yes, I just left a lobbyist party in the next room. Seeing the two of you sitting here, I lost my cool."

"I can understand that. How many drinks have you had?"

"A few–but that's none of your business. I'm upset and won't take an apology from you."

"Why not?" Realizing too late he shouldn't have said it, Jim angrily blurted: "We're not going steady, Lila. Why are you so possessive?"

Lila rose from the table, gave Jim a withering look and stalked off, cursing him.

Jim, left to face the music a second time, quickly summoned the waiter, paid his bill, and walked out.

Other diners turned back to their meals, buzzing about the give and take involving Jim and the two women–ready to spin gossip on the latest Sacramento happening. Since his name had been tossed around, they would learn later about his background–and how his difficulties now included women.

* * *

Jim postponed meeting with Juan to Friday due to the altercation, arranging to see his father, now living in Sacramento in semi-retirement, later that day at his home near the state capitol. He badly needed his advice on how to handle his problems with gambling, debt and women. He'd relied on his father to get him out of trouble before–and desperately needed his help once again.

Jim came from a tradition-laden family which felt public service was honorable and required. His grandfather, Nathaniel Robinson, developed the family credo which declared by word and deed that in pursuing his career, a man's first duty was to secure a fortune and provide for his family. Then, in the spirit of *noblesse oblige*, he later turned to public service. It was a dictum that Daniel Robinson, Jim's father, followed to the letter. It fit both the man and his times.

Not so for Jim. Not having to work for his fortune, he was spoiled rotten. Much had been given him without working for it. Painfully conscious of this, he donated some of his free time to making L.A. a better place to live. Unfortunately, his weaknesses were getting in the way. His explosive temper only made things worse.

* * *

"Dad, how're you feeling?" Jim asked, greeting his father upon entering his fashionable townhome.

204

"As good as can be expected for an old fart. Great to see you, son! You sounded uptight over the phone. What's up?"

Jim recounted the latest of his problems with women to his father, a man wise beyond his years, who'd struggled through the same problems. He also liked to spend all night at cards on the Strip, so he'd faced the same temptations.

"Jim, you've got to get control of yourself. Women and cards are much alike–you get addicted quickly with both while enjoying your fling. You've got to control your inhibitions." Sputtering, he self-consciously added, " I know I shouldn't be preaching something I've difficulty handling myself. But try. Life is a gamble in itself. Is this affecting your job–or political aspirations?" he asked, very concerned.

"Yes, Dad, it could, if things continue the way they have," Jim replied. "Have you heard some of the rumors out about me?"

"A little, since I still visit the clubs where I know many of the legislators–or former legislators. But rumors go with politics. Just don't overdo things," he said. "Say, I heard you're in trouble financially. Is that true?" anxiously looking him over.

"Yes, to a small extent."

"What's 'a small extent'?" his father snorted. " I'd heard the stock market, Vegas, horse racing, even extortion were involved. What's going on?"

"I guess I can't control my gambling urges anymore," Jim confessed. "I'm at wits end on what to do. I've even been advised by a friend that I should get help."

"You know I had that problem some 25 years ago," his father grudgingly admitted. "I finally got help from a group called 'Gamblers Anonymous'."

"I didn't know that," Jim reacted with surprise. "I always thought you and Granddad always knew the right thing to do and were never wrong."

"That's what you wanted to think," his father said with a chuckle. "We did what we felt was the best thing for us at the time–and felt we were never wrong."

"Why am I so arrogant?" Jim asked him for the first time. "Did some of it come from my upbringing?"

"That's the way we raised you, to be above the masses. It turned out to be wrong, plus we spoiled you in the process. Now, it's your job to undue things," his father stated. "I'll help–but it's up to you to accomplish it. You'll make many mistakes in the process, but it can be done."

"You know I want to, Dad. I've become more arrogant in recent years and it's hurting me. First of all, though, I've got to get rid of my passion for gambling," he stated with concern.

"Can you give me a contact at Gamblers Anonymous to get the ball rolling?"

"Of course, right away–but remember, son, it won't be easy. You'll be tempted to fall off the wagon. I know, I've suffered through all that," he said, shaking his head at the memories.

He made several calls to arrange for Jim to get literature and attend meetings of the Gamblers Anonymous organization, as well as providing its Web address and other information.

"What about your women problems, son? I hadn't heard you had troubles with them too," he said in wonder.

"Yeah, women seem to flock to me. Unfortunately, they aren't just women with unimportant jobs. One's a lobbyist with CIG and the other, a TV reporter and news woman. I know what I've done is not politically correct. Now they know about each other and, as you know, women can be vicious when they feel they've been wronged by a man. A triangle to end all triangles in this case. I've really got a tough nut to crack here. Any ideas?" he asked with resignation.

"You're really in trouble now. Gambling problems are easy when compared to women–especially politically inclined women involved with a man of your political aspirations."

"Yeah, I know. Any thoughts?" he asked desperately. This was the longest conversation he'd had with his father in years–and so humbling.

"Whatever you do, don't start telling them lies. They'll both see through that, and then, you'll really be in trouble," his father answered, shuddering.

Jim suddenly noticed that his father was sitting there with a puzzled look on his face. It had come on all of a sudden. What was going on?

"Okay, Dad. I'll try to smooth things over as soon as I can," he said, still looking at his dad. "Dad, are you all right?" he asked anxiously.

"What? Where am I?" his father finally responded. "I guess I wandered off. Jim, are you still here?" his dad asked with a befuddled look on his face. "Don't leave? Please stay awhile?"

"Okay, Dad. I'm concerned about you though. I'll stay overnight."

"Good. We haven't had much of a chance to talk."

Jim looked at his Dad, who seemed to have forgotten what they had been talking about.

He hoped that he wasn't becoming senile. He'd heard recently about how Alzheimer's Disease operated in its gradual penetration of people still in the prime of life. He doubted that was occurring now, but his concern deepened. Maybe he should stay around awhile to see how his father handled himself over the evening.

As the evening progressed, Jim became more apprehensive about his father's actions–normal at times but sluggish and disorganized at other times. As they talked more, he was glad he hadn't discussed the size of his debts with his father. He didn't want to worry his father about his problems. His father was apparently suffering from exhaustion. Upon further observation, he found that he also had problems sleeping, was easily irritated and had difficulty concentrating at times. He must get in touch with his father's doctor soon to have him checked out.

He must also continue to make his Sacramento contacts. With this effort to face his gambling addiction through his father, he felt ready to continue the meeting schedule he and Mike had developed, with Juan Rodriquez first on the list the next day. Then he would see his father's doctor and discuss his health.

* * *

Jim and Mike entered Juan's offices in the Capitol Building for their appointment the next morning. His previous humbling meetings and encounters with Juan weren't completely banished from his mind, but Jim put up a good front.

"Good to see you again," said Juan, shaking hands vigorously as they entered his office. Otto, his assistant, also greeted them. "I appreciate your changing our appointment on such short notice," Jim said. "An emergency that couldn't be anticipated."

"No problem. However, we'll need to move ahead quickly. I had to shift things around. What can I do to help you?" Juan asked quizzically, wondering what Jim was up to. He knew from past experience that he could be quite manipulative.

"Both Mike and I need to be brought up-to-date on your Regional Planning bill and see how its key provisions compare with our Regional Transportation Plan."

"Fine, Otto will brief you. It's been going through some changes as it passes through committee. But I think you'll both be pleased with its continued coverage on alternative plans, toll roads, transit, upgrading key freeways like the 710, 5, 10; regional airports; and other coverage like Environmental Justice. Give them the rundown, Otto."

Otto proceeded to give them, in fifteen minutes, the guts of the regional planning bill. After a few questions were answered, they turned back to Juan.

"Juan, you know we have critical financing needs that our two bills must pass to get through both houses. What's your position on them?" Jim asked.

"We need a strategy to lobby for these bills," Juan said. "The Northern California legislators won't agree to the amount you want unless we do some horse-trading with them. Nothing new. This happens all the time."

"Oh no, Juan, why get involved in this again? What caused all this to happen now?"

"The regional bill of mine–to be passed–must either be reduced in scale and impact, or your bills must receive five billion dollars less which would be shifted to Northern California projects. That's the gist of it," said Juan, looking Jim directly in the eye.

"My God! This will gut our total program, Juan. We'll be out of conformity and the state will end up taking us over. This just can't happen."

"It may be tough in the short term, Jim, but with my regional bill's extra features, you'll finally move away from all this horse-trading in the future. These short-term fixes California legislators get involved in don't work. That's why I've been touting my long range approach all this time with the added features of revenue sharing and other whistles," Juan said.

"I hoped this wouldn't happen. Isn't there some way to compromise?"

"Not this time. We've worked too hard to get this voting coalition together. You need to get away from relying on freeways to bail you out, Jim. Go to in-fill housing, transit stations, increased densities and other smart planning approaches. You'll be better off in the long run."

"I see your mind's made up. We won't take any more of your time," Jim said icily, rising to leave.

"Juan, I agree with you," Mike said, continuing to stay seated. "You understand just what we need to do. I'll stay and get your input on recrafting our bills so we can get them through the legislature." He had an excited look on his face, based on what Juan had just said.

"You mean that you're not backing me, Mike?" Jim reacted vehemently, glaring at his cohort who he'd taken for granted. "I can't believe this. I need your help to work out other ways to increase funding, like toll roads and similar private endeavors."

"No," Mike shouted. "That's where the subregions have decided to draw the line. I'm tired of the political games being played, and the planning process being hurt. Juan's regional planning bill is just what we need. Sorry, Jim, that's the way it is."

"All right, be a turncoat, Mike!" Jim shouted back, as he headed out the door. "I'm leaving. I'll get others to support my bills. You'll regret leaving me in a lurch."

"That took a lot of guts, Mike," Juan said as the door slammed. "He could really hurt you. I sort of expected him to react that way, but hoped you'd have a cooler head."

"Maybe he'll hurt me," Mike replied. "But I think the subregions will back me with the RC and policy committees. It's worth the gamble. Can you help us make the transition?"

"You bet. Otto and Joe know what needs to be done. We've talked about this possibility many times."

"I appreciate this–you don't know how long I've wanted to break the mold that Jim and other RC'ers have kept us in," Mike said, pleased at the prospect. "There's finally hope for regional planning for the L.A. area."

* * *

Jim returned to his hotel, angry about his growing dilemma. Entering his room, he poured a bourbon straight up. He knew he shouldn't be drinking so early, but these setbacks required something bracing. If Lila didn't contact him, he would get in touch with her some other way. Because she'd been a little tipsy, he hoped she'd call to apologize. Bea would be more difficult to assuage since he'd put her in an awkward spot. He needed to work out how to handle Juan and Mike now that he'd decided to go his own way. Also, how to handle his father's lapses. That was scary. He poured another drink. He needed it–and knew he could handle it. No sweat. He knew he would continue to be "King of the World."

Sitting down, he began to recheck his contact notes. He must make additional appointments since Juan put a crimp in his approach on getting support. Chances must be taken to stay afloat.

He planned to call a contact at CIG, realizing he would be in deep trouble if this ploy didn't work. He must get help to block Juan's regional bill in the legislature. With assistance, he felt he could, in turn, marshal the needed support to get his bills passed. A little trading of favors to get what he wanted. He called it "The American Way", or "Politics 101."

* * *

Jim phoned Abe Underhill, Director of Legislative Matters, at CIG.

"Abe, this is Jim Robinson. How are things?"

"Fine. What brings you to our fair city?"

"My annual foray on key legislation, Abe. You can help!"

"I can help kill the regional legislation, if that's what you need," Abe joked. "I'm kidding, of course, since you probably want it passed, don't you?"

"Well, not exactly. What do you have in mind if I help kill it?"

"What? You're against it? I don't believe it," Abe said, completely shocked.

"Can we sit down and work out some way to get my support to help kill the regional bill in return for support of my bill in the legislature? It would protect CIG's ability to guarantee the building of housing as rapidly as they have in the past."

"Maybe," Abe hedged, "We'll need something in return though. A favor for a favor since we never planned on backing your bills either."

"Fair enough. Can we get together this afternoon–say 4:00 PM?"

"If you can make it 4:30, you're on. Afterwards, we can go out for a drink or two. You know that's what a lobbyist is best at," he chuckled. "Just don't try to drink me under the table. You know from experience I've got a wooden leg."

"Yeah, I remember the last time we hoisted a few, Abe," Jim said, wincing at the memory. "Look forward to seeing you at 4:30."

* * *

"I never thought you'd see the light, Jim. I thought that liberal bunch at SCAG had snowed you completely. We can sure use your contacts to ensure California isn't sold down the river land use-wise," Abe said as they conferred in his office.

"It's taken me a long time to realize I didn't want to see Southern California cluttered with high density housing, transit and strict land use controls that take away our freedoms. I just don't believe those people who predict L.A. freeways are going to gridlock."

"Yeah, that crap is used to influence us to sacrifice our freedoms. Local cities have got to be protected. Otherwise, we citizens will lose our identity," Abe said. "That's why CIG wants to   preserve our way of life, and why KOPE has been working so closely with us."

"What does KOPE stand for?" asked Jim.

"'Keep Our Population Expanding.' It's an influential non-profit organization which has a strong base in the legislature. Its director, Judith Struthers, is committed to continued rapid suburban growth."

"Tell me a little more about them and her?" Jim asked, beginning to wonder where all this might lead. He jokingly could have better phrased her approach as a continuation of urban sprawl.

"KOPE was formed when some major corporations realized that the rapid pace of sales of cars, appliances, furniture, housing and other goods linked to population growth was threatened by efforts to increase housing densities and add more growth controls. Judith Struthers is known for her strong support for suburban development, as well as her strong advocacy for new toll roads. She just arrived and wants to meet you."

"I'd like to meet her too," Jim said, warily realizing this had been set up. Abe rose and went to the door. "Judith, come in. Jim wants to meet you."

210

A stern, gray haired woman with piercing, icy green eyes strode into the room. She exuded a strong presence. Quickly looking Jim over, she impatiently stated: "I'm glad you finally saw the light, Jim. Together, we can get a lot done to make sure citizens and local areas continue to support rapid, unimpeded suburban development."

Taken aback by her aggressive nature, Jim responded cautiously. "I agree that much needs to be done. I'm looking forward to learning more about you and your organization, Judith."

"There's no love lost between Juan Rodriguez and me," Judith said, her piercing green eyes riveted on Jim. "He's power hungry and leading California down the path to destruction of our vaulted lifestyle. I'll do anything to thwart his goals. Anything!" she emphasized, reaching for and lighting a cigarette.

"Juan and I don't see eye to eye either, Judith. We've tangled on things which I feel strongly about. I hope you and I can reach agreement on my bills so they can be passed by the legislature?"

"I think we can achieve your goals, but it may require some amendments to your bills to satisfy my backers. Are you prepared to compromise, Jim?" Judith asked searchingly, drawing hard on her cigarette while pacing back and forth.

Taken aback even more by her outspokenness, Jim nevertheless plunged ahead, realizing that he may have sold his soul to the devil by getting in league with her. But he had no choice now. He was already committed. "We should be able to work something out," Jim said. "What areas of compromise do you have in mind?"

"Well, we've got to gut this swing to transit at the expense of new freeways," she urged, lighting another cigarette and inhaling fiercely. "We also need to get a strong private toll road bill passed to open up more of Orange, Ventura, Riverside and San Bernardino counties. Those are givens," she emphasized, flourishing her cigarette.

"I'll have to take your proposals back to the RC and policy committees and see what can be done," Jim said. "Just how do you plan to torpedo Juan's regional planning bill?" he asked nervously.

"Continue our disinformation program to smear his past and totally discredit him," she answered, impatiently blowing smoke into the air. "You'll be privy to our plans as soon as we develop a suitable series of bills to substitute for his bill. Do you feel this is possible, Jim?" she asked with a cold stare.

"Should be," he responded, wishing he were elsewhere, but meeting her eye-to-eye. "I'll go back to L.A. and develop an approach. Have your people give me your requirements so we can move ahead," he added brash-ly. He wasn't happy about all this, not having known about KOPE and their plans. But he played along, keeping his face inscrutable as to his inner feel-ings.

"Okay, Jim. Abe has put together our needs. I have another meeting I must be at. Stay in touch," Judith said, cigarette in hand, quickly shaking his hand and Abe's as she departed on the run.

Jim got her requirements from Abe, thanked him for his efforts and strode out the door, bad feelings swirling around in his head. Lila had warned him about the consequences of getting in bed with CIG. He'd never considered KOPE would be included. Well, he'd burned his bridges with Juan. He must take the plunge regardless of the consequences.

* * *

Several days later, Evon requested a meeting with Juan and his assis-tants. Again, they met after hours in an out-of-the-way location to keep Evon's undercover role secret.

Evon came right to the point. "Jim Robinson has agreed to work to defeat your Regional Planning bill. He's met with both CIG and Judith Struthers of KOPE, and both plan to back his bills in the legislature."

"I'm not surprised," Juan said. "I don't think he realizes what he's sac-rificed though. They'll bleed him a lot of ways. I could have given him more than he will get from them–a better balanced program for example."

"What do we do, Juan?" Otto asked.

"We know things will get bloody now. We need to call Mike in L.A. to see how his bill is coming."

"What about me?" Evon asked. "How can I help?"

"You have an important role to play too. Find out what they plan to do, when and how? If we can find out their plans in advance, we may be able to reduce the impact and discredit the sources through the media. Keep in touch, Evon. You're doing a great job."

"What about you, Juan. Are you being hurt by this?" Evon asked, con-cern in his eyes.

"They're going to try to bleed me dry. We'll just have to keep hoping we can turn it around. It's never been easy for me, as you know. Let's move ahead."

* * *

Meanwhile, Mike notified his Subregion Coordinators in L.A. about the rival bills. They had worked to achieve 2001 RTP objectives with reduced funding and modified their bill so Juan could present it to the legislature in tandem with his Regional Planning bill. So far, Jim hadn't come out against him, although their two strikingly different bills would surface soon for endorsement by the RC. Mike knew Jim would make every effort to discredit him. He didn't think he had anything to hide in his past, but he knew that many things could be twisted to serve another's purpose.

Mike thought back to meeting Becky again after all these years. She came to California on a job with the Federal Highway Administration (FHWA), which she started yesterday. It worked out fortuitously since FHWA monitored the certification process on SCAG scheduled for May 2001. She might be supportive, especially since his bill complied better with Environmental Justice provisions than Jim's.

Mike had taken a big step with his decision to buck Jim. Several times he'd wondered if he'd been right to take this leap of faith. Friends admired his stand and felt he had made the right choice, and most fellow subregion coordinators stood by him. But, he had no idea how the RC would react, since they were unpredictable on controversial issues like this. He knew that Jim had greater recognition as a fellow RC'er than Mike could expect to get as a non-elected official. So Mike planned to equalize things prior to the vote by aligning himself with another important RC member. He would not, however, stoop to spreading rumors about Jim's problems with gambling, debt and women. That wasn't his style.

* * *

Jim's return to L.A. sorely tested him. In too foul a mood to work, he listlessly wandered around his home trying to make sense of his situation. He no longer had Mike's support, neither Lila or Bea had called, and his gambling and debt problems hadn't dissolved. In fact, they continually increased. Not hearing from either woman, he let time take its course with them.

Attending one Gamblers Anonymous meeting, he found its simplistic rules to be boring. Realizing this reaction could be expected, he decided to go slow on trying their approach. Once he got other more important problems resolved, he could pursue it further.

Jim knew he could weather the storm. No matter what others thought, he felt things would work out for him. His current indecisiveness could be attributed to his poor judgment in staying with Juan too long. He would fix him good by helping kill his Regional Planning bill. He couldn't wait to show him how he could one-up him in the political arena. He would gloat on this victory.

CHAPTER 17
TOWARD
ENVIRONMENTAL JUSTICE

*Environmental Justice holds many
definitions for those who struggle to
achieve it. To some, it involves air
quality; to others, noise issues; still
others, neighborhood quality and
toxic soils. Whatever the reason, it's
an important program which the Feds
have added to make sure the funds
passed on are used on an equitable
basis. Gateway Cities looms at the heart
of all this since it holds so many of the
problems tied to Environmental Justice.
Goods movement and port activity are confronted.*

"No one is free when others are oppressed."
Source Unknown

"Don't have them (children) if you don't want to raise them."
Source Unknown

Although Mike had lived in the Downey part of the Gateway Cities Subregion much of his life, he still had problems outlining ways to achieve environmental justice for its people. He had an opportunity to talk about this with Becky Sanchez, of the Southern California office of the Federal Highway Administration (FHWA), who oversaw how SCAG allocated its Federal funds. As they discussed it and other matters in her 30th floor office on Hope Street near City Hall in Downtown L.A. in January 2001, they looked out over a panoramic view of downtown. It was breathtaking, especially with the mountain backdrop visible on this rare smog-free day.

They tried to puzzle out an answer to a nagging question as they savored their coffee.

"Do you want to hear some horror stories about smog's impact on L.A. in the past?" Mike asked. "It took me a long time to come to grips with the

214

reasons why L.A. had such a problem in handling its poor and minority populations. The issue of air pollution provides a particularly vivid horror story," he said, clenching his hands tightly as he recalled its unfortunate history.

"Please do, Mike. I always enjoy learning more about the L.A. area," replied Becky.

"In late July 1943, halfway through World War II, a brown cloud formed over L.A., reducing visibility to a three block area. It caused people to cough, sneeze and complain of severe eye irritation. A gas plant thought to be the cause closed but the attacks persisted. Finally, a commission was formed to study the problem. Although reduced in severity, the smog problem remained."

Mike continued: "Finally, in 1947, the State legislature created the L.A. County Air Pollution Control District. In October 1954, L.A. was hit by another massive smog attack, worse than the one in 1943. Planes had to be diverted from the airport; children stayed home from school. Citizens vented their outrage in demonstrations. But when they discovered two-thirds of smog was caused by the automobile, combined with L.A.'s unique atmospheric conditions, public protests died down almost overnight."

"That's weird, Mike!" Becky replied. "People really are tied to their cars. Of course, if you look at the racial situation, that too is difficult to fathom. L.A. struggled with black migration over the 1940-65 period, along with school desegregation in 1963 and 1976. But the Watts Riots of 1965 and civil unrest of 1992 have continued this struggle to cope with minorities."

"You're right, Becky. Plus add the struggles over density and rapid transit by MTA over the years since World War II. This creates another dimension to historical influences on the way Environmental Justice is perceived today. No wonder L.A. and the larger region continue to have difficulty coming to grips with it. It's so completely built into the system."

"These are only a few examples of why Environmental Justice problems continue to dog the area. They are complex, and they mean different things to each person based on their own historical perspectives. How do we handle it effectively?" Mike concluded quizzically.

"It's sure tricky to administer," admitted Becky. "However, if we don't act effectively to resolve it, the poor and minority population will continue to get unfair and unequal treatment when Federal projects are developed in the region. That's just the way people are. Those in the know and the right positions get preferential treatment. It doesn't matter whether the poor and minorities need it more. They aren't on the radar screen when certain projects are considered because they don't have political clout."

As they continued talking in her office, they considered ways in which Gateway Cities and other subregions could participate equally in splitting the funds for transportation projects.

"Environmental Justice must be geared more to the needs of subregions and neighborhoods if it's to achieve the goals of the oppressed. We need to cite its goals and objectives, and develop the programs needed to carry them out," Becky explained.

"You're right," Mike responded heatedly. " I think they'll be demonstrated at the meeting tonight. Can you be ready by 7:00 P.M. to go to the Gateway Cities Environmental Justice Workshop scheduled at the Focus of God Church in South Central? Marcine and Sharon are putting it on in one of their grass roots workshop locations. Should be interesting."

"I'll be there even if I have to adjust my schedule," Becky said. "Wouldn't miss it for the world!"

* * *

Marcine arrived at the old church early to check out the visual-aid equipment she brought to show her Power Point presentation. This historic facility (circa 1900) had survived through several demographic shifts in race and income levels with the outward movement of L.A. Now, it was an architectural gem located in the heart of what looked like a run-down industrial area.

Marcine was excited about the opportunity to open up South Central and the Gateway area to improvements possible through Environmental Justice requirements applied to local neighborhoods and subregions. Both she and Sharon relished the challenge to introduce SCAG's regional process to their grass roots populace for the first time.

As Marcine continued her set-up, she thought back over the turf involved. South Central Concerned Citizens (SCCCLA) or C-LA, had a history of improving lives. As a non-profit 501(c)3 public benefit community-based organization originally formed in 1985 to fight the development of a mass waste incinerator, it won that battle and then turned its attention to other issues. Today, it continues to operate effectively.

Sharon arrived and helped Marcine finish setting up their presentation as early arrivers straggled in. They hoped to draw possibly 30 to 50 people to the workshop. Noticing Mike and Becky in the crowd, they caught their eye. The meeting room was old with rickety, uncomfortable chairs arranged in rows with a raised platform for the speakers. Although it was difficult to set up, they were happy to have such a facility available.

It looked like they were going to get a good crowd. Counting the crowd at five minutes to starting time, they estimated about 100 in attendance—with more still arriving. Mostly Blacks, with a few Latinos and whites, they were generally in their forties and fifties, evenly split male and female. It looked like a good cross section of the area. Outreach crowds of this number were unheard of, especially for early January 2001. Their word of mouth advertising through the churches and clubs seemed to have done the job.

Marcine ascending to the podium quickly to open the meeting.

"I'm Marcine Simpson, representing the Regional Advisory Council and SCAG. Welcome to this, our first Outreach session in South Central L.A. to get your thoughts on the Regional Transportation Plan. Our focus tonight is not on the preliminary plan itself, but on how Environmental Justice would be affected, especially along the 710 Freeway Corridor. This corridor is planned to be upgraded over the next few years."

"You're probably wondering what Environmental Justice is and how it will help you? I'll say a few words about it and then we'll open this meeting up to questions and your thoughts on how to ensure that you're all receiving the same treatment as those in higher income neighborhoods in other parts of L.A. and the region."

"First of all, what is Environmental Justice? To start things off, I'm going to give you some general definitions. If you want to improve on the definitions, please give us your ideas as the workshop moves along. Looking at the following charts, let me list the three fundamental principles of Environmental Justice considered most important by the U.S. Department of Transportation (USDOT).

No. 1: Minimize high and adverse health and environmental effects—including social and economic—on minority and low income folks like you,

No. 2: Full and fair involvement by all affected communities in the transportation decision-making.

No. 3: Prevent delays of any type in transportation benefits to any minority and low-income person."

"With that, I'd like to throw the meeting open to your comments and questions. We'll see how the discussion goes," Marcine said, ready for questions.

The questions came quickly as hands shot up around the room where some 120 people of all colors were now represented.

"Our community has suffered from decades of insensitive planning, poor environmental policy, inadequate city services and lack of affordable housing and economic development. What will this Environmental Justice program do to make others realize that our families' needs are no different than any other community's?" asked a middle-aged Black woman named Janice.

"A good question. You obviously have doubts about this program after getting promises instead of action for years. All I can say is the Federal government is now more closely watching how funds are being passed back to you. If they discover–or you claim successfully–that you aren't getting equitable treatment, then they'll find SCAG out of compliance with Federal guidelines, withdraw the funds involved, and cut off future funding of any sort until SCAG complies."

"I've heard that before. So easy to say, but they're in Washington and we're here. How're they going to monitor this? SCAG leaders failed before," stated Alex, an older, skeptical white.

"They have a representative from FHWA who has an office here in L.A. They check on fund disbursements and are available to receive complaints from people like you," Marcine replied.

"If we live under the LAX approaches and are subjected to too much noise–or have toxic soils which haven't been cleaned up, would Environmental Justice apply here?" asked Janeen, a tiny, dynamic Latino woman.

"Definitely. Also remember you have the South Central Concerned Citizens as a watch dog for programs like this. Keep in touch with them about any complaints you might have," replied Sharon.

"It doesn't seem like people living in poverty receive their fair share of transportation system benefits. Is this true?" asked Jackson.

"That's definitely true," Marcine replied. "Individuals living in poverty in Southern California represents 13 percent of the population, but according to SCAG, they receive only 4.5 percent of the benefits of the transportation system. To successfully get to work, people need better transit service. SCAG now recognizes the problem of inequitable transportation services, and is trying to improve the situation by upgrading bus service and funding transit alternatives, such as shuttles."

"We should have reasonable access to the basic needs of life, but we don't," added a middle-aged Hispanic man. "Why aren't we receiving these basic needs?"

"Low income and minority communities often don't have adequate access to jobs, loved ones, doctors, food stores, churches, parks, schools and other basic needs of life that many others take for granted," replied Sharon. "This needs to change by improving transportation, planning and the way our neighborhoods are developed and maintained," Marcine added.

218

Other similar questions were asked as the discussion continued. At its conclusion about two hours later, Marcine made plans for future workshops based on this very successful experience with enthusiastic audience participation.

* * *

SCAG's Goods Movement Task Force had met monthly at SCAG since it began in 1995. Its purpose is to establish workable transportation, infrastructure, land use and air quality policies for the region. Freight has become an increasingly critical part of the region's economy. It is even more important for the L.A. Region than many others because of the two major seaports and the need for major trucking routes to deliver and ship goods to and from the ports. In addition, goods movement involves the railroads, airports, trucking, and the sprawling freeway system. But all these systems were having difficulty in moving needed goods quickly to sustain the region's industries.

The committee's purpose focused on guarantees for maintaining and enhancing the region's competitive advantage in international trade. Truckers attending a recent Goods Movement Task Force meeting at SCAG illustrated the difficulty of achieving this. Their plight and importance were covered in their testimony as the first expert witness stepped to the podium:

"My name is Randall Pinkston and I've been a truck driver for 20 years, the last five on my own. I drive over 100,000 miles every year, serving cities from coast-to-coast, operating an 18-wheeler weighing around 90,000 pounds and costing over $100,000 new. My wages average about $40,000 per year after expenses. This makes me part of one of the lowest paying occupations in the U.S., although I average over 40 hours on the job per week."

"Randall, thanks for coming to give us an idea of how it is being a trucker. I didn't realize your wages were so small. How do you make ends meet?" asked Lori Petersen, the Chair.

"It's not easy. The tough part is that I don't get fringe benefits or retirement. I still have to pay medical costs, for example, for my family out of pocket."

"Wow! You guys really are underpaid. Are high truck fees and taxes part of your problem?" she asked.

"Yeah, we pay out an average of $14,000 a year in taxes and fees per truck. If you plan to add more taxes or require additional environmental equipment, you'll price us out of business."

"What about the L.A. freeways? Do you find them in good condition?"

"No. California freeways have the third worst patches of asphalt in the nation. Southern California's are the worst. I hate to handle orders in this area. That's one reason why I'm here today–to get some changes made soon. Hope you can help?"

"That's our objective. Get changes made. What about traffic in L.A. for trucking?"

'Traffic is horrible," he said. "I dropped off a load of luggage containers at LAX on the way home to Sacramento last week. You've got to be careful what time you go in and out of LAX or you'll be stuck."

"We've heard that California drivers are bad. Is that true?" the chair continued.

"Definitely. We cuss out drivers who cut us off all the time while chatting it up that 'we need to teach these four-wheelers how to drive.' California and Georgia head the list of the nation's worst drivers."

"What about the 18 wheeler drivers? Aren't they a problem too?"

"You bet," Randall replied. "We have drivers operating on drugs, deprived of sleep, and angry at the world. We're trying to weed out the bad ones–but it's not easy."

"What can be done to improve driving conditions for both truckers and the general public?"

"Improving the freeways would help a lot," Randall said. "Did you know that California highways are rated third worst by truckers–based on a recent national survey? More truck lanes would also help–especially on the freeways 5 and 10 –as long as truckers don't end up paying for them. I feel we're being unnecessarily penalized for congestion."

"Thanks for appearing today, Randall," the Chair concluded. "We're trying to make it easier for truckers and others delivering goods to accomplish this quickly, safely and profitably."

Other witnesses also testified as the Task Force moved on to other topics. Reports were made on railroads, intermodal terminals, trucks, airports and marine ports.

Many blue-collar cities south and east of downtown in Gateway Cities, according to one witness, are defined by the tracks that crisscross their neighborhoods, bisect residential streets, and paralyze traffic. The soundtrack for residents day and night are the trains' whistles, wheels rumbling and boxcar shudders. Rail traffic between the ports and downtown has increased 56 percent since 1989.

The witness, Larry, continued: "Livability in these areas will improve as a number of construction projects are completed. The Alameda Corridor will create a single high-speed corridor to replace four train lines that now carry about 30 trains a day–up to 8,000 feet in length–through six cities. By 2020, the corridor is expected to have 100 trains a day traversing it without obstructing street traffic. In addition, the proposed Alameda Corridor East area in the adjoining San Gabriel Valley subregion will eliminate train blockages at more than 50 rail crossings through construction of rail overpasses. These improvements will help deliver goods on time."

"What's being done to prevent gridlock from occurring?" the Chair asked.

"Much needs to be done to prevent total gridlock between the Los Angeles and Long Beach ports. These are the two busiest ports in the nation, and they tie in by freeway and rail to the rail yards near downtown Los Angeles. They did an estimated $300 billion in waterborne commerce in 2000–seven percent of U.S. gross national product. All sorts of efforts are underway to eliminate shipping empty containers, spread trucking schedules around the clock to utilize freeways and rail lines during slow periods of the day and night, and find other ways to reduce congestion. These containers are called TEU's (20 foot Equivalent Units) which if lined up would extend past the Grapevine in 2000 and all the way to San Francisco by 2020. Put another way, port-created truck traffic grew from 3 million trips in 1990 to 8.2 million in 1999, with a projected 24 million trips by 2020."

Larry continued: "Gridlock by growth of trucking serving the ports can be postponed with the Alameda Corridor's completion in 2002 and handling port traffic growth up to 2010. Freeway 710 upgrading will not be completed for at least ten years. Truck traffic was 36,300 TEU's of goods per day in 2000 and at least 65,000 TEU's by 2020."

* * *

"I've been concerned for a long time about the widening income gap between people," Boris said. "We used to have a big middle class but its declining rapidly. Increasingly, the wealthy virtually ignore the opinions of 'all others.' The 'have's' versus the 'have-nots'. The recent presidential elections demonstrated the power of unlimited soft money by rich and powerful corporations and individuals to buy elections and make sure once a person is in power, he or she gets preferential treatment for their programs and stays in power. Where will it all end?"

"You know, guys, all our talk has helped me crystalize an article that needs to be written to galvanize SCAG and the RC into action. I believe we've reached our worst crisis ever by a lot. Think about the impact of all these things. Struggles internally in 1998 and 2001 to get needed monies to carry out RTPs. Selling out to L.A. City and freeway enthusiasts at the expense of poor and minorities to make up the difference. Black Box problems–justifying things through model tinkering to justify plans. One example is not correcting for truck volume increases in models.

"Also, the models being used emphasize new growth–not infill. No alternative scenarios, although they're now talking about them. LAX expansion at the expense of surrounding neighborhoods and a balanced regional airport system. MAGLEV needs adjustments for speed. Emphasizing more mass transit development by MTA. Pushing this social conscience issue will help turn this around. It will also help to get the region into compliance. Do you think that's enough issues?"

"Terrific, Bea. That ought'a get their attention. You should devote a series to this. There's so much there for people to digest."

"Good point, Boris. I'll do it. Hope I can sell my boss on getting some front page coverage. Thanks for your ideas."

* * *

Bea pursued the series on this major crisis and got support from top management. Front page in the "Column One" location for five days. She was excited by the opportunity and wrote some great columns. One began:

SELLING OUT TO L.A. CITY AND FREEWAY
SUPPORTERS AGAINST POOR

Others focused on:

LAX EXPANSION AT EXPENSE OF
SURROUNDING NEIGHBORHOODS

BLACK BOX PROBLEMS AND MODEL
MANIPULATION AT SCAG

GROWTH VERSUS INFILL AS
SCAG PLANNING STRATEGIES

SCAG'S LACK OF COMMITMENT TO TRANSIT

Upon reading them during one of his weekly trips to L.A., Juan wanted to use some of the ideas in one of his speeches to a community group. After the speech, he talked with several members of the L.A. council.

"Were you upset by my use of the Times series in my speech," he asked Councilman Blumen?

"Yes. I thought it was completely out of line, Speaker."

"But it's true, isn't it?"

"Well–yes. But we are the central city and should get special treatment. Don't you agree?"

"No, I'm don't. I think it's way past time the City should realize that each integral part or subregion is equally important. Then, Councilman, L.A. will take off again–not fragment like it is currently," Juan exclaimed. "All of you need to realize this. Other major cities and metro regions have worked out a means of working together. Why can't you?"

"That's ridiculous, Mr. Speaker. The other parts of the region must follow the lead of L.A. if the area is to prosper. That's why SCAG gives us what we want. It's been true in the past and continues today. We have the leaders who count. L.A. City must receive special treatment or the region will fall apart. Just wait and see," the Councilman said vehemently, staring daggers at the speaker.

"You live in a fairy land, Councilman. No wonder the San Fernando Valley, San Pedro and North Hollywood want to go their own way. Wake up before it's too late," Juan exclaimed, turning away and striding toward the door.

The council representatives were stunned. No one had dared to treat them this way before. They had always been treated with reverence–or at least tactfully. Could he be right in his assessment? Had times changed as he said?

* * *

The March 2001 meeting of the Growth Visioning Sub-Committee continued to expose issues which needed to be aired. Included were 12 principles which had been hammered out to make Growth Visioning work. In addition, a presentation of "Sprawl Hits the Wall" by the Southern California Studies Center provided other thoughts on how Growth Visioning might be achieved. A series of needs were expressed: 1) social and economic consequences; 2) land and natural consequences; and 3) governance and fiscal consequences. Programs needed to resolve these consequences were also recommended.

Things began to coalesce with this meeting. Members began to get excited about the possibilities.

The chair, Mary stated: "The social and economic consequences of continuing the way things seem to be going are frightening. Regional job growth has concentrated in selected high-paying and low-paying sectors of the economy, creating a schism between the have's and have-nots. Even worse, job growth hasn't occurred in the same places as population growth. So, transportation infrastructure is becoming more crowded."

Wilbur jumped in: "Other factors concerning income and poverty make it still worse. Household income stagnated during the recession of the early 1990s, and poverty rates have continued to rise since the recession ended.

Frank W. Osgood

The growing income gap relates directly to race and ethnicity, as well as geography. In addition, the population of working poor residents is growing, and it's distributed across a large area of older communities. Compounding the problem, housing prices across the region are high compared to household income, and housing construction, especially multifamily construction, has declined dramatically. Metropolitan Los Angeles has many indicators of housing stress, including high rates of overcrowding and an affordability crisis. This is accentuated by the concentration of dollars of direct federal low-income housing assistance in the region's older communities of L.A. and Orange Counties as well as distressed outlying communities such as those in San Bernardino County."

"The educational system is also declining, with most public school students poor, Black and Latino, often with limited English proficiency," Sophia added. "Black and Latino students are concentrated in older, poorer areas of the region, even though the percentage of Latino students in some outlying areas is also expanding rapidly. And it's getting harder to create equal schools. School districts in older, poorer areas aren't receiving state school construction money equivalent to need. Finally, the pattern of school test scores corresponds with the general pattern of incomes with the region, often resulting in stark differences between adjacent school districts."

"When focusing on land and natural resources, the L.A. area consumes far more than its share of natural resources in order to sustain itself each day," Javier chimed in. " The region has consumed most of the raw land resources available for urban growth and is now running into severe environmental constraints. It's also facing constraints on other resources needed for future urban growth, especially water. In addition, residents of all income groups are at risk from natural hazards because of the spatial pattern of development. Air and water pollution also have differing but important spatial impacts on the region's public health. The L.A. area's pollution patterns place the young and poor at risk far more often than other residents."

"Proposition 13 and its spinoffs have dramatically altered the way local governments in the L.A. area pay for public services," Mary interjected. "In addition, the state's system of incorporations, 'contract cities,' and tax revenue distribution has created a pattern of fiscal inequity among local governments. The state's incorporation law has also created more small, affluent, Anglo cities throughout the region. To make things worse, many of the poorest cities in the region receive only a trickle of federal funds. The most disturbing finding was that older communities in the region's core are subsidizing the creation of newly developing suburbs on the metropolitan fringe through this perverse system."

All this evidence stunned the elected officials on the Growth Visioning committee. They only now began to realize they were part of the problem and their communities generally were taking advantage of other struggling portions of their huge region. They could now see, more than ever, the need for a comprehensive approach to guiding the growth of the region–with all portions sharing in the planning efforts.

* * *

"We've got to make Environmental Justice work, not on paper, but in the neighborhoods," Mike exclaimed to Marcine as they sat eating lunch at Gallaghers, a little eating place near the Gateway Cities office. "Any ideas!"

"I think your conversations with Becky should help, Mike. She's closest to the Conformity Committee which will be arriving in May 2001 to review SCAG's operations."

"Yeah, I know. But I'm thinking about strong evidence which can't be refuted. What can we put together which will 'knock their socks off'?"

"Good point. I'll work on it. We should have no problem on this since things haven't changed that much."

"Great. Make sure it can't be shrugged off–or discounted in some way. It's got to be definite proof in black and white, with strong witnesses."

* * *

Mike decided that the example of lack of Environmental Justice which took so long to be acknowledged was the 100-acre Brownfields site at Firestone and Atlantic in the Gateway Cities Subregion. It had everything imaginable wrong with it. It was bisected by the decaying 710 Freeway and flood-prone, concrete encased Los Angeles River. The 710 Freeway's heavy truck traffic had the highest toxins in the L.A. area, and it demonstrably polluted the surrounding neighborhood of poor single-family homes. Since it was one of the worst Brownfields sites, this meant that the soil was totally saturated with the worst industrial chemicals and other wastes. Add to this, the high noise factor and nauseous odors radiating from the site. In addition, visual pollution was extremely high, and the street system and condition of structures was among the worst imaginable. To cap it all off, efforts had been made at one time to build a new school on part of the site without taking care of the soil pollution. Plus, no parks were included and the encasement of the L.A. River made recreation impossible along the banks. How all this was allowed to continue over the years is disgusting, to say the least. There are many other examples of gross Environmental Justice pollution in the region, but Mike knew this had to be one of the worst.

Part Four

April–September 2001

CHAPTER 18
SUBREGIONAL
COOPERATION

*Coalition building, the key to achieving
effective change in the L.A. Region, came
through bills passed in the state legislature.
Beginning efforts are made regionally in such
areas as affordable housing, airports, and
transit to achieve needed change.
Increased efforts are made by subregions to
work together to get key programs through
which are mutually advantageous to those
cooperating in a joint effort. This was especially
true for those in the inner city and older
suburbs–even sometimes L.A. City. Continuation
of this trend is important to the entire region's
future development.*

"The first (lesson) is the choice of political
arena: the state legislature. Many Americans
do not fully understand that how local governments
are organized and what they are empowered to
do is determined by state legislatures."
David Rusk, Metropolitics (Foreword)

"A number of subregions are working together to get key legislation
passed–river conservancy, housing and even regional airports," Henry
said, talking with Carla and Mike over coffee in her office while glancing around at her memorabilia and pictures on her wall. "Could this be
considered coalition building? If so, shouldn't we do more of it?"
Looking at the calendar, he said: " I can't believe it's already May
2001."

"Yeah, time flies when you're busy. I'd say yes to both questions," Carla responded, glancing at Mike and all the work to do in her 'in' box. "I think coalitions encourage groups to work together that wouldn't ordinarily want to cooperate. We've got to encourage this give-and-take if we're going to create effective change in our cities and region. David Rusk said: 'Coalitions are held together by underlying social, economic, or political self-interest.' I really believe that. Don't you, Mike?"

"You bet. One example involves the river conservancy which brings together Gateway Cities, San Gabriel Valley and Orange County. Los Angeles City should have been included to encourage a multi-county riverfront park system which could help shape future regional growth."

"We need to figure out how to develop coalitions that include L.A. if we're ever going to break through with them, Henry. I guess the central city's always going to want to be the big cheese. We've got to figure out how to live with them without giving up the farm–so to speak"

"Any ideas, Carla?"

"I think we can come up with some coalition possibilities that will help both parties equally. One might be to develop affordable housing foundations together, since all cities need to provide a balance in housing to protect their economies. There are other ways to develop coalitions, whether it's in promoting regional airports, transit, balanced taxes, or greater fiscal prudence," Carla said, reflecting on some of her city's problems and how Compton and Los Angeles might work together. "Coalition building won't be easy though. We'll all have to do a better job of working together to make it happen."

"You're absolutely right. By the way, Carla, are you ready for the May MPO Recertification process?"

"It's fitting together–finally. I've got my complaints ready for the crucial series of meetings at SCAG on their 2001 RTP." These meetings permit the public, citizen groups and others to voice their concerns with the Federal reps.

"How's your regional planning finance bill coming, Mike? Do you think you'll be successful?" Carla asked.

"I think we're in great shape for presentation to the TCC Policy Committee and RC on April 5th. I don't know how Jim's doing on his version though."

"These meetings should prove v - e - r - y interesting. The L.A. Region will never be the same again. Henry, do you agree?"

"You've got that right."

* * *

227

"Just think what's happening, Becky," said Mike. "A coalition of sub-regions thwarting the continuation of LAX as the dominant and only regional airport for the L.A. Region. Who would have believed that the Inland Empire subregions and Gateway Cities could be helping pull off the approval of El Toro and Ontario as the additional regional airports for the region."

"It's amazing all right. Leadership has come forth on this. I think it's going to have even a greater impact. The City of L.A. no longer will have the dominance it's had. It will still be important but more like the other sub-regions. If it's going to exert continued influence, it will be through coali-tions. That's a great step forward."

This was a key happening at the April 2001 TCC Policy Committee meeting when the regional airport plan was finally approved after a tumul-tuous session lasting four hours.

* * *

Gateway Cities, in close cooperation with Caltrans, MTA and SCAG, finally got its 710 Freeway upgrading project moving ahead in April 2001. It had been a tremendous undertaking over two years. One of several multi-jurisdictional public projects which will slow movement of traffic during construction in the Gateway Subregion for a decade, it would cost $3 bil-lion to renovate the vital, aging highway corridor that will ultimately achieve freer flow of vehicles. Strategic objectives cited for the corridor included: enhance economic performance; reduce toxic diesel emissions, reduce freeway congestion and freight impacts on communities; build sus-tainable, more livable cities; and improve safety. This will make all 27 cities much more livable over the next ten years. The redesign and con-struction of the various interchanges and surrounding uses would virtually remake the Gateway Subregion. But Gateway would be torn up for quite some time as a result–probably until at least 2010.

* * *

Mike continued to grapple with SCAG transportation financing for the 2001 RTP. He knew Jim faced considerable problems in developing his version focused on freeways, with more limited funding for transit. Mike felt that a combination of bus, light rail and other forms of mass transit, along with emphasis on alternative fuel vehicles, and reduced environ-mental impacts of dirty diesel trucking were key to achieving the clean air goals needed by SCAG to meet federal requirements.

He met with SCAG's legislative analyst, Mort Jameson, Betsy and her FHWA assistants, and key RC members he needed on his side. He hadn't talked with Juan again or even considered contacting Jim to see when his version would be completed. He decided to wait and see what happened, ready to pounce at the right time when he knew what Jim planned. Mort Jameson did sketch out what Jim would propose, based on a meeting with him at SCAG, but things could change quickly, as they generally did in politics. He still didn't believe Jim would come out with an extreme approach, knowing he had to get approval of the RC and others.

* * *

Both Mike's and Jim's preliminary transportation financing bills were first on the agenda at the April meeting of the TCC Policy Committee. As expected, Mike's focused on transit extensions to achieve clear air goals, while limiting freeway improvements, street and freeway upgradings, and modernization. On the other hand, Jim's approach emphasized new and extended freeways that would encourage more sprawl; it included only limited transit improvements, similar to those in past RTP's. Jim cast his proposal as a combination of public/private cooperation efforts, using toll roads to stretch limited public revenues, even though he'd originally been against toll roads during the fiasco with them in late 1999.

TCC Committee reactions were more favorably disposed toward Mike's plan due to the clean air concerns, which Jim's proposal did not address. After a great deal of discussion, however, enough concerns existed about both bills that a final decision was put off until April 12. Obviously, a combination of the two bills would finally be necessary, but the striking differences between the two made it difficult to cobble together such a bill. Some behind-the-scenes maneuvering between Jim and Mike would be required.

Jim and Mike met afterwards to begin work on some sort of compromise.

"Jim," Mike asked, "do you have any way to modify either bill so TCC can present a joint bill to the RC?"

"Take away some transit money, especially to the South Bay and East Side, Mike. Then add two freeways to the east and south suburbs," Jim replied angrily. Haggard, with dark patches under his eyes and despair on his face, he looked like he hadn't slept for a week. "We've got to dramatically reduce congestion in the suburbs and serve the people who pay the taxes."

"That defeats the entire 2001 RTP program which will reduce the clean air problems and serve all of the region's population," Mike said with concern.

"I'm not going to back down from my position because it's right! Those who pay the most taxes must be served. It just makes sense," Jim replied vehemently.

"But if we do this, we'll end up out of conformity with the Feds. We can't afford this. We'll end up losing a major portion of our Federal allocation through TEA-21, Jim."

"That's not true! There's always a way where SCAG can, through its Black Box, make it work. They've done it before and they'll do it again," Jim answered dogmatically.

"The Feds are getting wise to how the Black Box works. They're going to require a complete reading on what's in the Black Box in 2004, which means that we've got to make sure we're not setting ourselves up for a fall in 2001," Mike shot back. "I can see we're not getting anywhere. If you'd indicate some areas where you'd compromise, I'd be willing to do the same."

"Sorry, Mike. That's the way it is. Consider the changes you must make and let me know next week. You're the one who's got to compromise." With that, Jim stalked out.

"Same old Jim," Mike said under his breath as he left to meet Betsy.

* * *

Gateway Cities continued to work toward meeting their many needs. However, this proved increasingly difficult. Both MTA's 2001 Transportation Plan and SCAG's 2001 RTP were scheduled to be adopted in April, and considerable disparity still existed between them. Mike Nelson, Carla Hawks and Gavin O'Neil of the Gateway group were meeting to determine how best to get SCAG, MTA and SCAQMD to come through for a subregion so desperately in need of improvement.

"We've worked to get as much as possible through Juan Rodriguez at the state level. Now we've got to focus at the regional level," said Mike.

"It's going to be tough, guys. They're going to say that we've got big improvement projects going for the 710 Freeway and I-5. Big bucks in the millions over ten to twenty years. What more do we want?" exclaimed Carla. "It's good in one way, but what a mess we'll have fighting through all the construction problems over this time period."

"Beglory, 'tis going to be a mess all right," Gavin said in dismay as he nervously broke into his brogue. "And the toxic soils issue with brownfields and the clean air problems from industrial and diesel fumes in neighborhoods along the 710 Corridor. Tis the price of progress. Every neighborhood torn up for years. Can we handle this?" he continued.

"We've got to," Mike responded. "And these improvements are only a small part of what needs to be done. Do you think the Gateway Partnership can handle the toxic soils and air pollution controversies, Gavin?"

"We must get through it by hook or crook, Mike. It reminds me of the

Belfast bombings at times, methinks. But the construction upheaval may improve things a wee bit better each year. Much better over time, not like the Belfast bombings."

"You're right, Gavin," remarked Carla, thinking of the construction messes that would occur in all the 27 cities–not just hers. "We've worked hard to get this opportunity, so we'll have to be prepared to suffer through it. We've just got to make sure that the money's available at the right times to keep all the construction and renewal on schedule."

"Just imagine what's happened along the Alameda Corridor. The connections to the two ports along with management improvements for cutting down the impact of truck travel on our neighborhoods," Gavin remarked in wonder.

"Right, Gavin. Well, let's summarize as best we can the reasons we need money for each project year-by-year, so the 2001 RTP will reflect our real needs. Otherwise, L.A. and other subregions will take our Federal dollars and tie our neighborhoods up with construction problems for forty or fifty years, not the ten or twenty years we specified," Mike stated emphatically.

They busied themselves in making plans to be presented at the next Gateway Cities meeting. Then, it would have to get pushed through the policy committee and RC meetings at SCAG next month without further amendment. The looming budget shortfall would make this extra difficult.

* * *

Jim continued to have sleepless nights and nightmares as he wrestled with his conscience. He didn't know how much longer he could tolerate his struggle to achieve a SCAG Transportation Finance Bill to his liking. He wasn't proud of how he had treated Mike at the last meeting. His bill had been changed considerably by Judith and KOPE when he had presented it to them. Even though his version was bad news, their amendments weakened it further. He also felt KOPE would not live up to their agreement to pay him $500,000 as the first installment on their bribe to get their version of the transportation finance legislation through SCAG. They were supposed to have paid it yesterday but hadn't made any contact yet. At this stage, he wasn't sure he even wanted them to pay him. Maybe he should go to his father and get a loan from him as Lila suggested.

Lila didn't think he should go through with it. She felt he was ruining his career and running the risk of being exposed. What was he going to do? He was approaching his breaking point. He knew Lila was losing faith in him through his efforts to achieve revenge from Juan and others. That's their problem, he thought. What difference did it make. He was finished anyway. So many people who once respected him had turned away. It didn't take much to alienate people. In comparison, it took a life time to build up the respect which could be taken away in the blink of an eye with one or two key blunders. He loathed himself for his intransigence and inability to face up to his problems and change.

*　*　*

The Transportation Finance Task Force met again to make final adjustments in their 2001 RTP financial forecast for the 2001-2025 period. Faced with a shortfall of 20 to 50 billion dollars, they went through some fine-tuning with Harry, the consultant. As Jim sized up the situation, they went through this process every time they developed the RTP. They realized that they wouldn't be able to balance projected revenues with expenditures. So they did as much in-filling as they could and somehow made things balance, realizing that three years from now they could tinker with it again in their 2004 RTP financial forecasts. Just a never ending process they went through. The day of reckoning never seemed to come as long as they did the best they could with limited revenues. Just do some creative bookkeeping, like the big corporations.

The debate involved adding a regional gas tax, coping with losses in gas tax revenues as alternative fuels eroded them more and more, and using private revenues to develop toll roads and Maglev.

"We've got to be more creative in increasing our taxes," said Harry. "It's difficult to get each county to agree to simple increases in taxes at the pump, since voters are increasingly resisting that option."

"How about creating a regional gas tax which wouldn't have to be voted on at the county level?" asked Jim.

"It might work if instituted at the state level by the legislature," replied Harry.

"Another problem we have is how to adjust for the loss in taxes as more alternative fuel vehicles replace gasoline fuel vehicles."

"Maybe we could develop a tax or charge which would replace the taxes lost by reduced gasoline consumption. This should be explored as an option," Harry answered, not too hopefully.

"We're going to have a significant shortfall unless we use private funds in certain cases. How could we justify this, Harry?" Jim asked.

"The only ways would be through the development of more toll roads, with toll fees paying for them."

"I guess we could do that even though they historically haven't paid their way. We could worry about that later," Jim replied unenthusiastically.

"Another approach would be to have Maglev financed entirely with private funds. Do you think that will make sense to the SCAG crew?"

"Possibly. Let's move ahead with that approach, and worry about it next year, when we start working on the 2004 RTP," Jim said with resignation.

"Okay. That's a way out. Looking at the chart on the revised 2001 RTP financial forecast, we see with Maglev and toll roads helping through private funding, this would take care of $22.5 billion. but we would still have to find $38.5 billion to finance other projects over the 2001-25 planning period (in constant 1997 dollars). We'll have to identify other creative funding sources to meet this shortfall."

"Looks great. Let's go with it if everyone approves."

"Unanimous," Jim said, counting the hands up when the aye vote was called. "Then it's final and will go to the TCC Policy Committee and RC for final approval. Thank you, gentlemen, for your patience on this difficult subject." Gaveling, he intoned, "Meeting adjourned."

* * *

The Regional Airport Plan continued to struggle in its fight for life as LAX and El Toro airport politics sucked blood out of the RC participants. It was a painful process since big money was behind efforts for and against. Public officials were caught up in some nasty situations.

"I understand that the forces against El Toro have spent over $40 million in PR and mailings in the past two years," Marcine told Gavin at an Alameda Corridor event on the airport mess. "Their Great Park for 4700 acres has snowed citizens who generally seemed to favor it over the airport."

"Wow! The power of PR and the snow job overcoming what's right. When the Navy was flying noisy jets over expensive neighborhoods as they were being built-out, they showed no concern," Gavin stated. "Human nature at its worst!"

"Imagine wanting to expand an already dangerous and overloaded John Wayne and its 500 acres when there's an already existing 4700 acre airport with protected runway approach areas ready to be used. It defies all logic!"

"Then you have LAX Airport, which was never supposed to handle even forty million passengers. They want to cram ninety million–and counting–passengers into its boundaries. It's also a small airport–less than a thousand acres–plus it's surrounded by thousands of small single family homes that have been subjected to growing noise for years. The minorities are really being 'had' here!" Gavin exploded. "Brings back memories of my bonnie Ireland and its problems."

"Plus LAX is choking with surface traffic on all sides, and highways

405 and 105 have become virtual parking lots during peak periods. They think it's going to get better by adding a couple million more passengers with cars needing additional space and parking?" Marcine sputtered in exasperation.

"You know, the simple solutions available at Ontario, March, even Palmdale, plus El Toro, should convincingly prove LAX traffic needs to be capped. The lousy self-serving politics of it all is pathetic, as shown by LA City Hall and south Orange County politicians. Where is it going to end?" Gavin shuddered in disgust. "We need some 'convenient deaths' or 'voted out of office' possibilities–and soon. We keep throwing good money after bad."

"You're right, it's money down a rat-hole, and we have less every year," Marcine exclaimed in dismay.

"To make things worse, there's areas in the Inland Empire with thousands of acres of cheap land where people are dying to get an airport to serve their own needs. Plus they need the jobs so they don't have to commute 50 to 100 miles to Orange County, throwing more traffic onto already over-loaded freeways."

"Gateway Cities and South Bay need to support a complete regional airport system which allows our residents to travel to the most convenient airport, whether it's LAX, El Toro, John Wayne, Ontario–or wherever, don't you think, Gavin?"

"Definitely. Plus our industries must be able to ship and receive cargo the quickest, cheapest and most convenient way, not all through a single congested airport."

"Our subregions must bond together to make this happen. Do you have any ideas on how to do this, other than through SCAG?" Marcine asked.

"We've got to harness the business leaders who can threaten the airlines and politicians, demanding a better system or they'll move their firms elsewhere."

"Do you think you could rattle some cages on this, Gavin? You've got a lot of business connections through your Gateway Cities Partnership, the L.A. Economic Development Association, the Ports, and others you know. You should be able to do some good here."

"It's crossed my mind a time or two. Unless I could get a 'bully pulpit' to organize this effort, I wouldn't be able to do much good. I can't afford to be caught up in the SCAG bureaucracy–that would be the kiss of death right away."

"Let me work on it, Gavin. I'll see what I can cook up through the non-profits, Regional Advisory Council and others. Thanks for your thoughts and interest," Marcine replied.

* * *

Heartened by Gavin's interest, Marcine moved ahead with attracting a blend of entrepreneurs, non-profits and others interested in making the regional airport system happen. She met with a wide range of people and organizations to enlist their support. Included were such supporters as Boeing and other big, influential industries which had the clout to start the ball rolling. In addition, she worked the phones to solicit support from as many congressional representatives as possible in both Washington and Sacramento.

* * *

The legislature also focused on tax-base sharing as part of their coverage of Juan's regional planning bill which was expected to move out of committee soon. Legislators made the following comments as the controversial tax-base sharing aspect was about to hit the Assembly:

"People of moderate means shouldn't have inferior public services because they can't afford to live in property-rich communities."

"School spending illustrates the need for equity. Low spending for schools coupled with the increased difficulties with single parenting and poverty, is the most likely contributor to high drop-out rates and low college attendance levels."

"Yeah, any community that can increase its tax base and limit its social responsibilities and costs (through exclusive zoning) will continue to want to maximize its advantages over less endowed cities."

"Besides promoting low-density development patterns, a fragmented metropolitan tax base fosters unnecessary outward movement."

"Since we don't have regional government, the common good and true regional perspective come through a fair contest of ideas, values, and perspectives which can't be decided by elected representatives. In the interim, however, changes can be made through solving regional problems, issue by issue, by building coalitions based on self-interest." This statement by Juan Rodriguez was a key to getting things done locally—and through the subregions, separately and jointly.

* * *

In late 1999, SCAG had asked a consultant to review how the new Workforce Investment Act (WIA) could be implemented on a regional basis. Although a program was proposed, SCAG felt it couldn't broker such a major effort regionally. It's still considering how it might possibly assist in encouraging retraining programs in certain key locations that are struggling with historic problems of high unemployment, underemployment, low education and subpar income levels. They sought guidance on how to accomplish such a program.

In a Gateway Cities Symposium, this issue burst forth.

"Gateway Cities has got to make this happen here and now! We have all the problems which WIA can resolve; we need to face up to them," said Gavin, addressing his Gateway Partners board.

"I agree with you, Gavin," remarked Don Bond, the chair from Boeing. "We've got to use the Skills Chart to its maximum. That means we've got to educate our youngsters better."

"You're right. Just what do you mean by that, Don?"

"Develop such basic skills as reading, writing, speaking, listening and math. Add to that thinking skills including how to learn, create, solve problems and make decisions. Consider such personal qualities of workers as responsibility, integrity, self-confidence, moral character and loyalty. These are really the building blocks of work skills."

"Plus they must learn how to use resources, process information, use technology, understand systems, and relate well with other persons," said Gavin. "On top of that, of course, they must learn company skills in machine tools and other industries, along with company-specific skills related only to how that company operates. Training for success is complex in this rapidly changing world."

"What can we do to encourage SCAG to get involved in these targeted needs for retraining?"asked Bob Finley, a small businessman on the board.

"SCAG must utilize its Regional Economic Strategies Consortium (RESC) to unify economic and workforce development planning for key industry clusters within the six-county region. It's had over six years experience with RESC, and that group brings together the employers, educators and training providers in key industries."

"Plus SCAG must use its position as co-chair of the Advanced Transportation Industry Consortium (ATIC) to provide a model for the industry panels that would be established under this pilot to develop skill standards and certification systems," said Don.

"It's going to be tough to honcho job retraining for the whole region. Obviously, SCAG can't do it all–or even a major portion of it. But it must provide the base and some of a robust framework for making sure the effort doesn't fizzle out if programs get at odds with one another throughout the region," Gavin emphasized.

"Let's push for the necessary meetings to get a regionwide effort going. Finding the money and staffing for it will be difficult but we've got to begin. Otherwise, we'll lose the narrow window of opportunity we have now," Don reminded the board.

"We've also got to work with Sacramento on this, to make sure the legislature provides the right legislation at the right time," said Gavin.

"So moved, as amended by the last two statements," said Don. With agreement, the meeting adjourned.

* * *

Further discussions continued on jobs/housing balance at the monthly CEHD Policy Committee meetings. Encouraging shifts began to move the group from the absolute feeling that jobs/housing balance wasn't possible to a growing feeling that strategies could be developed that could achieve some jobs/housing balance. There was even some optimism that they could encourage greater housing production throughout the region.

Eight strategies were hammered out:

1) more effective economic development;

2) increased infill efforts in key areas devoid of jobs;

3) adjustments/reduction in parking requirements when appropriate;

4) continued Brownfields efforts to bring decayed sites back into use;

5) use of transit-oriented development that arrays a mix of uses around the transit node, including residential, commercial, and businesses;

6) achievement of state and local finance reform to permit the development of critical housing and jobs;

7) use of state and Federal tax credits and other incentives when needed; and

8) creative use of mixed-use (Greyfields adapting of old, out-of-date sites) and other planning approaches through zoning changes to overcome lack of land.

Slowly, but surely, leaders of the various subregions increased their cooperative efforts through various forms of collaboration. Each had unique needs that couldn't be met without help from other subregions. They began to reach out and take chances by helping each other. The San Gabriel and Lower Los Angeles Rivers and Mountains Conservancy (RMC) as established by state legislation includes several of the subregions. They are in the process of adopting an Open Space Plan to protect the banks of these rivers, using money generated from various existing programs to carry out the plan. These efforts are important for reducing flooding, adding critically needed park space for both active and passive recreation, and meeting other needs stretching across a considerable number of communities and meeting other needs in the watershed.

* * *

On another front, the Growth Visioning Subcommittee moved ahead with its efforts to attract a larger, more powerful constituency to support regional planning goals. In preparing to move into Cycle Two (2003-2008), a public hearing was scheduled to begin involving an expanded mix of participants beyond SCAG and the subregions. Other levels of government, educational/ research institutes and professional peer group organizations needed to be attracted so a Technical Coalition would be developed.

This public hearing would focus on the proposals developed thus far by Growth Visioning leaders: objectives, growth principles, regional land use standards, what "if's", alternative urban forms, proposal scenarios, regional constraints, and other important aspects. The public hearing lasting all day at the Biltmore Hotel in Downtown L.A., took place on Thursday, June 6, 2002. Key members of a discussion group keynoting the event were Jim Robinson representing the RC, Mary Logan for the subregions, and Rudy So, L.A. City Councilman covering the City.

Initially, the meeting moved along well as the various findings were discussed. Once key issues involving urban form (compaction versus dispersion, transit versus freeways and growth principles) were introduced, the meeting began to bog down. This began with Rudy So, long-time L.A. City Councilman strongly complaining about the city being slighted:

"The City of Los Angeles needs help from the surrounding suburban areas regarding LAX, transit, affordable housing, downtown development and other problems. We've too long carried the lion's share of making the region work."

"I beg to disagree, Councilman," Jim jumped in. "Its suburbanites who need the help. L.A. too long has effectively taken vital resources (tax revenues, costs of adding needed urban infrastructure and other improvements) away from us without even an effort to try to work together. This has got to stop since our needs are growing more rapidly than L.A.'s now."

"Mary added: "Providing adequate affordable housing, infill needs, rehabilitation and redevelopment needs must be more adequately addressed by L.A. The City needs to handle its Brownfields and toxic air problems better, and provide its fair share of financing and planning to make it happen. Surrounding cities have long been victimized by L.A. on these matters."

"I can't believe that the surrounding region looks on L.A. as being at fault in this," Rudy lashed back, rising to his feet in indignation. "This disdain by you is why L.A. hasn't got involved in SCAG in the past. After all, we're the region's heart and its most important component."

The meeting degenerated from there into a heated debate. Finally, in an effort to get things back on track, Jim got everyone to defer further discussion of this issue to some other time so that some agreement could be reached to develop the Technical Coalition. Everyone agreed that considerable time should be spent on reaching a compromise for revenue sharing possibilities and related matters at a later date. After lengthy debate, the framework of a Technical Coalition was developed and the meeting adjourned.

The Technical Coalition was presented to the RC at its next monthly meeting for final approval. Approval came with little opposition, and the Growth Visioning group and SCAG's supporting staff moved ahead quickly to contact possible interested groups to determine their interest in being a part of the Coalition. Of the 50 some groups contacted, 20 expressed definite interest in sitting on the Technical Coalition Board to advise the Growth Visioning process in 2002.

CHAPTER 19
REGIONAL POLARIZATION

*Polarization is occurring more
and more in the region as some
subregions and even parts of L.A.
City (deannexation efforts) disagree
on what needs to be done. Efforts
are made in the state legislature to
break through. The regional
planning bill provides a key tool
to make the region work better.*

"Polarization on a regional scale
exacts its costs in terms of human and
governmental waste, overtaxed and
over-regulated business climate,
environmental destruction through
irrational use of land, and balkanization
of political life."

Myron Orfield, <u>Metropolitics</u>

"Few RC members feel that polarization could occur in SCAG, Carla," Mike said, as they sat discussing Gateway issues in her office. "Do you believe we're headed toward polarization?"

"I think so, Mike. There's certainly been opportunity for it. Several issues–regional airports and affordable housing–have created community activity which threatened to polarize the region. I think there are six issues which could collectively or singly polarize us. Firmer SCAG leadership is needed on regional airports, affordable housing, quality of education (schools), environmental justice, jobs, and air pollution (toxics). Situations on any of these issues could create the worst type of polarization."

"You know, Carla, some polarization on one or more of these issues could be healthy. It's often the only way to achieve effective change. Otherwise, everyone continues to blunder along with no sense of urgency."

"Hm... Interesting thought. Any examples you could cite?"

"I think quality of education is one. Until charter schools and use of public funds to develop strong private schools for minorities began, everyone kept saying that there were too many pitfalls to making public education better," Mike responded. "I believe that a little competition never hurt anyone."

"You're right, of course. You'd think that better education would be the easiest to achieve with all those bright educators involved. But it's been just the reverse."

"What should we do to make the educational system perform better?" asked Mike.

"How about making sure each school has adequate funds, qualified teachers and good facilities. Then ask the Board of Education to adopt a program that specifies what each school must do to keep its funds and adequately educate each student? If some schools don't meet these standards, then consider private schools to meet the need," replied Carla. "We've got to start taking chances so our mis-managed schools educate our students right."

"Great idea. All right, lets do it. Do you have any contacts with the state education department and L.A. School Board who might help us move this along?"

"I think I know a couple I can call. Maybe now's the time to get involved in breaking the log jam to get some things done. If this works, we can apply the same thinking to the other five issues we've cited. At least we can try to make a difference."

* * *

Jim's broker, Kent, dropped by after phoning him about a problem needing some answers. He came right to the point, attempting to break through Jim's hostility.

"Jim, your stock problems have mushroomed. I wasn't able to get you out of the market in time. You lost another $200,000 in the process."

"You've got to be kidding," Jim yelled. "Why can't my broker give me some good news for a change? Will my problems never end?"

"Settle down, Jim," Kent said soothingly. "I know it's tough. But these things happen. We need to sit down and calmly plot some strategy on your stock portfolio now. I can suggest–but you've got to make the decisions."

"It's my money going down the drain. It's easy for you to be calm. Well, you're right, I'm here–let's get this stuff over with, so I can face all my other problems," Jim sputtered, his face turning beet red.

They sat down and Kent meticulously worked out a temporary schedule and various options to consider, depending on how the various stocks did the next day. They planned to get back together again the following day to work out the final adjustments. But there was a sea of red ink regardless of the approach they tried. Things looked pretty bad.

* * *

Jim was caught in a crossfire of others' competing interests. He had to make sure he didn't lose his way. His financial problems increasingly grew in their dimensions. How could he solve his own problems while still satisfying those who were demanding he sell his soul? He had been wrestling with this dilemma for a long time. He must make a big decision soon, and never look back. Once he did, he reasoned hopefully, his problems with gambling, women and drinking might be cut down to manageable proportions. They all related to the same issue–lack of money. But was it only the money, he asked himself cynically?

He decided to contact KOPE and agree to help them if they would pay him $500 grand–with $100,000 up front. He knew money wasn't a problem for them with their deep-pocketed hidden interests behind them. They would do anything to achieve their purposes, so why should he do all these things for nothing. Plus, he thought that this would be the only way to get Lila. He knew his obsession for her muddled his thinking, since she was already in their camp. First, though, he must put together an approach that would meet all his objectives. Then work out how they could be achieved–while making sure he got adequate protection.

* * *

He called Lila. At first, she threatened to hang up on him. Finally she agreed to see him at her office that afternoon.

Arriving, he entered her office exuding false confidence:

"Lila, it's great to see you!" he exclaimed, reaching out to take her in his arms.

"So the prodigal son returns," Lila answered in a cold, steely voice, dodging his embrace. "What can I do to get you out of your latest mess?" she asked cynically.

"Aw, Lila, please forgive me," Jim said, trying to placate her. " I'm sorry I screwed up–and hurt you in the process."

"You think you can just walk in here and figure everything has been forgiven," she replied coldly. "I can't believe your nerve. You think I'm that naive?"

"No, Lila. It's just taken me awhile to come to terms with what I need to do–and you were right all along. Give me a chance."

"What do you mean, 'I've been right all along'?" she asked, still not biting on his pitch. "Bring me up to speed on your latest?" came her cynical response. "I'm all ears."

"Okay, okay. I get the picture. Just give me time to explain where I'm at, will you?" he asked contritely

"Go on," she said, relenting only a little.

"I've agreed to help both KOPE and your organization to get what they want."

"What does that mean?" she countered with a frown.

"It means putting together a regional planning bill that helps them to meet their objectives. But many regional supporters will feel they've been sold out."

"You'd do that? You must be either crazy–or broke and desperate," she replied in anger.

"You're right both ways," he muttered with contempt for himself.

"Do you realize what you're doing, Jim?" she asked, shaken. "You're committing political and personal suicide."

"Maybe, but my debts are huge. I don't have any choice."

"Let's go out and get a cup of coffee–and talk more about what this means," she said, her face chalk white, with a little compassion finally showing.

"You're my last chance, Lila. I hope–really hope–you can help me, " Jim said, as they headed out the door.

*   *   *

Settling into seats in a nearby restaurant, Lila gazed at Jim with concern showing clearly on her face. She decided to be 'straight arrow' and try not to lead Jim on anymore. He looked like he'd had it in terms of being manipulated, although he'd admittedly done more than his share himself.

"I'm just holding on myself dealing with these buzzards," she said. "They're doing a lot of things I don't like–to win. They'll use you and throw you away once they get what they want. They have no scruples. Do you realize that, Jim?"

"I guess so," he answered lethargically. "I'm just at wits end. I'll do anything if they provide me the money to wipe out my debts."

"Answer these questions. What requirements do they have for the bill you're putting together? Will it be good enough to pass the RC and the legislature? If not, they won't help you at all, Jim. Don't you realize the danger you're in without much hope of success?"

"I haven't looked that far ahead. It's too scary, Lila," he replied. "I'm in over my head."

"Let's look at the situation more closely, Jim," she said compassionately. "Why don't you finish the bill based on their requirements and get back with me. In the meantime, I'll check to see what else can be done," Lila said. "Oh, Jim, I'm so sorry," she said sadly. "I love you and want to help. You know that, don't you?"

"I guess so, Lila," he responded, with a defeated, anguished look. "I don't know what to think anymore. But I'll put together my response to the bill. Can we talk at your place this evening about eight?"

"Okay, Jim," she said, stroking his hand. "Go work on the bill and we'll talk more later."

* * *

Jim struggled, afraid for his future. His inability to know what to do worried him since he'd never been indecisive like this before. He felt trapped. Whatever he decided to do, he knew in his heart he would lose. Both CIG and KOPE were pressing him to produce a reworked bill for them. He feared the consequences if he didn't comply. But he also knew, his RC colleagues wanted him to provide the right revamped bill to meet their needs. They wouldn't be happy with a bill slanted to the needs of CIG and KOPE. They knew Mike through his sponsor would offer them a bill putting a different–and probably better–spin on things from their standpoint.

He finally decided in desperation, he had to at least attempt to craft a bill he could live with. Possibly then, meet with Mort James, SCAG's Legislative Analyst, to work off its rough edges before sending it to KOPE and CIG. He needed to face up to his dilemma.

* * *

Jim met with Mort James the next morning after convincing him of the importance of the meeting. He went over his recrafting of the bill and what he thought needed to be done to meet the Region's needs.

"I know that Mike and his RC co-sponsors want to focus on higher densities and a less spread out region, but that's not the solution."

"What do you believe is the solution, Councilman, considering the clean air and money limitations involved to get so many needed transportation improvements accomplished?" asked Mort, concerned that Jim wasn't looking at the whole picture.

"We've got to continue to provide the citizens of this region with the low density housing they want and need. They'll rise up in anger otherwise."

"I understand your concerns, Councilman. It's hard to determine the priorities to focus on considering all the needs the Region has."

Mort however couldn't stop wondering what drove Jim Robinson to this version of the Regional Bill. He thought back to the weird going-ons over the past year in Sacramento and the intrigue generated by KOPE and CIG in the legislative halls. His job involved stressing advocacy in his work. As a lobbyist for SCAG, he visited many legislators and developed strategies encouraging them to vote for SCAG favored bills. He even tried to influence votes by stressing SCAG's position. He worked closely with such organizations as CALCOG, League of Cities, Association of Counties, Transportation Commissions and the 14 subregions to create coalitions with the strength to

244

get legislation approved or blocked to protect SCAG's interests.

In effect, his job was to weigh political tea leaves and collaborate with legislators in Sacramento. He also traveled to Washington on Maglev, TEA-21 and other important bills, working with contract lobbyists. In Jim's case where there were competing bills involved, his job would be to collapse them into one package with adjustments to resolve differences. Modify them so the RC would pass a bill agreeable to a majority.

Mort saw this as the tricky part coming up. The two bills would be almost impossible to reconcile enough for all parties to support the final version. He saw all sorts of problems surfacing if Jim's bill as currently constituted was offered. He also had the feeling that if KOPE and CIG were behind this bill, they would make substantial modifications before it saw the light of day in Sacramento or with the policy committee at SCAG. What should he advise Jim to do?

"Councilman, do you see some way to modify your bill so it might more easily be integrated with the competing bill into something that could be passed in Sacramento?"

"None whatever. If SCAG doesn't back me on this, bad things are going to happen. You don't want that to take place, do you?" he said, looking Mort fiercely in the eye.

"Of course not, Councilman," Mort said, trying to calm Jim down. "but there are substantial, possibly unmodifiable differences between the two bills. I'm just playing devil's advocate, trying to get the parties to close the gap before colliding in committee. Any thoughts?"

"I'm not going to compromise. That's my final answer. You go back and get them to make some changes," Jim said, as he angrily leapt to his feet. "Thanks for your time! I'll see you around." And out the door he walked—slamming it behind him.

Mortified by Jim's actions, Mort hurried to see the Executive Director and explain what happened. They had to determine what, if anything, could be done.

* * *

Now that he had put together his recrafted bill, Jim called Abe Underhill at CIG.

"Abe, I've redrafted the bill to meet the needs of both CIG and KOPE. However, we never talked about compensation for this."

"Compensation, Jim—what're you talking about? We can't pay you for this. That would be corruption. If we were found out, we could go to prison."

"If you think I'm going to do all these things without receiving something in return, you're crazy. I've got debts to pay off and it's only logical that you people with everything to gain should give me some assistance.

Otherwise, I wouldn't be in this position."

"I'll check with KOPE on this but I don't think they'll be willing. They've got you where they want you. You know that," Abe replied. "If they ask though, how much do you want?" he asked, perplexed and frustrated with this turn of events. He now felt there wasn't any rational way of dealing with him.

"$500 grand with $100,000 up front."

"You don't want much, do you? But okay," Abe said resignedly. "I'll check and get back to you, Jim. You say you've worked over the bill so that KOPE will be pleased?"

"Yes, I have. I'll be glad to meet with them in a day or so to go over it a final time. But I'll need $100 grand deposited in my account prior to any meeting," he stated emphatically.

"Okay. You drive a hard bargain, Jim," Abe said. "I'll get back to you."

* * *

When Jim called Lila, he apologized for not being able to meet her the previous evening due to some problems with getting the bill reworked. She agreed to see him at ten at her place, and asked him to bring the bill so she could look it over. He agreed.

* * *

Jim was late as usual, finally arriving at Lila's at eleven. Tired and a little uptight, he thanked her for seeing him, especially at such a late hour.

"Sorry, Lila. I've been running late all day.

"Okay, Jim. Did you bring the bill? I'm really concerned about what you're doing. I thought, at least, I could review it and give you my opinion."

"Here it is," Jim said, handing her the file.

"Sit down Jim. Have a drink while I review the bill."

Lila opened the file and read the recast bill. Frowning some and rereading the bill, she looked up:

"Jim, you sure you want to go through with this?"

"Yes, I'm so sure that I've asked for some compensation to help me get out of debt."

"They're going to pay you for this, Jim?" Lila gasped. "I'm appalled. Do you realize what you're getting into? Corruption! Plus you don't know whether they'll string you along on this–or change the bill so you won't ever be able to get out of this mess."

"I don't think they will," he stated stubbornly. "They're committed too, you know?"

"You don't know these jokers like I do. Don't do this. Back out now before it's too late, Jim. Please," Lila pleaded, sobbing.

"Why're you so upset, Lila. Isn't this what you wanted?"

"Jim, I'm sorry if I've led you astray. I love you," she said with tears in her eyes. "And I don't want you to destroy your career. Even if you never want to see me again. I want you to get yourself straightened out. We'll work out something to handle your debt. Your father and others could help if you would stop gambling and stay out of trouble," Lila pleaded with him, her face white as a sheet, eyes haunted.

"I don't know, Lila. I've gone too far to back out now," Jim said, shaken by Lila's reaction. "I thought I was doing what you wanted. I love you too and would do anything to make you happy. Why are you saying this now?" he asked, confused by her apparent shift in thinking.

"Because I've recently been seeing things in a new light, Jim. I didn't realize just how overboard some people had gone–at CIG and especially KOPE. Money makes people greedy and willing to do anything to get their share. It's not worth it, Jim. You've changed for the worse since you got caught up in this. You're not the Jim I used to know," she said, not knowing what else to say. "I know I'm not the Lila that you knew at the start either. Let's step back and see what we can work out."

"Back off now, Lila? It's too late. I've closed too many doors and alienated too many people. But let me think about it. I'll call you tomorrow," he said, getting up and sliding out the door.

* * *

"God, why have you forsaken me?" he cried in desperation, his face contorted, as he looked heavenward. Agnostic in his beliefs, although brought up a Catholic in his youth, he seized on a rekindling of prayer as a last straw from the religion he had thrown away years ago when he thought it was meaningless.

Realizing he had done nothing to carry out promises made to God in the Capitol chapel several months ago, he felt it was too late. Why shouldn't God forsake him? He had left no place for God in his life. No wonder life had passed him by. How could God provide him hope?

* * *

Judith Struthers and Abe Underhill met with Jim at KOPE's L.A. offices that evening at seven. Although Jim wanted a neutral site, he knew they were upset with him for keeping them waiting so long while rewriting his RTP bill. The note through Willie also provided a warning.

"Robinson, what's this about you wanting something in compensation from us for your help. What's going on with you?" Judith asked abruptly, cigarette in hand.

"Judith, I'm taking a lot of chances politically to help you get your RTP bill through our RC and the state legislature. It's only right that I should get something in return. Abe has already told you that I want $500 grand for this with $100 of it up front."

"He said that you wanted something in return but–$500 grand for some corrections. That's preposterous and illegal. Plus we don't know what your bill will say. I can't believe you'd ask for something, much less that amount. We're not a money tree," Judith replied testily, casting darts at Jim while puffing deeply on her cigarette.

"Come on, Judith. You've got a lot to gain from all this. Your backers will reap even more," Jim responded heatedly.

"Why aren't you concerned by our threats to expose you, Jim, if you don't go through with this?" Judith asked, puzzled, reaching for another cigarette.

"I have a reason. I won't disclose why either. You figure that out," he stubbornly replied.

"I still haven't had a chance to read this redraft," she said, looking at the draft he had handled her. "Can you indicate what some of the corrections are so I can go back and inform my backers?"

Jim proceeded to recite a few of the changes. Somewhat satisfied, she agreed to send him their decision and requirements the next day.

*　*　*

Judith and Abe conferred after Jim left.

"Well, we have his bribe request on tape, Abe. We should be able to do what we want with him, but he's proving difficult. What do you think we should do? Should we pay the $100 grand up front to get the legislation and hang him in the wind?"

"I have no idea what else he has in mind, Judith. How does he plan to ensure that he gets the balance? Refuse to back the bill unless we go with his bill? What will he do when he finds we want major changes in the legislation? What will SCAG do as they consolidate the two pieces of legislation in one package to send to the legislature? There are a lot of questions we don't know the answers to. Also, he doesn't consider our threats to expose him as worrisome"

"You're right. He's a sly one. Am I underestimating how cunning he is?" Judith wondered, puffing away on yet another cigarette. She got up and paced around the room, her high heels clicking angrily. "We've got to make sure he doesn't slip out from under our control. Any ideas?"

"Yes, we've got to pin him to the wall. How about our stringing him along by providing the $100 grand after our changes are approved and the consolidated bill clears SCAG? Can we get away with that?"

"We can try. I'm not sure it'll work though."

"Well, let's try. When he sends us the draft of the bill, agree to the $100 grand after clearing SCAG and see what happens."

"Okay, let's do it," she replied, lighting another cigarette as her chain smoking continued. "This should prove interesting. There's not much time left to get everything to the legislature."

* * *

Jim continued to vacillate on whether to follow through on his obsession to get a bribe from KOPE and Judith in return for getting their provisions through in a regional transportation finance bill. He knew it made no sense in a lot of ways, but he was so obsessed by the need to kill Juan's regional planning bill, he had lost sight of reality.

He was determined to move ahead now that he'd finalized his bill. He contacted Judith and got her to agree to send him KOPE's changes in the bill, along with a statement agreeing to a $100 grand first payment. She said she would have Willie deliver these within the hour.

Willie arrived with an envelope. Ripping it open, Jim found the list of changes to the bill and a statement indicating that the $100 grand would be delivered only following his incorporation of the changes into the bill and their becoming part of the consolidated transportation finance bill which the RC must pass.

Although angered by the trickery, Jim saw a good omen here. He now had evidence of KOPE's involvement and with the promise to pay the bribe, he had a way out. Although the wording in the attachment was cleverly disguised, he felt he could prove its authenticity and origin. He decided then to continue his subterfuge by going along with Judith's proposal. He sat down and reworked the bill to include their amendments. He planned to sit on them at least 24 hours before sending it to them for their final okay. He wanted them to sweat a little.

* * *

Meanwhile, Carla and Mike continued their efforts to develop collaborative efforts on education and other issues. They felt that more cross-fertilization with other organizations outside SCAG and the RC were needed if the Regional Transportation Plan was ever to make sense. They should not continue to work within their transportation area alone but needed to branch out into other equally important areas. Growth Visioning was the vehicle for doing this. By inviting other professions and organizations into their development of policy for the region, they could start making a true plan possible.

In addition, they felt that regional polarization would most likely occur as each subregion developed their approach to Growth Visioning in their own area. Similar prospects could be expected with Los Angeles as they had demonstrated with areas desiring to be de-annexed.

CHAPTER 20
TAX-BASE SHARING

*Los Angeles faced an unique and crucial
issue which experts felt they would never
ever consider–contrary to their swashbuckling
days of the past. Considering, much less permitting,
growth guidance (through Growth Visioning) to occur.
But without it, the region can't prosper–much less survive.
What a difference a few years and tremendous growth
has made for a region facing gridlock of the
worst form. A key factor to achieving quality
growth guidance would be tax-base sharing
among communities to reduce the have/have not' problem.*

"You've got to take your time making these
judgments: you can't come to conclusions
solely on appearance. Be a skeptic–always.
Remember that most of the time, everywhere
in life, things are seldom the way they seem."

The Detective, Arthur Hailey

"Do not go where the path may lead; go
instead where there is no path and leave a trail."

Ralph Waldo Emerson

"I'm really uptight about what KOPE has done in their efforts to destroy our regional planning efforts, Joe. What's going on?" blurted Juan, nervously pacing back and forth in his Capitol office on a sunny day in April 2001.

"Unfortunately, nothing new since our last meeting with Evon. Hope he checks in soon. The growth guidance issue should help us though," Joe answered, concerned about Juan.

"Yeah, growth guidance is really heating up statewide. What's the coverage on the SOAR and CAPP approaches to growth management?"

"The Save Open-space and Agricultural Resources or SOAR initiative in Ventura County has been around two years and is the darling of the slow-growth crowd, but the scourge of developers." Joe said. They sat in Juan's environmentally-correct office, jokingly called that since it held so many plants, reflecting Juan's love for the out-of-doors. They were waiting impatiently to hear from Evon, while discussing how to make growth guidance more palatable to both Houses, as well as the citizens.

"What's the difference between them?"

"SOAR sought to halt suburban sprawl by creating urban growth boundaries, to contain new development. Unlike many previous land use initiatives, SOAR-style measures don't restrict a community's population size or its rate of growth. Rather, they stake out a growth boundary that can't be changed without the approval of voters. The assumption is that cities will grow but such growth will be accommodated to protect farmland and open space."

"So how does CAPP compare?"

"CAPP's effort mirrors SOAR's in two important ways. It involves a coordinated group of initiatives within neighboring cities, so as to shape growth patterns in an entire region or subregion with one blow from citizens. In addition, it's based on the idea that voters should have the final say over zoning changes and amendments to local plans. But the similarity ends there."

"So how does it differ from SOAR?" asked Juan, his eyes fixed intently on Joe, as he settled back more comfortably in his high backed swivel chair.

"Citizen Alliance for Public Planning or CAPP was spawned in San Francisco's East Bay area. The initiatives defeated there were tied to the belief that local residents should be able to vote on developments in their neighborhoods. There were a lot of people who felt that CAPP didn't make sense because it allowed the voters to say 'no' to more growth," Joe replied.

"So the CAPP defeats may have proved positive for the growth guidance cause?"

"Yes, many voters thought the initiatives went too far. They didn't want to go to the polls every time somebody wanted to build a few houses."

"Good thinking on the part of the voters, Joe. Voters seem to have become more selective in ballot-box zoning issues."

"Yes. They voted down a 'greenbelt' proposal for more development, but in another instance, approved a church being built in an agricultural zone."

"So where do you think we should go on this issue with our regional planning bill?"

"Probably piggy-backing on the SOAR initiative, although your bill has so many other issues which make it unique, Juan."

"Okay, let's keep in touch on these and other statewide happenings so our bill can be adapted when necessary."

"One thing we must seriously consider regarding growth guidance–or what is called growth visioning in L.A.–is how to handle impacts of the factors impacting growth," said Joe. "They vary by subregion within L.A.'s huge mega-region."

"Vary in what ways?"

"Regarding such factors as builtout-ness of subregion, age of housing, development density, citizen needs, income levels, balance of jobs to housing, as well as land use. L.A. will be a tough nut to crack regarding growth visioning," Joe replied. "A real test."

"Then we must keep a close eye on what's happening there," Juan replied. "Have one of our planners monitor their growth visioning committee full-time, especially regarding possibilities of adding tax-base sharing to their equation."

"That's right! Tax-base sharing is a crucial part of your regional planning bill," Joe agreed enthusiastically.

*　*　*

That evening Evon dropped by to update them on the two organizations' plans.

"They still haven't heard from Jim and are furious about his slowness to act–as well as his not keeping them advised about what he's doing."

"So he still hasn't made any changes to the bill," Juan noted. "Why not?" he wondered.

"I did find out some of the things they plan to do when they get his version of the bill. They, of course, will modify what they expect him to propose. Also, they will move to smear your name. It's going to get real nasty."

"It figures. Have they given out details of how they'll smear my name? I expect them to disclose my drug past but I've already gone public on that."

"Not yet. They're very close mouthed to prevent any leaks on their plans, Juan."

"I appreciate what you're doing, Evon. I also realize that your involvement is risky and your life's in danger if they suspect you ratting on them," Juan said, reaching out to him. "Thanks, from the bottom of my heart, for all your help. You know you don't have to continue as a spy?"

"I know, Juan, but I still want to help you in every way I can. They still haven't tested my loyalty. I expect they will soon by involving me in smearing you. If you hear that I have a vendetta against you, remember how we used to warn each other through statements we made. I'll alert you the same way," he said. "It's time I got back before they wonder where I am."

"Okay, Evon. Be careful. God bless you."

* * *

Concerned over what KOPE and CIG planned to do, Juan thought back to the efforts made several months ago through phone calls and e-mails to his home to intimidate him and his family. Although he still hadn't contacted the home builder involved, he knew that KOPE was behind it. Things seemed to have finally settled down, but he made sure his home phone calls and e-mails involved only non-sensitive matters. With KOPE planning to smear him in various ways, he felt uneasy about what things had been compromised, both past and present. He must be prepared for any possibilities, especially since many of his political activities could be slanted in a negative way, whether distorted or not.

He felt like a marked man. Being overly careful proved unwise at times since it made him insecure and cynical. His sense of humor saved him many times as he poked fun at himself. A fan of Shakespeare, he remembered the remark stated in one of his plays, "The fault is not in the stars.... but in us," at such times when his levity was threatened. After all, people were a little crazy, including himself. It helped to adapt in this world of fast-moving events mirroring efforts to survive one another's 'best laid plans.' The key thing to remember was to never take himself too seriously. He chuckled about that and moved on to handle the endless tasks his job demanded. He routinely had to deal with people of all types, political persuasions and temperaments.

* * *

Juan received some anonymous tapes in the mail that day. They had been screened like all other suspicious mail for Anthrax which had become a threat. They included rantings by Evon about Juan's manipulation of him prior to their getting back together, and also covered Juan's past involving drugs, suppressed juvenile sentences, and other matters he wished wouldn't be exposed to the public. Although posted in Sacramento, the source was unknown.

Exposure of these tapes could hurt Juan depending on how they were distributed to the public—by radio, TV, news program, scandal sheet, or what. The character of the persons spreading the word would also make a difference. The political game of smearing people had become very sophisticated and deadly.

Especially disturbing, they also indicated knowledge of Juan's past dug up by private detectives about his family and its problems. This information could also be exposed to the public unless Juan backed off from his proposed legislation. However, revelations from the tapes wouldn't change his plans. He couldn't be swayed through blackmail of this type. He prepared to go the extra mile.

* * *

Juan met again with Evon on the latest happenings at KOPE. They wasted no time in their efforts to smear both Juan and Jim with their divide and destroy tactics. To counter this, Juan knew he needed to develop countermeasures. Evon had also been preparing material on KOPE that he had developed from his work for them. So they sat down and pored over the information Evon had assembled.

"You've got some great materials on the big corporations behind all this, Evon," Juan said, propping his feet up on the bed in the motel room where they were meeting. "Let's expose them first since they have the most to lose."

"The auto makers are the biggest culprits," Evon remarked, stretching his legs. "There are major companies making kitchen appliances and furniture involved. Also, some of the largest home improvement centers, hardware, lumber and other such firms. They all want to maximize their profits from single family housing over higher density housing. Even some of the largest computer and software firms have bought in with soft money to influence housing legislation."

"You know, Evon, it seems like history repeats itself even in this arena," Juan replied. "Back before 1910, L.A. participated in the streetcar era where Henry Huntington built a $60 million real estate fortune around the Pacific Electric over a decade. He eventually built PE's "Red Cars" into the largest interurban rail system in the U.S. It stretched over more than 1,100 miles from Santa Monica to San Bernardino; from the San Gabriel Mountains to Newport Beach. In 1911, he consolidated his operations with the Los Angeles Railway Company, the streetcar system serving urban L.A. Although initially moving people around quickly, it eventually ran into problems since every line ran through the downtown area, creating gridlock at times."

"Just think, gridlock back in the early 1900's," Otto exclaimed.

"The auto makers realized that they needed to take over this market since California was expanding rapidly and people wanted to get to their destination quickly," Juan continued. "In addition, regulation of the streetcar line by the utilities board made things worse. Eventually, the story goes, political payoffs were made to politicians to elbow out the railroad. This resulted in L.A. entering into its still ongoing love affair with the auto to move people around more rapidly. Even much of the abandoned railroad right-of-way was sold off, preventing its later use for transit, if needed. Later, freeways were added to ensure that the demand for cars increased. Until recently, all the legislation at the state and Federal levels favored the continued development of roads, highways and freeways at the expense of transit."

"As I've said before, 'history repeats itself,'" Otto remarked, shaking his head in resignation.

* * *

Juan and Evon wracked their brains on ways to turn the corner on Judith and KOPE. They wanted to encourage efforts to reverse sprawl and its consequences. They would then leak information to Bea for a major article.

Evon would spread a rumor to the big corporations involved that Judith planned to set them up by threatening blackmail on their roles unless they paid KOPE to keep quiet. He would slip the word to some contacts he had who worked for corporations involved. He'd met key people through his previous legislative efforts.

Both he and Juan knew this was risky. Evon would be operating without any backup from Juan if things went wrong. He felt he still owed Juan for giving him another chance, and was unconcerned about these dangers. He had no family, and the risk involved excited him even though the strong likelihood that KOPE would trace the rumors to him was a "no brainer". He'd suggested this approach to Juan who wouldn't endorse it, knowing the risks involved for Evon. But, Juan couldn't talk him out of it. Evon did agree to disappear after planting these rumors. He knew KOPE would target him as a leading suspect and would go after him.

* * *

Evon proceeded to initiate his contacts by calling an old friend, Nick Brady, who he knew from college days. Nick worked as PR rep in the local office of one of the car manufacturers supporting KOPE, and knew the story. Evon explained his position with KOPE and his concern that they were ready to let Nick's firm and others providing funding to take the fall. He didn't like what they were doing and planned to get out.

"I'm glad you called, Evon," Nick said. "I've been following our funding of KOPE and haven't liked the crap going on, either by our company or by KOPE. I knew we couldn't keep this hushed up forever."

"Yeah, it's going to get messy–and I'm afraid you people will look bad no matter what's done. But at least you can beat them to the punch and say you want out."

255

"Right. We can indicate how they trapped us into this and blackmailed us to continue to get more and more involved. But how do we protect you?" Nick asked.

"Don't worry. They'll know I'm involved no matter what. Just move ahead on this as fast as you can. I can have Bea from the L.A. Times do an article on this if you like. Just call her and give her my name. She'll be glad to meet with you."

"Great. Thanks for the info, Evon. Take care of yourself. I owe you one. Feel free to contact me any time if you need help."

*   *   *

In the meantime, Juan presented the Tax-Base Sharing portion of his regional planning bill to committee. The opposition included representatives aligned with several home builders who got with their key backers in an effort to thwart the bill.

He opened his remarks by stating: "In all U.S. metropolitan areas, there is a dilemma –wherever social needs (welfare, schools, services) are growing, the tax base is uncertain or declining; wherever the tax base is solid, social needs are stable or declining."

Looking around at his house committee audience, he noted two types, those representing the needy inner city, and those from the prosperous suburbs. How could his bill be drawn up so as to create a bridge between the two? Make them realize they needed each other?

"You all realize, I believe, that providing basic services funded only by local property taxes fosters socioeconomic polarization and sprawling, inefficient land use. However, tax-base sharing creates basic services meeting the needs of every income level. This breaks the mismatch between social needs and, in California's case–where the state has taken away property taxes from the cities–necessitates the sharing of retail sales tax revenues."

"Otherwise, there's the undermining of local fiscal incentives supporting exclusive zoning and sprawl; decreasing incentives for intrametropolitan competition for tax base; and making regional land use policies possible. Basic public services such as police and fire protection, local infrastructure, parks, and local schools should be equalized throughout the metropolitan area. People of moderate means shouldn't have inferior public services because they can't afford to live in property-rich communities."

"My bill covers all these needs. With these remarks, I'll open up the meeting to your questions, comments and criticisms."

Hands shot up. The first question came from Ed Potter, a legislator from L.A.'s suburbs.

"Juan, our state's fiscal structure is so screwed up since Proposition 13 passed and the state absconded with the cities property taxes. Can we ever get this straightened out so local cities can get their budgets back to normal?"

"I agree, this is the first thing that needs to be done, Ed. I want to get this achieved as the first part of solving the state's fiscal crisis. What I'm proposing here covering tax-base sharing would come next."

"As another representative from the suburbs, I feel your bill would take away all that we've struggled to achieve through the years with our shopping centers and industrial parks. I resent what you're doing. It's un-American."

"I understand what you're saying, Bill. However, what I'm proposing would help save your city money in the long run. Otherwise, urban decay will set in and welfare problems will continue to grow in other parts of the region. As a result, local expenditures and taxes will have to rise. However, these would only be band aids. They wouldn't really solve the problems. My bill will allow the economic bases of all cities to become stronger in the long run. Future viability of all cities are interlinked when fiscal matters are concerned."

"Juan, the inner cities, which I represent, must get more help. This tax-base sharing proposal makes a lot of sense. Could you provide some examples of how it would help?"

"Certainly, Edwin. It eases the fiscal crisis in declining communities, allowing them to shore up decline. When people move to the suburbs, they are replaced by poorer families who don't have the income to fix the units up or pay enough taxes to finance the infrastructure improvements needed to keep the neighborhood viable. A vicious cycle already begun, accelerates, creating slums. With tax-base sharing, this cycle could be reversed.. If done early, even the outward movement may not occur."

"Juan, I feel that tax-base sharing is unfair. With the development of our new suburban communities, we're faced with significant local debt to create the infrastructure needed. Tax base sharing would only make it worse."

"In some ways, Roger, you're right. However, if people keep leaving the inner cities as their housing and infrastructure declines, the newer areas are only taking advantage of the inner cities by receiving state subsidies for new roads and sewer, while the older areas receive nothing in return. Do you feel that people bailing out to new areas should be rewarded while the lower income households are penalized?"

"No. You have a good point. Maybe we should take another look, and possibly encourage people to remain where they are by making improvements needed in their city."

"Aren't there also other forms of inequity that tax-base sharing would help resolve, Juan?" Edwin Perez asked.

"Yes, some other distributional inequities can arise. Some cities, in desperate need for tax relief, may have funds available from other sources which they cannot use to meet their most urgent needs. This was true for Maywood in the Gateway Cities Subregion which couldn't use Proposition A funds for public transit, but they worked out a sale at discount to another city which could use them. Maywood in return received funds into their general fund which would finance much needed local street repairs."

"Yeah, another possibility would be in sharing tax receipts from new car sales which might benefit more than the city holding the agency or agencies," added Smith. "Cerritos, with its concentration of car agencies, is an example of this. If an agreement could be worked out with abutting cities making some tradeoffs, all the cities might benefit. Lancaster and Palmdale almost worked out such an agreement. Creative cooperation between cities of this type could be beneficial to all over the long run."

"Also, cities with a higher than average commercial base, but with low-valued homes and increasing social needs, may be penalized," added Juan.

Other questions were raised at the hearing which dramatized the difficulties in resolving this issue. Before adjourning, Juan scheduled another meeting in two weeks. It proved to be a good beginning on clarifying how local areas might get away from the tax base fragmentation that encourages continued sprawl.

* * *

Further discussions continued at the monthly CEHD Policy Committee meetings on jobs/housing balance. Encouraging shifts of sentiments were emerging gradually. Statements of "impossible" began giving way to "possible with development of strategies" to achieve jobs/housing balance. SCAG staff worked hard to develop possible strategies.

The final group of eight strategies considered focused on two general approaches–planning-oriented and economic/fiscal approaches. The one offering the most promise was the infill/redevelopment approach in the planning area.

Gateway Cities leaders felt strongly that their future rested with the use of infill/redevelopment to achieve needed change. But there was considerable resistance to it, sparked by false preconceptions.

A workshop was organized to come to grips with the fears of many regarding infill, renovation and redevelopment. All of these techniques were in poor repute due to errors in how they had been used in the past.

"Many of you feel that developing infill housing will result in strangers taking over your neighborhoods. This isn't true. The housing developed is for people already living in the community," said George, the workshop leader.

"Yeah, the new housing is for the adult children of the residents, so they can live close to family in a nearby apartment without resorting to doubling up or over-crowding," Marie, another participant, replied.

"But development of infill sites will change the character of the area forever," Joyce said.

"Not necessarily," said Herman, a local planner. "It may entail taking abandoned lots and redeveloping them for housing, converting old buildings to new housing uses, adding to existing buildings, or tearing down existing buildings and rebuilding on the site. When planned right, infill can really add to the quality of the neighborhood."

"Yeah, but it'll increase the density significantly. Too many people in a small space." Joyce said.

"That's not a problem, since these sites must be near parks and recreation areas where people can get away to enjoy nature easier than in a lower density, lotted subdivision. You'd be amazed how much better the development will be overall," Herman replied.

"But housing will be more expensive per square foot, won't it?" Marie asked.

"No, actually cheaper since high land costs are a big factor in making housing prices so high. Here, the average units per acre may be double that in a normal subdivision. Plus, you won't have to spend as much time keeping the yard up and traveling back and forth to work."

"Can a wider variety of households live in the development?" George asked.

"Definitely. This is the beauty of such infill development. The new housing is for essential members of the community which are increasingly being crowded out of reasonably priced housing. This includes teachers, policemen, and public servants," Herman replied.

"Isn't infill housing less attractive than regular single family housing?" Joyce countered.

"No, that's a misconception. Often, infill housing design competitions are sponsored so the planners and architects can work closely with residents of the community to design housing that will be a valued part of a community."

"What are some other advantages of going with infill housing?" Joyce asked.

"New public investments are often provided to make the development work, especially if the increased density requires upgraded sewers and street systems. These should be provided to ensure that no problems occur later with overloaded public services."

"Brownfields could be redeveloped to be a real asset for involved neighborhoods. They are currently a blighting influence. But, with a good plan and design, they can be placed back in operation as a productive industrial, commercial or residential land use," Herman indicated.

"Also, there's often hesitation to introduce a mixed use plan into an older neighborhood. With good thought and design, it can have a revitalizing influence also."

"Neighborhood renovation can occur with a strong planning effort. Rehabilitation and spot clearance are also options to renew our communities," Marie stated.

"Other strategies needed include orientation to transit through transit villages and transit stations. Other cities have been very successful in this," Herman indicated. "For example, it permits a mix of uses including residential, commercial and business to be clustered in varying densities around transit stations in transit villages. Reports are that this is beginning to happen in the L. A. area. A number of developments are either completed, under construction or planned. From this, a big breakthrough for transit and affordable housing related to convenient services."

"All this could be helped by more incentives, such as tax credits or state and local finance tools," George added.

"Reductions in off-street parking requirement where increased transit is available could help reduce the cost of housing where high land costs dictate. This needs to be explored," Herman said.

Through these discussions, the ins and outs of infill and redevelopment promised to strengthen older neighborhoods–while also using existing under-utilized infrastructure.

* * *

Another Gateway Workshop was organized to cover synergy, an important issue not well understood by most members other than practicing planners used to grappling with land use issues. Most didn't realize that good planning had a synergistic impact as to how well things worked when land uses were designed to blend and harmonize with each other.

The same group met again to discuss this issue. George, the workshop leader, who had been a planner, began the session.

"Do you know what synergy means when dealing with land uses?"

"No, what does it involve, George?" asked Joyce.

"Basically, synergy reflects the combined effect of land uses working together which exceeds the sum of their individual impacts. For example, let's look at the uses in a Transit Village to see why they are so effective in carrying out its functions. People consider a transit station only as a place to catch a train, but it's much more, isn't it?"

"You're right," stated Marie. "A transit station can hold shopping, eating and working places for those catching train who need to buy things, eat or earn a living."

"Plus transit villages also can provide close by apartments, condos, and other housing so residents won't have to even drive to the transit stop to board the train,"said Herman. "That cuts down on congestion and the need for too many parking spaces."

"Along with offices and work places created, the added jobs will also reduce the distance traveled by many of the residents," Marie shot back, starting to understand what George was talking about when synergy was mentioned.

"Right!" George stated. "So all these activities collectively reduce congestion, clean the air and make the area more livable. What else happens at the same time?"

"We were talking about infill of housing and other land uses at our last workshop. Synergy also encourages area infill, creating a more attractive and compact area," Roger, another participant, jumped in.

"Yeah, schools, parks and other public and semi-public uses would also be encouraged to congregate where people can easily use them with minimal congestion," Marie answered back, getting excited about what was being learned.

"Absolutely! All these uses feed on each other due to their close proximity. If these activities were only considered separately or poorly sited, then urban living would be adversely impacted," stated George. "This same thinking can be used for lots of other groupings of uses which will result in the achievement of more than the sum of their parts. This is the essence of good planning!"

"You mean different types of housing, industry, campuses, shopping centers, and other types of uses which minimize parking, loading, and other needs to make urban areas more attractive and desirable," Joyce answered back.

"Yes, people don't realize how good planning achieves so much. Synergy does so much," George shot back. "Let's always keep this in mind when we try to simplify the design of things too much."

With that, they continued to probe the elements of synergy which saved money, cleaned the air, made areas more attractive and reduced congestion, among other things. Without efforts like this, our urban areas will continue to be more unwieldy and ugly as they develop.

CHAPTER 21
REGIONAL
PLANNING LEGISLATION

*A number of regional planning
bills providing the finances and
other means for sustaining the various
regions over their planning periods move
ahead in SCAG and state legislature.
Major political battles result as liberal
and conservative forces jockey for
position in shaping the character of
the L.A. Region.*

"I've been a fool. We're all
fools most of our lives. It's unavoidable."

Les Miserables

Juan arrived in L.A. by plane the following Thursday to present his regional planning bill to the Growth Visioning Committee at their request. It turned out to be perfect timing for everyone. When SCAG realized Juan would be the main speaker at the meeting, they contacted Mike, chair of the Subregion Coordinators and some others. They planned to have all the subregion coordinators and other key officials attend the meeting. They even shifted the meeting to the larger RC Meeting Room to handle the expected crowd.

The big meeting room was filled wall-to-wall with several hundred people and the adjoining meeting rooms were connected by video screen for the talk.

"Regional members, I'm glad that we could meet in this splendid facility," Juan began. "I've heard about the great things going on with your efforts to develop an effective growth guidance or 'visioning' process to make your 2004 RTP successful. What a great step forward, in contrast to the urban sprawl which has been typical of L.A. for so many years. I applaud your efforts."

"The other reason for appearing before you is to explain the Regional Planning bill we're pursuing in the state legislature. That and the need for tax-base sharing at the regional level. I know you're in the process of final-izing your own transportation financing bill to be presented to the legisla-ture. Two different bills, I understand, need to be consolidated into one to present to the State House and Senate for adoption. So, this is a perfect time, I believe, to talk about what's needed now for the 2001 RTP, as well as to look forward to the 2004 RTP."

Juan proceeded to present the ingredients of his Regional Planning Bill and the integral part that tax-base sharing would play in its success. He acknowledged that the chances of passage of certain parts of the bill were not good, but such improvements often take years to get approved. This was true in Minnesota and other leading states. He then opened the meet-ing to questions.

"How will your Regional Planning Bill help to put our 2001 RTP in conformity?" asked the Growth Visioning chair.

"It won't help you for the 2001 RTP. It's geared to carrying out your 2004 RTP. But it will provide some guidelines for your transportation finance bill which will ensure that it will be passed if our Regional Planning Bill is adhered to."

"Does it provide guidelines for our Growth Visioning efforts?" asked the new RC chair.

"Yes, it does. Including the authorization, if desired, to collaborate in the development of tax sharing with adjoining or interested cities or areas. I won't go into this in detail here but it could solve lots of problems which you're currently having between 'have' and 'have-not' communities. Also help ensure the provision of more affordable housing throughout the region, along with working toward achieving housing/job balance."

These and other important questions were raised and answered at the meeting. Some were barbed and definitely meant to put Juan and his bill down.

One example was: "You sure want to take control away from the locals again." Another zapped him by saying: "Can't you better spend your time in the legislature by giving the property tax monies back to local areas where they should be?" Juan acknowledged: "local areas must get more tax money to solve their problems and I'm working hard on possible solu-tions."

The meeting ended well, in welcome contrast to the late 1999 Long Beach meeting which had been a disaster.

* * *

Several assemblymen, mostly from the L.A. area, were sitting around waiting for the Regional Planning Bill to go through committee.

"Well, it's going to be interesting to see how Juan's bill finally evolves, especially regarding Growth Visioning. L.A. is an area which most people never thought would be willing to try Growth Visioning. Do you feel it will pass?" asked Carl, from Los Angeles.

"I think it might have a chance to be passed by the committee, although it won't get through the Assembly this time," thought Burl from Glendale.

"Just look at the size of the L.A. area to realize what an undertaking it is. They have 14 unique regions (called subregions) to satisfy. It's going to be quite an undertaking," was another thought by Dennis from Fullerton.

"I agree," replied Carl, "Because it developed in such a decentralized fashion, Metropolitan L.A. has always had a distinctive pattern of wealthy, middle-class, working-class and poor neighborhoods. Generally, the poor and working-class neighborhoods developed in the flats, along flood-prone lowlands near the rivers. Wealthy enclaves sprang up in the foothills and the coastal areas, where high ground and spectacular views increased property values."

"Right. The middle income and working-class homeowners often lived in the 'middle ground' between the poor lowlands and wealthy uplands," replied Burl.

"But recent trends have begun to alter these patterns somewhat, I believe," Tom said.

"Yeah, it's gotten more complex since other problems involving population, demographic change, along with key social and economic issues have evolved," said Burl. "Land and natural resource constraints, as well as governing and local fiscal resource dilemmas have been added."

"It's obvious that we must come to grips with how we utilize our resources–not just continue to expand outward as in the past," broke in Earl from Riverside.

"Yeah, we must guide our growth within each subregion in ways that maximize its potentials and protect their uniqueness. At the same time, we must do it in such a way that the overall region benefits and works in tandem with all of its parts," Burl indicated.

"How do we do this?" asked Dennis.

"Possibly use the regional center-oriented concept; or urban rail system; or redeveloped livable neighborhoods focusing more on the human scale–or a combination of these depending on their location, topography, history, and other factors?" said Earl, who seemed to be the most familiar with Juan's Regional Planning Bill.

"Well, we've got our work cut out for us if we're going to guide this growth," growled Burl, as he got up and prepared to leave. "Let's see what we can do about it, especially if Juan's bill gets out of committee and is voted on in the coming months."

* * *

Evon met Juan that evening at the Capitol offices.

"Juan, she's sending the message that she's going to play hardball. Tapes on you and your past, proofs of hard drug use and your sentencing as a youth."

"I'm not surprised. Well, we need to assemble the evidence of her skullduggery with the big corporations and efforts to develop state legislation by the bribery route. Let's focus on that."

"I already have key information on that, Juan. I'll leave copies with you to look at. In a day or two, we can counterattack effectively. We can really hurt them."

* * *

Evon, responding to Judith Struthers request for a meeting, met with Abe Underhill and her the next day. She asked for an update of his work to date. After providing it, Evon excused himself and went off to wrap up some assigned tasks which needed to be completed before he left that evening. He knew he'd outlived his welcome and should get out. He'd moved out of his Sacramento apartment that morning, so he could get on the road directly.

Leaving KOPE's parking lot near the Capitol building, Evon planned to drive to his old San Fernando digs, in suburban L.A. even though the weather had turned bad–rainy and foggy. Driving along a little later, looking through the rear view mirror, he noticed a car which had been following him for some time. He hoped this wasn't an indication of paranoia involving all his cloak and dagger work. He sped up, slowed down, changed streets, went through a light turning red, and even stopped for gas, to no avail. The car, a black 98 Mazda sedan, doggedly remained on scent, keeping in sight although dropping back some at times.

He drove along Highway 99 which provided more variety with places to stop along the way, as compared with the monotony of I-5. Near Fresno, he stopped at a restaurant for dinner. With darkness rapidly approaching and the weather worsening, he debated whether to check into a motel or continue on to San Fernando. Not wanting an overnight stay in a bland motel room, he opted to press on.

Driving away from the restaurant, he thought at first he'd shaken the black Mazda. After a few miles though, the Mazda reappeared. At the restaurant, he'd mulled over who his follower might be, concluding he was in trouble based on how Judith acted earlier. Dark now, the road became

265

more winding and hilly. The rain increased as visibility lessened. He was between Visalia and Bakersfield when the Mazda quickly moved up on him, not over two or three car lengths behind. He speeded up to 80 but was unable to shake him. He couldn't identify who was driving due to the dark tinted windshield. He figured it was a man because of his size.

As he approached a hilly curve with a drop-off, the other car accelerated to over 100 miles per hour, overtook and rammed into his car from the side. The quick hit threw his car into a spin, hurling it over the edge and down the ravine. He blacked out as his car rolled over and over, hitting the bottom with a sodden thud.

* * *

He regained consciousness strapped to a hospital bed. Doctors were working over him.

"Where am I?" he feebly mumbled, sedated and unable to move any part of his body.

"You're lucky, young man. We were wondering whether you'd ever regain consciousness," grunted one of the doctors.

"You're in a Bakersfield hospital, County General," remarked the attending nurse.

"How long here?"

"Almost two days. At first, we thought you didn't have a chance," the doctor replied.

"You're still in bad shape with a leg, arm and ribs broken, and bruises all over your body. You're lucky your car, which was totaled, didn't catch fire. No more questions," he said. "You need to rest and get well. The police will be checking back on you as you get better."

Henry drifted off as they shot him full of morphine to handle the pain. When he came to again, he was immobilized in a private room. Unable to move, he waited for a nurse to come. Finally one came to check his charts, noting he had regained consciousness.

"Glad you've finally come to," she said, straightening his bed and checking bandages which covered him. "We'll let the police waiting know you're able to talk now," she said.

A police detective arrived a little later, asking him some questions after telling him what he knew. They'd found his car at the bottom of a ravine after receiving a call from a motorist who came by soon after the crash. They knew Evon's name from his driver's license, but didn't know who to call, since his address and phone number were out-of-date.

"What happened, Evon?"

"I was rammed by another car and shoved off the road. Someone wanted me dead. You haven't published any report that I'm alive, have you?" he asked anxiously. "I want protection. Someone wants me dead–bad. I have a partial license plate number for you to check out."

"We haven't notified anyone regarding you, but we'll post a guard at your door."

"Can you make one call–to Juan Rodriguez, Speaker of the House, at the State Capitol in Sacramento?" asked Evon. "Let him know what happened, but make sure you talk only to him. Make sure whoever answers knows the call's important but don't let on who's calling. Juan may also be in danger, officer. I'll answer any questions, but it's important that he gets in touch with me as quickly as possible."

"I'll contact him right away and get back with further questions so we can begin our investigation."

* * *

Juan was quickly reached, apprized of Evon's condition and how the accident happened. He made necessary arrangements for protection. The detective questioned Evon, with the license plate number checked he had remembered from the pursuing car. After piecing things together, they found it was a rental car. They surmised the renter had been hired to make a "hit" on Evon, but were unable to determine who he was since he used a fake name and address.

Both Evon and Juan knew that KOPE and Judith had been involved in the altercation. They planned to respond quickly, but needed time to map out an approach.

* * *

Thursday, April 3, 2001, dawned with an overcast sky and a hard, pulsating rain lashing Downtown Santa Monica. The adjacent gray, pulsating Pacific Ocean provided a cold, austere backdrop as fierce winds up to 80 miles per hour swept in, sending pedestrians bent over and shivering, scurrying to get their business completed as quickly as possible.

A decision on a judgment against Jim Robinson loomed ominously on the docket at the Santa Monica Court House, a squat, ugly, four story limestone structure of unknown architectural origin. Located on the edge of downtown with its colorful open air mall, this facility had been the locale of the O.J. Simpson murder trial six years earlier.

A jury of six men and six women of diverse shapes and colors filed into the courtroom ready to render its verdict. The judge received their findings of guilt on all counts.

Grimly, Jim Robinson rose to face the judge for sentencing.

"Jim Robinson, we find you guilty of evading payment of $100,000 to the Racing Corporation, owner of the Hollywood Racetrack. This involves accrued gambling debts over the past year. Are you ready to pay this debt plus $50,000 fine plus interest at this time?"

"No, your honor. But I can assemble the money in several days," Jim said, not sure how.

"I'll permit you two days. If you fail to pay this within the two day period, you'll be sentenced to 60 days in the local jail." Her gavel came down hard. "Next case."

Jim left the courtroom concerned about how to assemble the money. Although he had resisted asking help from his father, he knew now he had no other option. He remembered now he'd forgotten to call his father before leaving Sacramento. He must call him at once.

Receiving no answer, he knew he must fly there now. He couldn't shake the puzzled look on his father's face when he'd last seen him. Chartering a plane, he flew to Sacramento that afternoon, taking a cab to his father's home. His father's maid, Millie told him that his father hadn't been acting right lately. He proceeded to his father's bedroom and knocked.

"Dad, It's me. Can I come in?"

"Who? Oh, is that you, Jim? Come in," came a shaky reply. He entered, finding his father slumped on his bed, his hair and clothing disheveled.

"Dad, what's wrong?" Jim asked, looking down at him with deep concern.

"Don't know–confused. Not sure what's going on," came an anguished reply.

"I'm your son, Jim. Dad, don't you know me? I've never seen you acting like this before."

"Feel weird. Have fuzzy thoughts. Difficulty recognizing you–or anyone. Things strange recently," came a disjointed, muffled response. Jim had never seen him acting this way. He'd always had been so self-assured in his dealings. Now, Jim saw fear and uncertainty on his unshaven face gazing wearily up at Jim.

"We'll take care of you, Dad. I'll call your doctor and have him come right over."

His father's doctor, Dr. Harrell, arrived 15 minutes later. He examined him, although his father didn't initially recognize him. After the examination, Dr. Harrell talked to Jim.

"He has all the symptoms of early stages of Alzheimer's Disease. I can't be sure until some tests are made. He should be admitted to a hospital at once for tests."

"Thanks, Doctor. Let's do it now while he's tranquil and willing to cooperate."

* * *

Jim had taken his father for granted over the years as an indestructible person without problems. It was a rude shock to realize he needed help, although he realized now that, at his father's age, a person's health could change quickly. After admittance, his father wandered back and forth between recognizing him and being confused. During lucid moments, Jim was able to make the necessary arrangements through his father for a loan to pay off court judgment and debts. In his current state, his father didn't question Jim about how or why he needed the money. It probably was just as well for both of them.

In the process of coping with his father's Alzheimer's, Jim realized how much he loved his Dad and appreciated, for the first time, how much he'd done for Jim over the years. Thinking back, Jim focused on what had happened over the last few months. He had lost touch with reality and how to treat the people he loved–Lila, his father and Juan, his old friend from college days.

It was puzzling now why this was so. His friends were only trying to help him become a better person–and he'd resisted. Lila, because he was afraid to get close to her; Juan, who he wouldn't help get his regional bill passed; and his father, who he felt was old and worthless.

He had failed them all, while blaming them for his arrogance and self-importance. All he really needed to do was return their love. It was obvious now what he should have done. He should have returned Lila's love and helped her grow with him. His lack of commitment and fear of involvement were destroying their chances to consummate any type of relationship.

Instead of his obsession against Juan's Regional Planning Bill, he should have worked to help him achieve it in a modified form. With his father, if he'd appreciated him more, he might have drawn him into his work several years ago, keeping his mind active and outlook loving.

He must work to turn things around in all three situations. God had finally impressed on him the error of his ways and the way to proceed. It had taken him a long time to realize it.

* * *

Mike and Betsy, needing to discuss important regional happenings, finally got together at her office. They sat discussing how the Metro Planning Organization (MPO), in which Betsy had become involved, would handle SCAG.

"Do you think the RC will be able to meet the MPO requirements and get the 2001 RTP approved and MPO re-certified?" Betsy asked.

"I don't know. It depends on which bill the RC supports. Neither bill has been introduced yet. In fact, I'm still working on my version with my RC supporters," Mike replied. "We won't introduce it until we know more about what Jim and his supporters put together."

Reflecting on their conversation, Mike thought back to the Gateway Cities Partners meeting at Long Beach that took place in February 2001.

He told Betsy about the conference and wide range of speakers at that meeting.

"Almost too many, twenty-two speakers in one day. Gavin apologized about the number and wished he could have scheduled it over two or three days. So much to cover."

"How did they handle the demographics for the 27 cities involved?" Betsy asked.

"They used a video focusing on a mythical city of Gateway–representing the entire region–which was effective, especially looking at air quality and educational problems."

"Do you think Gateway Cities can be brought back to its former health?"

"One speaker provided comparisons with Cleveland, Chattanooga and Tupelo's inner city declines, and their revitalization in recent years through enlightened leadership. He thought this indicated good possibilities for Gateway's resurgence in the coming decades. If those cities could reenergize and redesign themselves even in the face of the "gloom and doom" forecasts facing them, Gateway Cities certainly should be able to do the same. Leadership and development of strong strategies and programs were the key.

"I'm glad to hear that. The Gateway Cities COG is key, in my estimation, to the region's achieving conformity, and being recertified over the long pull."

"I can't agree with you more, Betsy. If Gateway can do it, L.A. City, the remainder of the inner city areas and the older suburbs should use Gateway as a case study of what can be achieved. They won't have any excuses for not reaching their goals."

* * *

Jim and Lila had problems getting together, primarily because of his guilt about his past actions. He seemed to be awakening from a long sleep involving a nightmare which just went on and on. He wished he could wipe away the memories of all the crazy, selfish things he had done. But he couldn't, even after prayer. He knew God should hold him accountable for all the terrible things he had done or participated in. There was no other way out. He must apologize to everyone he'd wronged. It would be tough, but he must do it–as soon as possible.

He must start with Lila.. He called her at work:

"Lila, this is your wayward Jim. Please help me work something out of this mess I've made of myself with you and others close to me?"

"Jim, are you sure you're going to go through with all this confessing?"

"Yes. I'm finally at peace with God and ready to take some humbling steps necessary to finally put this mess behind me," Jim replied. "The big question is whether you'll like the new me? Can I meet you somewhere?"

"Jim, I can't believe what you're saying," Lila replied. "I'm scared you're going to make a fool out of me again. I've heard you say so many times that you've changed, and then I've found I'd been lied to again. I just don't know."

"Please, Lila. Take a leap of faith and meet me. I won't disappoint you this time."

"Okay–but this is your last chance, Jim. Meet me at my place this evening at seven. I'll be waiting. But if you don't get here by seven, don't come. I can't take any more."

"Thanks, Lila, from the bottom of my heart. I'll be there. See you."

* * *

"I don't believe it. You're here on time. Are you finally serious?" Lila asked when Jim arrived.

"Yes, Lila, I'm serious, although I've got a long way to go and a lot of people to convince."

"Convince me first."

"First off, your faith and my father's condition convinced me the error of my ways. That and a lot of praying to the good Lord."

"What's this about your father, Jim. Has something gone wrong?"

"He has Alzheimers and needs a lot of help–which I'm ready to help with."

"Oh, no."she gasped. "I'm sorry to hear that. Is he in bad shape, like Reagan?

"Not that bad, yet," Jim replied. "But when I first saw him, I was shocked by the change he'd undergone almost overnight. Here I was, so wrapped up in myself with my small problems. I felt disgusted with myself on just how far I had descended into greed and selfishness. That's when I got down on my knees and finally prayed a meaningful prayer to God, asking his help in turning myself around."

"So what are you proposing to do? Or is that what you want to talk about?"

"Yes, I value your advice, Lila, although I'm not sure how you'll react to my plans."

"So you're not sure whether I'll buy in to the new Jim, eh? Is that it?"Lila asked, almost impishly.

"That's about it, Lila. If I do what I propose to do, and I will, would you still love me and be willing to change some of your ways too? Or have you?" he asked desperately.

"Wow. True confessions. We're sure a mixed-up pair." Lila answered , finally understanding his frame of mind. "To answer your question, yes, I have changed. Or I think I have. It may be like the blind leading the blind, but I saw a lot of you in what I had become. Jim, we may have arrived at the same fork in the road together. I'm ready to change too. Maybe we can help each other along the way–by leaning on each other as we try the straight and narrow. We'll probably need the help of others along the way too. How does that sound?"

"Sounds great. Let's begin."

They began talking about their problems and possible solutions.

"What're you going to do about your Transportation Finance Bill, Jim?"

"I'm going to drop it entirely and endorse Mike's bill, Lila. It's going to take a lot of 'eating crow' but I'm willing to do this. Also, I'm going to make sure everyone knows that I don't plan on taking a bribe from KOPE. Any debts I have, I plan to pay off through loans from my father. I've got to do a lot of confessing, apologizing and 'eating crow.' It may take time to get myself straightened out so people will begin to trust me again. But it's got to start somewhere. Now's the time to begin, with your help, hopefully," he added.

"I'm ready to help, even if I lose my job."

* * *

Jim placed a call to Mike.

"Mike, this is Jim Robinson. I've given a lot of thought to SCAG's transportation financing bill since our meeting yesterday and I wanted you to know that I've decided to back your bill and drop mine entirely."

"Really? You really mean that, Jim?"came back the disbelieving response. There was a moment's pause as Mike regrouped. His voice came back "Why the abrupt change of heart?"

"I can understand why you're having difficulty believing me," Jim stated. "All I can say is I've finally come to my senses. It's taken awhile, but a number of things have influenced my decision. First of all, your bill makes sense. Mine doesn't, in terms of considering all the people of the

272

region. Other factors that have influenced my decision include prayer, my father's declining health and the entreaties of the woman I love."

"Wow! You have had a lot on your plate," Mike said, still trying to digest why Jim would suddenly reverse himself on something he had been so adamant about. "I'm going to have to think things over. But I might want you to work with me on the final details of the bill. Would you be interested– no changes in the bill? Possibly co-sponsor it with me to show your faith in it, Jim?"

"You bet I would, although I'm surprised you'd want me involved, Mike. After all the flak I've given you and Juan on this."

"Politics are weird, Jim. We all need each other–and I need your help. Any way I can help you? "

"I do need all the help I can get after digging myself into a deep, deep hole. All the rumors floating around about my financial problems need to stop. I'm getting a loan from my father to take care of them. I'm not taking a bribe from KOPE to get their programs passed. I think that's self-evident by the fact I'm dropping my bill entirely."

"I'm glad to hear that, Jim. If you'd like, I'd be glad to pass the word once we get the bill finalized and through the RC."

They agreed to get together and work out the bugs in Mike's bill.

* * *

As is generally true in life, things didn't work out that easily for Jim. The next day, Judith and KOPE threatened to leak news on Jim's efforts to make them responsible for proposed changes in the transportation finance bill which he was authoring. They sent him tapes on his bribe demand and stated that he must agree to their terms or they would expose him.

He responded by stating that he had more damning evidence on them and friends in high places who could damage their relationship with the big corporations supporting them.

Charges and counter-charges were hurled. Tapes were played and Jim's reputation suffered. Finally, Bea contacted Jim for an interview. Based on her previous involvement with Jim, she felt a great deal more was hidden behind the accusations. They finally agreed to a meeting at his condo at eight that evening.

* * *

Bea arrived at his condo just before eight. To start things off, Jim handed her a glass of her favorite wine. They sat in his study and exchanged some small talk. Then, the questions:

"Jim, can you enlighten me about all the rumors circulating about you?"

"I'm ready to give you a detailed interview about my problems and situation. It's a story I'm not proud of, but I guess it's time you got my side of it."

"No holds barred?"

"What do you mean by 'no holds barred', Bea?" he asked with trepidation.

"Tell it like it is, warts and all, if there are any," she responded with conviction.

"There are warts but there's a story behind the story which needs telling," he answered defensively.

"That's what I want to hear," she indicated.

"Bea, up to now, we've met a few times but only exchanged pleasantries. I haven't told you much about my life. Let me bring you up-to-date."

"First of all, Jim, I'd like some answers to some basic questions on your background which should help me place your problems in better perspective," she said, trying to get a early reading on him. "First of all, why did you get so involved in SCAG and its regional agenda?"

"I became involved in SCAG after I won a seat on the city council in Beverly Hills in the mid-80's. Sitting on the council whet my appetite because it allowed me to expand my practice. I had graduated from USC with a law degree and after spending several years playing football in the NFL, I came back and opened my practice. Originally, my plans were to practice law, but I found it too dry and limiting, at least at first, as I struggled with my first few cases of rezoning and real estate closings. I thought running for public office might be more glamorous and open up new directions in my career since I had a big name as a former football star.

"Trying to help, a friend of mine invited me to attend a SCAG meeting or two to learn about regionalism. He felt small cities like Beverly Hills were lost in a suburban setting, and that only by looking at urban growth from a regional perspective could we find solutions to our growing urban problems. He was right, things clicked, I caught the regional bug and I haven't stopped since. It even whet my appetite to run for the state legislature–which I still want to do."

"So that's what makes you tick? That helps me understand you better. My next question concerns why you got involved in compulsive gambling which seems to be one of your big problems?"

"You guessed it. It's bad. In desperation I'm working to break the gambling fever through Gamblers Anonymous. It operates like Alcoholics Anonymous to get people off the habit. I've had this urge to get rich quick, relishing an emotional high on everything. It's exciting–like playing football and gambling on runs or catching passes in front of your fans."

"Hm. Your answer helps me better understand your situation at this point in time. Go ahead and discuss your problems and how an article I might write could help you?"

"I think some of the things I just said alluded to some of my problems. By going into some detail in an article, I hope to provide the reader with a balanced picture of what prompted me to do what I did. Plus, provide me an opportunity to apologize for my actions.

"Okay. Where do you want to start, Jim?"

"I think the thing that started my downfall came when I trapped myself into helping CIG due to my obsession with Lila Moore. I felt that I had no chance to win her unless I agreed to help CIG with its goals for housing and more freeways. This complicated things since I already had dangerous passions for taking chances in the stock market, gambling at the racetrack, and seeking other thrills to prove my manhood.

He went on: "Things got out-of-control rapidly from that point on. Even Lila didn't understand what I was doing–or why.

"What happened next, Jim?"

"I got into an ego battle with Juan Rodriguez over what was best for the L.A. Region. He obviously knows more about regionalism than I'll ever know. But I dreamed of being powerful and thought it was about time to cut him down a peg. Others didn't agree with me, and I walked out–twice. Then I got into a battle with God as to who was right. And of course, I couldn't be wrong. I only believed in Jim Robinson.

"When did you finally realize you could be wrong?" she asked.

"When everything and everyone turned against me. It's difficult to continue to believe in yourself when everything you do or touch turns bad," he said, bad memories rushing back.

"But it took you a long time to find that out, didn't it?" she questioned further.

"Yes, although I knew long before I finally admitted it publicly," painfully aware of the pride involved.

"What do you want to tell people now, Jim?"

"Don't struggle with God on things like this. You can't win–nor should you want to win."

"Sounds like you've done a lot of thinking about this, Jim," Bea said, impressed with Jim's new convictions. "Do you have anything else you want to explain to people who feel you let them down?"

"I want to explain what I did which sealed my fate."

"Okay?"

"I became so self-centered and obsessed with winning that I would do anything to achieve what I wanted. So I gambled in every conceivable way. Friendships weren't important. I didn't care what happened to my father, my lady friend or society in general. Only I–Jim Robinson–seemed important.

"You were really caught up in it, weren't you, Jim? I've found this happens to a lot of people caught up in the so-called 'power trip.' They lose touch with reality."

"You've got that right, Bea. Looking back on it, I'm totally ashamed."

"Okay, Jim, let's shift to another painful issue–Judith Struthers and KOPE. I've received a lot of information on their game from Evon through Juan which I hope will sink their ship, so to speak. I understand that you've also been strung along by them on your version of SCAG's transportation finance bill for the state legislature. Could you give me details on this so I can include it in an expose of them?"

Jim proceeded to give her details on his dealings with Judith and KOPE. When their interview ended, Bea had a complete picture of Jim's problems and turnaround. His coverage and Evon's episodes provided her with at least two articles on how greed, money and power in high places can get out of hand and destroy promising careers. It wasn't just a local problem but also a national, and even a fundamental human problem being played out daily in headlines all over the world.

CHAPTER 22
FINAL REGIONAL PLAN

*Completion of the final 2001 RTP
would be significant due to the number
of obstacles thrust in its path. Whether
conformity could be achieved was another matter.
Only time would tell–time and the willingness to
compromise on a number of important
decisions. The RC must make some big
decisions which would shape the L.A. Region
for decades to come. Whether they would all
be the right decisions, no one could be sure
until years later. Hopefully, they would
prove right on the most important decisions.*

"On matters of little importance,
swim with the current. On matters
of principle, stand like a rock."

Julian Dixon

Finally! Things had come together so the 2001 Regional Transportation Plan (RTP) might be attainable. The SCAG transportation financing bill had been cobbled together, sent to the state legislature and passed. Now they had their guidelines to focus on reorganization of transit and its routes, plus improvements, upgrades and integrated operation of the highway and freeway system, a new regional system of airports, and final corrections for other important aspects of the plan.

But many people were still critical of the RTP. Comments about it ranged from being "a rare glimpse into the obvious" to "receiving 1900 requests for amendment but ignoring all logical corrections" and "talking the talk but not seriously considering the needs of the various subregions." The minimal efforts to modify the flawed RTP were received with more than grumbles around the meetings. No one was excited about the plan–other than its sharper focus on transit.

Other comments frequently voiced included tagging MAGLEV with being "a high priced trophy which goes from nowhere to nowhere" and faintly justifying other elements as being "only minor technical changes."

No one finds out how or whether these "minor technical changes" ever were made in the heat of the final moments of the numbers crunching. The big, big riddle, still the talk of all subregion gatherings concerned "what was in the Black Box which so magically changed things for the better" by achieving clean air goals or balancing transportation financing costs with available revenues. In another three years, the Feds would require disclosure of all components of the Black Box. Its commands would no longer be hidden from view–but would be opened to criticism.

Concern grew in the Regional Council hierarchy about the handling of their last two big meetings on the 2001 RTP, April 5 and 12. Much seemed at stake and little had been resolved about the potential for a huge financial shortfall. How were they going to patch this plan together to pass Federal scrutiny for conformity and recertification?

Jim prepared for the April 2nd meeting of the Transportation /Communications (TCC) Policy group and its crucial regional airport plan. So much rode on getting unanimous approval for this plan that had emerged from two years of wrangling and intense debate. Not only did significant differences with the City remain over the LAX expansion problem, but so did disagreements with Orange County on El Toro and problems with the Inland Empire on potential airports there. Surviving all these highly political issues would be difficult.

* * *

"Down with LAX expansion! Down with LAX expansion!" chanted the anti-growth demonstrators from neighborhoods and communities surrounding the airport, followed by choruses of "We want El Toro! We want El Toro!" They had staked out a well placed group of seats in the crowded chambers at SCAG where the regional airport plan was set for the crucial debate on the Regional Airport Plan for the six county area. The room was so packed, people stood in the aisles. The demonstrators came with especially garish tee-shirts–pink, green and orange–condemning LAX and glorifying El Toro.

The TCC Committee chair attempted to keep things orderly but the people were determined to present their case forcefully this time to avoid a repeat of 1998 when their RTP effort had fizzled. They came early, promising to provide an orderly but memorable performance, and hoping to get their position highlighted prominently in the news. Inglewood Mayor Zack Wherry led the assembled bloc in 25 seats plus another 25 standing in the aisles, their T-shirts emblazoned with the same slogans they were chanting. It was a garish and impressive display of power by the common people.

At least 30 to 40 speakers signed up for three minutes each to provide their stories of how LAX had ruined their lives with noisy takeoffs and landings over the years. They paraded to the microphone as the chair called their names, and spun tales of how the noise and danger had grown over the years as LAX traffic expanded from 24 million to the current 76 million passengers (MAP). They dramatized increases in aircraft size and noise, and detailed how each runway is now handling so many more aircraft at all hours of the day and night. Reporters and photographers strained to get their stories and pictures of the unfolding drama.

After several hours of testimony, the meeting shifted into its deliberative phase. About 30 members of the TCC Policy Committee were positioned around a horseshoe-shaped platform to render their verdict about the region's future airport configuration. They intended to take the findings the Regional Airport Task Force had hammered out over the last two years and approve a plan today. Now it was time for each of the task force participants to voice their views on the eight airports under consideration.

The meeting droned on and on with no consensus. The committee's advocates and opponents of LAX, El Toro, Ontario and several other Inland Empire airports, Palmdale and Burbank, made their cases. Finally, after three hours, the chair asked for an initial vote. The first vote split several ways but a majority favored the plan which advocated no expansion of LAX, and placed passenger caps on the other regional airports. Since a consensus would be required, efforts were made to narrow the differences. After another hour of debate, a consensus emerged. A decision would be passed to the Regional Council for final approval at its April 5th and 12th meetings.

The consensus capped LAX at 78 MAP and achieved a truly regional system of airports, at least on paper, for the first time. Other airports in the system included Ontario and El Toro, along with March, Palmdale, Burbank and John Wayne.

* * *

Juan arrived to visit Evon in the Bakersfield hospital. He was stunned by the news of Evon's near death and rushed to see him once his condition had stabilized.

"Evon, you're a tough one to knock off. I've known that for years. I've talked with detectives in Sacramento and locally. They seem to have some good information on the people involved. We're going to play hard-nosed politics to get this straightened out soon."

"Thanks for coming, Juan. It was touch and go for awhile but I've turned the corner. They've got me all wrapped up in bandages like a mummy. I can't do much for awhile."

"What happened, Evon? You know we've got detectives in Bakersfield and Sacramento at work on this. We know they were out to get you."

"You've got that right, Juan. Judith and KOPE wanted to make sure I didn't survive. I hope we can nail them good."

"We think we can prove that your accident was really an effort to kill you and wipe out your knowledge of their complicity in an effort to screw the democratic process," reassured Juan.

"If you can do that, all this has been worth it for me," Evon replied wanly.

*　*　*

Juan met later with Jim. It was the first time they had talked in several months, and Jim apologized for his actions, promising Juan that he would make up for things later.

"It's been a difficult time, Juan," Jim said, walking up and contritely shaking his hand. "I've been so off-base for so long, will you ever believe in me again?"

"You know I will, Jim. We all make mistakes or 'errors in judgment', as I prefer to call them. The big thing is to admit them and move on."

"My ego. I just had to have things go my way. Everyone else was wrong. It was 'My way or the highway.' It's scary how we get locked into something and won't budge."

"Yeah. It's a problem that's kept civilization from achieving great gains without high costs over time. Our history has been littered with religious wars, ethnic disputes and many other tragic happenings as we fail to face up to a situation and compromise some."

"What can I do to repair all the pain I've caused, Juan?"

"Obviously, you've got to begin to get your life back together again, Jim. You'll need to find forgiveness for all the pain you've caused and get your reputation back. It'll take time, but I've found John Wooden's principles of success and happiness can help."

"That's what I'm looking for, Juan. I seem to have lost my way toward happiness. I've seen Wooden's good old fashioned principles on the Internet. I'll study them; maybe get with some focus group on them. I certainly can't teach myself. Thanks for the advice."

*　*　*

Bea met with Mike on his Transportation Finance bill after Jim had agreed to drop his bill and support Mike's.

"I bet you're glad you and Jim won't have to collapse your two different bills into one, Mike."

280

"Right. It would have been virtually impossible, since they were so different. Especially with the anticipated KOPE amendments."

"Do you feel that things will work out now?"

"Yes, I do," Mike said. "Jim has agreed to work closely to get my bill accepted. In fact, when I asked him if he would be interested in jointly sponsoring it, he welcomed the opportunity. He was surprised that I would be interested. I just felt we needed to get all this bitterness behind us and this might be one way."

"He must have finally really faced up to what a mess he had created. I have to take off my hat to him for his willingness to make this embarrassing reversal. I know how hard it must be for a proud man like him."

"I think he was able to do this only by reaching out to God in prayer and some real soul-searching."

"So you've got the bill together. What are its chances of passing?"

"It's been passed by the TCC Policy Committee and should pass the RC at its meeting next week. Then it goes to the state Assembly where Juan hopes to get it passed by the end of the month."

"Wow. It's simple when you've got a lot of helping hands. Otherwise, it's chaos."

"That's politics, Bea....... That's politics!" Mike responded.

* * *

Henry and Marcine finally were able to have dinner to catch up on SCAG matters.

"Where does time go, Marc?"

"When you're dealing with regional affairs, there's never enough time. What's new on the regional planning process? I hear you're still involved in Growth Visioning at SCAG?"

"Yes, so far it looks good. What happens next–looking ahead to the 2004 RTP is anyone's guess."

"Yeah, hope we can make some big inroads there."

* * *

The Gateway Cities 710 Corridor project moved ahead to test how several communities could cooperate on commercial uses developed in their portion of the Slauson interchange. Carla and Kent, the subcommittee chair developed a procedure using the Transit Oriented Joint Development (TOJD) approach that involves citizen commitment to make it happen. Each of the four cities selected citizens to represent them in the joint effort. They met weekly to thrash out commercial uses which residents felt their city needed in their portion of the interchange corridor.

Finally, they met jointly with representatives of the other cities to see how they could reach agreement on the uses involved. Gradually, they resolved their differences and agreed on uses each city needed to develop in their portion of the interchange. Then they submitted their recommendations to the Gateway board for final approval. Architects involved with the layout developed the needed street, utility and building patterns needed to make the corridor work for all four cities. After getting the necessary approvals from all the cities, the Gateway board and SCAG incorporated the design into the overall plan. It was hailed as a significant effort by all to achieve regional cooperation and promote tax-base sharing at the local level.

* * *

Juan and his staff continued their efforts to resolve the two issues which had made them such strong adversaries of Judith and KOPE. Although the investigators looking into Evon's accident had no way of knowing how it paralleled Jim's legislative struggles with KOPE and Judith, Juan was sure there was an overstepping of bounds in both cases, and he was in a position to create problems for KOPE through his Regional Planning Bill.

Work in committee continued on the bill. KOPE and Judith fought the bill tooth and nail every chance they got. Bad blood increasingly strained the deliberations, and it appeared that the bill would fail.

* * *

The April 5th RC meeting focused almost entirely on the regional airport portion of the 2001 RTP. It was a raucous affair, with some 50 speakers protesting various portions of the plan. There were so many speakers at three minutes each that they had to reschedule some of them to the April 12th special RC meeting already planned to ensure that the plan was adequately aired. The anti-LAX and El Toro groups showed up again with their gaudy T-shirts peppering the chambers, and were allowed to voice their concerns once more.

Finally, the time came for the RC to come to grips with the regional airport issue. Things promised to be difficult though, since the 15 L.A.City Council members who normally didn't attend were there. Obviously, they were intent on influencing the Maglev and airport votes.

Since the Maglev issue was interwoven with access between the various regional airports, it came up first. Councilman Steadman, an opponent of Maglev, asked to be recognized.

"Mr. Chair, I object to the inclusion of the Maglev issue in the 2001 RTP, especially as the means to connect the key regional airports, particularly from LAX"

282

"How do you propose to exclude it, Councilman?"

"By stating that there're insufficient funds in the 2001 RTP to involve it, especially since L.A. was not a finalist for Federal funds to test it locally."

"There is a reorganized proposal which will permit Maglev to be funded completely by private means. You realize that don't you?"

"Yes, but the public has not been allowed to provide input into this."

"I understand your concern, councilman. What do you propose?"

"Dropping the Maglev issue from the RTP until 2004."

"Since we've run out of time today, we'll continue this issue to the special April 12th meeting. If there is no objection, this meeting is adjourned," the chair intoned.

* * *

The April 12th special RC meeting convened to wrap up the 2001 RTP. It had been a long pull. Some additional speakers voicing their concerns on the RTP were given their three minutes before the RC focused on approving the final 2001 RTP.

The region was so big and complex—with its six counties, 16 million residents, multi-cultural, under-served populations—it was able to give only lip service to all the challenges facing it over the 2001-2025 planning period. This was illustrated too well by the recommended action to adopt Resolution No. 01-418-2 with its eight page summary of recommended actions and 63 WHEREAS's, culminating with its "NOW, THEREFORE BE IT RESOLVED that...".

No wonder people threw up their hands in resignation when the final plan was adopted. It wasn't a plan, it was only a band aid. The Maglev issue had been dropped from consideration in the 2001 RTP, creating problems with transit. There was a shortfall in financing for transportation improvements through 2025, plus other problems. It couldn't be anything else but—when one considered how complicated things became as the process evolved.

All the consultant reports were done separately without consideration of other key information impacting their findings. All the complex models involved components which were unknown and untested by those wanting to better understand and consider the results. No one could know whether what was done was sufficient.

So many people, groups and subregions felt shut out of the process that ground on day after day, month after month, year after year. How could the RC members and public really know how good—or bad—the RTP was. There was a general feeling that the 2001 RTP was better than the 1998

RTP but, what did that mean? Most people weren't pleased with the 1998 RTP. SCAG's top leaders could be faulted for the staff's need to rush to complete at the last minute, late at night, what needed to be amended and done.

Some comments by RC members were overheard as the final deliberations on the WHEREAS's took place:

"I'm glad this is over. I don't know what I'm approving but I guess this will somehow help the L.A. Region."

"I know what you mean. I guess I'm pleased about some of the policies we adopted on housing, transit, land use, freeways, and other things. At least we're focusing on some issues which need to be covered."

"Yeah, hopefully all the data, models and interacting coverage was appropriate. I'm not sure how good that is, especially for a region as big as L.A.'s."

"All we've been doing for so long has been extend the sprawl–organized or disorganized– out toward Bakersfield. I didn't feel like we were doing any effective planning."

"Yeah, all these categories listed: growth, finance, transit, maglev, land use and livable community strategies, highways and arterials, goods movement, non-motorized transportation, etc–just 'hiccups in the sand,' so to speak. It's too much. I wish we could devise a better way to cope with all this."

"Subregion deliberations are helping but they're often not being listened to."

"This is true of other forms of outreach: all the types of citizen groups including senior citizens, Native Americans, minorities, women, health and handicapped organizations, groups traditionally underserved by existing transportation systems, including low-income and minority households. Efforts are made to get their input but it's difficult to get these people to participate when they're just struggling to survive. Even if they come, they don't have the background or ability to adequately interpret what's thrown at them in a few minutes. They don't feel they can make a difference, arguing with professionals. It's difficult to get Regional Citizens involved."

"I agree. I guess we just do the best we can with what we have. Let it go at that."

* * *

The FHWA recertification team worked through the first day of their three days of meetings at SCAG in early May. The team of specialists from Washington and Sacramento covered a wide range of key topics in their questioning sessions. At least ten 'Feds' sat around the U-shaped series of tables in SCAG's Riverside Room. Covering such topics as environmental justice, outreach, economic development, aviation, transit and other transportation, SCAG staff answered Federal officials' questions following a short summary of coverage on each topic. Betsy was there as the local representative of FHWA. She helped guide the Feds questioning of SCAG staff as the hearings moved along.

The Executive Director, Mort Porter, downplayed the traumatic trials and tribulations SCAG had gone through during the 1998-2001 period of certification. Included were the six or seven lawsuits; the audit and reorganization; problems on RHNA Housing with the State of California and the Inland Empire; emotional hearings on LAX and the efforts to regionalize airports to serve residents closer by; problems with limited transportation funds; air quality, air congestion; efforts to get more transit facilities in place along with reorganization; focus on upgrading and modernizing existing freeways and highways; and other matters.

Discussion droned on for six hours with only a short break for lunch. The Feds questions were readily answered and there appeared to be little difficulty with the recertification process. After another short break, a public hearing was scheduled. Surprisingly, few people showed up to raise questions or protest parts of the 2001 RTP. Betsy, as the local representative of FHWA, tried to keep things moving by advising the Feds about the players representing community-based groups. James Snead led off the speakers by lambasting the 2001 RTP for not including many of the 1,900 modifications requested.

"I'm very concerned that the plan doesn't adequately cover the PM10 levels which are projected to increase by 39 percent by 2025, causing serious health impacts. I recommend that the staff present a final plan that will decrease PM10 levels, with strategies for significantly increasing transit services."

He went on: "The final plan should calculate the current and projected PM2.5 levels, which involve an even more dangerous pollutant not covered at all, and show how they will be lowered."

James continued his forceful coverage by ticking off some other modifications he considered to be needed:

"Double funding for such non-motorized transportation as bicycle paths which was needed throughout the region."

"Fund incentives for livable communities and transit-oriented development so more development can take place to encourage people to take transit and be closer to their jobs."

"SCAG should not support a tax on alternative fuel vehicles before

2010 to encourage more people to buy them."

"Restudy Maglev as an option but remove it from the RTP until Federal or private funding is secured to cover all costs."

"Even though needed, keep truck lanes out of the RTP until adequate funding can be arranged."

His next point was the most telling. Claiming that "baseline" costs appear to have dropped by about $10 billion since the Draft Plan was issued, he asserted: "staff must present an itemized list of all Baseline and Plan projects with projected costs before the RTP is adopted." He knew this wouldn't happen now, but he wanted it on record for later use for the 2004 RTP.

His thorough coverage included other key points until his three minutes expired. Other speakers continued the assault on the plan, especially on making the transit portion stronger.

One of Henry's last shots at trying to achieve change at SCAG came at this meeting. He felt not enough people knew of the public hearing since only about ten showed up. Perturbed by the secrecy encouraged by top SCAG leaders, which continued to bedevil SCAG's process, he included himself in the speakers providing their spin on problems with the 2001 RTP. Changing his mind several times on what he should say, he finally decided to focus on community-based organizations and Regional Citizenry when his time came to speak.

"I'm Henry Ferrotte, past chair of RAC but speaking tonight as a private citizen, urban and regional planner. My purpose here is not to protest but to request that more Regional Citizens be recruited. All the speakers here are Regional Citizens and should be respected for taking the time necessary to appear. I'm very upset that more people didn't show up. I know several who indicated they would be here but aren't. Possibly, they didn't know the time of the meeting or felt, probably correctly unfortunately, that they couldn't make any difference if they did come.

"We need to focus on the importance of ensuring that they do make a difference since my feeling is that regional planning in the L.A. Region won't be strengthened until many more Regional Citizens are in the process. Their opinions are important even when they differ from the popular opinion. Only then will more speakers willing to applaud the plan's strong points make their comments.

"Please make more efforts to publicize these public hearings and encourage more participation. Some of the most vital changes in the plan came when people did speak out, evidenced at what happened regarding the LAX controversy on the Regional Airports Plan. The RC's public officials are important, but when all's said and done, the Region's most important participants are community-based organizations and Regional Citizens. Hopefully, they will be allowed to more effectively react in the development and effectuation of the 2004 RTP."

Since the SCAG director had hurried back into the meeting when told that Henry planned to speak, he knew Mort got the message.

* * *

Polls show that the American public consistently favors public servants who have "integrity" and promote morality. Local politicians often had to home in on their conscience in their decision-making process to determine whether they were compromising too much–or being sucked in by a power frenzy which always tempted politicians.

It's a reminder of a joke on politicians. "Do you know the definition for politicians?"

"I'm afraid to say no." comes the reply.

"'Poli' means 'many', 'ticians' means 'bloodsucking ticks.' Many bloodsucking ticks." comes the answer.

"Very appropriate," the listener agrees, chuckling cynically about the situation, having worked for a number of politicians, good and not-so-good, over the years.

Public officials of faith and integrity are not, however, always literalists or absolutists. They often find parallel ways to deal with conflicts of conscience in public life. They made every effort to resist compromise by introducing options equally favorable to both parties. This is often necessary since to enter politics often involves painful compromise with conflicting interests and faiths.

* * *

True to his promise, Jim did pursue Wooden's Principles of Happiness through the Internet. He also got Lila interested and found a forum where they could discuss them with others searching for a more meaningful life. He was so weighed down with guilt and unhappiness about his wasted life, he desperately sought to make his life more meaningful.

They attended one especially diverse forum in Beverly Hills which seemed to represent all walks of life, ethnic groups, ages and interests. Dominating the meeting was a huge pyramid of the key components. Viewing the traits listed, Jim noticed several in which he was strong. He also noted several he definitely needed to work on. These sessions would be good for him if he could open his thinking to possible changes. He steeled himself to accept change so he could grow. He knew it wouldn't be easy but felt it could be done.

The forum leader, Gerald, welcomed them and explained the group's purpose and how they operated. First of all, it was important that they split up into smaller groups composed of people unknown to each other, with each explaining their background and reasons for coming. Jim and Lila split up but planned to pool their thoughts afterwards. This could be a wonderful opportunity for both of them to grow without leaning on each other.

Jim and three others were grouped together to begin the process. Fortunately, they represented a good mix, Jim thought. They started out with introductions:

"I'm Jorge Bergman," began a young man who probably hadn't been in the country over five years. "I'm struggling to become a leader after working my way up in my company. I'm having problems since I lack what you call 'self-esteem,'" he said nervously.

"Joyce Brooks, a woman fighting in a man's world. I've got all sorts of moxie, being labeled as a very 'ballsy' woman who's always getting men mad at her. I need to learn how to work better with others including women, if I'm to succeed."

"My name is Ned Orders, and I find myself always at odds with others due to my religion. I head up a small non-profit association struggling to attract people of good character. But my religion always gets in the way of keeping good people. Hopefully, you guys can help me."

"I'm Jim Robinson, well-known by many but unable to work well with others. I'm spoiled, love to gamble and take chances, but it's destroyed my reputation. I need to develop traits that will permit me to achieve and hold the trust needed to be a good leader."

"Wow! If we can help each other based on the needs expressed, we'll all be better persons in a lot of ways," Ned exclaimed in amazement.

"I guess we'd better get going," stated Polly the moderator. "Let's begin with you, Ned, with your religious fanaticism problem."

Ned proceeded to talk about his problem, and the others suggested ways to correct them. Joyce followed with her problem of getting along with people; Jorge received feedback on handling his lack of self esteem; and Jim concluded as the group proposed how he could develop traits that would permit him to achieve and hold the trust required of a good leader. After the initial discussion, they considered which traits each needed to focus on most.

Ned's key weakness was self-control, Joyce's seemed to be cooperation and friendship; Jorge needed more confidence and poise; Jim's lack of integrity raised a big red flag. All had the basic building blocks of being industrious, enthusiastic, ambitious and skillful. The more they talked about their weaknesses, though, the overriding problem for each seemed to be a lack of faith

How could this be? Each was so different, but each had the same need to prove themselves over and over to others. As they examined each other's personalities and traits, they discovered that their faith was shallow, whether it was in themselves or a higher being. They struggled with this issue since a lack of faith seemed to be a sensitive subject to each of them.

They finally focused on Jim's problems since his seemed to be the most difficult to resolve. Jim found his problems hard to resolve because he always thought of himself as a person in charge of his own destiny. His parentage and background had a lot to do with it, and wasn't comfortable going through his key traits. They were not flattering: he was overly ambitious; his loyalties to others could be questioned; he lacked skills in cooperation and team spirit; his honesty, sincerity, reliability and patience were suspect; he lacked self-control and integrity. Finally, he had no or little faith in a higher being, relying completely on his own ability to get what he wanted.

This lack of faith seemed to be the key thing. They had struggled with a lot of things that day, but they finally decided that faith was a personal thing that each would have to face and resolve through their religious ties. Lila's group had broken up earlier but she waited around for Jim so they could compare notes. As they talked, Jim and Lila realized what they needed to work on. It wouldn't be easy but they felt they now had direction.

Part Five

2003 Forward Into Future

CHAPTER 23
REGION AROUSED

*A lot has happened since the completion
of the 2001 RTP. Behind the scene, efforts
move along to organize the Regional
Citizenry to increase their effectiveness.
Big meetings were planned for 2003.
Strong leadership was needed between the central
city, Los Angeles and the various subregions.
Other undertakings outlined seem more
Important if the region is to prosper. Future
prospects for growth toward A REGION AROUSED.*

"The more things change, the more they remain the same."
Author Unknown

"If you can dream it, you can do it!"
Dr Robert H. Schuller

The huge old Forum in Inglewood, site of many Laker basketball tri-umphs in the past, pulsed with energy as people streamed into the building for a big meeting focusing on efforts to psyche up the struggling regional planning efforts. In the heart of South-Central L.A., the Forum was well located to serve the various community-based organizations, land use, environmental, and other key groups the organizers hoped to attract. A huge banner, emblazoned: "REGION AROUSED" stretched over the arena's front.

Juan, Marcine, Mike and Bea gathered to discuss their roles as the event unfolded. Juan was the principal speaker, while Marcine was to mar-shal the various community-based organizations into a unified force for this first of the REGION AROUSED meetings in 2003. Mike would cover subregional aspects while Bea would provide news coverage.

Everyone was excited as the animated audience arrived, ready to make things happen. Marcine had worked the phones to bring key leaders together on this exciting occasion. Juan had promoted it with speeches to many groups stressing how critical it is to arouse the Region and expand the effort beyond SCAG's narrow confines. Bea had boosted the event with maximum exposure in the press and on TV. The budding Growth Visioning effort by consultants drew other key businesses and non-profit leaders. Even the subregions had done their part to pump up awareness. The magnitude of what was happening hugely exceeded expectations.

*　*　*

As Juan looked over the multitude of groups before him, he could see it was time to get things moving. Their mood buoyed him, and he could hardly wait to begin. There must be 5,000 to 10,000 people, and they continued streaming in.

Striding up to the microphone, Juan began:

"Ladies and gentlemen! Welcome to this important REGION AROUSED rally. For you who haven't worked with me in the past, I'm Juan Rodriguez, Speaker of the House in Sacramento, and proud to represent the L.A. Region. Many of you have been attracted by the efforts of Marcine and Mike, and I want to acknowledge their yeoman work in the trenches to get such a great crowd to kick-start this new venture. My hat's off to them!

"As many of you know, my major focus in recent months has been on creating and expanding the non-profit Southland Regional Alliance which mobilizes support from prominent foundations. I'm excited about how well it's doing. The land use and environmental groups it brings together to protect forests and farmland at the metro periphery, the church and other religious groups to care for inner-city poverty, and the neighborhood councils—is truly amazing. The synergies they unlock are greater than I could have ever anticipated. They are focusing on regionwide solutions to such important issues as affordable housing, tax-base sharing, innovative land use planning and urban reinvestment, and they have generated tremendous interest."

Acknowledging that not everyone has been happy with these successes, Juan continued discussing his programs and then invited questions.

"Hasn't most of the Alliance's success been based on your efforts, Juan? You've put a lot of time and energy into it. Could you sketch out how it's organized?" asked one veteran L.A. citizen activist from the L.A. Charter amendment movement.

"It's a broad-based effort," Juan replied, "put together at the grass roots by some fine, dedicated people located throughout Southern California.

291

They've been recruited for their commitment to achieving a better living environment for all."

"But what are they attempting to accomplish?" came the rejoinder.

"Educating the general public and helping produce strong legislation to make it happen, coming from the local level," Juan emphasized. "These are the other two key elements of my efforts. If we can create a growing regional citizenry demanding such change and willing to help develop and implement the programs, then we'll begin to see some progress–with help from the legislature."

"What programs will you be focusing on over the next year?" asked a Southbay matron.

"I believe we should concentrate on Growth Visioning, Environmental Justice, Tax-Base Sharing, Affordable Housing and Jobs. Only then will we be able to turn the corner toward a truly livable region. All these initiatives are interwoven; the success of each is dependent upon help from the others. I believe that strong efforts in these areas will energize an increasingly vital and livable region," Juan concluded.

"So what approach should we give to achieve strong results?" came the next question, raised by a West Riverside representative.

"There's already been a strong start on this through the Growth Visioning Subcommittee at SCAG. It began about two years ago, and they already have a nationally-known consultant working on the initial phases of a extensive program for the whole six county region."

"SCAG hasn't had any success with Growth Visioning programs in the past," intoned a long time RC member from the Verdigris area. "Why should this effort provide better results?"

"Several reasons. They're broadening their membership to include many other groups, working to involve the media more, thinking finally about the importance of a truly innovative land use plan, and making the subregions a more integral part of the process. They now understand that if only elected officials are involved, the regional process won't ever spread its wings and soar."

"I'm glad to hear you say that. We've got to involve everyone and attract regional citizens if we're ever going to resolve our regional problems," responded an elderly man who Mike had seen occasionally at Gateway City meetings.

"Speaker, what're your feelings about efforts to develop your Regional Planning Bill?" asked a long-time legislative watcher from Orange County.

"It's been a wild three years in the legislature as we have been developing it. We're continuing to improve it, but we may still need another two years to perfect its growth guidance and tax-base sharing provisions. This is complex work, particularly in the L.A. Region. We dodged the bullet after significant problems with the 1998 RTP. Growth Visioning hopefully will provide the impetus to begin–I repeat BEGIN–to reshape the region by 2004 through the RTP. Only time and hard work will tell."

"What about important Environmental Justice issues?" asked a questioner from the Gateway Cities area. "Do you feel that SCAG needs to do more to improve the lives of those affected by noise, air pollution, lack of job opportunities, inadequate transportation options, poor housing, and limited incomes?"

"Definitely!" Juan stated. "One area which is getting increased attention is diesel toxins from trucks. This has been ignored too long and it's particularly lethal to minority areas within one-quarter mile of expressways. The 710 Freeway area abutting the Gateway Cities area is a striking example. These areas have many elementary schools and most of the minority housing where young children live whose lungs and bodies are being severely impacted by the U10 and U2 toxins in their growing years. Cancer, asthma and other major diseases result, robbing our children of their health at a critical period of their lives."

Warming up to the issue, Juan continued: "Since state and Federal standards for heavy-duty truck engines and fuels have lagged far behind similar requirements for cars, strong new efforts are needed. New diesel engines must replace older, toxin-sprewing ones, and improved diesel fuels must also be developed. The cancer risk in the South Coast Air Basin is 14 times higher than normal, and the Gateway Cities area rate is even worse. This is only one instance of how we must focus on Environmental Justice issues in specific places. It's no longer good enough to consider just the regionwide averages. They give us little guidance. We need measurements involving each neighborhood abutting these freeways where more and more trucks will travel in future years. Conditions are bound to get worse if we don't pay attention at this level."

"This is so true, Mr. Speaker," Marcine emphasized. "The Gateway Cities Subregion has real problems and their high concentration of children makes it worse. Housing problems, high unemployment and other issues continue to dog their efforts. Other subregions are also adversely affected, especially the areas around LAX Airport. Environmental Justice must be pursued, not just by lip-service, but by effective action."

"What plans do you have to achieve tax-base sharing within the region, Mr. Speaker? This, to me, would be the most difficult to achieve. What are your thoughts?" asked a middle-aged lady from North Los Angeles, likely either Lancaster or Palmdale.

"You're right. This will be the most difficult to achieve. It won't be easy. We won't be able to base it on a simple program that everyone could follow. It must come from a realization that individual cities cooperating, can achieve economic objectives they can't get by going it alone. It might be through efforts which almost succeeded when the two northern L.A. County cities, Lancaster and Palmdale, initially planned to share their auto sales tax revenues. It will depend on what seems important at the time. It might involve low-income central city and suburban cities banding together through their legislators to share tax revenues from wealthier cities in the region. I understand that the Sacramento area may be involved in tax-base sharing if a bill circulating at the state level to allow several local cities to cooperate is passed. It won't be easy, but tax-base sharing is a powerful tool for building regional alliances."

Marcine eagerly broke in: "Tax-base sharing means (for most of the region) what is always promised in American politics but never delivered: immediate lower taxes and better services. This combination can build firm coalitions quickly."

"We'll be developing a bill in the House this year which will begin to share taxes with the poorer communities," Juan continued. "It'll be a first step toward getting our fouled-up fiscal situation straightened out."

"Do you think starting tax-base sharing is wise at this time, Speaker?" a young man from Santa Monica asked. "I've heard that many in the legislature call this bill 'community socialism' and say that such bills 'are like Robin Hood–they take from the progressive communities and give to the backward ones.'"

"I'm sure many will feel that way, at least initially," Juan replied firmly, "but once more is known about the purposes and, especially the potentials, we'll get strong backing," Juan replied firmly. "You need to look into this issue thoroughly before making up your mind."

"Mr Speaker, I've heard some very reputable elected officials say it doesn't make sense," a member of the audience from a Verdigris high income area countered. "One asked how can metro government take away the revenues we earned and give them to those who can't operate effectively on their 100 percent? I understand his alarm. Why are you so sure that tax-base sharing makes sense?"

"Collaboration by all communities, rich and poor, will return all a great deal over time. The wealthy will benefit in other ways by sharing their revenues."

"Mr. Speaker, you also mentioned affordable housing and jobs as equally important?" queried a middle-aged woman from the San Fernando Valley.

"Extremely important. The need for a jobs-housing balance is crucial to the achievement of balanced growth, environmental justice and tax-base sharing. All these issues are so intertwined that each must receive equal treatment if they're all to succeed."

"Can we focus on them all at the same time? To do so seems like a tall order, Mr Speaker. Why jobs-housing too?" she asked again.

"Because without equitable distribution of jobs and provision of housing for all income groups throughout the region, there can be no effective guidance of growth and achievement of equity for everyone," Juan responded. "In fact, encouraging shifts are occurring, indicating that a better jobs-housing balance is possible. There's a growing feeling that eight key strategies can be developed on this through namely: 1) economic development, 2) infill activities, 3) reduction of parking where land values are prohibitive, 4) more focus on Brownfields, 5) use of transit village clusters, 6) state and local finance referendums, 7) tax credits and other financial incentives, and 8) creating mixed uses in certain areas. We need to really focus on these eight strategies which have been discussed recently with developers. It can be done if we really work at it."

"But can all this be done quickly?" a L.A. resident asked. "You and others have done a good job converting us to the need for and ways to give all citizens the good life. But this can't be accomplished overnight. Much needs to be done to make this happen."

"You're right. But we've got to begin now. Otherwise, we'll never get anywhere. It also takes both bottom-up and top-down approaches to be successful. I need the help of all of you at the local and regional levels if we're to succeed. We'll have more meetings on how to accomplish it, I'm sure."

"I think we're starting to come around, Speaker," a man from Santa Ana interjected. "We've just got to think about it some more. This tax-base sharing concept is not something that we can embrace quickly. We need to talk about it with others before we can buy in."

"Will the subregions be able to work well together to achieve such a regional effort?" asked an attractive lady from Malibu.

"That's an important element," Mike replied. "Working together regionally—while developing a strong subregional planning process, we can make it work," stated Mike, beginning coverage about his beloved subregions. "It'll be a herculean effort! Did you know that most of the L.A. subregions are larger than most U.S. regions–each by themselves. Just think about it. Most L.A. subregions being larger than other regions national-ly–and we've got fourteen of them!

"For example, the six counties in SCAG's region constituted the largest regional council in the U.S. in 1990 with twice the population of its clos-est rival, New York City. Los Angeles City Subregion, by itself is as big as Pennsylvania's Delaware Valley Region, which is nation's ninth largest region. And Orange County is the size of South Florida Region, which was the tenth largest. Gateway Cities' population equaled the Hudson Valley Region (21st), and three others (San Bernardino, San Gabriel Valley and West Riverside) were among the top 45 regional councils in population size. All told, eight SCAG subregions would equal in size any of the top 72 regional councils in 1990."

"Does that impress you a little, people?" Juan jumped in. "We have tremendous problems facing this Region, and more growth is anticipated over the 2003-2025 planning period?"

"Wow!" one delegate exclaimed, her eyes almost popping out. "I never realized the L.A. Region was that huge."

"It's breathtaking when compared with complete regions elsewhere. Now, we're working on developing plans for each and every subregion in our Growth Visioning efforts. It's tough to do since each subregion is so different in size, population and need," Mike reminded everyone.

"What're we doing to handle these differences? Are the subregions happy with the top-down approach?" asked a concerned San Gabriel Valley Subregion resident.

"Definitely not!" Juan stated. "They're literally frothing at the mouth. They don't like some of the approaches the consultants are using. And we're starting to listen to the subregions. The Chair and Vice Chair of the Subregion Coordinators have been made ex-officio members of the Growth Visioning group. Everyone knows now what the subregions do will have a significant impact on the success of the Growth Visioning effort. Some of SCAG's top leadership and RC members would love to see Growth Visioning fail. After all, it could adversely affect the future of their current orderly world," Juan said.

"Why do you say that?" a resident from South-Central L.A. asked, con-cerned by this possibility.

"Like any big bureaucratic body," Juan responded, "there're always those along for the free ride who don't want to chance such changes in direction. After all, change might take away their free ride. That's just human nature. We've seen it happen with MTA, AQMD and others–and especially with SCAG."

"You mentioned that there are a lot of differences among the various subregions. Could you or Mike elaborate on this some?" asked a San Bernardino resident who had traveled far.

"Certainly," Mike stepped in. "Based on needs, growth potentials, built-outness and innovative land use possibilities, all the subregions could have significantly different futures."

"Mike, can you give some examples of these 'futures' and which subregions might be involved?" asked a representative from Arroyo Verdugo.

"Good question. Well, to start with, the subregions we expect will change most, since their future population growth should be the greatest, are Western Riverside, San Bernardino County, Orange County and North L.A. County."

"That makes sense since they're the growth areas. But aren't they also the areas which have problems with the jobs-housing balance?"

"Exactly," said Mike. "So the growth visioning process, to be effective, must consider many things if it's going to be successful."

"Will they have opportunities to collaborate? It seems important for them to work closely together in some things where objectives are similar," a Gateway Cities resident asked.

"Absolutely, close collaboration is essential if the subregions are to prosper," Mike said.

"What are other types of subregions? Why the special treatment?" the Gateway rep asked.

"Another type of subregion, especially important in the L.A. Region, are those with strong environmental protection needs," Mike replied. "Places like Las Virgenes/ Malibu; Arroyo Verdugo; and Gateway Cities. The first two have beautiful ravines, canyons and mountains which need protection. Gateway Cities requires the resurrection of its toxic Brownfield sites which criscross its already built-up areas."

"Extremely interesting. How about other examples?" the Gateway rep continued to probe.

"Others have different types of environmental problems which need protecting. The Coachella Valley Subregion has special plants and animals which need protection, along with its threatened desert areas. In contrast, the Imperial County Subregion is sparsely populated but must preserve its fragile environment. Finally, Ventura County is battling to prevent sprawl from threatening its rich farm lands."

"Wow! Such a range of subregional types in one huge region," exclaimed a Southbay citizen.

"Hold on, there's still one more category," Mike replied. "This involves subregions which aren't expected to change dramatically. They are the built-out areas like the Westside Cities, San Gabriel Valley, South Bay Cities, the Gateway Cities, and finally, the Los Angeles City colossus. As you may suspect, a lot of changes would be expected even in these areas, but more focused on innovative infill, renovation and redevelopment approaches."

"It's obvious that subregions will be an extremely important part of the successful development of the Growth Visioning process and the regional planning program over the 2003-2025 period," Juan concluded as he ended the meeting. Participants seemed pleased with the range of topics and the give-and-take. They left buzzing with excitement about the many new opportunities they could see opening for them to participate in making L.A. a REGION truly AROUSED.

* * *

True to her word, Bea had a front page article in the Times the next day, and it was widely read. That afternoon, she got a call from FHWA's Becky Sanchez, who wanted to follow-up.

They arranged to get together for lunch at Bea's downtown office at the Times. As Becky entered the office, she was struck by the unusual decor. The focus of Bea's office wasn't fine furniture or pictures–but statements by people who had made the news over the years. Adlai Stevenson's "Let's talk sense to the American people. Let's tell them the truth, that there are no gains without pains," Will Rogers "All I know is what I read in the papers," and Ernie Pyle's "I write from the worm's-eye point of view," adorned the walls. Front and center was another Stevenson, "Those who corrupt the public mind are just as evil as those who steal from the public purse."

"I see that you're quite a Stevenson fan, Bea. How did that happen?"

"He just seemed, like Will Rogers, to 'cut to the chase' in reminding people that what they do with their life is important and certain things just needed to be said at the appropriate time. That's why I'm a journalist, Becky."

"Well put, Bea. Let me begin in that same vein. I'll start by saying that we obviously need to get Los Angeles City more involved in the regional process. What can we do to help make this happen, Bea? You seem to have that golden touch by working with many who are active the regional process to come together to reach a desired solution."

"I'd love to see it happen, Becky. One way might be by the Feds getting tougher with their requirements for using grants. Couldn't that press

Los Angeles to get more involved? The new mayor seems more interested in regional matters, so this may be is the time to get tough and prod the parties to work together more," Bea shot back.

"That may be possible now. I'll work on making something like that happen. Do you plan on more articles like the one yesterday, Bea? That's what we need to educate people about the possibilities."

"Yes, I'll continue working to keep regional issues in the headlines. We need to get more people besides elected officials and SCAG involved. Until we do, we just aren't going to get the public pressure we need to make things happen."

"Okay, it's a deal, Bea. I'll do more at my end and you continue to do your best. Maybe between us, we can get something going."

"Sounds good. Let's eat. I had a nice spread put together which has just been brought in. Hope you're hungry for a vegetarian meal? I know I've got to keep my weight down, Becky. As we eat, we can cover some other matters which need discussion."

*   *   *

Following the meeting, Bea talked to the mayor and key council members, and things started happening. This led to a joint meeting between the City Council, mayor and Regional Council leadership, including SCAG's executive director. They began to work out details of how they might combine in a real collaborative effort in the future.

A few days later, key leaders in all the subregions were drawn into the discussions and made to feel more like they were key players. Things began speeding up. Everyone finally began to realize that unless subregions could operate as important parts of the region, the Region would soon grind to a halt.

In another important move stimulated by discussions with key regional leaders, Juan and Jim convened an unofficial REGION AROUSED task force to keep citizen support growing. Key members included Carla, Mike, Henry, Gavin, Marcine and Bea. Not surprisingly, they were same people Juan had met with in two key meetings on his regional planning bill last year. He and Jim would have a number of sessions, along with phone calls and e-mails to keep the process going. He wanted to stir things up and keep things happening. Included would be Jim's twelve proposals to strengthen SCAG, the RC and the regional process.

The first meeting took place in April 2003 at a neutral site in Santa Monica. It was at the Grand Corporation, a national urban issue think tank, where Juan had a friend. Jim's twelve improvement proposals were first on the agenda.

Jim began: "I feel it's important to begin correcting certain problems that have occurred within SCAG through development of poor policy and technical decisions during the last few years. I wanted to focus on them to see if you agree."

"Great idea, Jim," Juan replied. "Let's get them on record; then figure out how to handle them."

RTP Principles

"All of these are important. First, the importance of finally looking at various scenarios in developing an innovative regional land use plan through Growth Visioning is a major move forward, especially if there is broad backing from the subregions' leaders and Regional Council.

"Second, RTP financial planning projections must be balanced to reflect the true situation for the 2003-2025 planning period. Any manipulations must be discouraged to ensure that 'creative bookkeeping' is not used to justify plan components which aren't financially feasible.

"Third, Subregions must be given first consideration in planning, especially within Growth Visioning's land use planning program involving each and every subregion.

"Fourth, Maglev's potentials must be truly stated, with their cost and likely achievements analyzed, so that desperately needed competing programs have equal opportunity to receive the limited funds available.

"Fifth, imperfections in the travel models must be acknowledged and corrected so that problems faced by the L.A. Region can be resolved. An example of this would be the truck volume undercounting that could have been adjusted when found deficient, but wasn't.

"Sixth," he continued, "SCAG's policy on toll road development needs to be reviewed and, if necessary, corrected to avoid embarrassing and sueable situations.

"Seventh, SCAG's straddling the fence on the LAX problem to placate the City of Los Angeles must be stopped along with similar problems on housing and other important issues.

"Eighth, there needs to be adequate funding and recognition of RAC's role so that Regional Citizen and other important citizen issues are adequately resolved.

"Ninth, 'conflict of interest' irregularities by individual members must be quickly resolved to avoid adverse impacts on SCAG that hamper effective regional planning.

Ooooh Dang!

"Tenth, SCAG's leadership efforts to control and manipulate the Regional Council through its top leaders need to stop. There may be denial of this issue but it still needs to be discussed and resolved. SCAG also needs to be rid of dead wood on its staff, as well as special interest influences that adversely affect its performance and regional harmony.

"Eleventh, the Black Box issue needs to be explored in depth to ensure that all its components make sense and result in sound projections.

"And finally, efforts must be made to ensure that large SCAG consulting contracts are given only to the most qualified firms. Smaller, often more qualified firms should be encouraged to submit and given truly equal opportunity."

"I'm anxious to know what you think of these issues and would be pleased to answer any questions you may have," Jim concluded.

"Wow! You've really focused on some important issues which SCAG and the RC must face, Jim. I can see why SCAG is involved in so many law suits," Bea stated. "Where do we go from here?"

"Great points, Jim," Juan said. "Are you prepared to work to make sure changes are made? You know, as well as I do, many of the points you made will be disputed or denied, other points will be justified as unneeded, and you will be ridiculed on any stand you take. However, this could be the best way to remake your image as the 'good guy'. It won't be easy though."

"I agree with you, Juan and Bea, and I'm ready to be heard on these issues. As you know, I love controversy. This gives me the opportunity to provide my viewpoints. I know I'll be doubted by some at first, maybe because of my checkered past. But I'm ready to weather the storm and prove my points. After all," he noted wryly, "I do know where most of 'the bodies are buried.'"

Juan moved on as he looked out at the audience. Juan had made sure that all the subregions were well represented since he felt they would "make or break" the achievement of a sufficiently aroused region. The large comfortable room in the Grand where they were meeting encouraged a relaxed environment in an academic setting, complete with wall-to-wall book cases and a fireplace around which to focus.

"I'm glad you all think this meeting is important," Juan began. "Jim and I have been working hard using both bottoms-up and top-down approaches to strengthen the regional process. We want your ideas and suggestions on how this can be accomplished. We're conscious of the past unsuccessful efforts to make good things happen, but let's get your suggestions."

Ideas began to pour out to address Jim's issues and arouse the region. Many participants aired their concerns and recommendations for making better regional plans and implementing them more effectively and equitably. Juan adjourned the meeting after scheduling another one in two months to discuss materials they had been given on ways to achieve a "REGION AROUSED."

FAST FORWARD TO THE REGION'S OUTLOOK IN THE 2007-2010 PERIOD

Things seemed to be improving after moving through the 2004 RTP and work to complete the 2007 RTP. Mike had retired, but remained passionate about achieving an AROUSED REGION. He put together an analysis of how the various subregions were doing in their work to achieve a regional plan. The region had continued its growth so its population now exceeded 20 million.

Meeting with the Subregional Coordinators at their monthly meeting in February 2008, Mike presented his findings so they could be forwarded to the Regional Council.

"I'm happy to report that the Region has turned the corner and can finally be considered to be a REGION AROUSED," he began. "It's taken some time, but the efforts we began back in the Year 2000 are finally paying off. We knew it would take time to get results, but now we have them. I'm excited by what I found."

"What are these favorable indicators?" the current chair asked, stirred by Mike's opening.

"We've more than doubled the transit trips to 75 per capita. This compared with projections back in 2000 of 72 per capita by 2025, with only 34.9 trips provided then per capita. Transit lines to Pasadena, East L.A., West L.A. and three non-stop Rapid Bus lines through South-Central L.A. have been developed.

"Transit Villages with a wide range of housing and commercial land uses have evolved at several key locations along light rail and subway lines. This has reduced unnecessary travel to shopping, services and jobs.

"The number of LAX passengers have been capped at 78 million in accordance with the 2004 Plan, and the emerging regional airports at Ontario, Palmdale and John Wayne are working effectively to handle the balance due to expansion and airline efforts to diversify flight schedules. Quite an improvement over the 94 MAP (million air passengers) sought by LAX originally.

"Air pollution has been reduced significantly, with notable headway made on toxins and other pollutants."

"Environmental Justice issues are being handled expeditiously, not on an average regional basis, but by subregion and neighborhood."

"Jobs and housing are better balanced, with unnecessary trips by highways and freeways cut back significantly. Levels of congestion have stabilized, and in some instances, reduced on some freeways as a result of increased transit use and greater jobs-housing balance.

"Housing for all income groups has been regionally dispersed and a wider range of housing types and prices available in all subregions.

"Innovative infill, renovation and redevelopment activities are taking place in many locations in all subregions to encourage increased densities and locations closer to jobs.

"Downtown L.A. neighborhoods have continued to strengthen as affordable housing and loft development, offices, industry, and more services are built, along with the creation of a better job mix. Long Beach and other regional downtowns have been strengthened.

"Growth and changes in population characteristics in the subregions have been bolstered without adding unnecessarily to congestion.

"Stronger neighborhoods are emerging with the renewal of grass-roots coalitions of community-based groups, religious organizations and non-profits throughout the region.

"These improvements plus corrections at the top levels in SCAG bodes well for the future of the L.A. Region over the next few decades. A REGION AROUSED NOW IS ACHIEVABLE! Let's continue to make it happen with our efforts!"

With this summary, the Subregional Coordinators endorsed Mike's report and forwarded it to the RC, and everyone realized the significance of all the efforts over many years in achieving this. The Region's future now was secure. THE REGION IS AROUSED!